A MATURE WOMAN

A MATURE WOMAN

Saiichi Maruya

Translated by
Dennis Keene

KODANSHA INTERNATIONAL
Tokyo · New York · London

ACKNOWLEDGEMENT
The publisher wishes to thank Rengo Co., Ltd., a member of the
Association for 100 Japanese Books, for its contribution towards the
cost of publishing this translation.

First published by Bungei Shunju in 1993 under the title *Onnazakari*.

ISBN 4-7700-2183-6
First edition, 1995
First paperback edition, 1997

97 98 99 00 10 9 8 7 6 5 4 3 2 1

A MATURE WOMAN

ONE

∴

The *Shinnippo*, or *New Daily*, began publication the year after the Russo-Japanese War ended, on 12 November, 1906, and the first number opened with a suitably sensational front-page splash, covering the murder the previous day by a geisha of her patron. The official history of the paper records that everyone on the staff 'rejoiced in this godsend', implying that the murder had been arranged by the powers on high specifically to provide the newspaper with a good story, which shows, in its total lack of sympathy for the unhappy victim, that journalism was much the same then as it is now. The paper has since had a checkered history, defying the government in the name of democracy only to support interventionism abroad in an attempt to stay on the right side of the military, sometimes winning applause for its bold exposure of the contents of political treaties, sometimes laughter for its massive coverage of news that turned out to be completely false; yet throughout all this it has managed to stay afloat in a fiercely competitive business, never being obliged to close down, never having to endure the gloom of bankruptcy or merger, and now, in this the ninth decade of its existence, recognised as one of the six leading newspapers in the country, with no decline in company fortunes—a remarkable achievement which undoubtedly deserves a measure of respect.

Naturally, there have been envious voices heard, and some of the paper's critics have maintained, whether in earnest or in jest, that the *New Daily* owes its moderate success simply to the fact that it followed a different pattern of development from the other big papers; by which they mean that the founding family of three avoided the kind of two-against-one split that would have occasioned a corresponding division in the company at large and bitter sectarian differences among the staff. And they are right, to the extent that there hasn't been a major rift, though as if in compensation the paper has acquired a great variety of minor factions, all in a state of constant strife; and even there one could argue that this skirmishing maintains a certain alertness to events and serves to keep complacency at bay.

Nobody can deny, however, that the founders went to great lengths to please the paper's distributors, positively vying among themselves to earn their favours, giving tokens of consolation or celebration whenever the occasion demanded, extending invitations to flower viewings at the family mansion, even going so far as to hold a golf tournament for them. All to good effect, for nothing decides the affairs of a great newspaper so much as winning the hearts and minds of the people who have to sell it. Once bound to you by the iron bonds of loving kindness, they are unlikely to fall easy prey to your rivals.

The most important factor, though, was that the company confined its sales area to metropolitan Tokyo and the three major cities in the Kansai region (Osaka, Kyoto and Kobe). By not aiming for nationwide coverage, they avoided competing with the local newspapers, thus saving themselves the expense of propping up business in areas where it was inevitable they would make a loss. Of course, not everything was perfect—there were, for example, real problems as regards the selling of advertising space—but on the whole it was obvious that the business was financially sound. There was no need to open any more branch offices, they were managing to hold the price of the paper down, and editorial policy was free to engage with a readership which, in the best sense of the word, was cosmopolitan. The *New Daily* owed its modest but undeniable success to its dedication to the principle that tangible results mean more than national reputation, that the proof of any pudding is indeed in the eating.

Even if the long-term decision taken in the early 1970s to limit the paper's scope had been recently relaxed, to the extent of allowing sales to expand over the Kanto and Kansai regions as a whole, the way it was done was felt to be in keeping with the founders' level-headed aims. Practical considerations had also been behind the decision made just after the Pacific War not to have a company baseball team, for though the stated reason was a fear that it might attract unseemly attention to itself, the truth of the matter was that they had more serious problems to worry about.

Problems had always been part of their history. But it would be tedious to devote much time to the numerous blunders and setbacks they'd experienced, so this account will move swiftly forward to the present day, to focus on the major problem on everybody's minds: namely, the lack of space. The building they occupied dated from half a century before, and although the purchase of a neighbouring block had increased the space available, it was still inadequate, particularly as each department began to fill up with photocopiers, word processors and fax machines. Even when the printing of the paper was computerised, this only seemed to make the place more awkward to work in. What with the traffic congestion at the back of the building, which restricted the movement of delivery vans coming and going, and the state of the air-conditioning, which was on its last legs, if not actually defunct, it was obvious that land had somewhere to be acquired and a new office building put up.

Still, with land prices in Tokyo being what they were, the company could not afford to pick and choose. So while moving was certainly a priority in the minds of the employees, the decision was up to the president and other executives, with the result that daily life went on as usual. Those most concerned with the problem, although they had virtually no say in the matter, were the writers of the editorial columns. And this wasn't because their work involved them in matters of national land policy—with the

9

pros and cons of moving the seat of government, with property taxation and so on—no, the reason was that their office was on the sixth floor, where the air-conditioning was at its worst. Although the room wasn't all that large, the system was incapable of maintaining an even flow of air at a steady temperature, so that in some areas it was chronically over-effective and in others it hardly worked at all. In summer, for example, the section chief was subjected to such icy temperatures that he was obliged to wear a thick cardigan and gloves, while in winter the writer of 'In a Pensive Mood', the short column at the foot of the front page of the evening edition, had to cool himself with a small fan in order to bring on his reveries. One of the weakest and most frequently made jokes at the fortnightly Saturday drinking party concerned the remarkable improvement the editorial columns would show if only the air-conditioning could be made to function properly. To avoid dwelling on this issue, though, we will open our story at a time of year when the air-conditioning in their office was not dominating the lives of the staff.

With the annual reshuffle which regularly took place on 1 April, two new members were co-opted into the team. This was no more than average, but what astonished everybody as soon as the news got out, immediately after the appointments had been made, was the choice. News travels at a speed proportional to the degree of surprise it causes, and the announcement that Juzo Urano was to join the editorial writing staff was certainly an eye-opener. Some people were moved to predict the end of the *New Daily*—now 'one of the six leading newspapers in the country'— if it could make insane appointments of this kind, while the majority of the employees, down to the receptionists and telephone operators, found it difficult to associate him with the work to which he had been assigned. Reporters from other papers responded with equal bewilderment, the reason being that Urano was notorious for his inability to write.

Not that he was a novice, by any means. Indeed, his abilities were well known and widely appreciated, and had earned him the president's prize once and the editorial manager's prize twice, as well as his appointment as head of the paper's crime-reporting team. But despite his astuteness in sniffing out stories, his pertinacity in following them up, and his penchant for filling notebooks with scribbled information, once sat before a blank sheet of paper with the intention of putting together an article, he dried up around the third short line or so and was quite incapable of writing anything that could be printed. What he eventually produced was always written up by a colleague, who would have to work with the essential facts transmitted by word of mouth. Urano himself attributed his inability to write to the way he assembled the material leading to his various scoops, and told people so, meaning presumably that his methods were quite different from those of other reporters.

Urano was born in the Kanto area and educated at a university in Tokyo, but when he joined the paper he was sent off to work in the Kansai office, just outside Osaka. It was while he was there, associating with police detectives, that he began to wonder if their interrogation techniques, using the alternation of mean bastard and sympathetic good guy, might not be borrowed by a pair of newspaper reporters out gathering material. He managed to put the idea into practice, however, only some years later, when he was posted back to Tokyo, first using it when investigating the affairs of a mayor in Saitama Prefecture who was suspected of corruption. When they interviewed this mayor, Urano began the questioning. Before long, it became obvious that the mayor was repeatedly ignoring some relevant fact, or blatantly lying about it, making his account less and less consistent, until Urano seized on an obvious contradiction and appeared to lose his temper. At this point, the second reporter, who up till then had unobtrusively just been taking notes, interrupted and tried to calm Urano down, exaggerating his use of the local accent with its soothing drawl and taking the mayor's side. Thus what seemed an irreparable breach, leading to the termination of the interview, was somehow papered over, allowing Urano time, while his colleague drawled soothingly at the mayor, to think up his next barbed question, until finally the mayor got himself into a corner from which there was no escape. The technique, extended over three interviews, led Urano to feel so sure of his conclusions that the newspaper was able to print a front-page exposure of the mayor the day before he was actually arrested. This initial success was followed by others, but, all the while, Urano's constant efforts to refine his two-way method of interrogation resulted in his neglecting the actual writing skills he needed, which was why he'd never even managed to learn the conventional house style. At least, that was his explanation, even if nobody else seemed prepared to accept it, since obviously it was ridiculous that the person who actually got hold of a story couldn't write it up.

Still, the fact that Urano couldn't write wasn't held against him, largely because his sleuthing abilities ensured the *New Daily* a place ahead of its five rivals on stories ranging from the murder of a young wife in Chiba, or the mysterious disappearance of an old couple in Kawasaki, or the teenage gang-rape cases somewhere in the suburbs, to some crooked financing by a certain bank which almost led to the downfall of the cabinet, only they were able to hush it up just in time. Presumably the upper echelons of the paper were as unconcerned that this reporter couldn't write as they were that the hero of the paper's serial, written by a literary person of some standing, should have started off his fictional life as a teetotaller, only to become a raving alcoholic halfway through.

As it happened, Urano had been made an editorial writer owing to factional divisions within the paper. The two deputy heads of the editorial writing section belonged to two different factions, and although this didn't stop them getting on with each other, since they enjoyed drinking together, supported the same baseball team, and preferred different types of women, so avoiding ugly scenes in bars, it was inevitable when two vacancies on the editorial staff occurred that they should announce to their chief the sensible choice of one person from the president's faction and one from the vice-president's. That was during the first week in February. Since their immediate boss belonged to the president's party, he accepted their proposal and passed it on to the editor-in-chief, who, however, belonged to the chairman's clique and refused to give his approval. Things became difficult from that point onwards: the two original names were struck off the list and other names were put forward, but no two could be found that satisfied all three factions, and the ages of the prospective candidates had gradually been lowered to a point beyond which they just couldn't go. By 10 March, further procrastination had become impossible, so they made up their minds, choosing Yumiko Minami, a member of the chairman's group but well liked by the president, and Juzo Urano, a president's man but also of strategic importance as far as the vice-president was concerned. The woman was forty-five and the man one year older, so that was all right, and while the vice-president's faction would have liked someone more firmly allied with them, well, there were other personnel changes to consider, the everyday job of running the paper had to be got on with, and the three factions were tired of the whole business anyway. So even though transferring Yumiko Minami from the domestic pages to the editorial writing staff meant breaking the unwritten rule that there should only be one female member of that team, not to mention the fact that the boss of the crime-reporting squad couldn't write, there was, after all, nothing very unusual about any of this, the matter was settled, and Minami and Urano were appointed.

This was a move upwards for both journalists, so congratulations were in order, but Urano for one was less than happy about it, and when he was on his own his face looked thoroughly dejected. The reason for this wasn't his awareness that he would now be obliged to write proper articles, or even the gloom that overtakes any child of nature used to roaming at will who finds himself tied down to a dreary desk job. Of course, both contributed to it to some extent, but the main cloud hanging over him was disappointment at the thought that the path to becoming head of the city desk was now permanently closed to him. If the truth were really told, the future Urano had envisaged for himself involved first a spell in charge of the city desk, then becoming editor-in-chief and finally, who knows, maybe even a board director; but it was a fact about this paper that people appointed to his new section were rather likely to stay there, and on no occasion in its history had any member of it then been appointed head of the city desk. Just how deep his depression went was indicated by his failure to realise how meaningless was any consideration of precedents in this case, since what precedent could there be for appointing to the editorial writing section someone who lacked any ability to write?

Slightly before noon on April Fool's Day, Urano entered the editorial office and seated himself at his new desk. Despite the small size of the room, everybody had his own desk—indeed, this was the first time since Urano had joined the paper that he'd been granted such a privilege, and he was happy enough about that. He had visited the room a few times since his appointment was announced, to pay his respects to his new boss and colleagues, to put his reference books and various writing materials in their proper places, and to stick a smallish calendar on his bookshelf, but this felt very different. His desk was near the window (in fact, the first away from it on the left), and on this bright spring day the limpid waters of the Sumida River could be, if not actually seen, at least easily imagined. The desk next to his was right by the window and belonged to the other new appointee, Yumiko Minami, although she didn't seem to have turned up yet. Urano, of course, knew her by sight, but for some reason their paths hadn't crossed since the appointments were made and he'd not had the opportunity to discuss anything with her. Her desk looked quite different from his, since all her writing things were very neatly arranged and a word processor was already in place, while on her bookshelf there were about a dozen dictionaries, all seeming much more used than Urano's, with a smudged, well-thumbed look to their pages and strips of tape binding their backs in places. Urano certainly noticed this, although he didn't appear to appreciate the significance of the fact that all the dictionaries were out and ready to use while his own were still stored away inside a cardboard box.

On top of Yumiko's bookshelf was something that had definitely not been there the previous day. This was a cuddly toy dog, large, white, with short hair and floppy ears. It was difficult to work out what breed it was supposed to be—some kind of mongrel probably. Urano stood up and gave the small blob of black plastic representing the dog's nose a light prod with his right forefinger (it obviously wasn't damp), grunting a dog-like greeting to it.

'His name's Shirobei,' a voice said. Urano turned round, and there was Yumiko, dressed smartly in a navy-blue suit with white pinstripes and a rose-coloured blouse. She seemed, in fact, to be dressed rather more elegantly even than usual, probably because this was her first day in her new job, and her face was carefully made up. Urano got to his feet and the two exchanged greetings. Then they both sat down and talked about the dog.

'It's a mongrel, is it?'

'So it would seem.'

'And male?'

'Well, according to its name.'

He picked the dog up, spun it round and peered up its backside.

'Yes. Its name seems to be the only indication.'

'Oh, really?' said Yumiko, frowning slightly, but not enough to put him off. 'My daughter gave it to me, to celebrate my new job.'

'You're lucky. My son didn't give me anything. Is she fond of dogs?'

'She's crazy about them. Even more than I am. When our dog died she was absolutely heartbroken.'

'When was that?'

'About a year ago.'

'And you haven't got a new one?'

'No. It didn't seem right to get one just after the other had died, and anyway we're not allowed to keep pets in the block of flats we live in.'

'That's the worst of those places.'

The first copies of the evening paper had arrived, and one man—bearded, around fifty, with a cardigan draped over his

15

shoulders—seemed unable to wait for them to be distributed to the various desks, and rushed over to the door from his place at the far side of the room. This was the author of 'In a Pensive Mood', and he stood by the door reading his short column intently, ignoring everything about him, even though he must already have read it countless times. The two new recruits, impressed by this enthusiasm, glanced at the lead story on the front page of the copies they received, then went quickly to 'In a Pensive Mood' so they could comment on it to its author.

'I never realised the new year used to begin on the first of April. How fascinating.'

'I like your idea that in some professions every day is like April Fool's Day. I suppose you didn't have journalism in mind?'

But the bearded man just gave them a satisfied smile, making no response.

By now the other members of staff had began to turn up, carrying a variety of briefcases. Most were dressed formally, like Urano, in suit and tie. As they came in, one man, with a bald head, got up and headed for the door, greeting everybody as he did so; the fact that he was wearing a sports jacket, with a copy of the evening paper stuffed in one pocket, and no tie, seemed to emphasise his going against the general flow. This was the author of 'News from Another Planet', the column that appeared at the foot of the front page of the morning edition, and it was his habit to go out every day at this time to a nearby cafe where he would drink two cups of coffee. Like the author of 'In a Pensive Mood', he wasn't obliged to attend staff meetings, even though he was a member of the writing team. Before he left the room, one of his colleagues quoted from the April Fool's Day haiku parody in that morning's column, and he said something cheerful back.

Just before 12.30 everyone began to get up from their desks and gather round a large table in one corner of the room. They formed a motley crowd, one holding a fat wad of notebooks, another a copy of the evening edition, various people not holding anything, some smoking, some with folded arms, some with their heads resting in their hands, one sitting on a sofa at a slight distance from the table with his notebook open on his knees. Yumiko Minami sat next to the only other woman among the twenty or so journalists, directly facing the chief, and Urano found himself fairly close to them, between two senior members who were, like him, originally from the city desk.

The chief had been carrying on an impassioned conversation with a man sitting near him on his right, about some German ointment that was supposed to be effective in treating a stiff shoulder, but he now abruptly abandoned this topic, cleared his throat and introduced the two new members of staff. They both stood up and bowed, and the chief then said:

'Right. I'm afraid we now have to get down to business, and that means deciding who's going to write tomorrow's lead articles, my suggestion being that our two new people should do the job. The first lead for Urano, and the second for Minami.'

Urano immediately roused himself.

'That's a bit thick, when it's our first day.' This was meant to be a straight refusal, but everyone just laughed, refusing to take him seriously, so he turned to Yumiko for support. 'Not really fair, is it?' he said, but she merely smiled, seeming not to agree. 'I haven't prepared anything, for a start,' he went on. But the chief and his two deputies had already thought of that:

'How about something on election issues?'

'There are a number of local elections this month.'

'There's masses of material you can use.'

'We'll all give you a hand.'

And it was decided he would write about that. The helping hand he was given seemed to consist of an hour or so's gossip about something to do with one of their branch offices, reflections on political theory obtained at second or third hand from some university professor, a few stock aphorisms from one political commentator, and some opinions on the political outlook for the country thrown in for good measure—all of which Urano diligently wrote down, managing to fill about ten pages of his notebook with these often flippant and highly subjective statements. Finally, after laughing loudly at a joke somebody had made, the

17

chief tied up the proceedings by saying:

'Well, that should just about cover it. All you need is to knock that into shape, making your own views the main thrust of the article, of course.'

Now it was Yumiko Minami's turn, and she was immediately on top of things, saying she wanted to write about women and work, and giving a three-minute outline of what she would say. The other woman member of staff said it was an interesting approach, but nobody else had any comment to make, apart from a deputy chief who felt someone had to break the silence and merely repeated the same opinion in different words. With this apparently agreed, all that remained was to decide who would write the feature on the second page of the evening edition called 'Starting from Scratch', before the meeting was brought to a close at around 2.00 P.M. Then they all trooped out, either to have a late lunch at the staff restaurant or a local soba shop, or heading off somewhere in search of a story. One or two of them even went to the cinema. Those who had something to write were, of course, obliged to get on with it, so Yumiko, who hadn't expected to do anything much on her first day and had promised to cook dinner that evening, immediately phoned home to tell her mother she wouldn't be able to after all, but that she'd certainly be back by 7.30.

By around 3.30 she had finished her article, which she showed first to the other woman there, then to one of the deputy chiefs. Since there didn't seem to be any problem with it, she went off and had a light meal before going to the library to look a few things up. When she got back to the office at around five, the monitor copy of what she'd written had arrived, which the deputy chief told her looked all right. Yumiko took the chair next to him and cast her eye over the ten sheets or so of copy, now in the form in which it would be fed into the computer, but nothing needed to be changed. The deputy raised his head and said the chief had already seen it and thought it was pretty good. She smiled in reply.

While waiting for the proofs to appear she returned to her

own desk to find Urano seated next to her, looking very different from the calm, confident person she remembered. He was sighing, deep sighs, and his desk was covered with crumpled bits of paper, as was the floor at his feet. He looked, for all the world, like a caricature of the artist in the throes of creation.

'You do seem to be making heavy weather of it,' she couldn't help saying.

'Hello there,' he replied wearily, looking up at her and trying, but failing, to hide his embarrassment and despair.

'What's gone wrong?' she asked anxiously.

'It's all gone wrong. I just don't know what the hell I'm doing any more. He's been getting a bit worried and came to have a look, but all he did was mutter at me, and that didn't help.' 'He' seemed to refer to the deputy chief, and Urano went on to mumble, 'God knows what I'm going to do. But I suppose there's still time.'

'Of course there is.'

'I just can't seem to think straight any more.'

'Ah.'

'What do you mean?'

'I suppose you haven't had lunch yet?'

'You're quite right. I clean forgot about it.'

'There you are, you see. A perfectly simple explanation. That can soon be fixed.'

On her way to and from the shop next door she felt secretly rather pleased. Not only was the crack reporter from the city desk living up to his reputation of being unable to write, whereas she had finished her own piece ages ago, but she had cleverly made up the face-saving excuse that it was all because he was hungry (though she did feel there was probably something in that anyway). It was also quite fun to go and buy this food for him—some rice balls, milk and Oolong tea—and find him genuinely grateful to get it; and she liked the way, when she declined his offer of payment, that he didn't boorishly insist on it. But a deeper reason for her feeling of contentment was probably the fact that she'd spent the previous night with a man, although she was quite unaware of this as a possible cause since, consciously at least, she had forgotten all about it.

Urano ate the rice balls and sucked up the milk through a straw.

'I've never been any good at writing. I was pretty hopeless at primary school, and never got much better. Even worse than I was at music. I wonder what I was good at? Can't think of anything. Nothing, perhaps. Look, I'm sorry, but would you mind reading it over?'

He passed her his manuscript as if it were the most natural thing in the world to do. And perhaps it was—certainly it was normal for any completed article to be shown to a colleague, and perhaps he had chosen her because the more approachable veterans of the city desk had already disappeared. At least, that was what Yumiko thought, so she quite cheerfully accepted the chore of reading a text which was littered with erasures and insertions, but which still seemed to read surprisingly fluently. She was curious to see what the star journalist who couldn't write had come up with.

> April this year is a month of various local elections. Japan can expect to steer a different course, with new people at the wheel, from provincial governors to councillors of cities, towns and villages, during the last balmy days of this week of holidays. And yet, needless to say, there are many local government posts that are not subject to the process of re-election or otherwise this month.
>
> The subject that is on my mind today concerns the violation of electoral law. Among these violations are bribery and free handouts, but it's the money bribes I'm going to talk about. This has been well publicised, over a period of some time, but we still haven't been able to stamp it out, which is a matter for real concern. Why is it a matter for concern? Because democracy is a system whereby we entrust government to a political group that seems close to our own outlook, and who are felt to be of superior charac-

ter and wisdom. People involved in bribery can hardly be people of superior character and wisdom. Some politicians, let's face it, just shouldn't be elected.

Still, that's just the theory. In reality, there's an awful lot of bribery going on. They say that if we got rid of all the people who had been elected that way we'd find the Diet was half empty. And that's no empty threat.

One also has to admit that offering bribes can make life difficult for members of the public, too. After all, it can be very hard to refuse, and it's not just a question of being greedy. No doubt that's a part of it, of course, but other factors are involved, which may be more determinative.

A colleague of mine, when he was working in one of our branch offices, was once asked by a man of some standing in that area, and with whom he'd been fishing on occasion, to vote for his candidate; he then passed over a plain brown envelope. This colleague said he was very sorry etc., passed the envelope back, and that was the end of it. Now, since he happened to be a newspaperman from Tokyo, it wasn't all that hard to refuse, because it wouldn't have looked too good for a man in his position to accept, but if he'd been a local there's no doubt it wouldn't have been so easy, that he'd have been in a difficult situation.

The difficulties would stem from the fact that the bribe represents recognition that you are a member of a certain group. Refusing the bribe would be denying your own place in society, it would go against the concept of social obligation, and all the time spent building up relationships with that group of people would go down the drain. Also, whoever was making the offer would take it personally if everyone else he had approached had accepted it and just this one person hadn't. There are all sorts of issues involved when it's a question of personal relations of that kind.

Let's assume our man does pocket it—well, of course he can still do what he likes in a secret ballot. But the fact is, there's a question of honour involved here. He can hardly

21

take the bribe and not vote for the person who offered it; it just wouldn't feel right. Some years back, during the presidential elections in the Philippines, a Catholic archbishop said on the radio that it was all right to accept the money so long as you didn't let it influence the way you voted. But even so an awful lot of people voted for Marcos. That's the way it goes.

I am not sure what the going rate in the Philippines was, but in this country it's rumoured to be around ¥5,000 to ¥10,000. The least you can put inside your brown envelope is one ¥5,000 note. Whether this modest sum is intended to buy the vote only of the head of the household or all its members is not clear, but since the custom of buying votes goes back to pre-modern times, we can assume the ¥5,000 purchases the entire family's votes. What's more, nobody is under any obligation to split the money equally, which is why you don't see five ¥1,000 notes being used.

Given this situation, it is clear that the number of ¥5,000 notes changing hands in this country must be huge. I have heard that there is a considerable shortage of ¥5,000 notes in most financial institutions, and if this is so—and it certainly seems likely—that is surely the reason why. No doubt the Treasury produces a special issue of ¥5,000 notes as an election approaches, but I haven't been able to check on that.

Once an election campaign has started, though, the purchase of a large number of plain brown envelopes may be seen as proof of political misconduct. The trick, they say, is to buy all your cheap envelopes before the campaign starts, at a stationer's outside your electoral district. Rather than go to all that trouble, it might seem a better idea just to hand over the money direct, but that is felt to be too crude, while the use of the more expensive kind of envelope used on special occasions is felt to be taking things too far, as well as making the overheads mount up. White envelopes are thought to be too conspicuous. The cheap, no-nonsense brown envelope is just the thing.

Still, all that aside, there's no getting away from the fact that bribery is a denial of democratic government and a breach of the law. Bought votes and representational government just don't mix. If anyone offers any of us a plain brown envelope we ought just to give it back, calmly and politely, perfectly nicely, without giving the bearer any cause to take offence.

Yumiko read this twice. The first time she could hardly keep from laughing at the way in which it was written, but when she went through it again she read more slowly, thinking about the content. By the end of it she felt oddly moved, and inclined to be self-critical. She felt that, in comparison, the article she had done on 'Women and Employment', which had received the warm approval of her chief and deputy chief, was just a confection of cleverly organised trivialities.

Of course, what Urano had produced was, by any professional standards, pretty awful. It was much too slangy in some places, oddly stilted in others, and repetitive about things that needed saying only once. Even given the fact that it came from the pen of a beginner it was too crude and immature to make a leading article, and the argument itself was badly reasoned. No good, logical explanation, for example, was given as to why it was wrong to accept a bribe. The article just implied that what was bad was bad, without bothering to argue the matter. After making play with the ¥5,000 notes and plain brown envelopes, it suddenly turned into a plain man's admonition to give the money back without upsetting anyone. And that was that. The reader was left high and dry.

Yet, despite all these obvious faults, there was something attractive, something lively about the piece. The fact that it was nothing like a normal editorial was a mark in its favour. Most articles on this sort of subject merely churned out idle platitudes, and yet Urano had come up with something that few, if anyone, had said before but everyone had known for ages: the ridiculous fact that electoral malpractice had less to do with any desire for

23

money than with a rather misguided form of socialising.

The story about the journalist being offered a plain brown envelope and handing it back had been provided by one of their colleagues, a man seconded from the arts pages and now close to retirement, who had simply been describing the embarrassing experience of a friend of his. He had told it as a funny story, and his listeners had responded accordingly. The broadcast made by the archbishop in the Philippines had been mentioned by someone in the foreign news section, as a similar kind of joke. Neither had had the faintest idea that what they were saying would ever appear in print, and it seemed unlikely that Urano, while listening to them, had been aware that he might commit the indiscretion of using these anecdotes in something written for publication.

Why, then, had he done so? Yumiko tried to think the situation out logically.

1) There was no other suitable material.

2) The anecdotes went well with the other material he had to hand, such as the ¥5,000 notes and the cheap envelopes.

3) Using their stories was meant as a sort of compliment to them.

4) Being a man who couldn't write, he'd become over-excited at having to produce his first leading article and had lost sight of what he was doing.

5) He may have been aware to some extent that one didn't include that sort of thing in an editorial, but this awareness hadn't yet developed into a guiding principle.

These arguments all made a certain amount of sense, but what must have been decisive was that:

6) His ideas about election violations came from personal experience. Instead of parroting textbook phrases based on Western theories on the subject, he'd used his own observations.

Having reached this still tentative conclusion, Yumiko began to feel a genuine stirring of admiration, to think that maybe this city desk journalist, this man with all his achievements in the real world, who faced up to the realities of present-day Japan as an

24

Asian country, who was indifferent to broad generalisations and transient fashions—this earthy, blunt and uncouth character might well amount to something, might even possess a remarkable and incisive talent. (Let me, as author, add at this point that the listing from one to six reflects Yumiko's own mental processes. She had a tendency to itemise her thoughts whenever she was giving anything her serious attention.)

While she was reasoning along these lines, Yumiko happened to glance at the neighbouring desk, and saw that this man of parts, this possessor of hidden talents, had his hands raised towards her in supplication. He had the look of someone at his wits' end—someone, moreover, who looked, not bright, but imbecilic.

'What on earth is that supposed to mean?'

'Write it for me. Rewrite it for me. Please.'

'Rewrite this?'

'Please. There isn't much time.'

'But it's very good. It's really interesting, and original—honestly it is. I couldn't write anything like that.'

For a moment this fulsome praise made Urano look pleased, but then his old woeful expression returned and, raising his left hand as if to hit her, he told her to cut out the compliments.

'All right, let's suppose it is interesting—you still know as well as I do that no newspaper would print it as it stands.'

'Well, there are a few things the chief mightn't be all that happy about.'

'Not a few things. The whole lot. The whole thing's got to be rewritten. I know that but I don't know where to start. Please—do it for me. I don't mind what you write, I won't complain.'

'Oh, come on.'

'Please. I beg you.'

He really did seem to have worked himself into a state, and she couldn't just ignore him. Little did she know, however, that if he hadn't realised how stupid it would make him look, while running the risk of failing anyway, Urano would have been prepared to prostrate himself before her. He had no idea how else to make her agree, as he was determined she should. In the past, he had managed to get other people—colleagues or underlings—to do his writing for him any number of times, in the Osaka office, in the press club, in the head office, and he'd not once had to grovel, although there was always a degree of discomfort involved. But this was the first time he'd made such a request of a woman, and he was on the verge of panic.

'The trouble is,' Yumiko said, 'I promised my daughter I'd have dinner with her.' Even so, quite casually, she picked up the article, which Urano had left lying in front of her. Rewriting this was going to be a nuisance, and it wasn't the kind of habit she wanted to get into on her first day. Yet she also felt it could be turned into a good editorial, and that it would be a pity to waste it. This ambivalence revealed itself in the casual nature of her gesture, but Urano read it as assent and blurted out:

'Thank you. Thank you. You've saved my life.'

'I haven't said anything yet,' she protested, but she only muttered the words, which anyway sounded unconvincing, suggesting she had effectively given in. So she rang home again, and apologised, and her mother and daughter agreed to wait a while longer, suppressing the pangs of hunger by nibbling biscuits.

When, an hour or so later, Yumiko read through what she'd written she wasn't particularly happy with it. She hadn't actually mucked it up, but the whole thing seemed to have been diluted and made somehow ordinary. Still, after she had passed over the printed version to Urano she got up quietly and headed for the door. Urano noticed and also stood up, expressing his thanks and bowing deeply to her departing back, before going on with his reading.

> The whole country this April will see a rash of local elections. A large number of electoral seats, from governors to town councillors, will have changed hands before the nation settles down after its week-long holiday.
>
> For many people, however, the word 'election' brings to mind the question of electoral malpractice, particularly that

involving the buying and selling of votes. At present, indeed, a surprising amount of this still goes on, and it is impossible to discuss the political set-up in this country without taking this factor into account. It is a matter for regret that a habit which has been effectively stamped out in the West should still be rampant here. Democratic societies are based upon free elections. Our leaders and representatives are chosen by the electoral method, and it is upon this system that we depend when it comes to the running of the country. Consequently, unless we vote for people whose political ideas we share and who are themselves reasonably trustworthy, the system can hardly be said to be functioning properly. If people allow their votes to be bought, then financial influence wins a victory over shared political ideology and individual integrity. And if that is the case, then there is simply nothing left worth trying for. The exchange of votes for money means the destruction of the democratic principle.

This, at least, is the officially accepted view. Like most views of this kind, however, while not necessarily being untrue, it addresses the situation in abstract terms, without dealing with the full reality that most of us face. As an illustration of the form that this reality can commonly take, the following anecdote may be of interest here. A colleague of mine, when he was working at one of our branch offices, was in the habit of going fishing with a man who was influential in the area, and one day he was dismayed to find this same man handing him a brown envelope and asking for his vote. Apparently, what he did was to apologise as courteously as he could and turn it down. Now, as a Tokyo journalist, he was in a relatively easy position to refuse, but if he had been born and brought up in that area there would undoubtedly have been awkward consequences, and his social life would probably have been disrupted in a number of ways.

Why should this happen? Namely, because the fact that

he was chosen to receive one of these envelopes implied his acceptance as a member of a particular social group. His refusal would constitute a breach of manners and a rejection. All his previous relations with the group, all his actions in that context up to that time, would lose their value, while any further contact might well be treated with at least restraint, if not suspicion.

I said it was a brown envelope that my colleague was given, without specifying its contents, which we can assume were much the same as in any other part of the country. The extent to which this particular convention has spread becomes clear when you realise that to buy such envelopes in a local stationer's while an electoral campaign is under way is considered proof of electoral malpractice. The choice of a plain brown envelope can be attributed to the feeling that anything more expensive would seem flashy, quite apart from adding unnecessarily to election expenses; but, however ordinary the envelope, it still serves to show that what is being offered is a gift, to demonstrate that the main intention is not to buy your vote but to offer a gesture of respect and friendship. Even so, it is only natural when accepting a gesture of this kind to feel obliged to do something in return, and if the other person involved is a candidate in an election, then there will be a strong inclination to let him have your vote.

A few years ago, during the presidential election in the Philippines, a Catholic archbishop stated on the radio that it was all right to accept money so long as you didn't let it influence your vote. This may seem a sensible piece of advice, but in practice it is very difficult to follow. One only has to look at the fact that, although Marcos did eventually lose, he still managed to get a sizeable number of votes, to find evidence of the particular psychological process I have described.

It is clear that two major principles govern the way we

28

live now. The first is what can be called the village principle—the desire to have our relations with our neighbours
run as smoothly as possible. The second principle is urban,
in that it governs the way we are obliged to behave in terms
of modern political life in our cities. Generally, when an
election is held, these two principles come into conflict. For
that reason, if someone hands you a brown envelope, you
should give it back to him, making sure you observe the village principle by doing this as calmly and cheerfully as you
can, so as to cause the least possible offence, before casting
your totally impartial vote.

As Urano read this, he felt himself growing more and more
cheerful, until by the end of it he was positively overjoyed. If
analysed à la Yumiko Minami, his state of mind would have
revealed three main components, each jostling the other to produce this powerful emotional response:

1) Relief that his editorial was, after all, written.

2) Self-satisfaction, on realising that his ideas, now they
were readable, were really rather striking.

3) A hopeful expectation that he would be able to get this
colleague to write other things for him in the future.

His happiness did not falter even in the editing process, when
the deputy chief made various corrections to what Yumiko had
already corrected, using even duller language, making the meaning in places hopelessly vague, and effecting all those other changes
for the worse which go under the name of editing. The feeling
lasted through the monitor printout, the first proofs, right up until he read it in the paper itself when it was delivered the next
morning—in fact, it probably increased, because the layout made
his editorial appear more impressive than when he had last seen
it, and by this time he had forgotten the details of what he'd
actually written and was again moved that his opinions should
appear to such good effect. This was a bit different from having
one's scoop written up by a young reporter; this was real writing,
the joy of creative expression—or so Urano was beginning to

think, for he was more and more under the impression that he had done it all himself.

Now, newspaper editorials are hardly ever read. There is even a theory that the number of people who read them is actually smaller than the sum of all the editorial writers in the country, but Urano's first effort prompted a genuine response. On the very afternoon of the day it appeared, it happened that the president of the paper was sitting next to one of the leaders of the ruling party at a certain barber's shop in Ginza, and this important man said the article was unacceptable, everybody was angry about it, and he himself thought it grossly exaggerated. This was immediately reported to the editorial section chief, who only smiled, pleased that the piece seemed to have hit home, and that its accuracy had been confirmed in this indirect way. What particularly pleased him was the idea that 'everybody' was angry: he wondered how many Diet members were implicated in that word, speculating with his deputies as to whether it might be less than five, or just possibly more than ten.

Not one reader's response was prompted by Yumiko's article. Her own reaction to this was complex, but she came to three basic conclusions:

　　1) Her opinion of Urano's editorial had been correct.

　　2) The editorial would have been better if they had left it as she wrote it.

　　3) Anyway, she hadn't done herself any good by it.

Two days after the encounter between the president and the politician, Urano was asked at the staff meeting to write something for the evening edition's regular column, 'Starting from Scratch'. This required little more than a few casual comments, and his turn had come earlier than usual because some of the other people were either ill or abroad. But another reason for the choice was a natural desire to use the writer whose first effort had provoked such a sharp response, coupled with an element of sheer curiosity as to whether he'd be able to persuade Yumiko to do it for him again. The staff was made up of experts in the acquisition and propagation of rumour, and most of them were aware of the process that had transformed Urano's editorial into something publishable.

'What, me again?' he muttered, sounding unwilling, but then adding: 'Actually I do have a bit of stuff about what goes on behind the scenes when the government awards get dished out.'

Everybody, from the chief down, thought this an excellent idea, since the awards were to be announced at the end of the month, and the meeting ended on a cheerful note. So Urano proceeded to phone a number of people to get further information, then, having learned from experience, went off to the local soba shop for a fairly substantial meal and, to make doubly sure, returned to his desk equipped with sandwiches, milk and Oolong tea.

Since 'Starting from Scratch' required only a few hundred words and was a series of observations rather than an editorial, he felt it would be reasonably easy to write, particularly as he had a personal interest in the subject. Among his relations was an old man who had been head of a village council and had lived for years in the hope that he would receive some kind of medal; but the years passed in silence, until he died at the age of seventy-five. It was in memory of him—and of the many who must have suffered the same fate—that he wanted to write this story. He also had an anecdote he could use from a career civil servant who once worked in the prime minister's office, and who hadn't added the disclaimer that what he was saying was off the record.

However, when he got down to it, Urano found he had so much material that the brevity of the article made it more, not less, difficult to write. He opened with what he'd intended to be a brisk account of the schedule for the spring awards, beginning with the announcement on 29 April, then going on to the actual ceremonies during the first week of May when the first-class awards were personally bestowed by the emperor, the second-class by the prime minister, the third-class by the various ministers concerned, followed by an audience with the emperor the same afternoon. This all became fairly confused in the writing, with Urano somehow implying that recipients in the second category weren't presented to the emperor, which called for a line tacked on explaining: 'Needless to say, those who are awarded second-class decorations also receive an audience with the emperor...' His sense of relief at having caught this blunder was then spoiled by the realisation that he'd used up practically half his allotted space by then, but he pressed on, telling himself that he'd cut it down ruthlessly somehow later.

Now, to qualify for an award you have to have reached the age of seventy. There are a number of people who, if they reach the age of seventy, can reasonably expect to get something, but if one considers the fact that life expectancy has grown in recent years, with the market getting more crowded every year, and if everyone continues to live for a long time, then, from the broader perspective, the present system has both its advantages as well as its drawbacks.

There was something wrong with that 'advantages as well as its drawbacks', and 'from the broader perspective' sounded stupid—still, it didn't matter ... he'd fix it later.

Now, the actual decisions are taken during the first week in April, and if nobody has phoned you by the 15th you can safely assume you've had it for that year. Considering the fact that the increase in the numbers of old people is causing extra work for the organisers, you could well be made to wait another four or five years. [Hang on—haven't I said that already?] Anyway, there are people who die waiting, and you can imagine just how mortified they must feel, and, in this connection, I can remember as if it were yesterday a letter I got from a relative of mine, the old-fashioned kind rolled up like a scroll, who'd been head of a village council and thought he was due for something, and could I help, because if so he'd see I was all right. And after that his son turned up asking me to put in a word for his dad in the right places, so off I went to the Bureau of

Municipal Affairs with a couple of bottles of best quality saké...

No, there was no need to go into all that detail, better cut it ... and he started to cross it all out. But while he was doing so the sandwiches on his bookshelf, which had been bothering him for some time, began to prey on his mind. It wasn't that long since he'd eaten a large meal at the soba shop, so there was no question of his being hungry. Perhaps it was an intellectual curiosity as to what they might taste like—but that seemed a bit far-fetched; a more likely reason was just that they were distracting him, and he didn't think he'd be able to work properly unless he removed the source of distraction by seeing what they tasted like. So he tried the ham sandwich, washed down with plenty of milk, and then the egg salad one, but now he was genuinely full up and couldn't manage any more. To help his digestion he took three brisk turns about the building—in fact, so brisk he found himself sweating heavily and felt he really ought to go to the basement and take a shower, stopping himself only at the last moment when he realised how much time he'd wasted.

At this point it is necessary to explain what these awards actually are. [I can get that out of a book.] What one mustn't forget is what determines the nature of the award, i.e. the kind of public office a person has held and for how long. Although they can be given to people in other jobs, the majority still go to people in some kind of public office. To speed things up, it might help if we give some examples: thus someone who has served one term as a cabinet minister gets the very highest level of the first-class awards, but right at the other end of the scale [that's going to upset somebody, it'll have to be changed], the fourth-class awards are given to headmasters of state schools, heads of tax offices, mayors etc.; the fifth-class is for deputy chief inspectors, heads of village councils, ships' captains, dentists, organisers of midwives' associations etc.; the sixth-class is for members of statistical research teams, local postmasters, chief wardens at reform schools; and the seventh is for seconds-in-command at fire stations, junior law-court officials, heads of committees for the investigation and preservation of objects of cultural value in remote prefectures…

Looking back over the paragraph, he sighed nervously, wondering what on earth he was going to do: he already had twice as many words as he needed, and couldn't think how to cut them down. Perhaps it was the sandwiches he'd eaten. And he should never have drunk a whole carton of milk. In fact he felt so sleepy he decided to take a rest and, stretching out on the sofa, fell into a doze, dreaming he was a child again, that it was summer, and that his dead uncle was with him in a room, pinning a beer top to his chest as if it were a medal. When he complained that he hated being treated like a child, the dream began to fade, changing from technicolor to black and white, from black and white to sepia, then off-white, and finally into a pure white, at which stage of this longish trance he decided that it should stop, so he got up, washed his face, and settled down to his writing again.

He read through what he'd already done, seeing that it was muddled and not very interesting, but deciding it would have to do. After all, the readership he had in mind was made up more of ordinary public servants than up-and-coming mayors and keen-eyed detectives, so it wasn't a bad thing to keep hammering home some points. Anyway, it was time to get to the main part of the story, the episode he'd heard from his informant in the prime minister's office:

Soichiro Honda, a leading figure in the world of finance and industry, was vice-president of the Automobile Makers Association, of the Tokyo Council of Commerce and Industry, and of many other organisations, but always in that capacity, never as a full president, so strictly speaking, as a second-in-command all he could expect was a second-class decoration. This obviously wasn't good enough for a great man like that, but luckily the awards-giving committee was able to dig up one instance where he was an actual chairman, even if it was only Chairman of the Action Committee against Prostitution, and so he could be given a first-class award. I think this story shows, in a nutshell, what the awards business is all about. So if you don't get one there's nothing to get upset about. The end.

When he re-read this he realised that the anecdote with which he'd expected to bring the article to a resounding close had fallen flat, and that the argument itself didn't seem to make much sense. So, all right, that hadn't come off, it couldn't be helped ... but he couldn't cut the rest down to the right length either. There was no point in starting from scratch, because he knew he couldn't provide the kind of noncommittal comment that was the staple of this column. He had things to say ... so what the hell was he to do?

The situation was desperate. Urano bewailed his lot, cursed God and his boss, and abused himself for the stupid way he'd cheerfully accepted the task in the first place. He was also, if the truth be told, annoyed with Yumiko Minami. She had disappeared after lunch, and it didn't look as if she'd be back again today. What on earth did she think she was up to? Even the deputy chief hadn't been to see how he was getting on. They'd all abandoned him. It was seven o'clock now and the deadline could probably be extended until eight, but the way things were going he didn't look like making that either. He supposed he'd have to find somebody else to rewrite the piece for him...

He was lost in thought when he heard a burst of laughter at his side. Looking up, he saw Yumiko Minami standing there. As soon as the staff meeting had come to an end she had left the building, first to interview the ambassadress of an African country, then to buy some curtains, a rug for her entrance hall, three lacquer bowls, and some shoes at a department store, and, after a light meal with a woman friend who worked in the Ministry of Labour, she'd dropped in at the office again. She had forgotten all about Urano, and found the sight of him sitting at his desk, head in hands, with the same dejected air she'd seen only a couple of days ago, extremely funny.

'You really shouldn't laugh, you know,' said Urano. 'Not when someone's in the mess I'm in.'

'I'm sorry, I really am. But you look exactly as you did the other day.'

'Yes. Ludicrous, I admit. Very amusing. But it was a definite breach of manners to laugh. As a penance I think you should re-write this for me.'

Urano passed over his article, inwardly rejoicing at the timing of her appearance, and Yumiko accepted it in the same half-accidental way she had before, aware that she was curious to see what he'd come up with this time. She read it through to the end, still laughing. It wasn't as interesting as the editorial he'd written, but it certainly had something; on the other hand, she felt the combination of anti-establishment feeling and inside information from a government source to be very much what one would expect of a Tokyo journalist, and was also struck that he wasn't so much congratulating people on receiving prizes as consoling those who hadn't. And with the best will in the world, it could hardly be called well written.

'It's very interesting. This story about Soichiro Honda is hilarious. Is it true?'

'Oh it's true all right, don't you worry.'

'I know it's exactly the sort of thing that goes on, but I just wondered…'

'Look, I realise we can't leave it like this. It's well over the word limit for a start. Still, I can't seem to cut it down or rephrase it. Writing's damn difficult, isn't it? You know, I was hopeless at composition when I was at school… But I told you that before, didn't I? Still, you'll do it for me, won't you?' He pressed his hands together in prayer again and, keeping this humble pose, went on: 'You can rewrite it as much as you like, I don't mind. Please do it for me. Please.'

'All right. I'll do it—only stop begging.'

Having reassured Urano, Yumiko questioned him minutely about the whole business, then sent him off to the sports desk and the library to research a couple of things for her. As a former chief crime reporter he was quick to grasp what was required, asking no questions that weren't relevant and finding exactly what was wanted. Once she'd got everything she needed, Yumiko started to write. She opened with the statement that it was now time for the spring awards, and that, although the awards themselves had meaning enough, the process that decided who got what was in many ways absurd. Put briefly, the kind of gong you got was determined less by individual achievement than by factors related to which service you had worked in, and particularly by how long you had been there and what rank you had reached. A glance at the pecking order ('I'm afraid I had to cut an awful lot here,' she said) showed that the top awards went to ministers who had served at least one term of office, above which there was a special order given so far only to two former prime ministers and that solely for length of service—Yoshida for five terms in office, and Sato for three. The logic behind the award-giving became quite clear in a case like that involving Soichiro Honda, of motorcycle fame, who had managed to get his first-class award only on the apparent assumption that his principal contribution to society had been as chairman of an anti-prostitution committee. Then came the concluding paragraph:

> This is very much like maintaining that a professional baseball star such as Shigeo Nagashima should be valued, not for the number of RBIs he hit, nor for the excellence of his infield play, nor even for the fact that the Giants won the pennant race a number of times while he was playing for them, but because he was president of the Old Folks Croquet Council. Surely it's about time this absurd, illogical system was changed.

There was no reference to people in their seventies who waited and waited and never received a thing, but Yumiko felt this was covered in the overall argument. Urano read the article carefully a couple of times, praised the way she had rewritten it, and thanked her again.

'So that's why you wanted that stuff on Nagashima. I was wondering what on earth you were up to there. That's clever, very clever.'

Yumiko was secretly quite pleased with that part herself, but she only smiled and said modestly:

'Nagashima's like Marilyn Monroe—mention them as much as you like, no one ever complains.'

'Just what one would expect of a very brainy woman. Sorry—I should have said a very beautiful woman and brainy to boot. It's a great piece of work.'

'You're wasting your talents in this outfit, you should be running the advertising department.'

Despite a slight feeling of anti-climax, she still felt the excitement that remains after writing something, even as short as Urano's article. Her eyes were shining, and she found herself making jokes; she certainly didn't look as if she were in any hurry to go home. Urano himself felt as happy as a schoolboy after having his composition improved for him by a woman teacher—which thought led unexpectedly to another. He began to wonder why Yumiko was being so nice to him. Obviously, considering the fuss he'd made, it would have been hard for her to refuse, but that didn't really explain it, and eventually he came to a tentative conclusion: that this was no ordinary kindness, not something attributable simply to the fact that they were both new members of staff, that their desks were next to each other, that she couldn't bear the sight of a grown man, an important journalist, going through such torments, or that she found what he'd written interesting (although clearly that wasn't an empty compliment). No, it was for some more interesting reason; this was a relationship qualitatively different from any he'd had with the people who had done his articles for him before.

While he was pondering these mysteries, a sudden and this time genuinely startling thought came to him. This woman must surely be in love with him. That was the obvious explanation—astonishing even to him, but inescapable. She had, after all, done him this favour twice by now; indeed, her behaviour at this very moment demonstrated the truth of what he was thinking, for in her obvious unwillingness to bring the encounter to a close he saw a deeper need—to give the man she loved a helping hand.

It was well known that Yumiko had married while still in her early twenties, but had divorced soon afterwards and remained single ever since. Although she had a number of men friends (none of whom, however, worked for the paper), nobody knew whether any were her lovers. All this Urano now recalled, before plunging into an extended daydream in which Yumiko broke off with her unknown lover at the very time when, as luck would have it, Urano appeared on the scene. He was a great believer in the workings of fate, and had always been in the habit, when investigating some large-scale crime such as fraud or corruption, of wondering whether he might have had some connection with the suspect in a previous incarnation.

At this point a tiny yawn escaped Yumiko, prompting Urano to the slightly hasty conclusion that she might be signalling a desire to go off somewhere and have a quick lie-down; this was in fact a misapprehension, but so confident was he of its accuracy that he felt it would be rude to ignore her wish and, with the invitation behind his words only thinly veiled, said:

'Well, I obviously owe you for the two articles you've done. Why don't we go and have a bite to eat somewhere? If you can spare the time, of course.'

Yumiko's reply was unexpectedly prosaic.

'Oh, don't worry. I've already had dinner anyway. Let's make it some other time.'

She did smile, however, and to Urano that smile seemed subtly provocative, even though her matter-of-fact rejection had shaken him. He'd misread the yawn, it seemed, but the smile said she was looking forward to being taken out in future, and was also willing to rewrite many more articles for him—all of which was only natural, seeing that she was crazy about him.

'Well then,' he said gallantly, 'till we meet again, adieu,' adding, when he heard the deputy chief's voice aimed in his direction: 'Yes, it's done. I'll just bring it over.'

He signed his name at the bottom of the article and stood up. The deputy looked through it, then smiled:

'That's not bad at all.'

'Someone wrote it for me,' Urano said, but the man only nodded.

There were only three places where corrections were needed. The title was contributed by the deputy, after two cigarettes to get himself in a suitably thoughtful frame of mind. It was: 'The Awards'.

When Urano returned to his own desk Yumiko was no longer there, but he interpreted this as a sweet desire on her part to conceal her feelings from him; and once he'd arrived at this conclusion he began to reflect on the merits of the mature woman, the woman in her forties, who retained only traces of the slender delicacy of youth in her features and frame, but had a physical ripeness—the fruit of masculine endeavour—as alluring as any virginal innocence. This panegyric, however, was interrupted by a thought even cruder than the headlines dreamed up by the make-up chief when they were suffering staff shortages. As he was preparing to leave, vaguely looking in the direction of the cuddly toy Shirobei, he realised this was going to be the first time he'd ever slept with a woman who had been to university.

Urano made a point of knowing what people's level of education was, whether they belonged to the paper or not. His first reaction, when someone came to mind, was to remember what college he'd been to, if he'd graduated or dropped out, sometimes even which school he'd attended, in just the same way that a baseball reporter had at his fingertips the career of any player, including whether he'd played in the high-school championships, where he'd been drafted and where traded. But this was the first time Urano had found himself thinking in these terms about a woman. The fact was that only two of all the women he'd ever known had got as far as junior college; and deep down he had always felt a sense of frustration at this lack of higher learning in them, which was probably why the present thought had popped into his mind.

The two exceptions were his wife and a woman who had been married to a detective sergeant in Osaka. At that period in his provincial career Urano had no longer been involved with the police as a crime reporter, but he still knew the face of the woman's husband very well. He could remember it all as if it were yesterday: one afternoon in mid-summer, he had been leaving a cheap hotel with her when he suddenly saw the sergeant leaning against a telegraph pole bang opposite the hotel entrance, just standing there, with what seemed to be an assortment of shiny objects dangling about him. It looked as if this was going to be a real showdown, and Urano decided to tough it out; but luckily, as soon as he dropped a broad hint that he knew all about the bribes the sergeant was taking from gangsters (something Urano had suspected for ages but for which he had never had any solid proof), the man turned deathly pale and, without a word, grabbed his wife's hand and led her off, as if he were taking her into custody. As Urano watched them go he realised that all those shiny things were in fact the silver wrappings of some toffees stuffed in the sergeant's pockets. The man had a sweet tooth. That had been over ten years ago—as long as that.

Urano went down in the lift, left the building and set off for his usual sushi restaurant, thinking about Yumiko as he walked, the tender feelings this inspired seizing on the difference in status between a mere junior college and a real university, and in turn enveloping the woman in a romantic haze which gave added lustre to her eyes, put a youthful glow back on her skin, but left her with the erotic maturity of a woman in her forties, thereby creating an image of the ideal lover to trouble and torment his mind.

TWO

. . .

As they walked the short distance from the concert hall to the Vietnamese restaurant under a clear night sky in mid-May, the three of them talked enthusiastically about the singer they had just heard. She was a soprano from Eastern Europe, and they particularly admired the way she sang operetta.

'It was like coming across a new species of bird,' said Chie Minami. As a graduate studying English literature she was keen on metaphor.

'Her voice is certainly a lot more expressive now than it was on her early records,' one of the young men replied more critically. He was an assistant professor who taught Japanese history, and his name was Takero Shibukawa.

'Oh, I agree,' said Masaya Miyake, by way of endorsing both comments, as was appropriate for an up-and-coming bureaucrat in the Finance Ministry.

Given this start to the evening, it was natural that the topic of conversation in the restaurant should be people's voices. They were shown to a table by the wall, and the girl, who was wearing a dress of a blue hydrangea colour, sat alone with her back to it while the two young men, in suits, sat facing her. Once they were seated Shibukawa immediately said:

'I got quite a surprise when I phoned you the other day: your mother's voice sounds just like yours—exactly the same.' The mother whose voice so resembled the girl's was Yumiko Minami of the *New Daily*.

'Our voices do sound similar on the phone.' Chie said, nodding. 'We look quite different, though.'

'Ah.'

'Mummy has fairly exotic features, rather like her aunt—my great-aunt, that is. She was a film star, you see.'

'Was she? What was her name?'

'Aeka Yanagi.'

'Never heard of her.'

Miyake, his eyes still fixed on the menu since he was ordering the food, said:

'Aeka Yanagi? I seem to have heard the name somewhere.'

'Yes, she's supposed to have been quite famous. For about ten years after the war, anyway.'

'Which gives *my* age away.'

'Still, it shows what a good memory you've got,' she said.

Miyake conferred with the waiter while Shibukawa said:

'It's interesting you should sound alike and yet look so different.'

'I take after my grandmother.'

'In that case she must be a very handsome lady.'

Miyake felt obliged to interrupt them at this point and said, looking up:

'Can't you think of a subtler compliment than that?'

They all laughed cheerfully, a little too cheerfully, but there was a reason for the slight artificiality that ran through their relationship. The two young men had been close friends since high school, and had made the acquaintance of Chie Minami at about the same time. They had also both been powerfully attracted by her slightly sad expression, by the girlish face that nevertheless was capable of showing a surprising depth of feeling; while she, for her part, had shown no preference for either of them, treating both with strict impartiality. It might perhaps be truer to say that she liked them both but loved neither, not having yet experienced

43

that emotion. Thus, since the two men were determined that their rivalry should not bring an end to their friendship, they found themselves in a rather strange relationship to each other: both getting the same treatment, and both seeing no reason why they shouldn't report back to each other from time to time on how Chie was responding, or discuss what their own reactions should be.

Today the two of them had invited her out to console her for her failure to be accepted for postgraduate studies at a national university, meaning that she would have to stay on at the women's college from which she'd graduated that spring. So although the evening was supposed to be a treat, the girl was still unhappy about failing her exam, while the two men had their emotional entanglement to worry about. They were thus all three determined to behave as if they had nothing on their minds and to make the occasion go as smoothly as possible.

Though it seemed a rather un-Vietnamese dish to order, they started off with some smoked salmon accompanied by a bit of sliced radish, and, after toasting each other in Chinese wine, they got back to the question of voices.

'Mummy's friends sound much the same too,' said Chie, which was interpreted by the others as a veiled reference to various boyfriends.

They knew a certain amount about Chie's home life, since she had once, unasked, told them something about it. Her mother, Yumiko, had married a man who worked in a bank, but a short while after Chie was born they divorced. Yumiko had taken custody of the child and had remained single, while the father was now the chief executive or president of some bank in Hokkaido. Having been brought up in a one-parent family Chie was unlikely, they felt, to be thinking much about marriage herself, although she was presumably not going to turn her back on the possibility if it arose. In fact their main preoccupation, in Chie's absence, was her mother's love life. When Shibukawa was an assistant lecturer at the university where he still worked, Miyake, who was then head of a provincial tax office, came across a picture of the mother in a magazine and sent it to him. It was this picture that had engaged their interest, since Yumiko was obviously a beautiful woman and, being unmarried, most unlikely to be without a lover; they were convinced, moreover, that he must be someone of note, someone with real status. But, as they could hardly ask Yumiko's daughter to find out for them, and neither knew anyone who worked at the *New Daily*, they still didn't know who this man was. And inevitably their interest in his identity had gradually faded into the background except when, as now, Chie came up with something that might shed some light on it.

'Musicians, though, seem to be quite different,' she said, referring to a conductor who performed mostly overseas and who had rung up the other day. After only a couple of words with Chie, he'd asked for her mother.

'It's not surprising. People like that can tell, just listening to a record, not only when one of the violinists has made a mistake, but what seat in the orchestra he's sitting in,' Miyake added, instantly casting this conductor in the lover's role, and thinking that as he wasn't often in Japan, Yumiko would be left on her own a lot.

'Must have a terrific ear,' muttered Shibukawa, also wondering if this might be the man, but assuming that as the daughter had mentioned him pretty casually there couldn't be much going on between them.

The three praised the wine, and the two men drank quite a lot of it while the girl sipped hers. Chie felt that, since the party was for her, she should be making interesting conversation, but she couldn't think of any more promising subject and resorted to her mother's men friends again, offering the names of a painter whose pictures had recently gone up considerably in price, a civil servant in MITI who was due to be made the next under-secretary, and a chemist who was rumoured to be a candidate for the Nobel Prize.

'When I pass the phone to Mummy they're all amazed it wasn't her in the first place. She says they all sound as if they find it rather disturbing.'

45

'She seems to have some pretty important friends.'

'And they all keep on telephoning?'

'Yes. She's rather popular. That's not the end of the list, either.'

Chie smiled, and went on with other names: an authority on cancer research, a second-generation Diet member who was said to be on the verge of taking over the leadership of one of the ruling party factions, a distinguished writer of historical novels (on both Oriental and European themes), another politician (this one in the opposition), an architect, and the president of a company known for its bold development of new technology.

'And all these act as a sort of guard of honour for her?'

'Yes, she likes them in a group.'

Miyake merely grunted in assent, thinking first that it would be a source of some pride to have a mother-in-law who led such an exotic social life, and then that it was hardly likely that a person like her would allow herself to be tied down by one man. Shibukawa, on the other hand, wondered why someone who so rarely said anything even faintly boastful should show off like this about her mother, but, catching sight of her enigmatic smile, assumed there was something else to come, and waited for it.

'Still, it's rather odd, don't you think,' Chie said, 'that they should all be older than her, and that there's only one each from so many different walks of life? Although there are two politicians, admittedly.'

'But they're from different sides of the house,' the civil servant put in.

'The truth is, there's a reason for it.'

According to Chie, when Yumiko was in her late twenties and had been working on the women's page, the new man in charge of the lifestyle pages (at that time men still held such posts) said jokingly that he thought it odd that the women's page didn't deal with women's favourite subject, namely men, and suggested a series called 'Men: the Pre-Forties' consisting of interviews with up-and-coming people from various professions all in their thirties. Yumiko was chosen to do the interviews and the series was a great success with everyone, her interviewees included. This was how she had got to know so many talented men. Since then almost twenty years had passed, and except for a strikingly good-looking Kabuki actor (specialising in women's parts) who had suddenly died, all of them were alive and well, and all were at the top of their professions—which only went to show, said Chie with a smile, how smart the idea had been and how much research must have been done by the staff to get all that information together. At least, that was what her mother said.

'Oh, she's just being modest. Obviously men like that would want to know a really talented journalist, particularly when she's good-looking and intelligent too,' said Miyake, although he didn't go on with what he meant to say, which was that, since most men want more than friendship with an attractive single woman and tend to drift away if there seems little chance of that, she must be extremely clever to have her 'pre-forties' still hanging around. Or did it just mean that middle-aged men were remarkably patient and prepared to wait a long time? He didn't say any of this, however, because it would take only one misplaced word to make it sound as if he were implying she was in the habit of sleeping around. And, fortunately, the other two didn't seem to notice the way he abruptly stopped talking.

'Hold on a moment,' said Shibukawa, who started counting on his fingers. He was working out how many men were involved. 'It's an odd number to choose, neither ten nor a round dozen. Eleven.'

'Is someone missing, perhaps?'

'Maybe,' said Chie. Personally, she was less interested in the question of who her mother's men friends were than in the difference in rhyming techniques between the Italian and the Shakespearean sonnet, or the number of novels Jane Austen wrote.

Some Vietnamese-style spring rolls arrived, and Miyake suggested they give the sweet wine a rest and order some beer. This went down so well with the jasmine-coloured rolls in their wrappings of perilla and lettuce that all three felt they'd be happy to go on drinking it. Favourable comments were also made on the food itself, before Miyake returned to their original subject.

'It must be quite a business keeping up with all those men, particularly people of that calibre. But they probably provide some pretty valuable information as well. She must often get asked things—to do favours, for example.'

'You think so?'

'It seems likely.'

'Maybe.'

'She must be kept pretty busy anyway, even if she only meets each of them once a year,' said Shibukawa, and Chie agreed.

'Invitations to parties and so on, tickets to the theatre and opera, things like that.'

Miyake washed the last spring roll down with a mouthful of beer and said:

'Still, even if they are a group there must be a pecking order.'

'You mean in terms of intimacy?'

'Yes. Who's she on best terms with?'

Miyake realised this could sound as if he were saying that any-one unmarried would be happier with one settled lover rather than a host of them. He did in fact think that, but he would have found it hard to argue his case, particularly in front of this girl.

'Well, I'm hardly likely to know something like that, am I?' Chie quickly replied, and Shibukawa tried to stop his friend, say-ing it was none of their business. But to no effect.

'I would have thought you could work that out by the way your mother talks about them.'

'Well, I can't.'

'Which means, perhaps, it isn't one of them?' Miyake said, looking at her quizzically.

'Maybe, maybe not,' the girl said playfully. Of course she had a very good idea who her mother's lover was, but she was hardly going to tell these two.

'You can't tell by the way they talk on the phone?' Miyake per-sisted.

'No. Important people like that never say anything revealing on the phone.'

'Implying,' Miyake said (perhaps falling back on a mode of

interrogation that belonged to his days as an inspector catching out tax evaders), 'that there is another kind of man who does tend to say revealing things on the phone?'

Chie responded in tax-evader fashion for a moment, going red and not knowing quite how to reply, and the inspector pressed his advantage home.

'Who? Who was it? Did he mistake you for someone else and say something strange?'

Shibukawa seemed to have forgotten his role as a restraining influence and was craning forward. So Chie smiled enigmatically again and decided her best course was to tell the truth. Apparently when she'd answered the phone the other day she'd heard the voice of a man she didn't recognise—an uncultivated, boorish voice—suddenly say, 'Thank you, thank you again and again—I love you, truly I love you,' in the impassioned, repetitive tones of an election candidate shouting from his campaign car. When she asked him to hold the line a moment he let out a cry of amazement and confusion, like a complete idiot. Her mother then came to the phone and Chie didn't hear what followed because the laundry arrived and she had to take care of it; afterwards, her mother signalled to her that the conversation was private, so Chie went to her own room. When the phone call finally came to an end she'd asked her mother who it was, only to be told that it was someone who had joined the editorial writing staff in April, at the same time as her; it seemed he'd been a crack crime reporter and had won lots of prizes, but he didn't know how to write and had to get someone to do it for him. Naturally he couldn't get away with this so easily now that he was one of the editorial writers, but since her mother was sitting at the next desk he got her to help him sometimes. The trouble was, each time she helped him out he thought it was because she fancied him, and the result was he'd fallen for her.

'She gave him a real telling-off, and he got all sulky and depressed. For her he's just a colleague, of course. And then he had the nerve to ask her to give his regards to me! He sounds crazy.'

This produced a burst of laughter from the other two, who

49

noted that 'regards' were a conveniently meaningless thing to give—as meaningless, in fact, as journalists who couldn't write, though there were plenty of academics who couldn't, either.

'Then I got this,' Chie said, showing them an expensive, dark green French handbag that went well with her bluish dress.

'He had it sent from a department store.'

'As a mark of apology,' said Miyake.

'It was supposed to be a thank-you present to my mother, but she felt if she accepted it herself she'd have to give him something in return, and that might lead to more awkwardness, so—since it'd be unkind to send it back—she gave it to me.'

'So you've done quite well out of it.'

'Yes.'

'Claiming to be a thank-you present but in reality…' Miyake broke off, because he meant it was really a gift from an admirer and he didn't want to say that outright, but the girl knew exactly what he was thinking and simply agreed, taking a small fan out of her handbag and using it lightly on her face. She looked flushed, perhaps to a certain extent because of the drink, but mostly from embarrassment as she realised she'd given away too much. Luckily the next course turned up at that point, fried tofu stuffed with mince meat. This was delicious, and she said so, and Shibukawa announced that it ought to become part of their own cuisine. Miyake, however, lowered his voice and suggested they shouldn't get too excited, since this was the high point of today's meal and the quality would probably decline from here on.

After a moment Shibukawa asked Chie if he might look at her fan. It had a line from a Chinese poem written on it, and he managed to make out what it meant.

' "A fresh breeze fans your emerald brows": just right for a lady's fan.'

'A friend of mine's grandfather wrote it for me.'

'Someone you know?'

'No. He saw a photo of me and said the fan was for this young lady. That's what I was told anyway. Sounds rather silly.'

'Both mother and child seem to be very popular,' Miyake put

in cynically, while Shibukawa was trying to decipher the name on the seal beneath the written characters.

'Looks like Banzan.'

'Banzan?' said Miyake in surprise, snatching the fan and staring at it for a while. It seemed the name had some significance for him, as he proceeded to explain.

Banzan Onuma had begun his career as a provincial schoolmaster teaching Chinese and brush writing, but after the war he had somehow found his way to the centre of things, opening a calligraphy school in Tokyo and becoming a university lecturer at the same time. It seemed one of the pupils he'd had as a schoolmaster had become a cabinet minister, and this minister asked Banzan for specialist tuition in calligraphy and the writing of Chinese poems; and since he eventually became the leader of a government faction, and then prime minister, Banzan soon added a number of politicians to his list of pupils. His method of instruction in the correct style of using the brush consisted mainly in sitting next to his distinguished students and bestowing immoderate praise on their efforts, but since they all seemed to appreciate this way of doing things his popularity soon grew. Similarly, his interpretations of poetry were easy to understand and highly quotable, and the fact that his pupils, including the prime minister, found themselves able to use such quotations in their speeches was another mark in his favour. When, for some reason, the prime minister was dismissed from office, his closest colleague was called on to form a cabinet, with the result that Banzan, now in the position of mentor to a second prime minister, found his self-importance considerably inflated and began (no doubt with the encouragement of his entourage) to consider himself a modern-day Yasuoka. (This Yasuoka was a scholar of Chinese who had been mentor to a series of prime ministers, starting with Shigeru Yoshida, just after the war; a man of great popularity, his lectures were widely attended by dignitaries from the worlds of politics, finance and the civil service. Most people would agree, however, that Banzan wasn't in the same class.)

'I've never heard of him,' Shibukawa admitted. 'His writing

doesn't look too good either, though it does at least have the virtue of being legible.'

'If I go and visit him it seems he'll do a large scroll specially for me. Still, what use is a thing like that?' said Chie, immediately feeling that perhaps she wouldn't mind one after all. 'I suppose they must be worth quite a lot,' she added.

'Can't really tell,' said Miyake, and while he was considering the matter the next course arrived, boiled red sea bream with some spicy seasoning, all in all quite tasty. It was Miyake who had been responsible for ordering this dish, so he remained noncommittal about it, but the other two dutifully said how much they were enjoying it.

Chie now changed the subject, wondering aloud, to neither of them in particular, why Japanese politicians had such a thing about brush writing. Shibukawa glanced at Miyake, who waved his hand to indicate he would leave the answer to his learned friend.

'That's a very good question, Chie. But shouldn't we be asking, not just why they do such things, but why people want them to do it *for* them? One has to try to imagine what kind of person actually wants some piece of writing just because it was done by a well-known politician—after all, neither of *us* would want that sort of thing, and it's surprising *any*body should.'

'I don't want any either,' Miyake interjected, and Shibukawa promptly apologised for not including him in their number before going on.

Receiving scrolls written by politicians was a ritual performed in countries that used Chinese characters in their writing system. Naturally the idea originated in China itself, where in ancient times anybody who wanted a career in government had to pass the higher civil service exams. There was no exam in writing itself, but people were obliged to do essays and obviously you couldn't get away with bad handwriting, even if you were unlikely to fail for this reason alone. So everybody who passed the exams and became a court official could write well, in addition to their general scholarship. It was as a result of this that the custom developed of asking such officials to write for those less skilled, the practice eventually spreading abroad. Finally, even ignorant soldiers, who wrote very clumsily, started to do scrolls for people. Chang Tso-lin, for example, the warlord who was murdered by the Japanese military, was illiterate, but once he'd subdued Manchuria he learned how to write, until he could produce his own scrolls on demand.

Since military men could write such things, it was pretty obvious that no artistic merit attached to these writings; the custom of putting them in frames, or fastening a roller to the bottom and hanging them on the wall, merely demonstrated that one was under the protection of such and such a person. Those who wrote them were perfectly well aware of how they would be used. And yet, beneath this surface function (which is rightly called political), was another, hidden from view. According to Chinese politics, the way a country was ruled depended for its success on the virtue of its rulers, and this virtue could be viewed, from one perspective, as an actual power possessed by the soul, a spiritual energy. The Chinese also believed the written word contained such power. For example, according to one traditional story, when a certain river flooded and even offerings of treasure to the river god failed to ensure safe passage across, the casting of a fan with some particularly fine example of calligraphy on it was enough to restore peace to the waters. Thus it was felt that the words written by important statesmen and officials were possessed of magical powers, and that if they were hung on the wall they invited good fortune and averted bad. At least, that must have been the unconscious belief.

This way of thinking found its way to Japan, and, particularly during the Meiji period, inscriptions by elder statesmen were highly valued. Most of these distinguished men came from poor families living in the backwoods, until, with the success of the Meiji Restoration, they suddenly found they had the whole country at their feet, so that anything connected with them would have been seen as having the power to grant similar good fortune to others. Thus you decorated your room with a specimen of their

53

brushwork and awaited results. It was this tradition that persisted in the demand for written scrolls by politicians of ministerial rank.

When the lecture was over, Miyake was quick to point out that his friend specialised in the second half of the nineteenth century:

'At first I thought you'd produced all this at a moment's notice and was terribly impressed, but you obviously had it all worked out long ago.'

'How much would you have to pay for a specimen of the prime minister's calligraphy?' asked Chie.

This question shook both of them for a moment, then made them laugh out loud.

'There wouldn't be any official charge, but obviously some not inconsiderable token of appreciation would be expected. He wouldn't write something for anyone who didn't seem likely to fork up,' said the civil servant, and the historian backed him up:

'I don't know about the really big names of the Meiji period, but even in ordinary cases it would hardly be free.'

'The perfect opportunity for making lavish bribes,' said Chie.

They were both delighted to be able to agree with her. Miyake went on to ask if the calligraphy of the elder statesmen of the years around the time of the Meiji Restoration was particularly good.

'Well, there's no comparison, of course, with the rubbish our politicians produce now. They were all pretty competent, and Soejima's work is quite remarkable. In the case of a complete mystery like Saigo, for example, it seems to me that, for the light they throw on him as a man, one could do much worse than go to those scrolls of his. They would provide excellent material for a research project.'

He explained that the main feature of Saigo's writing was the impression it gave of someone straining to appear tremendously competent.

'It's very eccentric—unnervingly, unpleasantly so. I find it rather distasteful, in fact.'

'Really? Distasteful?'

54

But this display of interest on Miyake's part was interrupted by the arrival of the next course, grilled lamb, and for a while food became the focus of discussion. After debating the merits of imported meat, however, they soon took a turn back towards the politics of the Meiji period, and began to consider why it was that a genuinely talented politician like Okubo should have been forgotten, while a total incompetent like Saigo was a national hero. It was puzzling, particularly as both had met with untimely deaths.

'Opinions are just about equally divided at the Ministry,' said Miyake.

'I think Okubo should be viewed much more favourably, but everyone gets their information out of novels, and nobody really knows anything about him. I'm the same, of course. What do you think, Chie?'

It was clear that the historian was all for Okubo, and as a mere first-year postgraduate at a women's college Chie was bound to hesitate, but she managed to find a way out of it by making a joke:

'I'm for Saigo, though I don't really know why. Perhaps it's because he always had that little dog with him.'

Naturally, they all laughed, then went on to discuss the well-known statue of Saigo with his dog in Ueno Park, wondering if it was male or female; and this led in turn to Chie describing the extraordinary antics the bitch she used to have at home got up to, producing more laughter, which Shibukawa interrupted by saying suddenly:

'You know, I like the Taisho emperor—I really do.'

This seemed a particularly eccentric change of topic, even when you considered that thinking about scrolls had reminded him of those the Taisho emperor had produced. It was even odder if you hadn't followed that train of thought, and the other two were justifiably confused.

'What?'

'Taisho? The one before Hirohito?'

'Yes. Now, he was remarkably good at writing, even if he was rather peculiar.'

'Peculiar?' echoed Chie.

While Shibukawa was trying to think how to explain, Miyake said:

'There's a story that once, at the Diet opening ceremony, when all the assembled members were waiting for him to read aloud the imperial rescript, he stood on the dais with the scroll still tied up in his hands, using it as a telescope to inspect them all.'

To illustrate this, Miyake made a tunnel with his hands, placing one in front of the other, and peered at Chie through them, observing the finely drawn features of the girl in the blue dress through the loose, wide tube of his fingers. Chie gave a cry of delight at this piece of information.

'I've never heard that before.'

For a moment, Miyake had the feeling that he was training his telescope on the whole household of women in which this girl, her mother and her grandmother all lived, not to mention the great-aunt whose flat was in the same block, and found himself wondering what they all talked about together. After putting his hands back on the table, he said:

'But it's the first time I've heard he was supposed to be any good at calligraphy.'

'He was,' said Shibukawa. 'He did some really good stuff. Free of any sort of emotional impurity … innocent, and calm. It shows in its precision and order. With an emperor writing as well as that, no wonder things went so well in the Taisho period.'

Both his listeners found this hard to swallow.

'What's that supposed to mean?' asked Miyake.

'Search me,' said Chie.

'Perhaps I'm being a little obscure,' said Shibukawa, grimacing slightly, and he tried to explain.

During the Taisho period, he said, a peculiarly Japanese form of capitalism was created, resulting in a high economic growth rate. The per capita GNP became equal to that of Austria and Italy, despite the fact that those two countries had started decades ahead of Japan, and that alone was an astonishing achievement. Genuine political parties were formed during this period, which is why we still talk about Taisho democracy, while in the field of culture the European tradition began to have an influence, producing distinctive works of real quality. Much seems to have been achieved in the short space of fifteen years or so, between 1911 and 1925, and even though one might have wished it had gone further, it still seems to have been a good, fertile period.

'This is the real problem when we think about modern Japanese history. It's probably true that the fifteen years after the Pacific War saw a much greater growth in national power and importance than the Taisho years, but in my opinion that was just building on the foundations of something that had been worked out before. I wouldn't go so far as one American scholar, who wants to go right back to the Edo period to find the roots of our success, because I think there are quite different questions involved, and also a real mystery about why things should have gone so well, particularly during the Taisho years. If you say it's just because worldwide capitalism was going through a boom at the time, then you're accepting the idea of economic determinism, which might be all right if you were a Marxist scholar.'

Miyake nodded and grunted in agreement, while Chie just held her fan still and listened; but just as the historian was about to get into his stride with an impressive 'Consequently…', the civil servant interrupted and completed his argument for him.

'You're saying, I take it, that while we don't know the real reasons behind the success of that period, we do know that the Taisho emperor was remarkably accomplished with the brush. And if we accept that certain people's writing has mystical qualities, then this will be particularly true in the case of an emperor's writing. Since he also suffered from some kind of mental disorder, these magical powers, in combination with his nature as a living god, would be that much greater. So, if we follow the reasoning of the ancients, we can account for everything that happened during that period merely by referring to the lines written in the emperor's hand on various hallowed scrolls—unless we happen to be contemporary historians, in which case we remain in a quandary. Am I right?'

'You took the words right out of my mouth,' said Shibukawa, and the two young men laughed pleasantly at each other, while Chie smiled. Shibukawa was feeling particularly pleased since he'd noticed that Miyake, on joining the Finance Ministry, had tended to curb his argumentative side, and hearing him talk like this took him back to the old days. But just at this point more dishes arrived—the elegantly named Spring Rain Salad (which was simply salad with sticks of bean jelly in it), shrimp rolls and other delicacies, until there was no room on the table for any more food.

'I haven't a clue where to start,' said Miyake, although he didn't seem to be having too much trouble, while Chie, using her chopsticks, neatly folded a shrimp roll, some lettuce and some thinly sliced cucumber inside a sheet of rice paper before asking:

'It must surely have been awkward being an emperor with that kind of illness?'

'Of course it was awkward. In fact it caused no end of problems,' Shibukawa replied, while Miyake looked thoughtful and, as he helped himself to more salad, added:

'Whereas Hirohito was a man of great intelligence.'

He said this with such conviction that Shibukawa was taken aback for a moment, sitting blankly with his glass in his hand, before deciding to agree with him.

'You're right, I suppose. There was no problem about heredity in his case.' Secretly he was hoping they might talk about something else, such as South-East Asian cooking, or what kind of salad they liked best. If they got on to safe ground the evening could proceed peacefully to its conclusion. But as it turned out, Miyake seemed to have more to say on the subject.

'I think he was a great man. We owe much of our post-war prosperity to him.'

Shibukawa was caught between the demands of social etiquette and his scholarly conscience, with a dash of political conviction thrown in for good measure.

'I'm not so sure about that. I don't want to detract from his achievements, but I should have thought the will and determination of the people had much more to do with it.' He spoke in a low voice, with little emphasis, since he had no desire to quarrel with his old friend and rival in love on this particular question. Miyake responded as if he was quite happy to keep the discussion friendly, but in no way prepared to water down his own opinions.

'Okay, okay—I'll give you that. But I still feel the emperor did a great service to the nation.'

'Yes, maybe you're right. That's certainly one view,' Shibu-kawa conceded, keeping what he really thought to himself. When he went on, it was with the intention of sticking to generalisations that could cause no offence to anybody. 'It's very difficult to speak objectively about the emperor system. Why should an ancient emotion like emperor worship survive in the modern world? Isn't it the case that the emperor just serves as an idealised reflection of the pride a people takes in itself? That he simply symbolises self-worship? Compared with the kings and queens of other countries, the concept of "emperor" is peculiarly vague, allowing this idealisation to be taken to extremes. And yet, even given this vagueness about his role, there are certain moments in history—in recent times as well—when the emperor clearly had some definite influence...'

While he was quietly pursuing this line, he noted with dismay that his remarks weren't being taken in the harmless fashion he'd intended. Miyake had in fact been annoyed by the statement that emperor worship was just a reflection of a nation's self-esteem, considering his own positive feelings towards the emperor as the objective judgement of an intellectual concerning a real historical figure. It was also demeaning to find his judgement lumped in with the response of the Japanese public as a whole, since he certainly didn't regard himself as a member of the common herd. Still, he made considerable efforts to keep his temper under control as he replied:

'Yes, but look, just consider the end of the war. If it hadn't been for the Showa emperor I can't imagine how things would have gone...'

However, when he saw that Shibukawa wasn't prepared to

nod in agreement at this, he went on, delivering a speech to the effect that there was little point in producing an idealised image of the ruler only to decide that actual emperors were inferior to it. Instead, they should look at four real emperors, the last four in Japanese history—Komei, Meiji, Taisho and Showa. (He chose to ignore the emperor before Komei because he couldn't remember his name, smiling at Shibukawa instead, who dutifully smiled back.) Komei, as was perhaps inevitable in the Japan of that period, had been aggressively xenophobic, apparently believing that horns sprouted from the heads of all foreigners and encouraging the idea of all-out war against the Americans, with what disastrous consequences they all knew. Meiji, being of an heroic nature and fiercely pro-war, with an apparent inability to be flexible on any question, was always prepared to waste the country's resources in the quest for some final decisive battle, and had been leading them down the road to ruin. As far as Taisho was concerned, well, he seemed to have been unfit to take administrative decisions of any kind, so he just didn't count. Miyake concluded by saying:

'Which means that Hirohito was the wisest of the four, and I think we were fortunate to have him as our ruler at such a crucial point in history.'

'All right, it makes better sense to compare four actual rulers, I agree,' said Shibukawa, although in order to make it quite clear he didn't do so completely, he added: 'Still, we'd all have been better off if he'd displayed his wisdom a bit earlier, don't you think?'

'Before the atom bombs were dropped?'

'Well, that would have been something—although I really meant before the war started.'

'Yes, but the emperor was bound by the constitution, and was obliged to let the cabinet run the country. He followed constitutional practice as it had been taught him by Prince Saionji, and had to defend the principle that political responsibility lay with the cabinet.'

'All right. But since we are, in fact, talking about the Meiji constitution, which was in effect at the time, I don't see how you can say he was obliged to behave like that. The military were quite happy to ignore the constitution whenever they felt like it, and even if *he* really thought he was following the British model of government, well, he was just blinding himself to what was actually going on in the country he was supposed to be ruling. All this trying to do something according to an ideal set of standards is absolutely typical of the twentieth-century Japanese intelligentsia. Maybe that makes him genuinely representative of that class, and you might therefore consider it unfair to criticise him on those grounds, but I can't see any reason to praise him either for his "wisdom".'

The atmosphere had now become quite tense, and Miyake looked down at his salad for a while, then raised his head as if about to produce some counter-statement, but instead looked at Chie and decided they ought to stop. He apologised for getting into an argument when they were supposed to be celebrating her entry into graduate school, and Shibukawa said the same. Chie replied that she didn't mind at all, and in fact, although her attempt at an easy smile wasn't entirely convincing, she had genuinely been enjoying the discussion, though her interest was purely intellectual and had nothing to do with which of these two rivals for her affections was going to win. Since she had never heard two intellectuals having a serious difference of opinion before, and assumed she wouldn't often get the chance again, she was delighted to have this opportunity to witness one. It is in the nature of Japanese society for everyone to try hard to avoid any subject that might cause the least offence, and it was inevitable that this should be even more the case in the all-women's schools in which Chie had been educated where, even if some kind of argument did occur, it was invariably over something trivial. She was sick to death of the silly chatter that surrounded her, and longed for intellectual debate. In fact, the prospect of their engaging in just this sort of argument was probably the main reason for her long association with these two young men.

Miyake realised that Chie had indeed been enjoying herself, and was somewhat conscious of this as he continued:

'I wasn't trying to claim that he was some kind of genius. If I've given that impression I must have been expressing myself badly.'

'No, no, of course not,' said Shibukawa.

'But I don't see that I'm indulging in emperor worship as some form of self-admiration.'

'No, I wasn't talking about you. I meant the general public.'

'Well, if Prince Saionji did encourage him to become a constitutional monarch of the British type, it seems unreasonable to expect him suddenly to assume autocratic powers and have a showdown with the military. After all, he wasn't a genius, and he would never have succeeded anyway. One small slip and they would have put him away.'

'Maybe.'

'As I see it, he did the best thing in the circumstances—bending like a willow before the storm, as he did before the war and during it. I think the way he read the situation and reacted to it was masterly.'

' "Masterly" seems to be going a bit far,' said Shibukawa, shaking his head, and then, knowing he was getting worked up but unable to stop himself, he added: 'Still, that really was a damn *stupid* war. There was no justification for it, and no hope of winning either. Okay, perhaps nothing could be done once it got going, but at least it might have been stopped before the bomb was dropped. After all, it *is* a fact that it ended when the emperor decided it should—or, at least, that's how it seems now. And if that's the case, then I want to know why he didn't come round to that way of thinking a bit earlier. I really think there are grounds for complaint there.'

'But I've already explained why that was impossible.'

'I know you have. It was a very difficult situation and all that. But if he was such a pacifist, as he later kept on insisting he'd been all the time, then why didn't he put an end to it much earlier? Look at the misery the Taiwanese and Korean troops had to go through. And what about the victims of the two atom bombs?...'

'That was the Americans' fault. They dropped them.'

'As if we didn't know. Look, an *uncle* of mine, just a bit older than my father, was in Hiroshima at the time. He'd been sent there, as a soldier. Much later, a year after my father died, my mother said to me, very casually, that she'd always preferred my uncle, that he was much more interesting than my father. In fact she'd wanted to marry him. That shook me—it really did. I mean, if she had married my uncle I wouldn't be alive now.'

His tone was still serious when he made this last remark, but Chie couldn't help giggling. She tried hard not to, gripping the table with both hands to restrain herself, to the extent that the plates and glasses began to rattle, but she couldn't stop herself and shook with muffled laughter, apologising at the same time, her face contorting with the effort. Miyake soon joined in with a snort of amusement, and Shibukawa, finally seeing the funny side of what he'd said, acknowledged it with a grimace which acted as encouragement to the other two to laugh out loud.

All three of them now spent a moment discussing the mystery of being alive at this particular moment, and though nobody had anything very profound to say, the mere fact of talking about life in this way gave them a strange sense of themselves, as they realised that normally they never gave it a thought. It seemed somehow appropriate to the setting and to the ritual of eating and drinking in which they were engaged.

'The funny thing about life is that, when you least expect it, something will happen, for no good reason … like a parcel suddenly being delivered.'

Chie decided to extend her academic friend's metaphor:

'Like a parcel sent by special delivery. People hardly ever send covering letters, do they?' Although she was eight years younger than the two men, she sometimes spoke to them as their equal, as if she'd lost any sense of the difference in their ages over the two years she'd known them. Perhaps this was something she'd picked up from her mother, who associated with so many men older than herself.

'Those kinds of unannounced deliveries are a real nuisance,' said Miyake. 'At the end of last year a box of five enormous salmon arrived and I hadn't a clue what to do with them.'

They had moved on to safer ground, talking easily of parcels sent by people they'd never seen or heard of. They then tried to decide when they could have another game of mixed doubles. Chie belonged to the tennis club at her college—in fact it was through tennis that she'd got to know the student who had introduced her to Miyake and Shibukawa, since they were old boys of his university's tennis association. But it was hard to find a day that suited everyone, and since the two young men, half in jest and half in earnest, both insisted on partnering Chie, they gave up in the end without setting a date. It would have been as well if the evening could have ended on this note, but Miyake, after another glass of Chinese wine, suddenly seemed to remember what they'd been talking about earlier.

'I still don't see how you can say the war was totally meaningless,' he said. Shibukawa remained silent, as if he hadn't heard, so Miyake went on: 'The least you can say is that it forced Britain out of India, France out of Vietnam, and Holland out of Indonesia. And it's the main reason we're enjoying our current prosperity.'

Shibukawa found this too naive to reply to, and simply muttered:

'Yes, I know there are people who think like that. But I have my doubts. I mean, just because the red pepper was introduced into Korea during the invasion by Hideyoshi in the sixteenth century doesn't mean the Koreans should be grateful for having been invaded.'

'You mean they didn't have red peppers before then?' exclaimed Chie in surprise.

'That's right.'

'A good debating point,' said Miyake. 'Just the kind of obscure fact one would expect a scholar to know. However...'

'No, hold on. Look—the aim of the Greater East Asia War was the invasion of the countries of Asia. Any talk about Asian liberation is just being wise after the event. The same goes for post-war prosperity. If we'd invested in industry and education instead of in war, we could have done all right without there having to be all those millions of victims.'

Shibukawa imagined Miyake would answer this point by saying that post-war prosperity was the result of American technical aid, and that that had been offered only because they felt a responsibility towards the country they'd defeated; but his reply was simply:

'So you're saying everybody who died in that war died for nothing? They died like dogs?'

'What?...' said Shibukawa, taken unawares and wondering how to react. 'Yes, I am. If we're going to be brutally frank about it, then they did all die like dogs.'

'But if that's the case, then the whole thing's too horrible to think about.' There was real pain in his voice, but Shibukawa wouldn't let himself be sidetracked. He felt it was his duty to speak out, although he did lower his voice a little as he went on:

'Because you feel their deaths are too awful to think about— because you feel sorry for them if they died for nothing—you want to twist the judgement of history and convince yourself the war had a meaning. I can sympathise with that. I understand your reluctance to think those people died in vain—but all you're doing is just making a ritual offering to the dead. It's history as an attempt to appease troubled spirits, a religious act. It's not what real history is about.'

'In real history they died like dogs.'

'That's right.'

'But if history won't allow those deaths to have any meaning, then history's view of life is incredibly bleak.'

'But hang on,' Shibukawa started to say, when Chie's voice interrupted him.

'Why do you have to go on and on about dying like *dogs*? Can't you see how it makes *me* feel?'

The two men, who had been facing each other up till now, turned and saw an expression of pure misery on the girl's face, her eyes full of tears, a couple trickling down her cheek. Seeing this, both realised, with a firm intuition founded on past experience when they'd had to try to redeem a number of equally awkward situations, that she was weeping, not for those who had died in he war, but for her dog which had died a year ago. Speaking passionately, interrupted from time to time by her own sobs, she went on to say:

'It was awful when Mariko died, gasping for breath all the time, with these great long shudders going through her body—I can still see her now… You talk about dying like a dog, but it was the first time I'd ever let her on my bed. She'd always wanted to get on it but I'd never let her. I used to shout at her and tell her off when she tried, and I wish I hadn't now… I had a cushion in the corner of the room with an old bath towel on it, and she used to curl up on that. And it was all my fault… I thought she smelled bad, and although it was a horrible cloudy day I made her have a bath. She hated being bathed, she kept on running away, but I caught her in the end. And the next day it rained and she caught a cold and wouldn't stop shivering… I took her to two vets, but they couldn't do anything. She was only twelve. She might have lived a bit longer, poor thing. Then, what made it worse, the second day of her cold I was reading a magazine—I think it was some article called "Dogs of the World", some kind of series— and there was a schnauzer in it, and I said, "Oh, what a sweet little dog," and Mummy told me not to say things like that because it would upset Mariko, and I laughed and told her not to be silly because Mariko couldn't understand—and from the very next day she started to pine away and wouldn't eat anything, until finally she couldn't even drink anything by herself. And she was in agony, struggling for breath, as if her chest were going to burst… And it's going to be just like that when I die, I know it is. That's why people talk about dying like a dog…'

The two young men hadn't a clue how to respond to this, so they just sat there until they were released from their unhappy silence by the arrival of more food: rice consommé with shreds of onion and pemmican floating in it, followed by coconut ice cream.

THREE

.
.
.

Yumiko Minami's lover was not one of the eleven former 'pre-forties'. He was a man called Yokichi Toyosaki who taught philosophy at a university in Sendai, up in the north. This university professor was fifty-five and married, and their relationship had lasted ten years.

Toyosaki's teaching load in Sendai took up the whole of Monday, and also Wednesday morning. Faculty meetings were held on Wednesday afternoon. On Thursday morning he would take the super-express to Tokyo to lecture at a university there in the afternoon. Yumiko would meet him in the evening, at the hotel where they put him up, generally returning home that night. On Friday morning he would teach again at the university, and in the afternoon attend an editorial meeting at the learned journal to which he was an adviser. When that was over he would eat something at a noodle shop nearby, then go to Ueno Station to catch the train home. That was an average week in the life of Professor Toyosaki.

The secrecy surrounding this relationship was partly a result of their determination that it should not get out, but had more to do with the prejudice of journalists towards the abstract world of philosophy. Considering the two professions to be light years apart, they extended that assumption to a point where, by definition, no woman journalist could ever fall in love with a philosopher. Thus Professor Toyosaki inhabited an area outside their gossipmongering, or at least only at its extreme periphery.

When, two years after Yumiko's divorce, a year after she'd given birth to Chie, she had come across her talented 'pre-forties', some of them had made passes at her and occasionally come close to getting somewhere, but nothing in particular had happened with any of them. Nor was anything happening with the men at the newspaper. This was due less to any puritanism on her part than to lack of opportunity, since no one there ever meant anything to her in that way. In her early thirties she'd had a relationship with an actor which lasted almost two years, but he was always forcing her to buy tickets for the not very popular adaptations of Western plays he appeared in, and when she objected, he started boasting about a woman he knew who was quite happy to take as many tickets as he liked, which seemed a good enough reason to break off with him. Then, a while after that, she met Toyosaki, and was fascinated, never having read a work of philosophy, by his philosophical pronouncements; falling in love with him seemed a natural progression, although clearly she must have found him attractive from the start.

What interested Yumiko about Toyosaki's way of thinking was evident on the occasion of their first meeting. This was at the preview to an exhibition sponsored by the *New Daily*, when she was introduced to him by a colleague of hers on the arts pages and the three of them had tea together. Then, on the afternoon of the next day, they happened to come face to face in the middle of a pedestrian bridge near the university where he taught, and talked for a while before separating. As they did so she looked back, and he looked back at the same time, waving his hand. The following day they happened to sit next to each other at a Noh play (each having received a ticket from a different friend), had dinner together and, after a few drinks, went back to his hotel room. Later, in bed, Yumiko commented on the strange coincidence of their meeting by accident three days in a row in a city as big as Tokyo, and even having seats next to each other at the theatre.

'Yes, I was struck by that, too,' he replied. 'Ever since the death of God—or, as we're referring to the current situation here in Japan, since religion has ceased to have any influence over us—people have sought a substitute for their lost gods and buddhas in the salutary power of romantic love. And the most potent demonstration of this power is the accidental occurrence, the amazing coincidence. Or so it would seem, at least.'

What amazed and impressed Yumiko was his ability to hold forth like this, even in bed. Only recently, indeed, when he had taken her to an Italian restaurant to celebrate their ten years together, he had expressed his feelings about the anniversary in the same style. He proclaimed that the energy driving their relationship derived from the balance it maintained between the social acceptability of the marriage contract and its essentially confrontational correlative, the socially unsanctioned component of the love connection. Translated into simple terms, that probably meant he thought they'd managed to keep going because the whole affair had been kept secret. But the real reason they hadn't grown tired of each other was almost certainly because they only met once a week, something Yumiko had started complaining about only fairly recently.

One Wednesday evening in the middle of June, when Yumiko was looking forward with some pleasure to the following day, she received a phone call from Sendai announcing a change of plan.

'You've cancelled your teaching?'

'No, I'm teaching tomorrow, but I've got to cut the next day's classes.'

'So you're still coming to Tokyo?'

'Yes. We're coming down together.'

'With your wife?'

'There's some business to be attended to.'

'What kind of business?'

'Nothing of any great importance.'

At this point it would have been better if Toyosaki had told the truth and said he was taking his wife, who had been in an acutely nervous state since the onset of her menopause two years ago, to see a specialist in Tokyo because her condition had been getting progressively worse. But he didn't, partly out of concern for his wife, partly because he didn't want to upset Yumiko by giving her so uncompromising a glimpse of the ugly reality of his everyday life, partly from straightforward male vanity, and perhaps for a number of other underlying reasons as well.

For two years now his wife had been suffering bouts of depression, and recently she had taken to shutting herself in her room. The only time she went out was on visits to the local supermarket. Last year he had made an effort to take her shopping in the city centre and get her to choose a sweater and tie for him, because she used to love doing things like that; but it hadn't worked out, as she was afraid of the shop assistants and simply hid behind her husband. Since she also refused to eat out, he was obliged to cancel the table he'd reserved at a French restaurant that evening, and they went home and ate some leftover stew for dinner instead. The final straw had been when she'd entered his study sometime earlier this month, an expression of deep gloom showing on her face, and handed him her savings book.

'Here. You can have it,' she said, much to his surprise, not only because of the blunt offer, but also because he found she had ten million yen in savings.

'I'm giving it to you because I don't think I've got much longer to go. It's my little nest egg. When I die there'll be quite a lot to pay for, so I'm giving it to you now.' Since she insisted he take the thing, he did so, before hurriedly phoning the Tokyo specialist for advice, and being given the appointment for Friday.

Yumiko wasn't sure how to respond, but said:

'Couldn't we meet somewhere else?'

'That'll be a bit difficult, I think.'

'I suppose it would look a bit strange.'

'Yes.'

'Let's make it next week, then.'

They both then made an effort to talk cheerfully about something else. Yumiko explained how her daughter had been upset by the phrase 'dying like dogs'; Chie had told her mother and grandmother about it at dinner, tears coming to her eyes again. Toyosaki promised to bring some Sendai cakes which Yumiko was particularly fond of when he came next week. Finally Yumiko said:

'Could you try and phone me again tomorrow?'

'If I possibly can,' he told her, but she knew when he said that it usually meant he wouldn't, and this in fact proved to be the case. The following night Yumiko realised she had been thinking all day about her lover in the hotel in Tokyo with his wife, and that she found this much harder to bear than thinking of them together in a different city.

On Friday after breakfast Chie went off to school, leaving her grandmother and Yumiko talking over a late cup of tea. Her grandmother, Etsuko, raised the question of getting another dog, pointing out that other people in the building kept pets, but Yumiko opposed the idea, just as Etsuko had thought she would. She had suggested the idea tentatively a number of times, but even with the backing of her granddaughter no progress ever seemed to be made. The reason Yumiko gave was that it was against the regulations, and that she felt an editorial writer for a newspaper should be careful to conform to all public strictures—although her seventy-year-old mother privately thought that it was a bit odd to be such a stickler for correctness over this and yet quite happy to turn her back on social convention when it came to relations with the opposite sex. Naturally enough, she had divined the nature of her daughter's relationship with the married university professor. After ten years of it, it would have been strange if she hadn't.

This morning it was Yumiko's turn to tidy up the breakfast things so Etsuko could go on drinking tea, but she kept up her side of the conversation as she went between the kitchen and the living-cum-dining room. They returned to the subject of the dog-like death, which still made them laugh after a lapse of thirty-six hours, although the grandmother was concerned that neither of the two young men would feel much like marrying Chie if she was always going to be so emotional. She was proud of her granddaughter's association with an up-and-coming man in the Finance Ministry and an assistant professor, but recently the girl's attitude seemed so lukewarm that Etsuko was worried she might have lost interest in them. Deep down, she had never been very happy about Chie going on to do postgraduate work.

'Well,' said Yumiko, now drinking tea again, 'if her heart's not in it, it can't be helped.'

'I suppose not.'

Etsuko appeared to have conceded that point, but then started on about marriage until finally, forgetting herself, she said:

'Perhaps an arranged marriage would be right for her…'

The words 'arranged marriage' were never used between the two women. Yumiko's failed marriage had been arranged by her parents, and as a young girl she had thought it quite natural that this should be the case. Among her relations was the director of a large hospital who, together with his wife, was constantly arranging all sorts of marriages, a task for which the couple seemed to have a genuine passion, and this may have influenced Yumiko's belief that marriage was a matter of someone else's choice, love marriages taking place only in novels and films. Also, her brother, who was three years younger, eventually married a girl in a trading company thanks to someone else's good offices—as, indeed, had her parents, although since we're talking about a previous generation this almost goes without saying. The only person in the whole family who hadn't had an arranged marriage was her aunt Masako (stage name Aeka) Yanagi, but that was hardly surprising since she hadn't married at all. All in all, it was only to be expected that, shortly after she'd joined the *New Daily*, Yumiko should agree to go to a marriage interview. Her prospective husband, Gen'ichi Nakahara, worked in the Bank of Japan, was twelve years her senior, and gave such an overwhelming impression of being grown-up in a way she wasn't that she mistook this feeling for one of respect and accepted him.

When she looked back on her marriage, from the engagement right up to the divorce, it seemed to Yumiko that the Pacific War had probably started and ended in very much the same way (perhaps even the Peloponnesian and the Opium wars as well): with a succession of minor misunderstandings leading to total disaster. In the beginning, for example, Yumiko had felt that somehow or other she would be able to work and run a household at the same time. She had assumed her husband and mother-in-law would sympathise with her, and that, at a pinch, they'd be able to afford to have someone in to help with the housework. In fact, at first it had seemed to be working out, since when Yumiko was eight months pregnant the middle-aged woman who helped her parents out three days a week agreed to come two days a week to her, and immediately after the baby was born Yumiko's mother arranged for her to work there every day except Sundays.

But three months later the woman announced she would be moving to Hokkaido. Her husband, who had an administrative job in a local crammer, was being transferred to Sapporo to set up a new branch, which was expected to open in a couple of years. Naturally a replacement was sought, but none could be found. There followed a period of intensive searching for a servant, never-ending discussions with her husband, and a steady stream of opinions from her mother-in-law, all far too elaborate and long-winded to go into here. Finally the husband announced that he wanted Yumiko to devote herself exclusively to the care of their child, to which Yumiko replied that she still intended to combine marriage and a career; and all the while the day when the middle-aged help was due to depart was coming closer. So Yumiko went back to her parents' house with her baby and got her mother to look after the child for the greater part of the week. A few months later the divorce went through. Chie's surname was changed to Minami a year after that.

Given this history, Yumiko was naturally opposed to the idea of an arranged marriage, even if only obliquely, but this morning Etsuko seemed less sensitive about it than usual and didn't appear to notice her daughter's reaction.

'It's not a bad idea. It seems to work in Japan, anyway.'

'You mean, you and Father?' Yumiko said awkwardly.

'Yes. I know it didn't work out in your case, but you know,

73

you did agree to marry him. It wasn't as if you were forced to.'

Yumiko's own opinion was that she'd been so inexperienced at the time that she could have done with some advice from her parents along the lines of: 'If you don't feel like it, you don't have to go through with it,' or 'It's going to be very hard making marriage and a career work,' or 'Perhaps you'd be better off not having a child for the time being.' But they hadn't said anything, and she felt it was pointless to complain about it now when it was too much to have expected anyway.

'It was my fault, too,' Yumiko murmured, but her mother jumped on that 'too'.

'What do you mean by that—your fault, *too*?... Well, I made up for it, didn't I, the way I looked after that child of yours.'

'I know. I'm sorry.'

'And you're glad you had the child, surely? Much better than having nobody.'

'Yes, of course.'

'That's all right, then,' Etsuko said, apparently mollified, but then bursting out in a way that sounded distinctly unmollified: 'Just think of the dreary life I've had, looking after a grandchild all the time.'

Yumiko vanished into her room, and when she reappeared she was wearing a white blouse with a pattern of tiny flowers, a dark blue flared skirt, and a single gold bracelet as jewellery. She left the house, saying briskly that she would be late that evening as she'd probably have an article to write. But this wasn't just a bad-tempered excuse to stay away, since it was coming up to her turn to write the 'Starting from Scratch' column, and she had some material so perfect for it that she was thinking of volunteering if no one else wanted to do it.

The other day her mother had gone to a wedding reception for a friend's granddaughter, and had heard someone sitting at the same table talking about some special blocks of flats for businessmen posted away from home. It seemed this man, who worked for a large firm, had been made manager of a branch office in Takamatsu. As Takamatsu was hundreds of miles away in the south, his wife and children had stayed in Tokyo and he had been obliged to live alone, but he was able to move into a flat (vacated by his predecessor) that was obviously convenient for a grass widower like himself. The flat had only one room, but there was a restaurant on the ground floor of the building where he could have breakfast and dinner. As it turned out, he didn't dine there often, since he was obliged to go out a lot on business, but the solid Japanese-style breakfast they served ensured he ate plenty of vegetables, and that helped him to avoid the dietary hazards a man runs into when he only eats out or cooks for himself. So in that respect, at least, he found himself well placed.

A major drawback was that, when he'd signed the lease for the flat, he'd had to agree that nobody outside his immediate family would be allowed to stay there, and that when he did have a visitor he would fill in a form giving name, address, age, sex, and the nature of the visitor's relationship to him.

'Somebody had been chucked out just before I arrived,' her mother heard him say. 'There was a notice in the lobby announcing that, regrettably, a certain gentleman—they didn't give his name—who lived on the fourth floor had been asked to leave, having infringed the regulations. That made me feel a bit uncomfortable, particularly as I was on the fourth floor myself. It's a smallish town, with a population of about three hundred thousand. Most of us tended to go to the same places, and someone always seemed to be poking fun at me. "You getting your oats all right, sir?" they'd ask. I got sick to death of finding an answer to the same stupid question all the time.'

Yumiko had found this very interesting. These blocks of flats for grass widowers must be everywhere, or at least in all the major provincial cities, and she felt that a little research into the kind of menu such places offered would give her enough material for an article along the lines of 'What the Branch Manager Has for Breakfast'. She had already got the punch-line worked out: 'Boiled spinach or middle-aged romance—that's the choice facing our branch managers'. She probably wouldn't get away with this crack about middle-aged men and their morals, particularly as

75

the deputy chief on duty today had no sense of humour, so she'd been racking her brains to come up with a less provocative ending, but without success.

As she travelled in to work she went over the column again in her head, thinking at the same time that, since she'd got the story from her mother, she ought to invite her out for a meal. Perhaps she'd ask her daughter if she wanted to come along, but then she smiled as she thought, no, that would mean asking her aunt too, otherwise she'd feel left out. Aunt Masako had always preferred Yumiko's younger brother when they were children, and had been quite cold towards Yumiko up until her divorce, but since then she'd been uncharacteristically nice to her. Perhaps she was impressed by the way Yumiko had put her career first, or maybe she felt here was someone else who'd strayed from the straight and narrow. It was probably her feelings for Yumiko that had led her to come to live in the same block of flats, albeit on a different floor. Yumiko was fond of her aunt, and felt that journalists and actresses did actually have a lot in common.

She was in the staff room reading the early printout of the evening edition when the other woman on the team, Nobuko Konaka, came over.

'Have you read these two articles?' she asked, pointing at two pages of another paper marked in red. 'What a lovely blouse—it's all right to sit here, isn't it?'

She sat down on Urano's chair. She was wearing a check skirt with a light blue shirt and a collarless white jacket. Her small gold earrings matched the two gold half-moons that dangled from the blue frames of her glasses. Yumiko praised this rather eccentric attempt at fashion, then read the two articles. The first was a short piece concerning internal politics:

Former prime minister Yamamura visited *** City in Kagoshima Prefecture on the 14th to unveil a memorial stone for the souls of aborted babies. In his dedicatory speech he said: 'The fact that so many memorial services are held these days for aborted babies is an indication of how unwelcome a social practice abortion has become. In the past, women cared for children. They loved having them. It is ridiculous to claim that if we didn't allow contraception and abortion there would be too many children. Look at Admiral Togo. His name was Heihachiro, meaning he was the eighth son. If his parents had believed in abortion the Russians would have won the battle in the Sea of Japan.'

The second article was on the city pages, and was similarly short:

Takeyoshi Nagatani, 53, unemployed, living at *** in Nerima Ward, former employee of the firm Tokyo Memorial Art of *** in Itabashi Ward, was arrested on the evening of the 14th on a charge of blackmailing the president of the above company, Mr Kawasaki. Under interrogation, the suspect said he had threatened to expose Kawasaki for not paying tax on the profits he had made from selling stone images of Jizo, which in this instance were apparently dedicated to the souls of aborted foetuses.

Yumiko looked up when she'd finished reading, and Nobuko said:

'Nothing that old fool says ever makes any sense.'

'I know. And it's weird to bring in Admiral Togo like that.'

'That's because he was in Kagoshima. They like to be reminded of their favourite son down there.'

'Yes, of course—and his generation loves remembering the Russo-Japanese War.'

'It reminds me of that American commentator—or was he British?—it doesn't matter. Anyway, he said somewhere that if people had always had abortions to spare children from living in a lousy environment, then Mary wouldn't have given birth to Jesus, there'd have been no Christianity, no Anno Domini and, worst of all, no Christmas.'

'At least that sounds as if he was trying to be funny.'

'They're both saying the same thing, though,' said Nobuko, and sighed. 'What can you say to a politician who's incapable of differentiating between abortion and birth control?'

'Maybe the reporter got it wrong?'

'I doubt it. No, this is about the intellectual level we can expect of our politicians.'

Yumiko agreed, then added: 'Still, it's strange there should be an article the same day about tax evasion on profits from selling images dedicated to unborn babies.'

'Isn't that horrible? They exploit people's feelings of guilt to make money out of them.'

'Are you going to write something about it?' Yumiko asked.

Since Nobuko had long been passionately interested in this question, and had written a signed article (not an editorial) about it when the legal period in which abortion could take place was shortened, while at the same time seeing that a woman doctor who opposed the new law was given generous space on the letters page, Yumiko assumed she wanted to write an editorial on the subject for tomorrow's paper. This assumption turned out to be wrong.

'No, that's the trouble, I can't. I'm chairing that symposium today on the role of the Japanese economy in Asia—the one the paper's sponsoring.'

'Oh, are you?'

'Yes. So could you write it up?'

'Well, I thought I'd be asked to do "Starting from Scratch" today, so I came prepared for that. It's about those flats for grass widowers. It's really quite interesting...'

She started to explain, but Nobuko's perfunctory replies showed she didn't think much of the idea, and Yumiko began to wonder if the other woman didn't have some personal interest in the subject—in fact, now she came to think of it, hadn't she heard something about it in connection with her husband or his work? But she couldn't remember what it was, and at that point Urano turned up and Nobuko moved away, saying:

'So you're going to let that old fool off the hook, are you?'

Yumiko smiled. 'I suppose it doesn't seem right, somehow, does it?'

The day's meeting began, but even before she took her place at the table she noticed something odd about it. For a start, there was a high level of absenteeism: normally you could expect to see over thirty people there, but today at least ten hadn't turned up. The chief himself was travelling abroad (Russia, Germany, France, Britain, Italy—at the moment he should be in Berlin), so inevitably he couldn't be present, and one of the deputy chiefs was also away, having gone to Kyoto for the funeral of some old and distinguished figure. Then, of the ordinary editorial writing staff, the tall fellow, originally from the political pages, had fallen down some stairs at a bar the night before and was in hospital, while that dwarf-like creature, the other one who dealt with politics, was laid up with gout. Another, from the financial section, was in Shikoku for his daughter's wedding, and his erstwhile colleague from the same section had gone to Seoul at the invitation of the South Korean government. Yumiko was rather relieved that the man from the arts pages, who always wanted to have the last word, had been invited by some obscure magazine to investigate the remains of whatever culture had existed in the very distant past on the Sea of Japan coast, while the elderly writer who had once worked on the sports pages had been invited by an ex-base-ball player to play golf in Sydney. But these were mostly planned absences, and didn't create any particular problems. What would make things difficult was the non-appearance not only of the journalist assigned to write that day's lead article, on the question of reducing air fares, who was in bed with a cold and a tempera-ture of 104°, but also of the man who was supposed to be lament-ing the rise in juvenile crime, who had got a bad hangover on top of a slipped disc, two perfectly good reasons for taking the day off.

The remaining deputy chief, now officially chairing the meet-ing, after giving a detailed account of the phone call he'd received from the chief in Moscow last night, complete with the vital infor-mation that the best black caviar tasted wonderful when eaten in large spoonfuls, lowered his voice to a tone of almost painful gravity and said:

'I'm afraid we have a serious problem on our hands. I wonder if anybody is prepared to volunteer to write either of the editorials?'

Clearly he wasn't looking for any probing analysis of the major issues in Japan and the world at large but just a quick piece to tide them over. What complicated matters was the fact that, on the day in question, the world seemed to be unnaturally untroubled: no one important in the U.S. State Department had commented on the Japanese economy; the members of the Japanese Diet had formed two teams (East and West) to play a friendly baseball match in the Tokyo Dome (so incompetent was the opening batter that the prime minister managed to throw a genuine strike with his opening pitch); nothing at all seemed to be going on in Africa or the Middle East; all the members of the Praesidium in Moscow were praising each other; and not one Chinese author had been attacked by the Communist Party. It was, as the deputy chief said ruefully, just the day for leaders on air ticket prices and juvenile crime.

'So, what are we going to do?' he asked, looking round the table to where their faces would have been had they not all had their heads lowered. When there was no response, he picked on a man who was notorious for his meagre output, an ex-reporter on the affairs of the imperial family. The latter, though, had little to offer of any significance, beyond the fact that the imperial gardens were in peak condition, which he mentioned in a tone of unctuous reverence. Similarly, when the deputy asked an old hand in the world of finance if he had anything, he was treated, at great length and in fine editorial writing style, to a lecture on interest rates, on what the Bank of Japan was doing and what the finance minister might have to say about it, on the situation in America ... and finally to the lame conclusion that the situation needed watching, that it would be some time before any public statements could be made. He was equally unlucky with the other journalists (Urano had learned the ropes by now and cleverly wriggled out of it, and Nobuko Konaka was able to use the excuse of that afternoon's symposium), until he came to Yumiko, who said:

'I did, in fact, come prepared to write "Starting from Scratch".'

She gave an outline of what she intended to write, but although the bit about the man being expelled from his flat for immoral behaviour was greeted with some amusement, it was only a half-hearted reaction, presumably because most of them sympathised with the fellow and wondered what they'd do in the same situation. Nobody urged her to write it up, and during the awkward pause that followed she suddenly remembered that Nobuko's husband was a university professor and was, in fact, in the States at the moment, in a similar grass-widower situation, so it was hardly surprising that she hadn't been encouraging.

The silence was broken by an ex-international trade reporter, who had excused himself from any direct involvement with a curt wave of the hand, but now said that the whole question of prizes at pinball arcades ought to be taken up, and, at almost exactly the same moment, by Nobuko saying to Yumiko in a loud stage whisper: 'What about that other thing for the leading article?'

Yumiko's reply—'You mean about Togo?'—aroused a murmur of interest round the table. Both pinball and Admiral Togo were subjects that could be relied on to stir the Japanese male, and there was a general feeling that a patch of light could finally be seen at the end of the tunnel. It was decided that 'Starting from Scratch' would go to the ex-international trade reporter, while Admiral Togo would do for the first leader, even if nobody had much idea of the context in which he would appear. Something could be concocted for the second editorial from whatever was left over from the discussion.

By now, to everyone's relief, it looked as if the meeting might soon be over, and when the deputy chief asked Nobuko or Yumiko to explain, Yumiko found herself being singled out as the one with the story. She first read the two short articles out loud and then, to the occasional dry rustle as individuals turned the pages of the evening edition, criticised what the former prime minister had said. Naturally Nobuko gave her full support.

In response, their resident expert on matters relating to the constitution pointed out that anything construable as an attack on memorial services for abortions could be seen as a denial of freedom of worship, and that it might be awkward, even dangerous, for the newspaper to publish an editorial, supposedly representative of its policy, that could be viewed as anti-constitutional. The religious expert then spoke at some length, saying in his slow monotone that the practice of holding memorial services for the souls of aborted or still-born babies was correctly seen as a form of spirit worship, and therefore as a form of folk religion, and thus a legitimate religious activity, though the issue was complicated by the question whether an aborted child, or any other kind of foetus, could be thought of as having a spirit or soul. Moreover, if seen as a form of ancestor worship, as it presumably must be, its social function could be thought of as a substitute for the more traditional practice which had declined with the breakdown of the traditional family. He went on to say a lot more, in a similar tone of voice, with the result that no one could work out what sort of conclusion he wanted them to come to, apart from a vague feeling that they should try, so far as humanly possible, to avoid attacking the practice.

The response to this speech might well have led the two women to feel that there was little interest in their suggestion, or even that it was actually being rejected, and yet the twenty or so men sitting silently round the table were registering little more than their complete lack of interest both in the relevant article of the constitution and in traditional folk religion. Uppermost in their minds was the question of who, if Yumiko Minami's outline was turned down, would write the editorial. If either the constitutional specialist or the religious expert took it over, that would be fine, but there seemed little likelihood of that, so their attacks were seen to be irresponsible in terms of the job in hand. Not only that: nearly all the men there had had the experience of getting a woman (their wives or other women) pregnant and having to arrange an abortion, and they felt it was just a matter of luck if anyone hadn't been in that position. The constitutional specialist was, in fact, not only childless but notorious for his experiments with traditional Chinese fertility potions, while the religious expert was a pederast. Thus their remarks sounded as academic and doctrinaire as the Pope's objections to birth control. Furthermore, all twenty or so of them, from the deputy chief (one abortion for his wife, two for other women) down, felt the former prime minister had opened his big mouth once again on a subject they'd prefer not to think about (did he insist that all his women followed all their pregnancies through, then?), and that at this stage in the proceedings the best way forward would be to let the pair of women here get on with what they wanted to write. At least it would spare the men the distasteful task of dealing with it.

When the religious expert had finished speaking, the deputy ignored Nobuko's raised right hand and said:

'Well, I think that settles it then. Clearly, the subject is important enough to deserve discussion, so we'll use it for the first leader. Naturally the views of our two experts will be taken into account, and we should tread carefully where this question of saying prayers for foetuses is concerned. Now, since Mrs Konaka has to chair a symposium on—what was it?—ah yes, the Asian economy, I'm afraid I must ask you, Ms Minami, to be good enough to write it. Personally, I thought your account of the grass widowers and their consumption of a healthy breakfast was of considerable interest, but perhaps the spinach and other good things can be put into the fridge for use another day.'

Everyone laughed dutifully at this little joke, and since Yumiko laughed with them she was assumed somehow to have accepted. The deputy chief then proceeded to ask those who had remained silent if they had anything they wanted to write about, but since none of them had, he undertook to do the second editorial himself. Both deputy chiefs made a point of being ready for such a contingency with an article of due weight but sufficiently uncontroversial to allow it to be published in any newspaper at any time—for example, on the fact that the housing situation in Japan had now reached crisis point, or that we, the public, were happy to pay our taxes but weren't prepared to put up with unfair discrimination within the system.

Shortly after the meeting had ended, Nobuko appeared at

Yumiko's desk with four scrapbooks, seven reference books, and a special edition of a magazine, all of which had some bearing on the editorial Yumiko was to write. Urano had slipped away somewhere, so his chair was empty, but Nobuko made no move to sit down, merely telling her to do her best and waving goodbye as she left.

The first thing Yumiko did was ring up the Kagoshima office of one of the news agencies to confirm the newspaper report. Apparently the former prime minister had been in very good form, despite the fact that the ceremony had taken place in the early hours of the morning, speaking off the cuff without even any notes. In addition to what was reported, he had expressed his concern regarding any future decline in the population, saying it would be a waste of labour to go on producing cars and electrical goods if there was nobody to buy them. At this point the man at the agency broke off, saying:

'I expect the weather's lovely in Tokyo. We're bang in the middle of the rainy season down here.'

'It's all right today,' said Yumiko, not wishing to be outdone, 'but it's going to start pouring here tomorrow.'

Then she started reading through the mass of material on her desk, skipping through most of it, marking passages that seemed worth re-reading, and making notes. Abortion was an extremely emotive subject, which tended to be argued, at home and abroad, in language that was little better than invective, even if European and American writers made a pretence at reasoned argument, and Yumiko felt she would have to be very careful about her own choice of words, particularly after her row with her mother that morning. A calm, disciplined prose was called for.

Yumiko had never had an abortion herself. Her daughter was the result of her first pregnancy, immediately after she got married. In point of fact she'd intended to avoid getting pregnant then, but for some reason the contraceptive measures she'd taken hadn't worked, and she'd persuaded herself that, since her husband was middle-aged, it was probably a good thing to have a child early. Since her divorce, throughout her relationships with the actor and

84

now with the philosopher, the occasion had not arisen. She had used contraception, but she still felt it was only luck that had prevented her from becoming pregnant again; she also realised that, if it had happened, she would have had an abortion. She knew there would be too many difficulties if she had another child, and that not only she herself but the child and its father would all be unhappy, in ways she could easily imagine; given all this, she found it hard to believe she would feel too guilty about such a decision. She also assumed she wouldn't offer prayers for the soul of her lost child, or worry that if she didn't the child would put some sort of curse on her. That was superstitious nonsense, just like believing your fate could be influenced by the direction the house faced in or by the sort of name you had. She didn't feel her thoughts on the subject necessarily reflected the fact that she was unmarried. If she had stayed with her husband she would have got pregnant again, and there would have come a time when she'd have had an abortion. It would have been inevitable. She also believed the reason she'd been able to bring Chie up properly was that she'd been responsible and had avoided having another child. If she'd had another she couldn't possibly have given it the care it needed, no matter how much her mother might have helped, because she just wouldn't have been in a position to do so.

Yumiko knew that—assuming one didn't simply reject the idea of each and every form of birth control—no contraceptive method was a hundred per cent reliable; this was something you had to accept, which meant you had to accept abortion as well. Not to accept abortion meant that people were effectively being punished for no good reason other than for being unlucky. To consider abortion a form of murder was illogical, since it was actually just correcting a fault in the contraceptive process, and thus one couldn't condemn it, little as one might like it.

To reduce the argument to a question of what sexual intercourse was for (procreation or pleasure) did not help either, if the answer had to be a simple choice of one or the other. Sexual intercourse included both functions and could have both aims, sometimes together, sometimes apart. Since the human race had evolved to a point where sexual intercourse took place all the year round, human sexuality had become infinitely complex. It was this complexity, together with a number of other factors in the human environment, that had created the need for discovering methods of controlling birth. If you accepted this obvious truth, then you had to accept the logical extension of birth control, which was abortion. This was Yumiko's belief, and as a result she naturally considered the idea that a human soul was created at the moment of conception, which would make all abortion a form of murder, to be a piece of pure sophistry. However, she had been on the paper for over twenty years now, and had learned that there are occasions—of which this was one—when hypocrisy is called for. So she was not just going to write down her beliefs, but would word her argument with caution, using subtle phrases and arguments that would foil the enemy, win over the uncommitted, and gain the approval, perhaps even the applause, of those who were already on her side. That was what she decided and, after a late lunch, she got down to work.

At least this was what she intended to do, but things didn't work out that way. After lunch two classmates from high-school days had the nerve to come and ask her if she could find a place where they and some friends could hold a karaoke contest. She managed to get rid of them, but just as she was breathing a sigh of relief she had a phone call from a woman friend in the Department of Economic Planning, who wanted to tell her that their old university tutor (aged seventy-five) had remarried (a potter of fifty-eight), as the prelude to an extended narrative involving another half-dozen bits of gossip. As soon as that was over, a man from Hokkaido arrived with a letter of introduction from her ex-husband, in the mistaken belief that she might agree to write an editorial supporting the development of land for use as golf courses. Together with other documents, he passed over a white envelope. Naturally she refused to accept it, but the incident did make her reflect gloomily on what could have happened to her ex-husband, to be writing letters of introduction for people like that, however much he might feel he owed them a favour, and also to wonder why he'd not thought to warn her of the visit and give some indication of how he expected her to respond. Perhaps he was just losing his grip, or turning senile, although he couldn't be sixty yet. This led to further gloomy reflections on the dead days beyond recall and the unknown future yet to come and such-like, all of which took up a fair amount of time.

By the time she got round to the material that remained to be read and was at last facing her word processor, it was four o'clock. Even more disconcerting was the fact that she still had no idea what she was going to write. Certainly she had her own opin-ions—she knew what she wanted to say, and she knew how to put it into words. What she didn't know was how to put it into words that would speak through the medium of the newspaper editorial to the general public. Ten minutes later, she began writ-ing her opening paragraphs, aware that nobody was going to get excited about the platitudes she was putting down, but unable to think of anything better.

At a meeting in Kagoshima on the 14th, former prime minister Yamamura made the following objections to birth control and abortion. 'In the past, women were fond of chil-dren and liked having them. Take Admiral Togo, for ex-ample: as one can tell from his given name, he was an eighth son, but wasn't aborted. And that's the reason why Japan sank the Russian fleet and won the Russo-Japanese War.'

He went on to express concern about the declining birth rate and regional depopulation, saying, 'If things go on like this we can make as many cars and electrical goods as we like, but there won't be anyone to buy them.'

This, of course, is complete and utter nonsense. And it is no excuse to say he was addressing his words to the people of Kagoshima, the birthplace of Admiral Togo, and was merely being polite.

The possibilities of historical speculation are endless. The game of 'What if?' can be fun to play—what would have happened to the Russian fleet if Togo had suddenly gone mad just before the battle?—but it has no place in any serious discussion of history, and any argument based on such speculation is based on a false premise.

Similarly, the answer to economic policies that are concerned solely with profit is to say that man does not live by cars and electrical goods alone.

However, a further conclusion can be drawn from these remarks: namely, that they reflect a way of thinking that is fundamentally male in outlook. The former prime minister seems to believe the reason contemporary women might not want to give birth to children is because they don't like them, but that is not the case. Women, rather, want to decide when to have children, in order to bring them up in the best possible circumstances, and they rightly feel the choice should be left to the person actually involved.

It is women who get pregnant, who suffer morning sickness, who give birth. As far as child-raising and housework are concerned, there has certainly been an increase in the number of husbands prepared to help, but it is still not high. The fact is, it is women who have to change their lives when they have children, and they are the ones who take responsibility for raising them.

Yumiko had found it a struggle even to get this far, with any amount of crossings out and rewriting, and much sighing and tapping of her cheek as she asked herself why she should have to write about this awkward topic and cursed Nobuko Konaka, the deputy chief and the two people who were supposed to have written today's editorials. She cursed all the rest of the editorial staff, too, for good measure. One need hardly add that her fiercest curses were reserved for former prime minister Yamamura.

Although she knew exactly how many words she still had to produce, she checked again, grudgingly conceding that she'd only written half and didn't know what to do about the rest of it, feeling she'd exhausted the subject already. Of course, she realised she couldn't possibly have done so; it was more that if she went any deeper into it she knew she could find herself in real trouble. She had enough to say—more than enough—but nothing that could be said to represent the views of the paper. What was needed was something to pad it out, but she couldn't think of anything. Her head was a blank space, much like those full-page advertisements a large company puts in the paper in a pointless effort to impress people. The five hundred words she needed were five hundred too many, even though normally she would have dashed them off without thinking.

Time passed, and now something really had to be done, but still the necessary words eluded her, and the thought crossed her mind that she was in the archetypal Urano situation. This admonishment reminded her that she'd meant to tell Toyosaki about the extraordinary line in a letter sent to her by Urano, but had been so disappointed by his phone call she'd forgotten all about it. All the same, it wasn't the sort of thing one could just mention on the phone, and not even something she would want to say in bed, either. In fact, it was hard to know quite what to do about it. The letter had been a fluent piece of work, with a lot of pretentious stuff about his 'longing' and 'love' for her, and had ended with a formal request for more 'kind instruction' in the future, followed by a PS which he'd carefully scored through with his pen. It was easy enough to read, however, when the paper was held up to the light. The PS said: 'I want to screw you.'

What amazed her was the impudence of the man, who must have realised she'd be able to make out that last line, and who could then, on the occasions when they were alone together in the lift, for example, declare he'd be quite happy just to have a brother-sister relationship with her, and nothing else. She began to consider how Toyosaki would react to her telling him something like that, and, in the process, she suddenly realised she'd been wrong to blame Nobuko Konaka and her other colleagues, even the two absentees, for the state she was in. It wasn't even the fault of the former prime minister, who couldn't help being a silly old fool; and if he wasn't responsible then presumably no one was—except for one person: Toyosaki. After all, if he hadn't cancelled their date at such short notice she wouldn't have had to quarrel with her mother, which had put her in a bad mood, and would have been able to do this stupid little article with the greatest of ease. Yumiko liked to believe in her own reliability, and to make something or someone else responsible when things went wrong.

Then an unexpected thought came to her. She ceased to think of herself as a woman unable to meet her lover, and instead started to wonder what it was like being the wife of a grass widower. How did all those wives feel? Weren't they all in the same boat as herself? The thought consoled her. In fact, she realised, most of them were in a far worse position than her, and she felt a wave of affection for them, thought with sympathy of those who could meet only once every one or two months, of how hard it must be for them; and about those with husbands overseas, who might see each other only once every six months—even once a year, like Vega and her boyfriend, the two stars of the Tanabata festival, who couldn't even manage that if it happened to be raining.

As she considered the unhappy plight of these women, she became aware that in the article she had been planning to write for 'Starting from Scratch', about the branch manager's boiled spinach or middle-aged romance, she had seen things from the male point of view, not the female. She wondered why this was so when, unlike her mother, she always insisted women should find their own perspective. Perhaps it had just been a bit of absent-mindedness, failing to imagine the wife left alone to look after the house. Then she recalled the custom of attendance at court in the Tokugawa period, whereby the samurai husband would spend a year at the shogun's palace in Edo while the wife endured a year of lonely nights out in the provinces. It was just the same now—a male-orientated society in which women suffered and were ignored. (Of course, men suffered as a result of this system as well, but Yumiko wasn't interested in that at the moment.) Then there was the puppet drama she'd seen once, in which a woman had been so lonely in her husband's absence that, seduced by the plangent tones of a samisen, she was led into temptation. She had been killed for it, which wouldn't happen nowadays, since nobody went around with swords any more as the men of the samurai class had in those times. If a woman became pregnant like that today, it was simply a tragic nuisance.

Yumiko was now clear about how she wanted to fill her remaining two manuscript pages—in fact she was so excited at the thought, she had to force herself to stay calm by ringing a woman reporter on the arts pages to check some facts. This done, she started typing away at her word processor.

> To get an idea of how male-orientated our society is, just consider the custom of sending men away from home to take up a position in one of the provincial branches of their firm. The ancient equivalent of this was the long attendance at court in the Tokugawa period, and indeed it has been the tradition in this country to remain indifferent to, indeed unaware of, the plight of the woman left behind. This is something that has not changed, remaining intact after the war and despite the economic miracle of post-war Japan.

> The tragedy of the lonely wife, one of the main themes in the literature of the Edo period, still pertains, even if our contemporary writers seem to ignore it. It seems fair to say, in fact, that this country, both at home and abroad, has depended and still depends on the sacrifices women have been forced to make when separated from their husbands.

> For men, there is an acceptable social convention which helps them to live through these periods of deprivation. In fact, society not only condones this practice but could even be said to encourage it. In the case of women, however, society is less generous, imposing a strict prohibition on finding similar consolations.

> Given this situation, surely no one could wish to argue

that birth control and abortion were wrong. The tragedies that would result from denying their use must be plain to anyone, not to mention the disastrous effect this would have on the family, the ultimate foundation on which our society rests and the main determinant of the way people live. Since everyone acknowledges the importance of the family, an awareness of the damage that is done when husbands are sent away from their homes would make it very hard for companies to continue this practice.

In terms of the future of this country, this is a question we cannot ignore. If we treat it lightly, as material for dirty jokes, we will have cause to regret our mistake in the years to come. If we wish our present economic prosperity to continue, then this is something we should think about very seriously indeed.

Yumiko read through what she had written, first on her screen, then on a printout, and decided it was all right. She thought so for the following reasons:

1) She had been critical of the former prime minister's remarks, and supportive of both birth control and abortion.

2) She hadn't touched on the question of prayer services for aborted babies, thus avoiding any religious controversy.

3) She had dealt with the women's perspective historically, by linking the Tokugawa period with the modern world.

On those three points she felt she could be congratulated, but that wasn't all:

4) She had made some contribution towards protecting women who became pregnant through chance sexual encounters. (She felt quite proud of herself for this one. She herself, although college educated and reasonably intelligent, had still drifted into marriage because her parents had told her to, given birth to a child because that also was expected, and ended up going through a divorce. So she was well placed to see how easily a woman could find herself in a potentially tragic situation, right down to the miseries

a teenage girl could be put through because she thought she'd fallen in love.)

5) She had implied that it was quite natural for a woman to commit adultery while her husband was away on business, but had done this so skilfully the casual reader would probably not even notice.

She thought, quite objectively, she could be pleased with herself on these five points, although if someone had come along and praised her to her face she probably wouldn't have shown it. But if she were perfectly honest about it, she would have admitted that she wasn't at all clear what she was arguing for, particularly in the second half of her editorial. All she was really concerned about was that:

1) She'd been able to write something on the given topic.

2) She'd written it from a woman's perspective.

3) She'd written the required number of words.

She was certainly not happy that she'd conformed to the principle that:

4) One mustn't write what one really thinks because society expects newspapers to be suitably hypocritical.

And what she remained in complete ignorance of was the fact that her choice of theme for the latter half was:

5) An expression of her own unhappiness at being deprived of the presence of her own companion, projected into the emotions of others.

She could therefore hardly have known that the very ambiguities imposed upon the wording of that second half by the workings of her own subconscious would ensure her article's unobstructed progress through the organisation on its route towards acceptance as an editorial.

'I've done it,' she whispered to herself, and smiled at her own competence, congratulating herself for not behaving like the star crime reporter, winner of the president's award, on being given the same task. But then she became aware of something strange. It was only 5.30, and yet the office was almost deserted, only the deputy chief and two secretaries remaining, apart from herself, whereas normally it would still be full of people; this meant she wouldn't be able to have one of her colleagues read her editorial through for her. But she soon dismissed it from her mind, giving it about as much thought as one gives a misprint of some well-known name when reading the paper. She sent in her article to the central computer, then called the deputy chief.

'Oh, done it, have you? Good,' he said, starting to read it on the screen and the printout almost simultaneously. His dominant feeling at that moment was envy of the men who had left the office ahead of time. He knew very well why they had gone: not one of them had any wish to be in the awkward position of being asked to read Yumiko's editorial, aware they would be representing not only the male population of Japan but perhaps that of the world at large. He'd had to make only a few hasty alterations to the article he'd written all that time ago and kept in his desk drawer for just such an occasion as this (his thesis being that, since it was a good thing for elderly people to partake in such educational activities as writing haiku and waka, learning foreign languages, chanting Noh choruses and playing croquet and golf, these activities should be subsidised), but even so he had only just been in time to grab hold of a former financial-pages man who was on the point of leaving and have him read it. After he'd gone, the only other person left besides the few already mentioned was the bald-headed character who wrote 'News from Another Planet', and when *he* finally worked out what was going on he also left in a great hurry. On a normal Friday he would have made a draft of his weekend articles, finishing these together with the Monday article on Saturday, but he decided that now was not the time for such indulgence—if he didn't get out now it would be too late.

So the deputy chief started to run his eyes over Yumiko's editorial with great reluctance, even distaste, at the thought of all the unpleasant things she must have written. He was expecting there would be considerable abuse aimed at men, so when he came to the phrase 'way of thinking that is fundamentally male in outlook' he felt the world about him suddenly darken. There had always been three things he particularly disliked: pumpkins, earthquakes and hysterical women; and what he particularly disliked about these last was their tendency to abuse the male sex. Every time he encountered phrases like 'masculine oppression' or 'feudalistic concept of womankind' it made him feel depressed; sad, at first, that they should take such a narrow view of things, for there were certainly some men (himself, for example), who treated women with respect; but then ashamed to be giving himself good marks at the expense of other members of his sex. It was this conflict that led to the depressed feeling.

When his eyes fell upon 'As far as child-raising and housework are concerned ... the number of husbands prepared to help ... is still not high', he winced and stopped reading, sensing a deliberate, indeed spiteful, criticism aimed specifically at him. This was exactly the kind of nagging he'd been subjected to by his wife for a quarter of a century now. Partly as a result of this unpleasant association, he was unable to give his undivided attention to the critique of the system whereby husbands were posted away from their families, merely glancing at what was written. This kind of sidelong perusal was encouraged by the fact that he was still reading with one eye on the screen and one on the printout, which made it inevitable that his grasp of the editorial would be only superficial. In fact, he was now reading it as casually as he would have done an article or a phone call from someone on the political pages relating the remarks of one of the leaders of the ruling party as reinterpreted by another of its leaders. It was only natural, then, that when Yumiko wrote of similarities between the conventions in Tokugawa and contemporary Japan, he should fail to grasp that she was saying that, although men were able to get away with illicit love affairs and using prostitutes, if a woman had an affair she had to pay for it by pregnancy. The words 'disastrous effect on the family' did get a long nod from him, but he was quite unable to appreciate that by 'disastrous effect' she was referring to a situation where the grass widow would be obliged to have any child conceived by sleeping with another man. Anyway, by the end of it he decided the thing was probably all right, even if there were some parts that seemed a bit dubious—after all, it was inevitable they should see things differently (perceptive of him to work that out). So when Yumiko, still flushed with pleasure at having finished her article, took the seat next to his, he said to her cheerfully:

'This is fine. Not bad. Not bad at all. A bit harsh, of course. A bit below the belt at times, hah, hah, hah. Still, if the pheasant squawks the hunter will shoot at it. This whole business of posting husbands away from home has always been a nonsense—I've always been highly critical of it. But there are things to be said on the other side, you know. There's the question of the children's education for a start. And it could be worse: in socialist countries, for instance, diplomats are sent abroad alone by order of the state, to cut down on expenses. Now that is inexcusable, don't you think? Anyway, I entirely agree with your conclusion: "this is something we should think about very seriously indeed". That's the policy I've been pursuing for years now.'

Yumiko was always glad when what she wrote got past a deputy chief, and she said calmly:

'Does anything need changing?'

'Well,' he said, doing his sidelong scrutiny again. 'Well, um, yes, uh, that looks all right... Ah yes, this part here: "... it has been the tradition in this country to remain indifferent to ... the plight of the woman..." I think that would be better expressed as "to be on the whole indifferent..." '

'Yes, I see what you mean. Let's change it,' Yumiko agreed.

The deputy lost himself in contemplation for a while, then asked:

'How about "It's Women Who Give Birth" as your title?'

'Oh yes, that's fine, I think. I like it,' she said, secretly thinking that almost anything would have been better, but that she'd have to put up with it. So the deputy turned to the word processor, typed in the minor revision and the title, and pressed the button that meant the editorial had officially been submitted for publication.

On the fourth floor a woman proof-reader in her thirties was

soon checking Admiral Togo's name in the dictionary. 'Heihachiro Togo (1847–1934)' was there, so the name was right, and
although it didn't say if he was the eighth son or not, she decided
there was no need to look further. After all, newspapers were not
responsible for the truth of what politicians said. Eight boys,
though, she thought as she peered at the article on the screen—
that was pretty good going, especially as there must have been
some girls as well. She was curious to know just how many children had been born into that family, but not to the extent of going
to the library to find out, as a real researcher might have done.
She herself had been married for three years, without even one
child to show for it. Stimulated by the example of multiple births
in the Togo household, she wondered again if she should go and
see a doctor to find out why, whether it was her fault or her husband's; but then, as always, she felt it would be better to wait a bit
longer and see how things turned out.

On the same floor, in the makeup department, the man in
charge of the second page of the morning edition was also reading the editorial on his screen, and he clicked his tongue in irrita-
tion at yet another piece of feminist propaganda. His mother
had always been very hot on the subject, and since she had chosen
his wife for him it followed that his wife was too, and he was
pestered by the two of them night and day. He knew straight
away that a woman had written it. Naturally, he found what it
had to say pretty offensive, but he read it with as much care as he
devoted to the nagging of his wife and mother, concerned less
with understanding than simply with putting up with it. On top
of that, he had always disliked the former prime minister, not for
any political reason but because he looked so unimpressive and
spoke with an accent. His satisfaction at seeing him take a hammering therefore clashed with his aversion to feminism. Just to
complicate things, his wife loved children and they had five of
them, a fact he at times deeply regretted, at others felt very happy
about, being unable to decide one way or the other even after all
these years. So he finished the editorial with a cheerless expression
on his face, reflecting that if he'd been trusted with the headline,

as he was with all the other articles, he'd have chosen 'It's a Man's World', since the present headline would put most men off reading it (although that would actually be doing them a favour). But as nobody read editorials anyway, why bother?

Seated next to him was a man with prematurely greying hair who paused in his own reading of 'It's Women Who Give Birth' when he reached the words 'a way of thinking that is fundamentally male in outlook'. It had occurred to him that Purrs was a male, and maybe that was why he hadn't come home for such a long time. Purrs was the name of their cat—or at least he wasn't really theirs, since he belonged to his parents who lived in a separate building in the garden, but since they only fed him tinned cat food, while he and his wife gave him the real stuff (only dried sardines, but still), he had come to live with them. It was this cat that had disappeared a week ago. His parents didn't seem bothered about it, and he, his wife and daughter just assumed it was some untimely love affair and hadn't worried too much either. But that morning at around dawn he had dreamed that Purrs sat by his pillow and, instead of purring, gave a plaintive *mrmrmew*. This dream had thoroughly upset him, so at breakfast he'd suggested to his wife and daughter that they should get a notice printed, complete with photograph, and pin it to the telegraph poles in the neighbourhood. Of course, when he'd explained why, they'd just laughed at him, not knowing how pathetic the poor cat had sounded in his dream. But Purrs was probably lying sick and miserable somewhere, perhaps even seriously injured, after losing a fight over some female. Or maybe someone else had taken him in. It was vital that they get a good photo of him, he decided, wondering if they had any decent ones at home.

On the same floor, about twenty feet away from these two, was a young man who sat gazing at a full-page display on the large screen in front of him. Page two of the morning edition had both editorials on the right-hand side, with rules placed round them. He was pleased that the two headlines weren't exactly the same width, but he could have got an even better balance if the first one had been longer. 'You can't muck about with it, though,' he muttered to himself, feeling vexed that the editorials were 'off limits' as far as he was concerned, but reminding himself that he was taking the one o'clock flight to Hong Kong the following afternoon, and deciding that once he'd finished work at two in the morning he wouldn't go for the usual drink in the staff canteen but would head straight home; otherwise he might be there all night, or at least till four or five.

He ran his eyes over the two editorials a second time, stood up, leaned to the right in order to see round a pillar obstructing his view, and shouted to the man sitting twenty feet away.

'Yama. I'm going to let the two "off limits" roll. Okay?'

Yama stood up and started to say something to the grey-haired fellow at his side, but saw he was on the phone, looking a good deal more cheerful as he listened to whatever was being said at the other end.

'He's not too thin, then? Dirty? Well, he's bound to be… Okay. Yes. He ate all the sardines? What about milk? He should be all right, then. Still, funny sort of cat, just putting in an appearance then pushing straight off again. Don't worry, it couldn't be helped. In the circumstances, you could hardly have got him to wipe his paws before he came into the house…'

At that point the cat-lover, who also happened to be the senior person there, noticed that the fellow next to him was looking at him questioningly, so he nodded, raising his right hand with the thumb and forefinger forming a circle to indicate everything was all right. It was by way of misunderstandings of this kind that Yumiko Minami's dangerously controversial editorial came to be printed in the *New Daily*.

FOUR

⋮

On the second and fourth Saturdays of each month, at six in the evening, the conference table in the editorial staff room would be prepared for what looked like a celebration of some kind: on it would be a couple of bottles of whisky, plenty of mineral water, a glass container full of ice, sometimes saké, shochu and beer, and slices of cheese, ham and fish sausage, plus sandwiches. When all the arrangements had been made the team would assemble, and these fortnightly get-togethers were referred to as 'the booze-up'. Someone had once suggested it might be given a more dignified name, but this idea had been countered by the suggestion that they should ask Yasuoka for one, and the loud laughter that greeted this ensured the name stayed the same. This Yasuoka, in case you need reminding, was the scholar of Chinese, mentor to successive post-war prime ministers in the Wisdom of the East, to whom politicians used to turn when they needed an appropriate name for a new party faction.

Nobuko Konaka was a teetotaller, so she hardly ever attended these parties and thought them a waste of time, but Yumiko Minami did occasionally drink a little and always tried to put in an appearance for about half an hour. The men would go on drinking for a couple of hours; some of them would then move on somewhere else.

On the evening in question they were joined by Ichiro Anzai, an expert on economics, who had been made an editorial adviser in April. He was a cheerful character, popular with most people, and a crowd always seemed to gather round him, even the secretaries remaining behind (something they almost never did) to hear him talk. His speciality was telling stories that left his listeners uncertain as to whether they were true or not, and this evening's had been prompted by someone asking why he hadn't taken a post in a private university after reaching retirement age at his national university the year before.

Seated comfortably on the sofa, whisky glass in hand, he replied in his jovial way that he and two friends had made a vow when they were university students. All three had been confident they would become economics professors at national universities, and they had sworn to each other that, not only would they never accept doctorates (such titles being a desecration of pure scholarship), they would also, when they reached retirement age, decline to accept a position in a private university (because that would mean blocking the promotion of the junior members of their profession). As it happened, though, one of them had gone into banking, eventually becoming a top executive, which might have been excusable had he not written a dissertation in his spare time and been awarded a doctorate. And as if that wasn't bad enough, the other one had not only got his doctorate but had moved to a private university *before* reaching retirement age, excusing himself on the grounds that the promise applied only to what was done after retirement.

'It made me so angry I made up my mind never to take a job like that, just to show the two of them,' he said, laughing, although the truth was he was so busy with lectures and magazine articles he didn't have time to take up such a post anyway.

By way of a sequel, an old hand from the city desk then came up with a strange story about the gubernatorial elections in Kyushu (which couldn't be published, however), and this was followed by a financial reporter talking about the way the beer companies carved up the market between them. Apropos of nothing in particular, the overseas news specialist mentioned that some Scandinavian newspapers received financial support from their governments, a fact that everyone seemed to have something to say about.

'It's just like opera and ballet.'

'Like subsidising an orchestra.'

'In socialist countries all the newspapers are government-funded.'

'I think I heard somewhere it's the same in Holland.'

'I suppose it just shows that newspapers are as likely to lose money as orchestras are.'

'Let's hope it has as little effect on performance as it does with opera and ballet.'

'What about freedom of speech?'

'All universities get some form of state funding, yet they insist they have academic freedom.'

'Still, if you're getting government money it's difficult to be critical.'

'There's a difference between freedom of speech and academic freedom.'

'What? How?'

'It must be virtually impossible to attack the government if they're funding you. It's hard enough when you're not getting anything.'

'It's the carrot and the stick—eating the carrot means giving the government the stick.'

At this point one of the staff, his mouth full of cheese, asked Anzai his opinion.

'Any sort of gift implies the concept of "reciprocity",' he replied, using the English word.

'What's that—an illness?' said Urano (in fact Yumiko had thought the same at first, although she knew it couldn't be).

Anzai gave a chuckle and stood up, squeezing behind two chairs to make his way over to the blackboard which stood beside the television set. He wrote the Japanese translation of the English word on the board, then explained.

'It's the idea of both doing well out of something. Give and take, if you like. Mutual interdependence. The idea of exchange.'

Urano made a bemused sound, indicating he was well out of his depth, and everybody laughed; then the economics expert went on.

'Sociologists call it the "exchange theory", beginning with the idea that if someone receives a gift he feels obliged to give something back, and then explaining everything as a form of reciprocation of goods. Well, there's a good deal in that, of course; all the exchanging of gifts that goes on in this country in June and December is a prime example, with its roots in a much older social custom. The exchange of Christmas cards and presents is another imported form of it. Exchanging business cards when we meet for the first time is another.'

'What about when a politician bribes a constituent to get his vote?' asked Urano.

'A very clear case of reciprocity at work in the exchange of gifts. But there's another, rather quaint, academic theory about that, to the effect that a Diet member shows his appreciation for the votes he's received by doing good things for his constituency—building new bridges or railway lines ... and other projects of less obvious benefit. If you investigated what our politicians were really doing, though, I think you'd find cases of that sort of thing much less common than you might expect. The average Diet member, surely, finds it hard to meet all but a few of his constituents' demands. Anyway, I like to think that people vote for better reasons than that. Or am I being idealistic?'

Anzai looked in Yumiko's direction, over on the other side of the blackboard, and, catching her eye, said with a little smile:

'Now, how about love? Some vulgar people would maintain that the same principle of reciprocity applies there. The man falls for the woman, sends her flowers and jewellery, and she reciprocates by giving him her heart. That's one theory—not mine, of course, far from it. I'm just an old-fashioned romantic at heart, I suppose. As an explanation it's much too prosaic, and it overlooks something much more important. At least, from my own modest

103

experience I like to think it misses the point.'

The men laughed at this, while Yumiko smiled and nodded. This seemed to satisfy Anzai, and he went on:

'I'm glad to see you all agree with me. The theory is grossly simplistic, and fails to explain how things really are. Let me just make two further points about it. First, although exchanging gifts *is* economically important to this country, it's absurd to overlook actual productivity. The economy isn't kept going by people taking in each other's laundry. Secondly, the giving of gifts is a social phenomenon, and the form it takes varies considerably from culture to culture. It therefore lacks the universality that would allow it to work as a valid economic theory. Also, if taken too far, it actually prevents serious thought, and that can't be a good thing.'

'Yes, I appreciate all that,' said Yumiko, 'but what about in the case of newspapers?'

'You mean when a newspaper receives a subsidy from the government? Well, one can hardly deny that if a gift has been received, something has to be given back. Still, that doesn't have to take the form of subservience and sycophancy. There are other ways of responding.'

'Such as?'

'Plain speaking, honest advice, constructive criticism, noting what's wrong with government policy and getting it put right. That should be seen as a way of paying for services rendered—or at least, so I'd like to think, though perhaps I'm being idealistic again.'

Judging from the way they smiled, they seemed to agree with his self-assessment.

'But isn't it true, sir, that the basic idea behind the repaying of any gift is that the recipient should be pleased with it?' This came from the edge of the group, a man who had been a resident reporter at the Ministry of Transport for so long it was said he was personally responsible for all the new appointments made there.

'That's how it's supposed to be. In reality, things don't quite work out that way, do they? Just look at the traditional gifts some people receive—a couple who loathe pickled onions get a jar of them; a teetotaller gets a bottle of brandy...'

'I know...'

'And, in the past, the retainer showed his loyalty to his master by giving him advice that could hardly have pleased him, however politely it was phrased—to lay off the women, for example, or to avoid flatterers. That was a genuine form of repayment for the stipend he received. There are lots of examples of that kind of thing. So why shouldn't a newspaper behave in the same way—repaying its subsidy by saying things that may be unpalatable, but with the best of motives? But none of you seem to think it would work. I suppose the government would take offence, and assume you were just trying to be unpleasant.'

Everyone laughed again and Anzai finally sat down, reaching for the bottle of whisky to pour himself another drink, thanking Yumiko, who had offered to do it for him, but saying he could manage, while the discussion continued rather half-heartedly around them.

'Obviously, first you have to educate the government in this exchange theory.'

'Then get hold of a government subsidy...'

'Post Office New Year cards give you numbers for the state lottery, so that means they're a double return gift.'

'He's a bit over the top, isn't he?'

'Loyal retainers were always committing ritual suicide. That was their contribution.'

'Paying with their lives...'

Anzai himself only smiled at all this, and when he finally spoke again his words were not directed at the group, although he didn't lower his voice.

'I believe, Ms Minami, that you wrote this morning's editorial?'

'Yes.'

'And extremely entertaining it was, if I may say so. The first time, I think, that the post-expansionist period of the Japanese economy has been significantly linked with sexual behaviour. A genuinely original statement.'

Yumiko's face flushed, and she expressed conventional surprise and gratitude that he'd taken the trouble to read it.

'But your point of view is pretty radical.'

'Oh, d'you think so?'

She noticed that Urano was standing nearby, helping himself to more ice from the bowl.

'When you read something like that,' he put in, 'you can't help wondering about the sex life of the writer.'

'That's what's known as sexual harassment,' she promptly replied, making Urano duck his head in embarrassment and Anzai laugh out loud, and providing Yumiko herself with a good opportunity to leave, which she had to do anyway since she was due in Kyobashi, where she was to attend the first day of an exhibition of minor pieces by the traditional painter Sakon Ogino, one of her eleven 'pre-forties'. When she reached the lift, however, she turned round and saw Urano coming after her.

'Hold on a moment,' he said. 'I don't want to seem nosy, but isn't this your daughter?'

He produced the evening edition of one of the financial papers, which she took, seeing immediately that it wasn't bad news, although still surprising. Occupying a third of a page was a large advertisement showing six girls extolling the virtues of various makes of tea, biscuits, peanuts, crackers and so on. The one recommending the tea was 'postgraduate student Chie Minami', and the picture showed her smiling happily, though somewhat artificially.

'Yes, it is. Clever of you to notice.'

'But she looks like you.'

'Does she?'

'Yes. That was my first impression. Then it says she's a postgraduate, so…'

While she was looking at the photograph, thinking that Chie was the best-looking (or seemed the best-looking) of the six girls, Urano said:

'You can keep it if you like. I don't suppose they'll have sent her a copy yet.' He then went away.

In the lift Yumiko smiled, looking for a moment rather like the picture of her daughter. She was happy enough about seeing the girl in the paper, but also felt some satisfaction that a man should be preoccupied with her to the extent that Urano obviously was. But above all she was pleased about her editorial, for Anzai's and Urano's comments were the first she'd heard.

Something like 'Starting from Scratch', being little more than a set of casual asides and easy to read, generally got a good reader response, either by telephone or letter. But editorials very rarely received that kind of attention, and if they did it was considered quite exceptional. The same applied to the writing staff: they would comment on 'Starting from Scratch' because it was signed by an individual, but since editorials were unsigned they were impersonal and hardly anyone ever read them. In fact the only two colleagues who did read them fairly regularly were the authors of 'News from Another Planet' and 'Something on My Mind', but that was only because they were desperate for material and would look for it anywhere. At first Yumiko had been slightly unhappy about this lack of feedback, but she'd got used to it now and thought nothing of it, although on this occasion it had struck her as a bit much that the person who had virtually forced her to write it, Nobuko Konaka, should have said nothing about the piece, even though they'd come across each other at least once today. She didn't begin to consider that there might be a reason for this—that Nobuko thought the piece badly done or too outspoken, for example. Actually, the authors of 'News from Another Planet' and 'Something on My Mind' hadn't said anything either, but perhaps that was because they were so impressed they couldn't think what to say. In the case of Urano, well, he was always looking for ways to please her, though without much success, and he had merely used Anzai's comments to get in his own—but at least this showed that someone had read the thing.

She was still feeling pleased with herself when she got to the exhibition. Most people had already left, and only those invited to the reception remained, holding glasses in a loose circle around Sakon Ogino. Yumiko looked attentively at about ten pictures, all with red labels on them indicating they were sold, then paid her compliments to the artist and his wife. Ogino was wearing a dark blue pin-striped suit, a light blue shirt with thin white stripes, and a paisley bow tie (dark green on a reddish background). His wife wore a kimono with a pattern of clematis on a white ground, tied with a simple crêpe sash. This obvious attempt at sartorial restraint was presumably meant to encourage their guests to concentrate on the pictures.

Mrs Ogino had been suspicious of Yumiko's relationship with her husband up until a few years ago, and somehow they hadn't seemed to hit it off until, at another reception, she had heard that Yumiko also had a teenage daughter. Since then, she had seemed to accept her, and now they always tended to talk about Chie; today was no exception.

'I suppose she must have graduated this year?'

Here we go again, thought Yumiko, but without any real displeasure.

'She's staying on as a postgraduate. In English literature.'

This eventually led to the subject of the newspaper photograph. Yumiko showed it to the artist's wife, who praised it and handed it to her husband, who looked at it thoughtfully; it was then passed from hand to hand, everybody having something nice to say about it, until finally it came back to Ogino, who had another long look before returning it to Yumiko.

When Yumiko got home, however, neither Chie nor her grandmother had a good word to say for the picture. Chie frowned, and was annoyed with her mother for having passed it round at the reception. Then Chie's great-aunt Masako, former film actress Aeka Yanagi, turned up with some cakes, earning an invitation to have some tea so that they could eat them together, and gave it as her opinion that the angle was wrong, this leading to an endless account of the dreadful experiences she'd undergone at the hands of incompetent photographers and cameramen.

The next day being Sunday, all the family had a lie-in, and

they were eating a combined breakfast and lunch when there was a phone call from Ogino, who said he was planning a mother-and-child portrait and would like Yumiko and Chie to pose as models. He would show it in his spring exhibition next year, and since he'd already done the designs and sketches for his autumn exhibition, and was to start working on the actual pictures in a couple of days, he hoped to start on the portrait when these were finished, sometime towards the end of August.

Yumiko refused on the spot, though very politely. She was busy, as was her daughter, and it hardly seemed worth the trouble of trekking out to the suburbs in order to spend hours closeted in an artist's studio. The artist laughed, and asked her not to be so quick to decide, but to talk it over with her daughter; he seemed to have a pretty good idea what the outcome of such a discussion would be. Indeed, the outcome was that they did agree to model for him. Etsuko said it would be wrong to turn down an opportunity like that, since the painting might become famous and Chie would get dozens of proposals of marriage. Masako alias Aeka, who just happened to have dropped in again, said it would be tremendous publicity and that there was money to be made out of it, since even though one couldn't hope to be presented with the actual painting, there were always the sketches, and they could be worth quite a lot. Chie herself, who at first hadn't sounded very enthusiastic, gradually began to waver, until she finally said the experience of being painted by Sakon Ogino might be rather interesting. So later that afternoon Yumiko rang and explained that her mother, aunt and daughter had talked her round and that they could do the sittings sometime in September. As it turned out, in fact, the four women were to spend a good deal of time over the next two months discussing what they should wear, how they should do their hair and so on, all of which provided Yumiko with an unexpected and very welcome form of relaxation, for from the height of summer into autumn she was to go through a difficult period at work, the first really unhappy experience she'd had since joining the paper.

There was no work for her to do on Monday, and in the afternoon, when she was about to leave the building in search of material, she ran into the president near the ground-floor reception desk. They chatted a little, and she noticed nothing strange about his behaviour: his face was as floridly cheerful as ever as he asked her to explain a few things about the vocabulary young girls used nowadays. She did so, and he thanked her, and when she thought about it later she realised he couldn't yet have read the editorial. Indeed, it was normal for him not to read such things.

On Tuesday there was still no specific response to her article. When the editorial meeting was over, she went to the bookshop on the eighth floor of the next-door building, and found the vice-president there looking with deep interest at a volume of animal paintings. When she addressed him, he smiled, and said he was too old now to be interested in nudes, and she smiled as well. He couldn't have read the editorial either. Then, that afternoon, as she was leaving the staff room and about to get into the lift, she was stopped by a man who used to be one of the paper's directors and was now chairman of a television company. He seemed to be complimenting her on something, though she couldn't work out what, which left her feeling slightly rattled.

On Wednesday the head of the editorial writing section, now back from his business trip, told her he'd met the historical novelist member of the 'pre-forties' quite by accident in a three-star restaurant in Paris, but that, apart from some small talk about their health, sales, and what presents they were taking home, nothing of any importance was said. Since the editorials would certainly have been faxed to him while he was away, one could only assume he'd read Yumiko's but failed to see what she was getting at, and so had noticed nothing out of the ordinary.

Late that same evening, while she was watching television by herself, she had a phone call from a reporter on the financial pages, who told her that her article had been discussed at a joint conference of the Three Economic Organisations and had come under attack. Apparently a member of a watchdog committee had announced that, although he didn't object in principle to her criticism of the system of posting husbands away from their fami-

110

lies, her encouragement to wives to indulge in immoral behaviour during such absences could only profit their competitors, since it would undermine the businessmen's morale. The conference decided not to draw attention to the matter, so as not to upset the absent husbands unnecessarily (or provoke any corresponding action from the wives), and that was the end of it. Naturally, nothing would appear about it in the paper—in fact, he wouldn't even bother to make an official report—but he just thought he ought to let her know what had happened. He owed her a favour, since Yumiko, when he first joined the paper as a reporter on the lifestyle pages, before moving to the financial section, had introduced him to two of her 'pre-forties', one of the bright sparks at MITI and a businessman known for his development of new technology.

As soon as she put down the phone Yumiko got out her scrapbook and read through the offending editorial. Although she'd written it herself, she now saw it with new eyes, and an alternative interpretation became very clear. The piece could all too easily be seen as implying that female adultery was a reasonable weapon in the fight to get abortion accepted. She found herself impressed by the intelligence of the member of the watchdog committee who had worked this out, even if, as was likely, he had nothing better to do. And if he could work that out, then he'd probably also guessed that the writer of the editorial was a woman who was feeling deprived of a man. She could imagine all the old men at the joint conference, seated in their padded armchairs and sofas, chuckling as this was put to them, and had she been ten years younger she would have blushed with shame; as it was, she merely felt slightly embarrassed, and then relieved to think that the matter would go no further. If the sly old things in the Three Economic Organisations were prepared to overlook the matter, then so would everyone else.

Two days later she had dinner with Toyosaki in his hotel room. When she blamed him for making her write a bad editorial because he'd cancelled their date, he apologised, then said:

'But, you know, that's just arguing after the event. Theoreti-

111

cally, there's no good reason why it shouldn't have inspired a good editorial.'

There was no arguing with that, so she changed the subject, telling him about the economist's views on gifts.

'Anzai can be quite amusing,' he said. 'He bought me dinner once, in Kyoto—in fact, I've just realised I haven't paid him back yet. I don't rate him all that highly as an economics teacher, and I'm not prepared to buy his theory on reciprocity, but I suppose, since I owe him for that meal, I'm not really in a position to criticise him. Still, the fact is that gifts are usually an expression of goodwill, and since lovers are presumably in a goodwill relationship, then naturally their presents to each other come into the same category. Academically, the subject of exchanging gifts became popular with Mauss, a French anthropologist who did his research in the South Pacific—or was it Africa? Somewhere like that, anyway. He studied private gift-giving rituals, and made the point that the soul of the giver was supposed to live in the gift. It was that aspect that he stressed, so obviously lovers' presents to each other would be a prime example.'

'It's not the gift that counts but the thought?'

'Basically, yes. When we wrap our presents up carefully and tie them with string, we're binding the soul so that it can't escape.'

'Oh, are we?'

'Well, that's the idea. I don't know how well it stands up.'

They ate all the cakes he'd brought from Sendai, and went on talking late into the night. She mentioned that she and her daughter were going to be models for a picture in Sakon Ogino's spring exhibition. He replied by recalling the time Yumiko had introduced him to Chie when he'd met the two of them in Ginza a couple of years ago; he'd also seen a photo of her sometime later, and found it easy to remember what she looked like, which set him wondering about her father's appearance; but as Yumiko insisted her daughter didn't take after her father but was more like her grandmother, his attempts to put a face to the bank president in Hokkaido could hardly be expected to be successful. He then talked about Hegel's ideas on phrenology, and she laugh-ingly confessed that, when she heard him speak on any new subject, she always thought she'd like to read up about it but had found from experience that it was much more fun to listen to him talk. Then she mentioned the crossed-out postscript to Urano's letter, which startled him into a very unphilosophical, high-pitched laugh, and he immediately began to analyse her fellow journalist's aims and intentions, using the point-by-point method she favoured:

1) To challenge the boundary between coarseness and courtesy.

2) To promote a sense of complicity between them, by making her an accessory after the fact to the thought of a forbidden act.

3) To make the act itself an inevitable sequel to this sense of complicity.

There were other motives involved, but those were the main ones. She said she'd already worked that out for herself, and all he'd done was make things less clear by using longer words. He ignored this, and said he imagined the man had used similar methods before, to which she nodded meekly in agreement, making them both laugh. She didn't mention the fact that her editorial had been discussed by the Three Economic Organisations, in case he thought she still blamed him for it; she was also inclined to be amused at what now seemed the obvious connection between her private life and what she'd written, and since none of this was going to be made public it didn't seem worth bothering about.

One day at the beginning of July she was talking to a visitor in the cafe on the ground floor, when the vice-president entered with a couple of people around the same age as himself. Yumiko nodded in his direction, and he returned her greeting with a slightly dazed expression, which she thought a bit strange; but when her meeting was over and she rose to leave, she was reassured to see him give her a little wave, as he usually did. She also took it as a good sign that she hadn't bumped into the president for some time, or been called in to see him, and there was no apparent change in the attitude of her immediate boss towards her either.

Nor could anything ominous be read into the fact that in mid-July, the very day after her mother had pointed out how lovely the evening primroses were in the next-door garden, both the morning edition's 'News from Another Planet' and the evening edition's 'In a Pensive Mood' were on that subject, a coincidence that was discussed at the editorial writers' meeting. But just as the meeting was coming to an end, Yumiko had a phone call from the personnel manager, a man called Hasegawa, who said he wanted to see her. Since she had to go out that afternoon to interview someone, she went off to his office immediately.

Hasegawa was a man of unhealthy complexion with narrow eyes that made him look constantly on the verge of sleep. Even before his secretary had shown her in, he was on his feet, cheerfully directing her towards the large reception room next door. Since he took his jacket with him, she assumed this was going to take some time, for compared with the tepid warmth of his office the air-conditioning in the reception room worked very efficiently.

Despite his appearance, Hasegawa was a sharp talker, even a wit, and soon had her laughing with various rumours about the boards of directors and presidents of other papers, before praising the promotions section of one paper, condemning that of another, and lamenting that their own wasn't really up to scratch. He mentioned the fact that over the past few years all the exhibitions the paper had been the main sponsor for had ended up in the red, and although he admitted that the *New Daily* could weather some losses as a result of such activities, he was less happy about their cultural level, which was disappointingly low.

At that point he sneezed, put on his jacket, and asked Yumiko if she was cold, saying that if she was he could borrow a cardigan for her from one of the secretaries. She thanked him for the thought but said she was all right, at which he nodded gravely and went on to explain the importance of special promotions to a large newspaper. They demonstrated, in the most graphic way,

114

the cultural mission of the paper, getting right through to the masses—no, sorry—to all levels of society. If things were going badly, they could generate enormous—well, not enormous exactly, but considerable sums of money, as well as making a massive —well, perhaps not massive, but at least a major contribution to the circulation of the paper, being potentially the most profitable feature of the company. It was at this point that Yumiko began to wonder why she was being given this particular runaround.

Hasegawa now changed tack, praising her fulsomely, first for her series about the 'pre-forties', then for her reportage on the car-manufacturing cities in America, her interviews with the wives of land racketeers, and her coverage of the lifestyle and opinions of senior women officers in the armed forces and of new businesses run by women in Tokyo. These articles were a credit, he said, with a very plausible look on his face, as if he really believed it, not only to the *New Daily* but to the journalistic profession as a whole.

Yumiko made some modest response, feeling one part pleased, one part bemused, and one part downright suspicious, but Hasegawa ploughed on, saying her achievements went beyond mere writing skills, indicating a penetrating assessment of what went on in society and an ability to influence it which the company hoped to encourage in the future.

"That's the point, you see. What we'd like you to do is come and work in the promotions department, with full department chief status. Full status, mind you. We'd like you to play as active a role as possible there. How about it?'

Yumiko was amazed. She'd realised the conversation must be leading somewhere unexpected, but hadn't got beyond imagining she was going to be asked to provide some publicity for an exhibition of objects borrowed from the British Museum or the palace of Topkapi, or about some woman tennis or golf player or marathon runner, or maybe even about a fashion show. She had rather hoped it might be a fashion show, since she knew next to nothing about sport.

She devoted the following hour to trying to find out more, managing to decline the offer in the course of seeking out the reasons that lay behind it. But Hasegawa's answers were evasive, and no matter how persistently she questioned him, his skill at avoiding the issue ensured that, at the end of their meeting, she was none the wiser. Yumiko left to his repeated assurances that they would discuss the proposal again next week.

Yumiko's reasons for refusing the new appointment were, above all, that she wanted to go on doing the job she had chosen, namely journalism. Ever since she'd been a child she'd dreaded the idea of spending a lifetime shut away at home, just because she was a woman, and had felt the attractions of an active life in society the more strongly for that reason. This was why she had chosen to read sociology at university, although the very first lecture by the head of the department had made her realise it had been a mistake—one that she continued to regret throughout her university life, and that prejudiced her against working as a businesswoman or becoming a civil servant. Preferring to avoid such direct participation in society, she decided something like journalism would suit her better, particularly as she had a gift for writing. It was hardly surprising, then, that she viewed the work of the promotions department—arranging exhibitions of gold and silver screens assembled from various museums in the States, planning some monster relay race which would extend all the way from Tokyo to the furthest point Basho had reached on his journey north as part of the three hundredth anniversary celebrations of that famous walk—with the same distaste she'd once felt at the prospect of working in business or the civil service. It was also a fact that on the *New Daily* (and no doubt on other newspapers too), those who were transferred into something like the publications department rarely made their way back to the paper proper—and surely this would be even more the case when the posting was to the promotions branch. It would mean her career as a journalist was over.

Quite apart from her own personal inclinations, however, there was something distinctly fishy about the whole business. Surely it was unusual to move someone out of her section only three and a half months after joining it, particularly as she'd been told editorial writers could be sure of a long tenure and the freedom to write what they wanted. There was an unwritten law, in fact, that they wouldn't be moved around any more at random, but would most likely stay put until retirement. Of course there had been various exceptions to that rule, but to break with custom in this manner was surely treating the whole department in a very cavalier fashion. No, it was all too hasty, too sudden. There could be no good reason for it. She feared it indicated a renewed intention to limit the number of women on the writing staff. For that reason alone she would stand her ground, since this tendency (albeit only hinted at and never officially stated) was one to which she knew she must never submit.

And, finally, she couldn't accept the explanation given for this transfer. She knew there were situations where a journalist who was becoming a nuisance had to be kicked upstairs, into research or historical records or whatever, and in such cases it was usual to promote them by a grade, which would explain the offer of department chief rank. But since she had never once clashed with either her immediate boss or the two deputy chiefs, it seemed unlikely to be their doing. In fact, everything had been going pretty smoothly in the company generally, so far as she could tell, and although it was conceivable she had somehow annoyed somebody or other, she couldn't think of any names. No, she must have ruffled some feathers *outside* the paper. That must be the source of the pressure, and the upper echelons of the administration had submitted to it. The only thing she could think of was the Three Economic Organisations business, but why would they want to rake that up again? And if personnel decisions inside the *New Daily* were to be dictated by the financial world, then the editorial system was under genuine threat—not only from an attack on the right of free expression, but from an act of discrimination against women, since the person involved was a female staff member, namely herself.

This was the conclusion she had reached by the following

morning, and which she presented to her boss. As his astonishment on hearing what she had to say appeared to be genuine, she assumed the decision had been made without consulting anyone in her section. That made the business even more puzzling, for the situation must have demanded remarkably quick action for them to have been prepared to bypass the chief in this way. Naturally he was extremely annoyed and spent some time telling her so, saying he would take the matter up with Hasegawa immediately. The following day, however, his attitude changed, and she realised he was trying to avoid her and that someone must be putting the screws on him.

He wasn't the only one. When she got hold of Nobuko Konaka immediately afterwards, not so much to ask advice as simply to talk to someone, Nobuko responded positively, saying she should refuse point-blank, she mustn't give in, and so on—only to undergo a similar transformation a few days later. This was something Yumiko had seen before, not just on the *New Daily* but on other papers as well, when criticism of a government's financial policies ceases to appear and the tone in which some major political figure is discussed becomes suddenly conciliatory. Obviously something was up.

As things now stood, there was nobody she could trust. There was nothing to be gained from talking to the president, and although she did think of two people who might be worth approaching—the advertising manager, who had formerly been head of the city desk, and the top man on a sports paper, who had been her boss when she was on the lifestyle pages—she decided it would only create trouble for them. But the advice she ended up giving herself, to try just to stick it out, only made her feel more isolated, like one of those tiny advertisements for Kewpie Mayonnaise you see standing on its own on a page full of political news, a pathetic little cupid figure, with its sad forelock and shorn wings, adrift in a sea of newsprint.

Despite her resolution not to make herself more vulnerable by protesting, she still had no intention of going along with the company's decision, but was aware that if she was to put up a decent fight she needed information. So she tried the reporter who had given her the news about the Three Economic Organisations, to see if there had been any further developments on that score, but he said he hadn't heard of any, and there weren't likely to be any, either, since the instigator, the man who'd brought up the editorial in the first place, had gone into hospital the week before to have an operation on his wisdom teeth. He asked her if anything was wrong, and although she didn't like concealing the truth from someone who had been so nice to her, she said no, nothing in particular, she'd just phoned because she was a bit concerned.

The next person she tried was a company president, one of her 'pre-forties'. He had just got back from the States the day before but was already on his way out to the golf course when she phoned early in the morning, and listened to what she had to say on the car phone. He got back to her an hour later, merely confirming what her journalist friend had said. So it seemed the problem lay elsewhere, though she found it difficult to let go of the idea that the financial world was mixed up in it in some way.

Another of her 'pre-forties' was now in charge of the Industrial Trade Bureau, and he had plenty of time to listen to her when she phoned, since a couple of meetings planned for that day had been cancelled. He said he knew nothing about the business with the Three Economic Organisations, but he had heard that the key shareholder in the *New Daily* Corporation, a woman, who was now head of the founding family, had conceived a great passion for opera and apparently wanted to build an opera house either in Tokyo or in one of the three main cities in the Kansai area. Perhaps the appointment of a senior-ranking woman to the promotions section might have something to do with that? This was the first Yumiko had heard of such a project, and she didn't know what to make of it, since she found it hard to believe the corporation had the financial clout to underwrite anything of that scale. Also, she hardly knew the old lady in question, being on little more than nodding terms with her. She congratulated the bureau chief for being in possession of such little-known information, and although she wasn't prepared to lend any credence to his hypothesis regarding her 'promotion', she did go to the arts department a day later, to ask the music reporter if there was any truth in the idea. He merely waved his hands in the air in an exaggerated gesture of denial before saying:

'It's just one of those dreams of hers that must have taken wing. Probably mentioned it in passing and somebody picked it up and made a big thing of it. She certainly is a great opera fan—she goes umpteen times a year, to Vienna, New York, Milan. But the idea of building an opera house with our financial resources is ridiculous. After all,' he added, pointing at the ceiling, 'what comes first is a new building for us. How's that coming along?'

She managed to parry this final question, thanked him, and left, to the accompaniment of one of those long, quizzical looks peculiar to journalists which serve as a way of seeing one off the premises.

Naturally she discussed the matter with Yokichi Toyosaki. In his case, needless to say, it wasn't with the aim of acquiring information, but seemed to come up naturally when they next spoke, just as she might mention that the flowering dogwood in the patio garden of the block of flats where she lived had died, or describe how she'd been drinking tea on one of the top floors of a high-rise building during the earthquake two days ago and had wondered what he'd been doing. The philosopher's advice was to play for time, since obviously they would want to get her to agree to the transfer, and just as obviously, whatever was behind this business, it wasn't in the paper's best interests to go along with it. If she let things drift, it was possible something might happen to allow events to take a different course. This was, in fact, just what Yumiko was thinking herself, but she told him it was pretty commonplace advice for a philosopher to be giving.

All this time, Yumiko was being called to Hasegawa's office regularly once a week to be asked if she accepted the proposal, and to reply that she had no idea what was going on—would he mind telling her? Had she perhaps committed some kind of faux pas in one of her editorials? But all he ever offered was a renewed invitation to join the promotions department at a higher rank. He used a considerable number of words to say this, but that was what they boiled down to.

By August, Hasegawa had evidently worked out that she was going to be a tough nut to crack, and had the head of promotions sit in on their meetings. This was a man with very dark jowls who made a couple of jokes at the beginning but then fell silent, staring at the flowers on the table. There had been lilies in the vase for two weeks.

'I didn't know where to look,' Yumiko told Toyosaki later, 'so I stared at the vase too. Lilies are very depressing flowers.'

Toyosaki's summer visits to Tokyo were taken up with his obligatory attendance at various seminars and symposiums; this year, it seemed, he also had to put up with Yumiko's tales of woe.

'I don't see why they couldn't have some other flower occasionally—roses, for example...,' he said, but was unable to think of the name of any other flower that bloomed at that time of year.

By the second half of August, even Hasegawa seemed to feel they needed a break, and she was left alone for that fortnight, but the sessions began again in September, this time with yet another person present, the man in charge of printing the paper. Compared to the other two, he was fairly informative, occasionally letting things drop that made Yumiko feel uneasy. For example, he said that, if she didn't consent, the corporation would be put in a very awkward position with regard to 'a certain party'.

'Which party? Are you talking about the imperial court, or what?'

This kind of reply would reduce him to silence as he sat there facing her, on the other side of a vase of Turkish bell flowers, and her challenge would be left unanswered.

It was now clear to Yumiko that the corporation was not going to change its mind, and as a last resort she decided to tell Urano the whole story. She probably would have done so sooner, since his remarkable detective abilities made him an obvious source of information, except that over the past month his attitude towards her seemed to have cooled a bit. On the surface, he was his old self—unrestrained, personal, making jokes that at times came very near the bone—but she nonetheless felt there was something odd about him, exemplified by the fact that he had stopped calling her Yumiko and reverted to Ms Minami. She had no idea what had caused this change in him, and even though she occasionally suspected he might have heard something about her from Hasegawa or another of the high-ups, she felt he wasn't the type to change the way he behaved because of something like that, although she appreciated she could have overrated his integrity. Still, if she was wrong and he had heard something, then maybe she could wheedle it out of him. So she offered to buy him lunch and took him to a French restaurant some way away from the company building.

The truth was, Urano had finally decided to give up trying to find his way into Yumiko's affections. The reason for this lay with a man called Hashizume who had joined the paper at the same time as Urano, worked together with him for a while on the city desk, then been transferred to the publications department where he worked on the weekly magazine, various club magazines, and was now one of the editorial staff attached to the books section. Not only did he genuinely like books, and was indeed a man of some culture, he also had a good eye for the market, and had recently been responsible for publishing a best-seller by some celebrity. Urano didn't in fact feel particularly close to him, but Hashizume himself seemed to regard him as a good friend of his, perhaps because he had no other friends on the paper. He was very pale, with a long face, and given to making cynical remarks. He had married a woman who had once been someone else's wife—an illustrator's—and this gave him a slightly shady reputation which was supported, rather than the reverse, by his remarkable talent for sniffing out suspicious goings-on.

One afternoon in July this Hashizume turned up in Urano's section during one of its slack hours, and was shown to the sofa that played such a vital role in the editorial get-togethers. After the usual pleasantries, he lowered his voice and started on the subject he'd come to talk about.

'I know I've no right to say this,' he said with an awkward

122

smirk which, however, quickly changed to a look of honest determination. 'But I think I ought to tell you, as a friend. You'd better drop that one.'

He looked in the direction of Urano's desk, which meant, in effect, he was directing his attention to the chair where Yumiko sat. Of course she wasn't actually there at the time, having left the room immediately after the editorial meeting to go and give a lecture in Yokohama.

'Oh, her. I suppose you were bound to hear about it.'

'I'm not trying to shove my nose in where it's not wanted, but I still advise you to give that one up.'

'You do?'

'Have you made it yet?'

'Uh-uh.'

'That's all right, then.'

'What's up?'

Hashizume gave a little nod, then stroked his right cheek with his index finger.

'There's this involved, if you see what I mean.'

Urano did see what he meant, all too clearly. Hashizume's crude gesture was meant to indicate that Yumiko was mixed up in one of the rackets. He was so astonished he didn't know how to respond—indeed, he wouldn't have known how to respond even if he hadn't been astonished. Hashizume went on to explain.

Towards the end of April, he said, late one night, he had been sitting in the lounge of one of the central hotels, right next to the main lobby. He'd commissioned a second-rate scholar to write an economics primer and, since this scholar was a great pro-wrestling fan but had only ever seen it on television, had taken him to see a few bouts. They'd gone on to a cheap drinking place, and after there his guest had insisted on a few more to round off the evening, so they'd ended up at this hotel. But the bar up on the twenty-fourth floor was full, so, after trundling all the way down again, they settled for a drink in the lounge. By that stage, the scholar, who'd been chatting away cheerfully enough till then, drifted into silence, leaving Hashizume listening to the deep, regular breathing of a sleeping man. His attention was therefore free to wander, and he looked about him, noticing at a distant table a group consisting of two women and a man, sitting in a row facing him, all with drinks in front of them. He didn't recognise the man, who was middle-aged, wearing a quiet but obviously expensive suit with a plain tie of some thick material. He could have been a company director, or perhaps a politician, though he somehow didn't seem to be either. In fact he was hard to work out. But both the women were known to him. One of them had been married to a famous baseball star; she'd been quite a well-known film actress for a while. The other was Yumiko Minami.

Although the man was seated in the middle it was the two women who were doing most of the talking. They seemed to get on well together, the film actress speaking animatedly, using her hands a good deal, Yumiko joking in a rather skittish way that was very different from how she behaved at work. Since he couldn't hear what they were saying, Hachizume just sat there wondering what kind of man would bring these two women here, apparently just to drink and listen to them chat, nodding or laughing from time to time.

Then his gaze shifted slightly to the left and he happened to notice another table, partly hidden by a pillar, where five men were sitting. They were all heavily built, with drinks on the table which no one had touched, and one of them was speaking into a mobile telephone. They were obviously the junior members of some gangster's mob, and it struck him suddenly that the man sitting between Yumiko and her friend must be the boss himself. The image of the company director or Diet member vanished, to be replaced by that of a godfather, some major figure in the underworld.

It was a depressing discovery to make, particularly as Yumiko had seemed such a nice, intelligent and good-looking woman, and a fellow journalist too, but it wasn't the first time he'd been forced to revise his opinion of someone's character. But he told himself to try to keep an open mind and go on watching them, which he did, with the result that he saw the actress say something to the boss, who summoned the sidekick with the mobile phone. The actress then made a call on it and started a conversation, smiling as she spoke, and finally passing it over to Yumiko who spoke into it in the same cheerful way. Unfortunately, the pro-wrestling fan woke up at that point and said he wanted to go home.

The next day Hashizume went to see a reporter in the entertainment section and asked him if he could find out the identity of the gangster with whom the ex-wife of a famous baseball player was associating. Since the man refused to take his request seriously, he then approached a reporter on the city desk who had been a regular at police headquarters for donkey's years; this one promised to ask around, and after an interval of ten days came back with an answer. The man was probably Heigoro Asaoka, leader of the Friends of Justice Society, a gang that controlled one third of the Ginza area. The next step was to establish whether this was the same man he'd seen in the hotel lounge, although he hardly expected to find a photograph of him in the files since it was company policy to dispose of anyone's photograph if they had a criminal record. However, since it seemed a bit dodgy to approach the police directly, or even via a weekly paper that made its sales principally on the strength of its accounts of gangster rivalries, he thought he might as well start with the research photo files. The envelope labelled 'Leaders of the Major Gangs' produced nothing, but when, half convinced that his search was a waste of time, he looked casually through the file of individual names, he was excited to find under 'A' a grey envelope with 'Asaoka' written on it. Inside were five portrait photographs, obviously posed, which implied that permission had been obtained for them, and dated 1973. And there indeed was the face (a remarkably handsome face) of the man in the lounge, albeit as it must have looked nearly twenty years ago. Other than these, however, there was nothing, not even a casual snapshot, and although he checked through the newspaper files, he couldn't find anything on him, even a mention of his name. Hashizume thought this looked suspicious, and asked a number of old hands about it, but they couldn't help.

The mystery, however, was eventually solved quite easily. Every time he bumped into one of his old colleagues he would ask about this Ginza boss (without mentioning Yumiko, of course), and one day when he was sitting at the same table as the sales manager in the soba shop near the company building, he got a reply. The man sprinkled a generous amount of mixed spices over his bowl of noodles and said:

'Yes, he was clever, that one. He knew what he was doing.'

This was the prelude to a story about something that had taken place, he said, when he was working on the lifestyle pages. It must have been sometime in the early or mid-seventies, when the chief had his idea for a series of interviews called 'Men: the Pre-Forties' about up-and-coming people from various walks of life. He had been told to draw up a list, which he did, but, this being a period when student rebellion was still fashionable, he was told to include a few anti-establishment figures as well. So he racked his brains, and found a cartoonist who was popular with disaffected students; then a well-known Kabuki actor (of women's parts) who had caused a sensation by playing the lead role in a film about homosexuality and was rumoured to be that way in-clined himself. Some of the drama critics said he had a great fu-ture ahead of him.

The chief had convinced himself that the reason his son had failed to get into a good university was because he read too many comic books, so the cartoonist was out. The chief was also not well acquainted with Kabuki (all he had seen was one rather crude example of the genre on television) and was against includ-ing the specialist in women's roles. His wife, however, happened to be a great fan of this beautiful young man, and her powers of persuasion led to his being back on the list the next day. The actual compiler of the list, annoyed that the cartoonist (a great favourite of *his* son, who was getting good marks at his high

126

school) should have been dropped, then suggested cynically that they ought to get hold of a gangster, only to find that his boss loved the idea.

'A gangster! Perfect. That's it,' he cried.

Naturally there were objections: it was thought such exposure might be seen as encouraging the criminal element; that reader response might be bad; that police headquarters might have something to say about it; that other criminals might be jealous of the man chosen and take it out on the company somehow. But the chief was now totally sold on the idea.

'I'll take full responsibility,' he insisted, and the younger journalists supported him, since gangster films were very popular with students at that time. So eventually a member of the underworld was included among the twelve, and after a fair amount of research the second-in-command of a gang operating in Ginza, Heigoro Asaoka, was chosen, with the tacit consent of the guy in charge.

The interviewer was Yumiko Minami. The interview was held in a Japanese-style restaurant, in the presence not just of a photographer but of the deputy chief of her department (as he then was) as well. Yumiko asked some frank questions and received some equally frank answers; for example, she asked Asaoka how many women he had in addition to his wife, and he said five, though when it came to the group's main source of income he was less forthcoming, saying only that they weren't involved in narcotics. He seemed very taken with Yumiko and was obviously enjoying himself, while she in her turn appeared well disposed towards the gambler (clearly his main source of income) and wrote a very clever and amusing interview, avoiding anything that might cause offence, just as she had in all the other articles.

The first interview to appear was the one with the Kabuki actor, and since he committed suicide for unknown reasons three days after the article came out, the series was widely talked about. But by the time the last article, the interview with Asaoka, was scheduled to appear, the chief started to get cold feet, partly because the series had already attracted so much attention, but also because, on re-reading the copy, he came across a passage that he felt went too far. When Asaoka had been asked if he considered his activities criminal, he'd replied: 'Well, if you push the point, I suppose you could say I've done a number of things that could be called crimes. But that's true of politicians, too, isn't it?' (Yumiko had crossed out 'politicians' and put 'other businesses' instead.) As a result, the chief had gone to see the boss of the Friends of Justice Society to apologise for having to withdraw the article, and the deputy had gone with Yumiko to say the same thing to Asaoka, and the matter was settled with pleasant smiles and no ill feeling.

What was strange was that Hashizume, on hearing this story, decided it confirmed his belief that Yumiko must be Asaoka's mistress, and that what he had witnessed late that night in the hotel lounge was a man treating himself to the company not just of one, but of two of his mistresses. This was certainly jumping to conclusions—some would say pure fantasy—but such speculation is meat and drink to our journalists, the result being the considerable amount of misinformation that fills the papers. Hashizume had obviously been shaken by what he thought he saw going on at that distant table, which was made more sinister by the lateness of the hour, and it was perhaps inevitable that his view of things should be distorted. But he was also a cynic, as he acknowledged himself, and the cynic in him was willing to accept, even admire, the idea of a Ginza gangster getting two of his women to meet on such friendly terms.

Even stranger than this, however, given Urano's skill at separating true information from false, and his general integrity, was that the former crime reporter should swallow this concoction too. Despite the persistence with which he'd pursued her, pestering her with gifts, love letters and dinner invitations, he had sensed that things weren't going his way and come naturally to the conclusion she must have a lover, coming just as naturally to suspect one of the 'pre-forties'. But this unexpected solution to the question of who it was seemed so grotesque it left him, not only

128

aghast and quivering in amazement, but inclined, since his own experience of the world was by and large grotesque, to accept the information at face value.

He thanked Hashizume profusely, muttering that it had been a close shave, acknowledging the friendly rebuke that, while on paper it might be all right to risk everything for the sake of love, real life was rather different, and making up his mind that he was going to stop chasing after that woman. He was also, it might be said, relieved that he had an excuse to abandon this totally one-sided love affair.

It was from that point on that, although happy to continue their bantering conversations, he refrained from the sexual innu-endoes, dinner invitations, love letters and presents that had for-merly marked his encounters with Yumiko. He even refrained from asking her to help with his articles, although the real reason for this was that, in order to impress Yumiko, he'd worked hard to improve his style and by the end of June had suddenly found himself at a stage where he could write them all by himself, much like the time when, as a boy, he'd discovered all at once he could swim. He still occasionally asked her to read them through for him when they were written up, since she was sitting at the desk next to his, but on the whole he tried to avoid even that. Thus it was only natural she should have thought something was up.

At lunch in the French restaurant, however, when he heard what Yumiko had to say, his feelings started to change again. For one thing, he was flattered that she trusted him enough to ask him to investigate something of this nature for her. Also, it stirred his professional instincts, which told him that something funny was going on. More importantly, though, he felt encouraged to hope again that, if he managed to be of any help, she might come round and accept him as her lover. So, having drunk nearly all the half bottle of red wine they'd ordered, he ordered another glass for himself, cheerfully agreeing to help her and assuring her he would do all he could.

That night, just before he went to bed, he decided that the rea-son Hashizume had indulged in those groundless suspicions (if that was all they were) was because he himself was keen on Yumiko and was jealous of Urano's success with her. He also came to another conclusion, which slightly contradicted the first but followed the same broadly optimistic trend: namely, that a big shot with plenty of women at his beck and call (as he surely must have) ought to have grown tired of a woman in her forties, and would probably (if he got to know about it) be grateful to Urano for taking her off his hands.

The first thing he did in the morning was get the chief to let him off editorials and 'Starting from Scratch', and also from attendance at three editorial meetings. He said he was onto something big, only he wouldn't be able to handle it as editorial material but would have to give it to the city desk when he'd got it right. This blatant lie went down surprisingly well, so that even when he did put in an appearance at a meeting he was allowed to get away with saying nothing and leaving the minute it was over. The sight of his empty seat next to hers made Yumiko feel not only that it would have been almost impossible for her to find anything out if someone like Urano was as hard put to it as he seemed to be, but also that she must still be quite attractive if a man could spend all day rushing around on her account.

A number of days passed in this way, until finally she couldn't contain her curiosity and asked him for some kind of interim report.

'Well, I had intended to tell you all about it when I'd got everything worked out. Still, all right,' he agreed with some reluctance, and they arranged to meet at a small restaurant not far away for dinner. As it happened, Yumiko was again called in to see Hasegawa that afternoon, although he had absolutely no new proposals or suggestions to put forward, having presumably decided that there'd been no change of any kind in her attitude.

Urano turned up slightly after the appointed time, sitting down with his back to the cheap hanging scroll (pampas grass under the moon), ordering beer, drinking two or three glasses one after the other, and then beginning what he had to say. When the waitress turned up, he easily changed his style to one of smiling repartee, then returned to his original expression and theme as soon as she'd gone away, giving the essentials of everything he had found out so far, although naturally not the sources from which he'd obtained it. This he did with admirable clarity, making Yumiko understand how easy it must have been for his various ghost writers to do his articles for him if all the material was given in so coherent a form, though it did occur to her that it might be a talent more recently acquired—from learning to write for himself.

The first thing he had to say, which was obvious enough, was that the source of this disturbing business was not inside the company itself. There may have been people on the paper who thought her editorial was unsuitable or even dangerous, but no one had actually said so in public. Neither the section chief nor his two deputies had said a word against it. It had raised no repercussions in the advertising or promotions departments. Urano had thought the advertising people might have made moves to sell space to firms selling buddhas or things like that for aborted babies and perhaps been refused, but there hadn't been any such approaches made. No, the problem wasn't inside the paper; but knowing it was someone outside exerting pressure didn't unfortunately provide any leads in itself, and no amount of poking around in the company or pumping other sources had led to anything.

Still, there were certain negative conclusions to be drawn. It seemed to have nothing to do with the Three Economic Organisations. That man on the economic watchdog committee had been busy getting his wisdom teeth fixed, and when that was over his son had demonstrated his own lack of wisdom by looking as if he was going to be arrested for drug abuse, so he'd clearly had other things on his mind than leading articles. Also there were people on the board of the Three who'd never taken his objections seriously in the first place.

Urano had sounded out a number of religious organisations, but none of them looked suspect. This admittedly was a difficult area to investigate, since there were so many of them and they all had so little in common, but he could definitely say there were no signs at the moment that any of them had done anything, so he felt they could safely be dropped from the list of suspects.

What seemed most likely was that pressure had been applied from the political world, specifically the ruling party. The link man was probably either the president of a television company who had once been managing director of the *New Daily*, or the head of a sports paper who'd also worked at the *New Daily*, as editor-in-chief. Urano had discovered that, round about the time the whole business had started, the company president had met the chief secretary of the party at an exclusive restaurant in Aka-saka, while the head of the sports paper had met the same chief secretary's right-hand man in a similar restaurant in Tsukiji, and discussions had taken place, although it wasn't clear if they included this matter. The same people had met again quite recently. Since both of them had formerly been political journalists, their associating with politicians was perfectly normal, indeed a common enough occurrence, but it was still something worth bearing in mind. After all, it was one of those two, and possibly the pair of them, who had managed to hush up the scandal when the former president of the *New Daily* had died while on the job—meaning in bed with a woman.

'Oh, was that what happened?' exclaimed Yumiko with an excited squeal. 'I didn't know.'

'Really?'

'No, I mean I knew there'd been some kind of cover-up, but I didn't know the details of who'd done it. The whole thing was kept very hush-hush. No gossip at all.'

'When did you hear about it?'

'The night of the funeral. I'd already thought it was a bit strange that they were holding the funeral so soon. Normally with the president of a paper like ours they take more time over it, in a larger place as well.'

'Yes. I found out on the morning of the funeral, just before it started. Our president was quite a lad, was what I thought. I admired him for it.'

'Still, it was a good thing for his wife it was all kept quiet.'

'I know... And she was properly grateful. It was thanks to her, apparently, that the managing director, the one who's now a TV company president, got as far as he did.'

'Who was the woman? A bar hostess?'

'No, an amateur. A young woman, intellectual, graduated in French. They paid for her to spend a year in Paris to keep her quiet. While she was there she became the mistress of some French theatre producer, whose name escapes me, and never came back. The company, obviously, was very relieved.'

'Oh,' said Yumiko, feeling a bit put out at the thought that the reason she hadn't heard any of this before was because she was a woman. She would have liked to know who the French producer was, but Urano didn't seem likely to remember so she didn't bother to ask again.

'How did they manage it, then? The official version was that he died in a restaurant on the eighteenth floor of a hotel while dining in a private room with a friend. Does that mean he actually died in a bedroom, and they put his clothes on him and moved him to the restaurant?'

'No, no, they'd never do that,' said Urano, grinning and waving his hand. 'They just fixed it with the police.'

'Fixed it?'

'They got in touch with the chairman of the National Security Committee, a man called Zenroku Sakakibara, who was also a cabinet minister at the time, I think I'm right in saying. He agreed to keep it quiet, and once he'd taken care of that it was all plain sailing, the head of the National Security Committee being somebody with real clout, you see. The police just had to do what they were told, and when the official police announcement spells out the facts, dotting all the i's and crossing all the t's, everyone has to write it down just like that.'

'Well!' said Yumiko in astonishment, then added: 'This Zenroku Sakakibara is the present chief secretary?'

'That's right. The chief secretary of the party.'

'Still, I'm surprised he was prepared to tell a lie as big as that.'

'There was a reason for it.'

At this point Urano switched to shochu, a stronger sort of drink, urging Yumiko to join him, but she refused and he didn't insist but went on with his story. Two months before the president of the *New Daily* had passed away, the incumbent minister of education had been struck by lightning on a golf course and died. The natural reaction was that he'd been a damn fool taking such risks just for a game, yet the real problem was that, not only was the day he died a weekday, but it just so happened that only a week earlier an official reminder that members of the government were forbidden from playing golf had been circulated. Now obviously this incident could have been a considerable blow to the respect in which all ministers should rightly be held, and the whole cabinet would have suffered. It was also judged that the news might have a deleterious effect on the student community, both at school and university level, so the chairman of the National Security Committee, who was not of the same political faction as the deceased but, by good chance, had often drunk with him and played mah-jong too, announced that he had suddenly died of myocardial infarction at work in his office. A few days later, however, there was a sneak phone call to the paper from somebody presumably employed at the golf course in question that gave the whole game away, but the story was turned down for lack of sufficient back-up evidence. So when their president died, either the managing director at the time or the editor-in-chief (or both of them) used this information as a concealed threat held over the head of the chairman of the National Security Committee, with the result that their president didn't die of overexertion in bed but dropped dead having dinner in a hotel.

'But the news got round quickly enough, all the same. Everyone on the paper knew, so I can remember wondering just how they managed to hush the whole thing up officially. I never thought they could have got at someone as important as Sakakibara.'

'That's the kind to go for. Shut off the whole system at the mains. It only means turning one handle. Makes it all dead easy.'

134

'But then we owed him something back, and when Sakaki-bara approached the paper with this request...'

'There's no proof.'

'But let's suppose it did happen. Except it's difficult to work out why. I didn't write anything nasty about the government.'

'Someone's angry.'

'Who?'

'That's what I can't work out. Still, someone somewhere got in touch, and the politicos went along with it.'

'Some financial group?'

'Already ruled out.'

'A religious one?'

'Doesn't look like it.'

'Who, then?'

Urano replied in a voice that had little confidence in it:

'Well, it just might conceivably be the Americans.'

Yumiko didn't reply for a moment—for about as long as it would take to turn a globe round to find the country in question.

'The Americans? You mean the White House?'

'Well, somewhere thereabouts. They can get very upset about abortion in the States. It's a pretty sensitive issue. I tried the embassy and a few other places, but didn't get very far. It's not easy working on your own; I can't use the methods I'm good at.'

Urano gave an account of his investigation techniques, which were loosely based on police methods. This was the second time Yumiko had heard it, but she smiled dutifully for a while before reverting to normal and saying, as if she were wondering aloud:

'Still, if the chief secretary can put that kind of pressure on the paper, then there must be some weak point inside it.'

'Yes—if it *is* the chief secretary, because we don't know for certain. We can't even be absolutely sure it's his party that's involved.'

But Yumiko wasn't to be distracted.

'What's the weak point?'

'I don't really know. We don't print anything for any religious groups that take the souls of aborted babies seriously, so at least that's not it.'

'How about debts?'

'It's a possibility, but I haven't heard of any big ones lately. And I don't think the politicians have been squeezing us in that area.'

'What else could it be?'

'Well, the new company building is going to be put up on government-owned land. I mean, we're going to get it from them. But that's all tied up already. The head of the political section did all the preliminaries, the high-ups approved, and now the accountants are handling it. It's to go before the National Property Commission quite soon, and will be passed unanimously. Nobody's going to rock the boat at this late stage.'

'You're quite sure?'

'I'm sure.'

Urano explained how this state-owned property would be transferred to the private ownership of their company. What was being transferred was a piece of land in south Shinagawa, a bit removed from the centre but not all that far away, and in such cases one acquired the land for other land of equivalent value, which the *New Daily* had to find. The present company site, being bang in the centre, was worth more than that being acquired, so it would be foolish to offer it, and it was in fact being retained. What they'd done was put together a package that included a disused bowling centre in the suburbs, the company sports ground (arable land before the war) in Chiba Prefecture, a warehouse in Saitama Prefecture, and some land in the Osaka area that had been bought some time before. This last item was just behind a station and was bound to go up in value so it was a pity to have to get rid of it, but that couldn't be helped. Finally there was some woodland way out in Gumma Prefecture. Even all this, apparently, still wasn't enough, but they'd 'made up' the balance. The appraisal team was composed of three members, one recommended by the state, one of a neutral status and one chosen by the *New Daily*. The first two had made a fair, realistic valuation of the land involved, but the *New Daily* man had put much too low a price on the state-owned property and heavily overvalued the land offered by the company. Since the rule was to average out the figures set by all three, things would work out in the company's favour.

'But that's crooked, surely?' Yumiko said in a shocked voice.

Urano didn't seem bothered by it.

'All the other papers have done the same thing at some time.'

'I suppose so.'

'We're too honest, if anything.'

The former star crime reporter then told her a few stories he'd sniffed out about the goings-on at other papers. The pick of the bunch was how one paper had acquired a first-class piece of land for their new offices by throwing a scare into the prime minister of the day with a series of veiled threats about scandalous disclosures, and followed this up by revealing all the facts of the case in a biography of their president.

'You've got to admire them for it. Our people wouldn't have the nerve to do that. We're too gentlemanly.'

'Are we, now?'

'Perhaps not all of us,' he said, and laughed, inviting Yumiko to go on with him to a bar, a nice place he'd discovered recently where you weren't pestered by hostesses; but she turned the offer down as this was the night she spent with Toyosaki. Urano took it like a man.

'I guess what I've turned up ain't worth a date,' he said, but this was only a veiled way of saying the opposite, that he'd done his research so well he felt his invitation was very difficult to refuse, and he wished to make this quite clear, both to himself and to her. He knew there was still a danger of her being a gangster's moll, yet even if she were one, he now confidently believed that a member of the underworld who fell in love with an intellectual type like her must himself be a man of some discrimination, and too civilised to want to rough up or bump off a rival in love (as Urano considered himself).

The answer that Yumiko was looking for didn't, however, come from Urano but from a quite unexpected quarter. On a weekend afternoon she went to Seijo with her daughter to sit for the picture that was to be part of Sakon Ogino's spring exhibition.

They sat in a corner of his studio, which was impressively cluttered with paints, palettes and other tools of his trade. Her daughter was wearing a dress of light green with pink flowers scattered over it, while she herself wore a yellowish blue kimono with a figured brocade sash whose hazy white was nicely brought out by the light yellow-green of the binding cord. Both of these rather genteel outfits suggested they'd been invited to a tea ceremony, and indeed Yumiko had dressed them to give that impression.

On the second day of the sitting, which consisted of twenty minutes being sketched, then a thirty-minute break, then another twenty minutes and so on, Ogino during one of the breaks was telling various amusing anecdotes connected with his role on the selection committees of certain exhibitions, which led to his complaining that he had too many of such time-wasting chores these days, and he made the following remark:

'It's the same in any occupation, I suppose. I was talking to old Tamaru the other day and he was grumbling about the fact he hardly had any time to think about policy any more, he had so much of that kind of nonsense on his plate, like who was going to get what job in some company, whether government land should be transferred to private ownership or not, that sort of thing.'

'By old Tamaru you mean the prime minister?'

'That's right. We both come from the same part of the world. Sometimes get together, you know. He likes paintings.'

'Be nice if he could arrange for you to get your culture medal ahead of time.'

Yumiko felt a chill twinge about her heart as she watched him laughing loudly at her joke. So it was true: the transfer of that land to the *New Daily* had somehow been screwed up by that editorial of hers. This was her direct and sudden intuition and, as she thought about it during the next twenty-minute sitting, and then the next, she could see no way of getting round it. When they got home in the evening, she left her daughter to start the cooking and immediately phoned a colleague on the editorial staff (originally from the political section) who said he'd check it for her. Then, while she and her mother were shelling some ginkgo nuts, the phone rang, which seemed surprisingly quick, but it turned out to be from Asaoka, the Ginza boss. Yumiko responded with her usual greeting, but immediately got the impression this was no casual call and decided to take it in her own room.

'Miss Yumiko,' he said, 'are you aware of what's going on?' The way in which the president (as he now was) of the Friends of Justice Society addressed her varied according to his mood and ranged from Miss Minami to plain Yumiko; but as if to give the impression he came from good, even aristocratic stock, his manner was always remarkably polite.

'What is it that I'm supposed to be aware of?' she asked.

'That somebody wants you dismissed.'

'There've been efforts made since the beginning of this summer to have me transferred to the promotions department. Is that what you mean?'

'That's it. But are you aware of what's behind it?'

The account of the affair Asaoka gave was that the government party during the last election, which it only won by a small majority, had received secret financing from a religious group making money from memorial services for aborted foetuses. These funds were not expected to be repaid, at least not in cash. The fixer in this business had been the party's chief secretary, and it was he who had arranged that the former prime minister should attend the unveiling of the memorial stone in Kagoshima, as a token of their thanks. When the editorial appeared in the *New Daily* criticising this event, the head of the religious body had been incensed and complained to the chief secretary. The latter, conscious of the debt his party owed them, quite reasonably decided that the way to calm them down was to get the author of the offending article shifted to a different post, but since the offender refused to move, pressure was now being applied to the paper in the form of a threat to cancel the agreement already made about the transfer of government land for the company's use.

'Is that what happened?' muttered Yumiko, feeling astounded that the truth was so close to what she'd only recently supposed.

'More or less. What about your side of it?'

She explained the way she had read the situation and he listened quietly, complimenting her on her judgement. Then he said something very remarkable:

'If it's acceptable to you I should like to offer my assistance.'

'What?'

'In a totally non-professional way, of course. Just helping out an old friend, as they say.'

'But, really…'

'And no friendly recompense would be expected.'

'But for heaven's sake…'

A summary of the very elaborate and roundabout way in which he explained how he proposed to help her (probably wary of being bugged) would be as follows. One of the chief secretary's subordinates, a Diet member, had received a large sum of money from an organisation in the Kansai area in anticipation of his assistance in a certain affair, but as he hadn't done anything, they were now asking for their money back. Asaoka intended to meet the chief secretary for a little discussion of this matter, and then of another. Yumiko was fortunately able to refuse his offer after an appropriately polite pause because her breath had literally been taken away by it for a minute or so.

'I really am very grateful, and flattered by what you've said about me, but there's no need to put yourself to all that trouble. This isn't something just concerning me, you see—it concerns the paper as a whole. I'm not quite sure how to say this, but I think they would appreciate it if perhaps you didn't get involved.'

'All right, then, but if you just stand by and do nothing they'll get their own way in the end. Doesn't that bother you? Because it certainly bothers me.'

At that point a call came through from someone else.

'Look, there's someone on the other line—I've been expecting it. Could you hold on for just a moment?'

But Asaoka declined to do so, giving the impression that beneath his usual courtesy he was feeling rather ruffled.

'No, I'll ring off. If you should happen to change your mind just call me. Any time will do,' he said, and quickly put down the receiver.

The phone call was from her colleague at the paper. He said that what had been causing a stir in government circles over the past ten days was the question of who was to be made president of an airline company in which the government owned a large number of shares. A short article would appear about it in tomorrow's morning edition. So it was exactly as the prime minister had let slip to the painter: the two things bothering him at the moment were who was to get some job in a particular company and whether government land should be transferred to the *New Daily*.

During dinner, and after it as well, Yumiko kept thinking about what Asaoka had said about being 'bothered' if nothing was done to stop them. He sounded as if he really meant it, and she decided there were three things implied in it, which she listed in her usual way:

1) Even if one's going to lose, one still fights.

2) If one's bound to lose then the fighting itself is mere ritual.

3) Even if it is mere ritual, the fact of fighting itself means that something can always happen that might sway the balance in one's favour, turning defeat into victory.

She knew he was right: one did have to fight. But as she sat lost in such thoughts alone in her room, she couldn't help remembering—and it made her sigh at the time—that he belonged to a profession which depended mainly on fighting, in the plainest sense of the word.

That evening she phoned a number of other people from her room. Of her 'pre-forties', the government politician was nowhere to be found, the opposition member was in Africa, and the man in MITI rumoured to be the next under-secretary listened to it all very politely without saying a single thing of any use. She then remembered her daughter's boyfriend who worked in the Finance Ministry, so she had her ring him, but all he had to say apparently (not having got back home till after twelve) was that he was working in a different department and knew nothing about it, the end result being that Chie just had a long chat with him.

The next day, a Monday, Urano wasn't at work owing to a cold, and she was surprised to find how much she missed him and relied on him, for no matter how much she thought about the problem, during the meeting and afterwards, no brilliant solution offered itself. After lunch she went for a walk round the block, and when she got back she decided the only thing she could do was take her problem to the president of the company himself; but when she tried to get in touch, his secretary bluntly informed her that he was confined to his bed (he was seventy-five years old). This curt reply must have upset her because, immediately afterwards, on an impulse, she phoned the chairman's secretary and was told he was away on a trip abroad. Fortunately, this brought her to her senses, making her feel quite angry with herself. She knew these people would do nothing for her; she'd told herself so umpteen times and by now it was absolutely clear to her that it was so; and yet she had still made a fool of herself like that. What did she think she was up to?

That night she tried the government politician again, this time at his home number. A young man answered the phone.

'Father's not here, and I don't have a contact number,' he said and rang off. She'd never seen this young man, in fact she didn't even know his name, and she sat for a while wondering why he should sound so bad-tempered. Had she interrupted his studies for some important exam? Had his girlfriend turned him down? While she was imagining a number of possibilities the phone rang, with her pet conductor on the other end calling long distance from Paris.

'Hello, Yumi.' (He was the only one who called her that.) 'How are you?'

'I'm feeling rather down, maestro, as a matter of fact.'

She gave an outline of the situation.

'Well, even if I were in Japan, and I'm obviously not, I couldn't

142

be of much help,' he said helpfully, and then: 'Yumi, why don't you give up that paper?'

'Give it up? What would I do instead?'

'You could always find something.'

'What exactly?'

'You'd be all right. Things would work out.'

'Would they?'

'Yes. And don't forget, wherever you go and whatever you do, my friendship for you remains unchanging and eternal,' he said, as if he were translating word for word from some foreign language. In his case, particularly when he was phoning from abroad, it didn't sound all that embarrassing, and she accepted it unembarrassed as a verbal gift that gave her considerable comfort, both when she heard it and after she put the phone down.

The next day Urano turned up at work, standing by her desk and tapping her cuddly toy dog on the nose and saying good morning either to it or its owner.

'I think I've worked it out,' said Yumiko.

'Worked it out?' he echoed, sitting down in his chair as she gave a fast, detailed account of things in a low voice, concealing the names of neither the artist nor the gangster.

'Cancelling the land transfer? I don't see how they can. The chairman's due to pay a formal visit to the finance minister any day now.'

But they all had to troop over to the meeting table so the conversation came to an end there. Urano sat through it all, head bowed, thinking about things, ashamed that the investigation he'd made hadn't been thorough enough, and aggrieved that the mobster Asaoka had made one more unwelcome appearance on the scene. When the meeting reached the point at which it had to be decided who was going to write that day's editorials, the chief mentioned his name as a possibility, forgetting the fact that he'd already been asked not to, but Urano simply raised his head abruptly and, with a violent gesture of the hand, indicated that he should be counted out of the discussion. So bad-tempered was his manner there was an awkward silence all round, until a former film critic remarked in what was meant to be a conciliatory, amused tone of voice:

'Well, that's one way of refusing. As it seems to work, I must try to remember it.'

This got a laugh from everyone, and even the chief managed a grudging smile.

Soon after the meeting had ended Urano said in a lowered voice to his neighbor:

'You've got some impressive friends. The boss of the Friends of Justice Society for a start.'

'Well, yes,' said Yumiko in a normal voice, explaining about the 'pre-forties'. 'And that's why it became eleven.'

'And you've kept up the acquaintance ever since?'

'Yes. When I forget about one of them, something to remind me always seems to turn up. Like it did a little while ago…'

She gave an account of the incident in the hotel lounge. That evening, she said, a friend of hers from high-school days who was now running a hospital in Nagoya had come to Tokyo and invited her out to dinner at a French restaurant, and she'd gone back to her hotel and stayed chatting with her until quite late. (This was actually a lie; what had really happened was that she'd met Toyosaki at this hotel, which the university had booked for him because the cheap place he usually stayed in was full.) As she came out of the lift into the lobby and was heading for the door, a rather exotic middle-aged woman had called out to her. It was a film actress, who had split up with a well-known baseball player. Just after her recent divorce, Yumiko had been asked by the weekly magazine her paper put out to interview her, and the resulting article had presented the divorced couple in such an attractive and sympathetic light and been so well received that the actress had had no trouble making a comeback, for which she was obviously very grateful. The man with her (or just behind her) was Heigoro Asaoka, so the three of them agreed to have a drink together, in the course of which Yumiko noticed that they seemed

144

to be surrounded by numerous large, broad-shouldered men. Apparently this strangely conspicuous group had been turned away from the bar on the top floor (for no other reason than that it was full up), and so had settled in the lounge. Having a drink with a yakuza and his henchmen hovering in attendance felt embarrassingly like being on stage, she said, taking part in a melodrama of some kind.

When the story reached this point Urano broke in with odious relief, calling her 'Yumiko' for the first time in quite a while, and this alerted her, in one sudden insight, to the likely reason for it.

'Ah, you've been thinking there was something going on between me and him, haven't you? Somebody was in that hotel lounge and saw me, isn't that right?' She stared straight at Urano, and all he could do was raise his right hand like a little boy and admit it was. 'Well, you amaze me, you really do. Who was it? Come on, who was it? And that's why you became so stand-offish all of a sudden.'

'Right.'

'You're obviously quite a coward at heart, despite appearances.'

'I wouldn't say that. I mean, I'm not afraid of that thug of yours... All right, I am a little, as anybody would be. But what worries me more is the person who can associate with him.'

'Associate' is hardly the word. I'm not likely to be having an affair with him, am I? I only like intellectuals, anyway.' Yumiko let this slip out quite unintentionally, but Urano took it up.

'Intellectuals, eh? How do I stand, then? An intellectual, or not an intellectual; that is the question.'

Since Yumiko only smiled and didn't answer, he looked around for somebody else to ask but there was no one nearby. Just at that moment, though, the author of 'News from Another Planet' came back from the coffee shop, and Urano called out to him in a loud voice:

'Now, answer me this: am I an intellectual or not?'

'I'd've thought the answer was obvious,' the baldpate replied unsmilingly, and went off to his own place at the far side of the room.

'Obvious? Obvious is it? That kind of reply doesn't help at all,' he muttered, shaking his head. 'What's obvious is he's in a bad mood. Can't think of anything for tomorrow's column.'

Yumiko went on smiling for a while, thinking that even if he had got the wrong end of the stick (with help from whom?) and built an absurd fantasy of his own out of it, at least he hadn't let the attitude of the company towards her affect him; and she was impressed by the fact that his infatuation with her had survived despite everything. Yet this thought only made her feel even more depressed about herself.

'What am I going to do, though?' she burst out. 'The only course that seems to make any sense is to resign from the paper...'

'Don't make your mind up too quickly,' said Urano, clearly taken aback. 'Look, I'll find out what's at the back of this by tomorrow. Then we can think of what's to be done about it. No need to be in any kind of hurry.'

'I suppose not.'

'Don't tell Hasegawa anything about resigning. Don't even hint at it.'

That evening she went to see a performance at the Kabuki Theatre with her mother, and when they got back home she again shut herself up in her room, brooding about things and ringing up various people, such as a woman who wrote editorials for another paper and one who was a department chief in the Ministry of Labor. Still, none of this led to any progress, and she felt the whole business would remain at a standstill unless some clear information was forthcoming which would indicate what she should do. So she decided to ring up the head of the political section of the paper, assuming he'd be able to tell her exactly what the situation was with regard to the transfer of government land, and finally managed to track him down in a Ginza bar; but he said this wasn't quite the place for a discussion of that kind (he was perfectly right) and he'd phone her when he got home. But she waited until two, then three, and he still didn't phone, so round about dawn she treated herself to a glass of sherry, as she still couldn't sleep and was worried that she'd be unable to do any work in the morning.

The next day, Urano didn't turn up until the daily meeting was in progress, furtively taking a corner seat; but as soon as it ended he hopped over to where she was sitting by the blackboard, to say there wasn't much time and they'd have to discuss the matter there; which they did as soon as the others had moved away, Urano talking at great speed.

The information she'd received from Heigoro Asaoka was by and large correct, although the situation was a bit more complex than that. For a start, the nominal leader of the sect was just a puppet figure, and it was his uncle who was in charge. In fact the original idea to create a religious sect dedicated to the souls of aborted foetuses had been his, and he had fully expected to be its leader, but his wife had persuaded him that he was unsuited for the role, his face lacking the dignity required in someone wielding authority, so he'd used his nephew in his place. Now this man with the undignified face had been obsessed with politics from an early age, and had made a point of cultivating the larger factions in the government party. The trouble was that there were powerful members of the sect—not blood relations of the leader—who didn't share his interest, and who were using the editorial in the *New Daily* to attack him not only for having invited the former prime minister but, behind that pretext, for contributing to party funds. Consequently the uncle had complained about this to the chief secretary of the party in writing, saying he wanted the money back, and Sakakibara was trying to put him off by showing he could do something, that 'something' being at least to get the author of the offending editorial transferred to another job.

'Well, I like that! So I'm just a pawn in their little game?'

'Looks like it.'

'It may be just one move to them, but it's affecting my whole life.'

'Exactly. But think how Sakakibara feels about it: he'd got everything nicely worked out, with the hushing up of the deathbed scandal on the one hand and the transfer of government land on the other, then this woman comes along and screws it all up because she doesn't like telling fibs.'

'And I was right not to.'

'And she won't let them make her change her mind so he ups and says right, I'll put a stop to them getting their land.'

'That's despicable.'

'Well, I'm inclined to share your opinion, but nobody likes being made to look a fool.'

Urano began speaking at high speed again, indicating that he was going to make no more irrelevant comments but stick to the essential facts, the main one being that the projected meeting of the National Property Commission had been suddenly postponed. Since there was no precedent for this occurrence, the relevant officials were in a great dither about it.

'He's just doing it out of spite.'

'That's as it may be, but he does seem to be quite serious.'

'So if I just go on refusing what happens?'

'There'll be more pressure applied; much more. On the company, that is. It's a face-saving operation.'

'Aimed at the aborted babies trade?'

'That's right. He's almost certainly promised them he'd have the writer of the editorial removed.'

They were both silent for a while, then finally Yumiko said, more or less to herself:

'What am I going to do?'

'You'll have to do something.'

'Something?'

'My suggestion is, go for the prime minister, not for the chief secretary. It's the chief secretary's idea, after all. He's been handling it so far, and it's going to be hard to make him change his mind. He'll just stick to the same line. The only chance of getting him to change is to have him told to do so from a different quarter.'

'But what am I supposed to say to the prime minister?'

'Ask him what he feels about the women's vote. Tell him if

you get fired there'll be such a rumpus among women through-out the country his popularity with them will plummet.'

'Well, I…'

'Everyone's keeping pretty quiet about abortion at the moment. Does he want the whole country exploding in debate about it? If that happened, which way would the women's vote go? What would happen to Japanese-American relations? It could be the start of real trouble.'

'Surely that's going a bit far?'

'You never know with things like that.'

'Perhaps not.'

'All that Japanese politics is really concerned with is not stirring up trouble.'

'I agree.'

'So there's your way in.'

'Still…'

'There isn't any other way.'

'I suppose not.'

'I've checked up on the prime minister, and that's about the only sort of material you could use to approach him; a direct, frontal attack.' Urano opened a notebook. 'I'll give you a general picture. He's sixty-nine. Eldest son of a brewer. The second son took over the business, the third is a lawyer in Kyoto. The relationship between the three brothers is fairly amicable. Elected member for the Toyama second district. Topped the poll at the last two elections. He's a strong campaigner, no doubt about it. An American writer spent a year with Tamaru following his campaign and wrote it up in a book called *Japanese Diet Member*, so it's all gospel.'

'I've read it. Interesting enough, but a bit too easy on him.'

'Well, he was a guest of Tamaru's for a whole year, so there you are. His wife is sixty-three, daughter of an old party politician; in fact he took over his father-in-law's constituency. They have a son and daughter. The son is a scientist, professor at an American university. The daughter's husband used to work for a trading company, but is now secretary to the prime minister. He'll no doubt become a Diet member himself sometime. When Tamaru travels abroad his daughter goes with him. Ten years ago his wife got a herpes spinal infection that's made her as helpless as a child.'

'I heard about that.'

'The only thing that interests her is food. She's with a divorced sister of the prime minister's in his private house in Seijo, and before he moved into the official residence he was living there with them. She was a real problem then; her husband would be entertaining visitors and leave the room for a while to fetch something, and in she'd come and, without a word to anyone, start helping herself to somebody's cake or whatever.'

'Oh, God.'

'And just when she'd finished stuffing it in, back would come the husband with some documents, and drive her away, saying "Mother, would you mind going somewhere else?" '

Yumiko drew a deep breath, shaking her head as if she found the whole thing almost too painful to imagine.

'You can't use that.'

'Of course not.'

'Good-looking in a way. Up to professional standard in traditional dance. Very intelligent; at least they say she was. Well known for the way she'd tip all and sundry in any situation.'

'Lots of politicians' wives are like that.'

'Not in my experience. Most of them are damn tight-fisted.'

At that point one of the office girls summoned Yumiko to the phone. It was Hasegawa saying he had something to discuss with her and would like to take her out to dinner. Since she was due to meet Toyosaki that evening she asked him to make it sometime the next day, but he was all tied up then so finally she agreed but only on condition that it was over by eight-thirty. Perhaps one reason why she didn't decline with more persistence was that, due to her other assignation, she was dressed adequately to go out to a restaurant. She had on a charcoal grey pleated skirt, a light blue knitted T-shirt and a wine-coloured jacket, set off with long silver earrings in the shape of a lily. When she returned from her phone call Urano was writing something in his notebook, but he looked up and went on from where he'd left off.

'He has a woman; ex-dancer, round about thirty-eight or -nine, maybe forty. Used to be the mistress of a Kansai businessman. He meets her at weekends in a hotel in Hakone. All the political reporters know about it, but no one writes anything. That can't be used either.'

'No.'

'His niece—his youngest brother's youngest daughter—has gone wrong. Kicked over the traces, if you like. She's at a women's college and she runs after Sumo wrestlers.'

' "What does running after Sumo wrestlers mean? Confine your answer to one paragraph." Sounds like an exam question.'

'It means being a girl Sumo fan. These girls follow them round wherever they happen to be, at tournaments, on tour, at training sessions, and get on friendly terms with them.'

' "Friendly terms" meaning?'

'They sleep with them.'

'So their aim in life is to get married to one and finally become the lady in charge of her own stable?'

'No, nothing like that. All they want is what's there in front of their eyes, a young man, good strong body overflowing with energy. So they don't particularly mind if they're not all that famous. I suppose anyone would do really.'

'Well.'

'There's nothing much going on during the tournaments since there are too many journalists around, but from the last night onwards it's frantic, apparently. There's not one empty room in any of the hotels around the main Sumo hall. A novelist I know rented a room in a building next door to one of them and said he couldn't write a thing; the building was shaking so much he couldn't read what he'd written.'

Yumiko laughed, and Urano gave a quick laugh too.

'Then it's "Thanks very much" ' (said in the peculiar wrestlers' grunting voice) 'and goodbye. Nobody's going to make a respectable woman out of any of them. They're just like the fans of rock

151

musicians. There must be an awful lot of people having trouble with daughters like that, but still…'

'It can't be used, of course. It would be blackmail.'

'There's nothing wrong with a little blackmail, in moderation; although that particular one wouldn't work. But the scandal the boss of the Friends of Justice mentioned seems to be genuine. The mob is onto something down there in Kobe. I don't think we can count on much coming to light for some time, though.'

'This may be a long shot, but is it true that Banzan Onuma has some influence over the prime minister?'

Urano's reply was given with his usual bluntness.

'Influence? Not a bit of it. He was the previous prime minister's old teacher, and Tamaru probably learned a bit of brush writing from him, but he's so busy now I imagine he's given that sort of sideline up. Why do you ask, anyway?'

Yumiko explained that Banzan's granddaughter was a classmate of her daughter's, and he'd admired a photo of her, saying if she'd like to visit him he'd write something for her. Urano smiled at this, but shook his head.

'I think you'd be much better off going straight to the prime minister, although it might be something to bear in mind, just in case. Banzan's ancient, so at least you needn't worry about him doing anything funny with her.'

'Don't you ever think about anything else?' she said.

Urano looked at his watch and said hurriedly that he had to go. Yumiko thanked him politely for all he'd done, and as he was leaving he told her to give it a try anyway, a remark that was meant to be encouraging but sounded as if he felt there was only a slim chance of its succeeding.

That evening's dinner in Akasaka was a pretty weird affair. Those attending it weren't just the usual pair from previous meetings, but also the chief sales clerk and the head of the promotions department. No explanation was given for this. Yumiko assumed Hasegawa must have exhausted his own resources and was hoping to make some kind of breakthrough by enlisting the aid of greater numbers and the enlivening atmosphere of a restaurant; and at the appropriate moment he said:

'Well, I think we've just about reached the stage where some kind of decision is needed. I'm sure we can count on your support.'

He spoke pleasantly enough but didn't smile as he did so, merely making a formal bow. Yumiko and the others received this in respectful silence, but the chief printer, either because it made him feel uncomfortable or because he was just in the habit of shooting off his mouth, said in a frivolous tone of voice:

'It's a matter of life and death for the paper.'

'What's that supposed to mean?' asked Yumiko, and Hasegawa hastily explained that the paper was relying on her to reorganize the whole promotions operation, which made the head of that department look slightly downcast. Yumiko naturally said that the task was quite beyond her, etc., before remarking:

'This isn't about the new company building, by any chance?'

'No, nothing to do with that.'

'Not connected with the transfer of government land to us?'

'No. Not connected at all…,' Hasegawa replied with a sour look on his face. 'This is purely a matter of your being needed in promotions. I am in no position to offer opinions about questions other than that. All the paper wants is your consent.'

He bowed his head again in courteous appeal.

Naturally enough, the dinner party wasn't going with much of a swing. The head of the promotions department drank almost nothing, and although the chief printer remained his chatterbox self the only subjects he ventured to discuss were the well-worn topics of travel and food. As Yumiko started on a dish of coarse tofu and mushrooms steamed in saké, piled high in a small square bowl of elegant design, she tried to prod the other three into some sort of reaction by saying what a pity it was they had to discuss a matter of this kind in such tasteful surroundings with such excellent food, since it really spoiled the taste; or by asking if there was a nationwide consensus in this country over the population problem. To all such leads Hasegawa alone would reply, always evasively and slipping in reminders that there wasn't much time left, and of how he hoped to be of service and would be forever grateful and so on.

Since the company didn't seem to be willing to compromise, Yumiko wasn't either, maintaining the same stance as before until the party came to an end at the appointed hour of eight-thirty. As they walked down the passage towards the entrance she could feel how tired of this business the four men were, and was aware of just how much enmity she must have aroused in a mere two hours.

Later that night, as she and Toyosaki were drinking beer together, she reported on the situation, and the philosopher said:

'They don't know what to do. They've played all their cards. So now they invite you out to dinner. It will be French cuisine next week, Chinese the week after, and then Italian. All I had this evening was a cheap curry.'

'I've already realised that.'

'You would, I suppose,' he said, and nodded. 'But I wonder if you're wise to approach the prime minister and not the chief secretary.'

'That's what he suggested.'

'How far can you trust his judgement? The chief secretary, what's his name—ah yes, Sakakibara—he sounds a better bet, surely?' Toyosaki gave his reasons for this assurance, which to Yumiko seemed a bit simple-minded. 'When all's said and done, it's he who started the whole business. He may be supposed to be second-in-command, but he's the one running the show. Sakakibara makes things move; the prime minister just moves. "The Mover and the Moved": might be a good title for a thesis. Anyway, didn't you say the PM had been complaining about being sick of wasting his time on things like who gets what job and what company gets what land? So anything you have to say on the subject is not going to be very welcome, is it? Also, the chief secretary's bound to have more time at his disposal. The prime minister's too busy; he won't be able to fit you in.'

'Won't he?'

'He won't. What matters is having time. The chief secretary's got bags of it. Look, there was this woman working in his office, unmarried, and she was having affairs with two married journalists at the same time. Two of them, at the same time. Two love affairs, two *ménages à trois*; although she was forced to resign in the end, when the story was leaked to the press.'

'I heard about that.'

'Well, then, doesn't that just demonstrate how much time the chief secretary must have to spare?'

'It may demonstrate how much time *she* had to spare. It doesn't say the least thing about how much he might have.'

The philosopher laughed.

'How do you know about that, anyway?' she went on.

'I read it in a weekly magazine. Philosophers absorb a variety of knowledge. It's important for them. Aristotle and Hegel would have read the weeklies just as the modern Japanese philosopher does. They'd have been reading them all the time.'

'Don't be silly.'

'It's true. Look at Socrates. The man was like a weekly magazine himself.'

'A walking weekly.'

'Yes. And finally publication was banned.'

Yumiko decided Toyosaki was making suggestions as intelligently as he could but was so far removed from reality that in the end he had nothing to offer but these stupid jokes. This was borne out by what he said next:

'The whole issue seems to have turned into a demonstration of the gift theory. The government makes a gift of some land to your paper, and your paper makes a gift of your head in return. Although the initial form it took can be seen as one of presentation and disposal, its true gestalt is that of the contract. The fact that the contract by which freedom of speech is guaranteed should take the form of a gift is a fine irony, but characteristic of a society that can still be called primitive in its essentials, ours being a country that from earliest times has been organised on the basis of the reciprocal gift as its principal mode of expression.'

Yumiko claimed she understood about half of his academic analysis of the situation.

'Only half?'

'Maybe two thirds.'

'That should be enough. Still, theory apart, how are you going to negotiate with the prime minister? What route will you use to approach him?'

'I'm trying to think about that, but I don't seem to be getting any brilliant ideas. I had thought perhaps…'

She proceeded to give him an account of the Banzan business, but the more he heard the gloomier he got.

'Listen,' he said, finally looking her straight in the face.

'What?'

'Are you seriously thinking of sending her?'

'I don't feel all that happy about it, I must admit. I don't like having to ask something like that of a child of mine.'

'Thank goodness for that. The thought of your being in such a bad way you have to use your daughter as erotic bait was beginning to make me really unhappy.'

' "Erotic bait" is a bit of an exaggeration, isn't it?' she said, looking sulky.

'All right, then: the appropriation of goodwill by the stirring of sexual desire.'

'It's the same thing. I told you I'm not happy about it.' The tone in which this was said indicated how annoyed she was with him, but she quickly added: 'Perhaps I'll stay the night, if it's all right with you.'

He was pleased to see how quickly she recovered her spirits.

'Fine. I shall be reading a good book, however.'

'Absorbing a variety of knowledge?'

The next morning, on her way to work, Yumiko went to a Ginza department store to buy a light grey woollen skirt and some small gold earrings with a green stone set in them, as well as some foundation powder and lipstick. There was nothing wrong with her old foundation, but she'd been using it for some time and she bought the new one to give herself a lift. She changed her clothes in the tiny changing room, putting her pleated skirt in the store's paper bag, to take with her.

That day she was asked to write an editorial, which she hadn't done for some time, and spent the afternoon lost in thought on the question of whether wives should take their husbands' names. It was only when she'd completed her article that she had time to reflect that obviously no order had been given not to let her write any more editorials, although she then promptly revised that thought since everything that went on in a newspaper was such a mess that the command could well have been given and the result would still have been the same.

Meanwhile, on the super-express back to Sendai, Yokichi Toyosaki was reflecting on the relationship between Hegel and Napoleon, which he'd lectured about that morning, and also on the question of which of Husserl's disciples was the most significant, which had come up in a seminar that afternoon; but mostly on something quite unrelated to these topics, namely what he could do to help Yumiko. Up to then he had certainly not been indifferent to the question of her being shifted to another job, but he had refrained from making any real suggestions about it, and Yumiko had seemed to look on that as only natural. Yet lately he'd felt that this somehow wasn't good enough, for he sensed very plainly in the way she was confused as to whether to get her daughter involved in this or not, and also in the way she had offered to spend the night with him (a suggestion she'd never made before), the extent of her distress. So that evening, when he arrived at Sendai station, it was not a philosopher who got off the train but a man whose main purpose in life was now to find some practical means of helping the woman he loved.

Just before noon on Saturday he went shopping, then prepared a lunch of fried eggs, boiled spinach and miso soup with tofu, and took it on a tray to his wife Setsuko's room. When he spoke to her she was still in bed and, face still turned to the wall, she only made a brief reply. Toyosaki had his own lunch in the living room, reading the paper while he ate. After washing up the dishes he sorted out the mail, and noticed on the back of a sealed letter addressed to his wife the words 'Sakakibara Supporters' Group'. This astonished him for two reasons: firstly because it reminded him (a fact he'd completely forgotten) that Zenroku Sakakibara was the Diet member for this constituency; and secondly because he guessed immediately that his wife must be a member of his supporters' group. So he went back to her room.

'Here—do you belong to Sakakibara's supporters' group?' he asked.

'Oh, that was because Fumiko asked me to join.'

'Who's Fumiko?'

'We were at school together.'

'Is she interested in politics?'

'She does it for her husband.'

'What?'

'What's the matter?'

'You mean she's Sakakibara's wife?'

'That's right.'

So he explained, not without a certain degree of misgiving, that a friend of his worked on a newspaper as an editorial writer, and this friend had written an article which had offended Sakakibara and so been fired. He wanted to do something to help.

His wife rolled over and looked in his direction.

'That was a nasty thing for Mr Sakakibara to do. And yet he's normally such a nice person—although I admit he doesn't look nice.'

'He has to make people think he's nice otherwise he wouldn't get their votes.'

'Well, I'm very sorry for your friend. The family must be in a dreadful state,' she muttered, then got up. 'I'll telephone Fumiko.'

This was the first time since she'd become ill that she'd suggested phoning anyone. She had grown afraid of other people, and the very sound of the phone ringing made her tremble. This sudden transformation made Toyosaki a bit suspicious.

'Yes, if you would. Tell her I'd like to meet Sakakibara as soon as possible.'

But on his way to his work room he realised that, of course, Setsuko could only imagine a man writing editorials for a paper, and she sympathised with the wife of the man who'd been fired. It would never have crossed her mind that this friend might be a woman, and he had carefully avoided mentioning that point.

Later, while he was getting dinner ready (pork, fried vegetables, tinned soup), there was a phone call from Sakakibara's office saying he would be visiting Sendai on Thursday of next week, and would be able to see him at 9·00 P.M. at a restaurant called Kohagi. Naturally Toyosaki agreed, and at almost the same time made up his mind he wouldn't go to Tokyo that week. He had already come to the conclusion that the only way he could help Yumiko was by using the methods of philosophical argument to bring the chief secretary round to the right way of thinking. And he felt there was a good chance of this taking place, as he was quite convinced his own mental powers and persuasive abilities were of a very high order.

That night, around eleven o'clock, while Yumiko's mother was watching television, she heard the fax machine in the same room start to rumble, and one sheet of paper emerged, which she took to Yumiko in her room. Yumiko, who had been sitting at her desk, head propped on her hand, with a morose expression on her face, let out a little shriek as she read it.

> To: Ms Minami   1 sheet only
> From: Toyosaki
> I am to meet Zenroku Sakakibara in Sendai on Thursday night. Consequently I shall not be visiting Tokyo next week.
>   I hope to have good news for you.

When her mother asked her if it was bad news she merely nodded, deciding it was better to say nothing about it. However the projected meeting turned out, she could only imagine it making the situation more complicated, and thus worse than it was already.

'Yumiko, are you in some sort of trouble?' Etsuko asked.

'Um.'

'Something at work?'

'A bit.'

'Something outside work?'

'Well…,' Yumiko said, choosing not to go on with the sentence, and her mother finally lost her patience.

'What's wrong with you? Why don't you stop treating me like a fool! So far I've said nothing, nothing at all. When you were out all night recently and didn't bother to tell anybody, I didn't complain, did I? All these years you've been coming back late once a week, and I've kept quiet, even if I have thought it set Chie a bad example. I know perfectly well what's going on. Still, you're a grown-up, and you go your own way. There's nothing I can do about it. You're forty-five; or is it forty-six?'

'Five.'

'All right, you're forty-five, and at that age you ought to be able to behave a bit better. For two or three months now you've hardly had a civil word to say to anybody. What's getting you down like this? Even Chie's getting worried. She says it must be the menopause. She said it just the other day. Now what is it? What's wrong with you?'

There was no reply so she went on.

'Particularly the past week you've been almost hysterical all the time. There must be something wrong, and yet you won't say a word to your own mother living in the same house. I think it's horrible of you. What's the point of having a child if this is all it means.'

Her mother had been standing while she produced this outburst, and she now slumped down onto Yumiko's bed.

'I'm sorry. That's not what I meant at all. I just didn't want you to worry. I thought I could manage it best by myself.'

Yumiko rose from her chair and sat on the bed beside her, and then explained, taking down her scrapbook and showing her the offending article. Her mother went off to get her reading glasses and then read it with great care, although she didn't seem to be able to make much sense of it despite nodding thoughtfully in places, but she listened intently enough to the account of what had happened after the editorial was published. Yumiko then told her everything else about the problem and, except for a certain reticence over her relationship with Toyosaki, she concealed nothing. During this account they got up to make some tea and get a tin of rice crackers, munching these as they talked. When Yumiko had finished, her mother thought for a while, then said:

'Yumiko, this is a matter of great importance for all of us. We've all got to discuss it, all four.'

'Four?'

'Yes. Your aunt Masako included. If we four women all put our heads together we can think of something. We'll make it after lunch tomorrow.'

'But won't Aunt Masako be away, seeing it's Saturday?'

Aunt Masako, the former film star, spent most of her weekends with a boyfriend in Izu.

'I'll get in touch right away. Whenever she goes somewhere she always leaves a contact number.'

FIVE

⋮

She must have done something wrong, as she was being scolded. The man seemed to be her husband, and it was before they separated, but the face was only vague in the semi-darkness and she couldn't be sure whose it was. She didn't know what she was being scolded for, either. This not very painful dream continued its fragmentary progress for a while, until Yumiko woke up, realising it was Sunday and that she could go on dozing like this if she wished, or she could go and get the paper; and as she was wondering which to do, she heard the sound of the paper being slid under her door.

'Chie?' she called out, and the door opened.

'Sorry. Did I wake you up?'

'That's all right. Open the curtains, will you?'

The light flooded in, revealing her daughter, not yet made up and wrapped in a scarlet dressing gown which made her look like a goldfish. She put the paper beside Yumiko's pillow and said:

'Miyake just phoned. He said you were quite right, and asked me to tell you the meeting of the National Property Commission has been postponed.'

'I see. Thanks.'

'He said he was sorry he'd taken so long to let you know.'

'Yes, well, never mind... So it was true. We'll have to talk about that at the family meeting today.'

'It seems the fate of the country, and of our family, is at stake.' Her daughter smiled. 'I'm cooking today, so I'm making a special salad. There's a really good cartoon in the paper.' With this, she left the room.

The strip cartoon formed their first topic of conversation when they sat down to eat, although Yumiko didn't find it as funny as her mother and Chie seemed to. This in itself was in its way amusing: that in their three-generation household the taste of the eldest seemed to have skipped a generation, something they noticed not only in the matter of cartoons but in other things as well.

Just as they started eating the phone rang, and Chie answered it, saying she'd ring back.

'That was Shibukawa. How's the shrimp salad?'

The two were quick to praise it, competing in their comments.

'Very nice. I was just about to say so.'

'Especially the dressing—it's quite professional.'

'Yes, it's delicious. Well done!'

'Oh, good,' said Chie, who went on to explain (or rather boast about) how she'd made it. It was the combination of crisp lettuce, endives, white onions, very ripe tomatoes and herbs that gave it its attractive colour, but the important thing was to mix the salad very lightly, and just to warm the shrimps in the frying pan. Her grandmother and mother were not in the mood, however, to take in the details of the recipe, since their minds were on the meeting they were about to hold. Yumiko was wondering how much, if anything, would be gained by talking to these two, while Etsuko was worried about discussing something that might be slightly risqué in front of her granddaughter.

The meal of fried eggs, salad, bread, Indian tea and grapes came to an end, and Yumiko did the washing up. Chie went to her own room to make a phone call, although she came out again halfway through.

'Will our get-together be over by three? He wants to drop in around then to bring back a CD or something.'

'It should be.'

'Is Masako coming?'

'She said she'd arrive sometime after twelve.'

'That's all right, then.'

But things didn't go according to plan. Chie's great-aunt, Masako Yanagi, didn't turn up until well after one, wearing a white suit and a red hat and standing in the hallway for some time as she treated them to a blow-by-blow account of the traffic jams she'd met with on the way. Then, when she'd finished expatiating on the merits of the dried fish she'd brought them, Takero Shibukawa showed up, explaining that the business he'd had to attend to had been settled earlier than expected.

Chie, dressed in a dark blue shirt and denim trousers, introduced the young man to her great-aunt. The assistant professor of Japanese history was clearly impressed by the former film star, with her exotic clothes and make-up, perhaps even rather dazzled by her, but he made a suitable response to her cheerful greeting. Chie intended to tell him that, as they were about to start their family meeting, it was rather a bad time for him to have come, but her great-aunt got in first, urging him in her loud voice to come in, with the result that Shibukawa found himself taking off his shoes and putting on the red slippers that had been set out for Great-Aunt Masako, the pair she always wore when she came there. This turn of events certainly disconcerted Etsuko and Yumiko, but they decided to make the best of it and produced some new grey slippers that were meant for guests, which Masako used instead. So it was five of them who went into the living room for a cup of tea.

There were two brown toy dogs, one crouching and the other in a sitting posture, on the sofa, and although they weren't particularly big they still took up most of the space, so that Shibukawa was obliged to hug them to him in order to sit down. Then, when Masako sat down beside him, he stuffed them both in a corner. Chie sat on the chair next to him, and Etsuko in the armchair next to her. Yumiko made the tea.

There was a marathon race on television, and while they were drinking their tea they watched a bit of it, commenting on the bleak, shabby-looking town the runners, with ten men out in front, were passing through. Masako was obliged to twist her neck slightly to see the screen.

Speaking to Chie in a low voice, Shibukawa said:

'Look, I wonder if you could do me a favour. Do you think you could introduce me to Banzan Onuma sometime? Apparently he has some rather fine scrolls by Soejima.'

'Of course. I've got a standing invitation.'

'Yes, you told me.'

'We can go together. Hold on a minute.'

She promptly rang up Banzan's granddaughter to explain the situation, and quite soon the granddaughter rang back to say they were welcome to come on Thursday or Friday at around four o'clock. Neither could manage Friday, but Shibukawa was free on Thursday afternoon, and although Chie had a Middle English class she decided to skip it.

While this was being arranged, Yumiko, perched on the arm of her mother's chair, asked their young guest about Banzan. He said he'd heard about him but never seen any of his work, and chose instead to talk about Taneomi Soejima.

'Some people say he's the best since the Meiji Restoration, although for some time it was the Chinese poems he wrote rather than his brushwork that were most admired—content rather than form. During the Russo-Japanese War, apparently, Soejima was ill in bed when the news reached him that Port Arthur had fallen, on New Year's Day, but he was determined to get up and write a few lines to celebrate the occasion. Everyone said he wasn't well enough, but when he was on his own again he got out a large sheet of drawing paper and wrote his poem: four lines, seven characters a line. I can remember the last line, I think. Yes—'From ancient times, the first day of the year has been auspicious,' or words to that effect because he was writing in Chinese. The calligraphy itself is superb, among the best things he ever did. Then, on the thirty-first, he died.'

'Really...'

'He must have been particularly pleased with this work, be-

165

cause he told his son to use every seal he had on it—though oddly enough there are only four showing. One would have thought he had more than four.'

'Just being finicky, I suppose,' Masako said. It was her favourite word of condemnation, along with 'mean' and 'stingy'. But Etsuko stood up for Soejima's son.

'If he'd used too many it would have looked silly.'

On the TV screen the leading group of runners was now down to three, one of whom was shown trying to snatch up a bottle of water but bungling it. The conversation moved back to marathon running, then tennis, and while they were all laughing at a joke Shibukawa had made, Chie said to him:

'Look, I'm awfully sorry, but I'm afraid…'

Yumiko stopped her.

'It's all right, Chie. Your friend is welcome to sit in on the meeting if he wants to. In fact it might be a good thing if he did… Oh, I'm sorry, you must be wondering what I'm talking about. The fact is, we're having a little family discussion today, on a subject not entirely unconnected with Banzan.'

'But, Mummy, I really can't…,' said Chie, though before she could say what she really couldn't, Shibukawa interrupted:

'That's okay, don't worry. What's on the agenda?'

'Well, it isn't easy to explain…'

This was a signal for Etsuko to come in, saying in a fidgety kind of way:

'Yumiko, I really don't think this is a good idea. I'm sorry, Mr Shibukawa, but for various reasons this matter has to be kept in the family, to avoid awkwardness all round…'

'But what's so awkward about it?' asked Yumiko. 'After all, he's going with Chie to see Banzan, and he'll have to be told about it then, won't he? My idea was that he might be able to help, seeing he works on political subjects.'

Now Etsuko looked even more uncomfortable.

'I still feel it's a private, family problem. I do hope you understand, Mr Shibukawa.'

'If you're worrying about me, Etsuko, don't,' her sister said casually, in a slow, sing-song voice. 'You're worried about my affair with Shingo being made public. But ever since I got your phone call I've been thinking I should be the one to try to settle this. Really—it's all right. If Yumiko's in trouble, then obviously I've got to do something.'

She looked at the four of them, three of whom were duly mystified by what she'd said.

'So nobody knows anything about it except you, Etsuko. I suppose I'd better explain. I don't like the way old people go on about the past, but I don't really have much choice in this case. You'll just have to be patient, that's all.'

She bowed in Shibukawa's direction, and he gave a polite nod of acknowledgement:

'Yes, well, it was my fault for coming early, before I was expected.'

He was aware that this wasn't particularly relevant to what she'd just said, and that he hadn't grasped what she meant. Fortunately, as a historian, he was unfazed by situations in which total comprehension was lacking.

Yumiko, who seemed to be chairing the meeting, said:

'That's all right, then.'

She looked at Shibukawa, who agreed, as did Masako; even Etsuko nodded. So she turned off the television and Masako began her story.

It all began during the war, in the autumn of 1942, when the young film director she was in love with was drafted into the army. The following summer he died from some illness contracted at the front. It was a terrible period in her life: the man she'd intended to marry, dead, and the only parts available those of nurses, or wives seeing their husbands off to fight, or sisters waving goodbye to their brothers. Everyday life was symbolised by the ban on wearing long-sleeved kimonos and double-breasted suits—and if you went to Ginza in long sleeves the Women's Patriotic League would be lying in wait with their scissors, happy to cut the offending parts off for you.

Just after she'd heard the news of her lover's death, the exemption for university students reading arts subjects was abolished in what was referred to as the student draft. One day two students who were joining the same regiment the following week came to see her; being fans, they asked her to sign a rising sun flag for them. She showed them into her living room and served them the beer ration she'd just received. One of them was the son of a headmaster, a large young man with a good voice who could do a fair imitation of Dick Mine, the jazz singer. The other, of average height and size, was rather good-looking, and told quite funny jokes. He was the eldest son of a brewer. Masako put on some jazz records, although this was frowned on at the time as being enemy music, and danced one dance with each of them. They left after a couple of hours.

In February the following year, on a cold afternoon when it looked as if it was going to snow, she was sitting alone with the lower half of her body in the kotatsu, the only source of heat in the room. Her old nanny had gone out shopping, having been given a tip-off about some food. Masako started to feel hungry and was just thinking of eating something when she heard the sound of a flute outside the house—someone selling baked potatoes, she assumed. So she dashed out, but it was only the man who mended tobacco pipes. The old-style pipe, with its long stem and tiny bowl, had come back into favour because it could be filled with cigarette butts, ensuring no tobacco went to waste.

Chuckling to herself, she went back to the kotatsu, her mind on the war, wondering how long it would go on, how long the film studio would stay in production, thinking how she hated bit parts and not having enough work, but also how awful it would be if she had to join one of these touring vaudeville groups. This soon had the effect of making her feel miserable, and even hungrier. She then saw out of a side window that she seemed to have a visitor, and was astonished to find it was one of the two boys from last November, the good-looking one. Her first thought, despite the fact that he was dressed in a student's uniform, with a student's cap and a rucksack on his back, was: oh God, he's deserted. In fact, conceited as it might sound now, she imagined that it was because of her that he'd made this desperate decision, the idea of dying without ever seeing again the beautiful face of the actress he was madly in love with being more than he could bear.

She blurted out her suspicion that he had deserted, but he said no, he'd joined up but failed the medical and been sent home again; his family had just got in a new supply of rice, and as he thought she might be having trouble finding any he'd brought her some. She told him to wait a minute, quickly applied some make-up, tidied the room, then let him in. To her delight, she found he was carrying four quarts of rice and ten eggs. The young man sat with his legs in the kotatsu, remarking that the Tokyo custom of putting the warmer directly on the tatami matting meant it didn't work properly, which was why it felt so cold. So she put it on a floor cushion instead, and noticed the difference immediately. Then she shook his hand, congratulating him in a hushed voice on failing to be drafted. He said he'd gone to the hospital back at home to have a check-up and been told there was nothing wrong with him, so either the army doctor had got the diagnosis wrong or he had deliberately done him a favour. When she asked what had happened to his friend, he said he hadn't been so lucky and had been called up. By this time Masako was feeling a lot happier, as was Tamaru (which was the student's name), so she boiled some rice and made omelettes for them, and everything tasted delicious.

They started talking about films, mostly foreign ones but sometimes those he'd seen her in, which was perfectly all right with her. Before long she decided to open the little bottle of whisky she'd been saving for a special occasion, but at some point, though they'd been telling jokes and laughing until then, his mood changed, and he confessed he had some awful news he'd kept from her. His friend, the big boy who sang so well, had been killed in action. His troop ship, sailing for Manchuria soon after he was drafted, had been sunk. Along with everyone else who had joined the division, he'd been given a brand-new uniform to make him look the part, and they'd all seemed pleased and had larked about. He would have been twenty-two this month.

Masako, who was six years older, was very upset by this, saying over and over again how sad it was. Eventually, to change the subject, she asked if men also enjoyed getting new clothes. Tamaru immediately understood, and made sure the subject stayed changed, telling her about an odd thing that had happened after the army medic turned him down. He went first to the regimental HQ and reported the news. Then he undid the bundle he'd made up that morning and was changing into his student's uniform when an NCO approached and said it was a crying shame that such a fine-looking soldier boy shouldn't be allowed to serve his country but should be sent away, feeling rejected and downhearted. He then said he would have a personal word with the MO. So Tamaru spent a nerve-racking twenty minutes waiting on the bench outside the office until the NCO came back. When he asked him what the verdict was, the man looked startled, but then assumed a solemn expression and told him that, unfortunately, he couldn't be accepted for active service yet but should go home, get himself in tip-top physical condition, and wait for his call-up papers. When Tamaru thought about this later he came to the conclusion the soldier had just been having him on, especially as he heard that a number of other people had had the same experience. But he was certainly taken in at the time—the man was a genuine actor. This made Masako laugh; in fact she laughed so hard her eyes filled with tears and before long she was really crying. She was remembering her dead lover, but she couldn't talk about him, only weep. The young man had no idea what he should do, and clumsily tried to console her. This turned into a lasting embrace.

From then on, until the war ended eighteen months later, Masako had no clear memory of things. She was more concerned about the air raids than her love affair. In February 1945 her old nanny was persuaded by her son to move into the country to escape the bombing, and was in fact bombed there, but luckily survived. In her absence, the young man moved in with Masako, travelling from her house every day to work in the factory where he was part of the conscripted labour force. There weren't that many of them, since the majority had by now been drafted, and they were dispersed among a number of factories. Then the plant was burned down and he was put to work removing books from a university library for safekeeping, until ordered to go to another factory. Sometimes he would be taken off factory duty to build air-raid shelters or work in the fields.

The actress still did occasional work at the film studio, so she managed to get by without joining a touring company. The parts were as bad as ever, but she gradually got used to that. Once she was delighted to be given the role of a spy working for Chiang Kai-shek but the plot had her involved with a naval officer, and the Imperial Navy raised some objection, so the part was finally cut out of the film altogether.

By now the bombing was really bad, but the area surrounding her small house always seemed to escape unscathed. Rice and other provisions kept arriving regularly from the country, and although she didn't have enough, she never actually starved, the main reason being that Tamaru had established a very efficient bartering system with his friends and acquaintances. In that final year of the war she became more and more angry about the news on the radio, exclaiming every time the announcer said anything that it was a pack of lies, the man must be a complete fool, and making other equally insulting remarks. Her young friend warned her to be careful, knowing that if she went around saying things like that she could get herself into real trouble.

Then, on 11 August, 1945, being off duty that day, he went to a friend's house to deliver a bottle of saké as repayment for some beef they'd been given, and heard from this friend via a relation of his who was a privy councillor that Japan was going to surrender on the fifteenth. The old saying, 'The man who sees three days ahead will make his fortune', seemed almost too appropriate here, for all he had to do was buy up property before the fifteenth and he was bound to make a lot of money. Another friend of his had told him just the other day that the black market operating in front of his local station was charging ten yen for one rice ball, and yet the price of land in that area (a couple of stations from Shinjuku) was ridiculously low, only one or two yen per four square yards. This meant you could get half an acre for the cost of a hundred balls of black-market rice. Tamaru decided he would phone his mother the next day and get her to send him five thousand yen, or preferably double that amount, and even though he knew his guardian (his uncle) would object, he was determined to go through with his plan and clean up on the property market. He kept Masako up half the night telling her about it, but as luck would have it, having borrowed a neighbour's phone and finally got through to his mother, he was told she was glad he'd got in touch because his call-up papers had arrived and he was to report to his regiment on the fifteenth. So all his plans came to nothing because of this pointless summons on the very day the war ended. If he had managed to buy four or five acres in that part of town, he would never have needed to work again.

When peace was declared, Tamaru joined the debating society at his university, and was such a hit there he decided, after discussion with his younger brother, that he would go into politics, leaving his brother to take over the family brewing business. He went on to become secretary to a Diet member. In the meantime, Masako's old nanny came back from the country, so the two lovers had to live apart again, but their relationship continued, even though both had other affairs. Of the two, it was the man who seemed to suffer more from jealousy.

In the general election of 1952, Tamaru, now thirty years old, stood as a candidate in his local constituency but failed to be elected. Immediately afterwards he turned up at the actress's house and, after being teased by her for reverting to his local accent, told her he might be getting married—almost as if he were talking about somebody else. The girl was twenty-four, the daughter of a former Diet member of the old conservative party. He was an elderly man, ill and unlikely to recover, whose considerable support in the constituency would pass to the 'incumbent bridegroom' (as his uncle put it in his old-fashioned and rather unappealing way). Masako, herself now thirty-six, wasn't particularly upset at this news, since she'd never had any intention of marrying this friend of hers, six years younger than herself, and appreciated that without local support a prospective candidate had no hope of being elected. The marriage, she recognised, was unavoidable. It also appeared that Tamaru expected their relationship to continue after his marriage to the old politician's daughter.

But in February of the following year, when she was filming a comedy on location in Izu, she received a phone call from a man claiming to be Tamaru's uncle, who said he would very much like to pay his respects to her sometime in the near future. She arranged for him to visit her house in Tokyo three days later. Tamaru had been behaving recently as if things weren't going as planned, constantly travelling backwards and forwards between his constituency and Tokyo, and visiting her a number of times. He'd even stayed with her over the New Year. Since he never once talked about his marriage, she thought perhaps it had been called off.

The uncle was a mixture of bluff integrity and bland prevarication, just as one would expect of a local building contractor. After the usual courtesies he got straight down to business, saying that his nephew had decided to settle down, as she may already have heard, that if he didn't he'd never get elected, which was his main ambition in life, and that he hoped for her understanding and support in the matter. She had been very good to him so far, but now he was beginning to make a name for himself and a scandal would be a serious setback; so would she agree to a separation? And would she accept this small token of his esteem? Whereupon he produced a fat envelope enclosed in the usual formal wrapping. He then laid before her a sheet of typewritten paper and handed her a fountain pen. She was so taken aback that, although she went through the motions of reading what was written on it, she failed to take in its meaning and could remember nothing of it now. She asked, with a forced laugh, if she should stamp it with her seal, but he said that wouldn't be necessary. After he'd gone she opened the envelope and found it contained five hundred thousand yen.

Feeling deeply humiliated, she sat in a daze looking at the blue flame of the oil stove. All she could think about was that, if this was what he felt he had to do, Tamaru should have come himself and handed over the money in person—and did he really think he had to buy her off? Late that night, she lay a long time in the bath and then, in desperation, drowned her sorrows in drink.

Her face looked very strange when she looked in the mirror the next morning, and she was glad she wasn't doing any filming that day. She had no appetite at all, but tried to make herself eat. She then spent a long time just sitting by the stove, and around noon decided to send Tamaru a telegram. She took some care over the wording, finally coming up with: 'WOULD HAVE PREFERRED LITTLE MORE DELICACY. MASAKO'. At first she thought this was rather good, then changed her mind. After all, it could just possibly be taken as saying she wanted more money, which was how that building contractor who'd come yesterday was likely to interpret it. But no matter how hard she thought, she couldn't find a better way of saying what she felt, and ultimately decided not to send it. Then, as she went on thinking, she was surprised to find she wasn't really upset by the way the separation had been handled, but only by the fact of the separation itself. She didn't want to give up this man.

Everything now went according to the uncle's script: the Diet was dissolved and a general election called. During the campaign Masako was playing the role of a resort geisha in a film, a performance widely praised by the critics for its 'degenerate beauty' (meaning sexiness). Off-stage, however, she had no sex life at all, having convinced herself that, no matter what anybody might say or have said, once the election was over Tamaru would come back to her and the smouldering embers would catch fire again.

Since he was assured of adequate local support this time, he seemed certain to get in, and she thought a good deal about whether or not to send a telegram of congratulations. Although she finally decided against it, when she actually heard the news of his election on the radio she was so excited she wrote the message and sent it off just like that. But days passed, then a week, and still she heard nothing from the new Diet member. Instead she accepted an invitation from a wealthy acquaintance to go to Yokohama, and they spent the night there; and the following night. Since then, for almost forty years, she hadn't met the politician once.

That was the gist of what Masako had to tell them at the family meeting, and although there were obviously places where her account was vague or ambiguous, she made no attempt to hide anything and her listeners found it gripping. Clearly Chie's great-aunt didn't think the girl was a complete innocent, and Chie was pleased to be considered old enough to hear these revelations but was also pretty shaken by them. Yumiko herself had known nothing of this affair and finally, unable to restrain herself any longer, exclaimed:

'And I never knew any of this!'

'I could hardly tell you, could I?' her mother protested. 'It would have…'

'Set her a bad example,' Masako put in. 'Still, Yumiko was born the year after the war ended, and I gave you quite a lot of the rice we got from his family. That's probably why you were able to breast-feed her.'

'So we should both be grateful?'

'If you like.'

'What a ghastly time that was—rice boiled with corn to make there seem more of it, then dextrose rations in place of rice…' Etsuko thought back over the years, more than four decades ago, and was amazed that she had survived.

Yumiko interrupted these reminiscences by asking tentatively if she could say something which might seem out of place. Masako generously gave her assent, without knowing what she was assenting to.

'Surely, even if you haven't actually met him over all these years, you've still seen him on television, or in the papers?…'

Masako laughed. 'Not to mention cartoons. Well, I don't mind the cartoons or the caricatures—that's what they're for, and I've had enough experience of them myself. But I won't look at any photographs or television. Particularly close-ups. When I see that face, all spotty and flabby, it really makes me feel ill. For someone so dazzlingly handsome to turn into that! Still, the point about Shingo was that he had a good head on his shoulders, not just a pretty one—they had plenty of those in the film studios. And he had a lovely smile, too, but when he smiles now he just looks vulgar. I had a good look at him on television once, by accident. I was just going to switch it off when the phone rang and I only turned the sound off by mistake, and while this long phone call was going on I was looking at his face, and, I promise you, it made me feel sick.'

To back her up, her sister said:

'I can remember a young man coming to our house with rice once, and you say now that was Tamaru, but I just can't see it. They're two quite different people. He was very good-looking— like someone from a good family who's decided to be a bit of a rake.'

'That's him. That's him exactly. But since he's gone the way he has, it's best not to see him. It just spoils my memories.'

Etsuko smiled wryly at this, but said nothing. Yumiko smiled as well, but there was nothing wry about her expression. Chie was all ears, looking completely enthralled. Shibukawa, after deep consideration, half raised his right hand (like one of those porcelain beckoning cats, thought Chie) and said:

'Um … excuse me.'

'Oh, you want an ashtray,' said Etsuko quickly. 'I'll go and get you one.'

She began to get up, but he waved her down.

'No, that's all right. I don't want to smoke, only to ask a question, if I may.'

'Of course,' said Masako.

'The Shingo you mentioned is the present prime minister…'

'Yes.'

'… Shingo Tamaru.'

'Of course. Oh, I'm sorry, perhaps I should have made that clear…'

'I thought so,' said Shibukawa, nodding.

'W…ell,' breathed Chie, lost in admiration.

'I realised that right away,' murmured Yumiko, and her aunt, aware that Shibukawa was watching her closely, kept her head modestly lowered as she drank her tea. He waited until another cup had been placed in front of him, then said:

'My next question is … why have I been treated to these rather special reminiscences? I mean … uh … what exactly is the connection between the present prime minister and your family meeting?'

'Yumiko, you'll have to tell him what's been going on at work.'

Yumiko promptly gave a full account, although she refrained from saying she'd written the editorial that had started it all because she'd been suffering from sexual deprivation. What she did say was that an article intended as a defence of women's rights had somehow turned into an argument in favour of marital infidelity, that a member of an economic watchdog committee had been upset by it, and that, although this seemed to have gone no further, somehow the article had also offended a certain religious sect, with the result that government land which had been promised to the *New Daily* was now being withheld, and the person at the head of the political party responsible for this was Shingo Tamaru.

When she reached this point, Shibukawa interrupted.

'Right, I'm with you so far. You know, it's like when you've been abroad for a while, and you come back and switch on the TV and the news makes no sense at all, and you wonder what everyone's making such a fuss about. But if you read the newspapers that have piled up while you've been away, then it all becomes clear.'

'What a good comparison,' said Yumiko admiringly, although the relevance of his metaphor seemed dubious, even if it did have the merit of favouring newspapers over television. Still, her mother had also given an exclamation of approval, and Chie looked as

177

proud as if her pet dog had performed some clever trick in front of a visitor.

Since it all seemed to be going satisfactorily, Etsuko felt she could now make a somewhat indirect request.

'In that case, how about it? Will you?' she asked her sister.

'Of course I will,' came the cheerful reply. 'I'm not sure how much good it will do, but I'll certainly meet him and ask him to do whatever he can.'

'Thank you. I don't know what we would have done if you'd refused.'

'Is it likely I'd turn down the first good part I've had in years?'

'Thank you very much, Auntie. I'm really grateful,' said Yumiko, bowing her head.

'Don't worry, it's no trouble for me. And if it doesn't work out, well, at least nobody will be any worse off.'

'But it *is* very nice of you.'

'Stop thanking me, child, or I shall begin to feel like a stranger.'

Yumiko smiled. 'Then I won't say any more about it.'

'It's a fascinating situation,' said Shibukawa. 'Have you ever played a part like it in a film?'

'What, meeting an old flame again?'

'Yes. You meet, and then…'

'Try to screw him?'

'A less ambiguous word might be better.'

'All right. The two meet again, and then she tries to blackmail him. That kind of part?'

'Yes, something like that…'

'I once played the owner of a bar who goes to complain to a gangster and gets killed. I wonder what she was complaining about?… I seem to have forgotten.'

'That wasn't very clever, getting yourself killed.'

Masako laughed. 'In the screenplay I came out alive, but when I saw the rushes I seemed to have been done in. I'm still not quite sure how it turned out in the end.'

When they had all stopped laughing, Yumiko said:

178

'I'm not asking you to put pressure on him, just to appeal to his good nature. If the government and their party people would stop poking their nose in, I'd be able to get on with writing editorials and they wouldn't need to worry about what's going to happen to the women's vote. Seriously—if this thing does blow up it could make a very loud bang. Obviously *I* couldn't expect the prime minister to give me an appointment, but in Auntie's case…'

'That's right. An appeal—a petition. That's the way I've been thinking,' Etsuko insisted.

'An appeal is all right,' Shibukawa put in, 'but this would be more like a caution, a warning even, to him.'

'There's nothing wrong with that,' said Masako. 'But what am I going to say? I don't seem to have a script.'

'I'll write down the gist of it for you,' Yumiko replied. 'Then you can improvise along those lines.'

'And you'll come with me?'

'Of course, I'd be glad to. But I'm afraid you'll have to do the talking.'

'Suppose you ask and I just back you up?'

'No, you'll have to be left alone together, a third party would just make it more awkward, and I wouldn't like him to think I was being a nuisance. Besides, I don't think he'd let you in with a chaperone.'

'He wouldn't?'

'I don't think so.'

Masako thought about this, then said eventually:

'Do it in nice big handwriting.'

This seemed to be her way of agreeing. Yumiko thanked her, then Chie asked her mother:

'Is the Banzan operation still on?'

'Yes. I was going to ask you. Is that all right?'

'Of course it is. But will it do any good?'

'As much good as approaching the prime minister, you mean?'

'Yes.'

'It's hard to say.'

'According to Miyake, he's got no real clout,' said Shibukawa, playing down the whole idea. 'Still, it's probably worth trying. Fire off enough shots and one's bound to hit the target.'

'That's what I was thinking,' said Yumiko to Chie. 'So if it doesn't go well just let it drop—don't get involved.'

'Apparently he's a great admirer of Chie's,' said Shibukawa, 'so he's quite likely to agree to ask Tamaru. Whether the PM will say yes or no is another matter. In this case, of course, I'll be the one who's the nuisance. Banzan will want to be alone with Chie.'

'You've got to stay by my side all the time,' said Chie, 'and give me support.'

Etsuko, however, seemed to feel a formal request was in order, and spent a while thanking him and apologising for all the trouble they were putting him to, which Shibukawa answered with a formal bow.

'I don't mind in the least, I assure you. After all, I was the one who asked to be involved in the first place. I'm sure everything will be all right.' And he bowed his head a few more times.

'I can't see any problem as long as he goes with her,' said Yumiko, trying to reassure herself. 'And talking of firing off shots— and a very long shot at that—Professor Toyosaki, whom I think you know, Chie, but I'm not sure if you do, Mr Shibukawa…'

'Professor Toyosaki…'

'Oh, you know,' said Chie. 'He's the one who wrote *Indifferent Phenomenology*, *Indifferent Hermeneutics*…'

'Ah, you mean Yokichi Toyosaki,' said Shibukawa, and was going to add 'the indifferent philosopher' but managed just in time to change this to 'the indefatigable writer'. 'His books are rather fun. They sell well, too.'

Yumiko smiled. 'They're all cheap paperbacks, so the royalties are minimal. He's always complaining that the prices of books don't rise with inflation.'

'They could hardly do that!'

'Still, I prefer his paperbacks, because I can at least understand them a little, unlike those terrible hardbacks. I always feel slightly embarrassed when he gives me a signed copy of one—it's completely wasted on me.'

'Isn't it rather difficult having a philosophy teacher for a friend?' her aunt put in. 'Doesn't it give you a headache talking to him?'

'We don't talk about things that make my head ache.' Yumiko smiled at her, then said to Shibukawa: 'Toyosaki's going to see Mr Sakakibara for us on Thursday.'

'The chief secretary. What a good idea.' But Shibukawa was thinking less about the chief secretary than about the relationship between this philosopher and Chie's mother. The suspicion she'd aroused was at once perceived by Yumiko, however, who added with an innocent expression on her face:

'Their wives are old school friends.'

'Really? Still, what an odd meeting that's going to be!'

'I know.'

'The chief secretary's going to end up with a splitting headache probably.'

Everyone laughed at this except Etsuko, who didn't even smile, forcing Chie to explain to her grandmother why a meeting between the party's chief secretary and a professor of philosophy was considered funny.

'Is that what you were laughing about? I must have been thinking of something else. You know, even at that time, five hundred thousand yen wasn't a great deal of money. I can remember being quite furious when I heard about it two or three years later.'

'Yes, you did have something to say about it, didn't you?' her sister said, seemingly with mixed feelings, though she didn't look upset. Yumiko felt the ground was safe enough to ask:

'What actually was it worth in the mid-fifties?'

This typical journalist's question was taken up by Etsuko.

'In 1955 I had my little kitchen repaired. I can remember quite distinctly that the carpenter charged seven hundred yen.'

'Nowadays it would cost you twenty-five or twenty-six thousand,' said Shibukawa. 'Um ... that makes it forty times as much, so in today's money it would be worth twenty million—although you can't really generalise from one example...'

'I had a bowl of noodles at a little place near the hospital the other day and it cost five hundred,' Etsuko interrupted. She remembered the price because she didn't eat out much.

Yumiko was getting into her stride now and said: 'I wonder what it would have cost in 1955. I'll ask the research people…'

She started to get up, but Shibukawa stopped her.

'I can tell you that exactly, since it cropped up in a comic book I was reading recently. In 1955 or 1956 it would have cost you forty yen.'

'So, that would be…'

Since she had problems with mental arithmetic, Chie did it for her.

'That's about thirteen times, which makes it six and a half million.'

'You see—there's too big a gap between that and twenty million. You can see why historians have so much trouble over this. The thing is, it's almost impossible to get a real sense of what money was worth in *any* period … though that's not something any historian is going to admit.'

Shibukawa made these remarks with some energy, but nobody showed any particular interest in this fundamental problem of historical research.

'The big change is labour costs,' said Yumiko.

'About the only things that have got cheaper are eggs,' said Etsuko.

'Only because of the battery system.'

'The taste's gone right off, too.'

'Eggs were dreadfully expensive before the war, you know.'

'That's what really astonishes me when I go abroad, the eggs and milk. They taste so much richer.'

'The ice cream tastes quite different, too.'

A lively discussion began, with Etsuko noting at some point:

'Still, the price of land has gone up even more than the cost of labour.'

'It's the main reason for our high cost of living,' said Yumiko.

'What a pity he didn't buy those four or five acres on August

whenever-it-was. If he'd held on to them he'd have been able…'
Shibukawa stopped. He had been going to say, 'to fork out more
separation money', but when he glanced at Masako he noticed she
was looking into the distance, a sad expression on her face. He
began to regret the cheerful conversation they were having about
the cost of living, particularly his own contribution to it. All this
talk of money was ruining Masako's memories of her love affair,
and he felt she must be feeling hurt by it, so he said, clearly, to
attract her attention:

'All I seem to be able to talk about is money. It's awful. I'm
very sorry.'

'That's perfectly all right,' Masako said, looking at him. 'I was
thinking about something else, that's all—something not unconnected with this matter. But I wasn't annoyed or upset. Why
should I be—it was I who brought the subject up in the first
place.'

The other three all started to apologise as well.

'It's all right, I assure you, it was something else,' she protested,
smiling; and then, after a moment's thought, she went on, as if
determined to prevent any misunderstanding: 'I've always been
very casual about things. Probably all actresses are the same. We
don't like to think about anything very seriously. But two things,
when I was young, really shook me. The first was when that boy
went into the army and got killed. He just wasn't there any more.
Gone. It wasn't so much a feeling of sadness—although of course
I was sad, utterly miserable—as a sense of strangeness, of mystery.
Do you understand that? Chie, can you understand that? That
sort of feeling? I don't suppose you can. I was two or three years
older than you at the time.'

Chie judged rightly that it would be best not to say anything to
this, so she just looked a little puzzled, and her great-aunt nodded
at her and went on:

'The other was when I got the money we've been talking
about. I was dreadfully upset by both these things, and I worried
and worried about what I should do, but never seemed to find an
answer. To say "seemed" makes it sound as though I'm talking

about somebody else, but that's what it was like. I didn't seem able to understand what was going on in my mind. Perhaps nobody does—nobody knows what's going on there. I fell in love again but a part of me always felt bothered by it. I suppose I must have been—deeply bothered by it—and that was why I started to think like that: difficult thoughts, of a kind I've never had before or since, a strange kind of logic that nagged and nagged at me. It was the summer after he'd been elected, around mid-September.'

'In 1954?' asked Shibukawa.

'Yes, I suppose it must have been. I was going to a party or gathering of some kind, I can't quite remember, and left the house around four or five. My dresser—Satake, her name was—was with me, and we were walking down the main street. They were having a festival in our neighbourhood that day. The eaves of the houses were hung with paper lanterns, the grown-ups were wearing identical yukata, although for some reason there were still no children around, and the local district office between the electricity shop and the fishmonger was the centre of attention, the festival headquarters, with the greengrocer and the barber solemnly sitting there in their yukata. There was a hanging scroll with the name of the local god written in large letters, and various offerings were lined up, three large bottles of saké, melons, rice cakes piled on a plain wooden stand, and peaches. Just a little way further on was a small shrine, between a cafe and a tofu shop, and I stopped there and put a coin in the box, giving a tug on the bell rope which wasn't too dirty, clapped my hands, and prayed. But while I was doing so, it suddenly seemed so strange to see the offerings, the bottles of saké and beer, even Coca-Cola, the wooden stand with tomatoes on it, the onions, rice cakes and melons. Not strange, in fact, but comic, ridiculous. What was the god going to do with all this stuff? Wouldn't he be offended by it? I remember the red tomatoes in particular, they looked so gaudy, and the Coke seemed completely out of place, making everything look somehow cheap and vulgar. Anyway, that's what I suddenly felt. I'd been going to festivals ever since I was a tiny little girl, but never before had I looked at one in that way, as if I were really

184

seeing it for the first time. I suppose we all have experiences of that kind…'

They all nodded in agreement, even Shibukawa.

'Then I decided that the barber and the man who ran the cafe and the lady at the tofu shop just didn't know how to behave towards their god, so they gave him things like this, not knowing what else to do. And then I thought, that god doesn't really like having this stuff offered him, or people asking him favours, but, people being what they are, he knew not to expect too much of them, since they were bound to do something in bad taste, and so he put up with it. Then I thought, it must be awful being a god, and I felt sorry for him.

'At that moment, just when I was sympathising with the god's problems, a housewife who'd been shopping at the greengrocer's came and stood at my side with her shopping basket, flicked a five- or ten-yen coin into the box, rang the bell and clapped her hands, mumbling a few words, no doubt asking for something, of course, and then dashed away. And as I watched her, it struck me it must be a hell of a business just listening to all these prayers, let alone going to the trouble of answering them, and the very next moment I realised her five or ten yen, my hundred yen, the tomatoes, the Coke, the onions and the melons—they were all exactly the same. There was absolutely no difference between them. What I'd done was exactly the same as what the barber, the fishmonger and the lady in the tofu shop had done. We had all acted in equally bad taste. Money is no better than material things—it's all the same, all vulgar, everything… And when I realised that, I felt a sense of shock. And then Satake suggested we ought to go.'

She took a sip of tea, then continued:

'When we got to the station there were no taxis waiting, and we were wondering if we shouldn't go by train, just standing about, not quite making up our minds, when suddenly I had this flash of insight, if you can call it that, and I thought that, just as people offer things like onions and pears and melons and tomatoes and peaches and money and bottles of saké to the god, knowing they ought to be able to find something better to give him but

185

unable to think what, so had Shingo finally decided to send me that half a million yen. There just wasn't anything else he could come up with. And I thought that I'd just have to be like the god—I'd just have to smile, a slightly bitter smile, and keep quiet and accept it, even if I did feel it was in bad taste, because that was the way things were; and I also thought I didn't mind things being like that either. Ridiculous, of course, comparing myself with a god. Absurd—isn't it? Enough to make you burst out laughing—which is what I did. Well, only a kind of snigger, but enough for Satake to ask me what it was about. Naturally I didn't say anything.'

Nobody said anything in response to this, either, no doubt because they were lost for words, and also worried that anything they did say might cause offence, but mostly because they'd all been genuinely moved. Etsuko just sat nodding throughout the narrative. Yumiko was so surprised she was sitting with her mouth half open. Chie was leaning forward in her chair staring at her great-aunt, while Shibukawa, having removed the two dogs from their corner and placed them on his lap, gave a deep sigh as he leaned back against the sofa. The former actress went on:

'If you're honest about it, money is always worth having. I admit I frittered away most of that half a million yen, but still, money is useful, you can do lots with it, so I was able in my way to accept the fact that he'd sent me money when he didn't know what else to do. Someone more intelligent would have grasped that straight away, but I was so stupid it took a festival to make me realise it. Still, although I'd worked that out, and knew I ought to be like a god—sad at heart and yet putting up with it, not kicking against it but detached, forbearing—yet I couldn't. I felt angry still, really angry. It's funny, really. He'd left me over a year before, and I'd never thought I was that keen on him anyway. But I suppose I was still in love with him, in some way I don't quite understand. Anyway, even if I couldn't manage that god-like state of mind, I did gradually settle down, bit by bit, very slowly. Even now I still sometimes remember that festival day, the only day in my life when I've really tried to think a question through, to reason something out. It's like an anniversary for me, although I can't remember the actual date, except that it was some time in mid-September. It seems like yesterday, but it's over thirty years ago. That's what I was thinking about when I looked the way I did. I wasn't upset by anything you said, you needn't worry about that.'

They were all silent for a while, then everyone started to speak at once. Etsuko said, so quietly they could hardly hear her:

'When all's said and done, that student was the one you really cared about—at least, that's what I think.'

Chie said: 'You sound so different today—so thoughtful.'

Shibukawa said: 'That wasn't just fascinating, it was moving.' He nodded several times, then picked the toy dogs up and shoved them back in their corner.

Yumiko nodded in agreement before saying: 'Still, there's one thing you haven't mentioned. Wasn't the real problem that he didn't bring the money himself but got his uncle to do it? Surely that's what hurt.'

Both the younger two agreed with this, and Masako replied:

'Yes, I didn't like that at all. It left a bad taste, as if it had been intended as an insult. But that wore off as well after a while. I accepted it, as I accepted the whole thing. It hurts to have to part from someone—nothing can ever really make up for it, there's no consolation—but life is like that. What I understood at the festival was that it was better to have had money from him than to have had nothing at all. Money and material things don't mean much in themselves, but as ways of showing certain feelings, well, that's about all we have. It's sad, but it's true. When the man I was going to marry was killed in the war the country did nothing for me. I wasn't his wife, and I know I had no reason to expect anything. But compared with that—compared with the people who took my man away without offering anything in return—the people in Tamaru's family, who'd also taken my man away from me, were a bit better; in fact, a great deal better. At least they gave me some cash.'

Shibukawa breathed another deep sigh and lowered his head,

as if he represented both the house of Tamaru and the nation as a whole, and felt a painful responsibility for what Masako had suffered.

'It took a while for me to stop blaming him for not bringing the money himself. One moment I'd forgive him, then I'd feel angry again. I forgave him because I imagined he thought that if he came himself he might have weakened, and things would have gone on just as they had before; that he couldn't trust himself, and asked his uncle to do it for him. I think that was how I explained it to myself, although it sounds big-headed, and you'll probably laugh at me for saying so. But, you know, I was the one who taught him about love. He couldn't have wanted to leave me. He just had to, because he wanted to be a politician, and to get elected he had to "settle down" in a place where people would vote for him. That's all it was. He probably cried his heart out over it. I myself, well, I never expected it to go on for ever, but even so…'

Her voice softened as if she were remembering all those far-off nights.

'At first he was really clumsy, quite hopeless. He didn't know a thing, you see. I had terrible trouble getting…'

'Please, Masako,' her sister put in hurriedly, and then, after the briefest of pauses: 'Aren't you hungry?'

But as she spoke, the small machine in the corner of the living room began to make a dull rumbling sound.

'Ah, it's a fax,' cried Chie delightedly, and stood up, while Yumiko and Shibukawa breathed inner sighs of relief, Yumiko saying:

'Oh, the fax.'

'They're very useful machines,' Shibukawa added.

Chie passed the sheet of paper to her mother, who saw it was in Urano's handwriting.

> To: Ms Yumiko Minami   1 sheet only
> From: an acquaintance
> Have received fresh information. Company will adopt a
> new approach to the problem of your reassignment. To-

morrow they will announce that you are to be attached to the chairman's office with the status of department head. This is just to give you advance notice.

The message was signed with a crudely drawn heart.

'The company's going to offer me a different job tomorrow,' Yumiko said, and read aloud what Urano had written. 'I'm not going to buy it,' she added. 'They might just as well give me early retirement.'

'So you're not prepared to settle for that?' Etsuko asked rather diffidently, and Yumiko shook her head in silence.

'Has this post been available for some time?' Chie asked.

'Of course not. It doesn't exist. They've just cooked up something in a hurry, like a lot of the positions in that company.'

'You're right to turn it down,' her aunt said. 'No job attached to the chairman's office can be any good. You'll just be writing addresses on envelopes and sticking on stamps.' She spoke as if she knew all about it, no doubt assuming it would be like the equivalent job in a film studio.

'There's probably a bit more to it than that,' replied Yumiko with a smile, 'but it's still only a way of getting me off the editorial team.'

'Whatever it means you mustn't let them push you around.'

Etsuko thought for a while, then said:

'Yes, well, you may be right. Anyway, the first thing to do is to find out if the prime minister will see you.'

'What do you think?' Yumiko asked Shibukawa.

'I agree. I think the best thing is to continue with our present plan.'

'Then will you write him a letter?' Yumiko asked her aunt. 'A short one will do. Just say you would very much like to speak to him about something. I'll give it to a reporter who's been assigned to the PM tomorrow.'

'Okay, I'd better write it this evening, then.' Masako nodded to confirm her acceptance of this request, while Chie, who had been reading the fax over her mother's shoulder, said:

'What's that funny squiggle at the end?'

And indeed the shape Urano had drawn in place of a signature was strangely deformed, and didn't look like a heart at all.

SIX

·
·
·

Chie was dressed in a formal kimono, rose coloured with a discreet, splashed pattern, and a sash of clove green with a powdered pearl-shell overlay. She'd had the outfit made for her sittings with Sakon Ogino, but since he had decided he wanted the girl to wear Western-style clothes, it was the first time she'd worn it. Shibukawa had on a dark blue blazer with a white shirt and polka-dot tie, in a conscious effort to humour the supposed sartorial tastes of the distinguished calligrapher they were about to visit.

The two granddaughters of the great man greeted them in the entrance hall. They were dressed in striking contrast to their guests, both being in identical frilly white blouses with red cardigans and extraordinarily brief black mini-skirts. The only difference between the two was their lipstick, the elder of the sisters favouring dark red, the younger a pale cherry colour. It was the former who was Chie's classmate, although she'd never seen her looking so trendy at college, and wondered if it was because she was at home or just conforming to her younger sister's tastes. The girls also chattered away with a surprisingly similar, affected-sounding lisp (again, Chie had never heard her classmate talk like that before) as they showed their guests into the living room. The walls were hung with a jumble of temporarily mounted scrolls,

191

and it was in this rather confusing atmosphere that the two visitors handed over the presents they'd brought, in Chie's case a bunch of roses, in Shibukawa's a bottle of white wine. The younger sister adopted an informal manner with Shibukawa from the start, and the elder soon followed her example, much to the bemusement, even dismay, of both the other two, and they all sat round the living room table which appeared to serve as a dining table as well. After the introductions had been made, the younger sister stood up as if to leave the room, at which point Banzan Onuma appeared, dressed in a loose brown kimono bound by a stiff sash. He was a tall man, with white hair, white eyebrows, a white moustache and a grey face.

'Surprise, surprise,' said his granddaughter. 'He usually makes such a fuss before coming down.'

'And I know the reason why,' cried the other. 'It's because he's dying to see Chie.'

Banzan ignored these cheeky comments, merely motioning to his guests to remain seated.

'That's all right ... do stay as you are.'

He sat down himself.

'How good of you to come, my dear. I can't tell you how delighted I am. It's a privilege for an old man to see your sweet face again. And how beautifully you're dressed.'

He beamed at Chie, then turned his attention to Shibukawa, who was seated in front of him.

'And who might you be?'

This provoked an immediate response from the sisters.

'Don't be so grumpy, Grandad.'

'You're just jealous, that's all.'

It was to a chorus of these and similar remarks that Shibukawa placed his card in front of the calligrapher and, while Banzan proceeded to read it with the help of a large magnifying glass provided by his elder granddaughter, said respectfully:

'As a student of the pre-Meiji and Meiji periods, I would be most grateful if I could be allowed to see the scrolls of Taneomi Soejima that I believe you have, sir, in your possession.'

'I mentioned it when we spoke on the telephone the other day,' put in Chie, and the two granddaughters joined in as well.

'Yes, she did, she did.'

'And you've forgotten again, Grandad.'

'Ah, so that's what it's about,' the old man said, nodding slightly, then more deeply as he thanked his visitors for their gifts. He went on: 'Yes, Soejima's distinguished ancestors were of Han lineage, and for that reason the first name he took was Ryoshu, which means a descendant of the emperor, but out of respect for our imperial family he changed it to Taneomi, to make his status as a retainer clear.'

'So he was a descendant of the Chinese emperor of the Han dynasty?' asked Chie.

'Yes. A long time ago, of course. The family came to Japan around the middle of the third century, when Himiko was empress, I think. Perhaps that accounts for his prowess in things Chinese. Japanese diplomats sent to China were generally inept at calligraphy and incompetent at writing verse, whereas he shone in both fields. No doubt those abilities contributed to his very real diplomatic achievements.'

Shibukawa modestly acknowledged the truth of this, but the granddaughters felt it called for more banter from them.

'You ought to have been an ambassador, Grandad—I bet you think so, too, don't you?'

'You're a natural—the perfect diplomat in everything you do.'

'No,' Banzan replied quite seriously. 'It wouldn't have done for me. Ignorant of the law, you see. Now, even before the Meiji Restoration, Soejima had the Chinese version of international law by heart.'

The old man's failure to see that he was being teased made Shibukawa want to giggle, his efforts to control himself affecting Chie, who couldn't help smiling. This Banzan did notice, but also misunderstood.

'The smile of a beauteous woman is worth a king's ransom. Yet all an old artist like myself has to offer you is this.'

He pointed towards the corner of the room. The granddaughters stood up, one bringing his inkstone and rubbing away at it to produce some ink, the other bringing poem cards and a pot bristling with brushes. Banzan went on gazing at Chie, muttering to himself what appeared to be lines of poetry, although no one could work out what he was saying. Finally the old man with the grey face reached out with his left hand, picked up a card made of stiff white paper, and took out a brush with the other hand. Then, suddenly, a large tremor passed through his body, like some great cat getting ready to pounce, and he produced eight characters written in the square, very legible, Chinese style. The girls then hung it in a frame fixed to a pillar for that purpose, and Banzan slowly transformed himself back from a large cat into an old man. He translated the two lines of Chinese verse.

' "The moon rides out, pure white / Beauty is her companion." Which is to say that the moon is lovely to look at, and a pretty young lady equally so. It's from "Songs in Praise of Beauteous Women".'

He looked at what he'd written.

'Not very well done, I'm afraid. The writing lacks interest.'

Shibukawa found himself agreeing with him. The characters were, of course, skilfully drawn, but they looked like a teacher's copybook exercise, with no intrinsic interest. However, his grand-daughters reacted in their usual cheerful manner.

'Oh, he's fishing again…,' the younger of them said.

'Just wants a drink…,' chimed in the other.

'No, no, that wasn't what I meant. Well, it's all a matter of taste, I suppose,' said Banzan, blinking as he made this statement, which in fact did nothing to clarify what he really thought of the lines he'd written.

One of the girls got up and produced a bottle of saké from somewhere, while her sister brought two small glasses. Chie's classmate then filled them both, putting one in front of Shibu-kawa and one in front of Banzan and urging Shibukawa to drink up, which he did, half emptying his glass in one gulp. Banzan, however, sipped a little of his before saying:

'That reminds me…' Catching sight of Chie's polite, if fleeting, response to this, he went on happily:

'When I first came to Tokyo—that would be in 1925—the place I lived in was very close to where Soejima's son was. Of course, the great man himself had already passed away by that time. And yet, either by coincidence or fate, whichever one cares to call it, a person very closely connected with Soejima, by the name of Mori…'

At this point he gave a sigh, trying but failing to remember the rest of the name. He took another sip from his glass, but still memory wouldn't come to his aid.

'Ogai?' suggested his elder granddaughter, but apparently he didn't mean the distinguished Meiji novelist. Then she winked at Chie and Shibukawa and suggested 'Ranmaru', one of Oda Nobunaga's loyal young retainers who died defending his lord when he was assassinated at Honnoji in the sixteenth century, and Banzan seemed prepared to take this preposterous suggestion seriously, shaking his head and saying no, he was talking about someone from the present century. The younger girl's suggestion of 'Ishimatsu', another loyal retainer of considerably lower rank who was the virtuous and half-witted hero of a number of second-rate films, produced a fiercer rejection. Banzan frowned and took another sip. Chie couldn't help laughing, but the granddaughters were like well-trained actors in a farce, managing to restrain even the faintest sign of mirth. Shibukawa, however, found it hard to remain a mere spectator and at last gave the right answer.

'Are you perhaps thinking of Kainan?'

'Yes, yes, Kainan, that's it. He wrote Chinese poetry. Meiji period. A very representative figure.'

Delighted to have resolved the matter, he downed the remainder of his drink in one mouthful. His granddaughters immediately praised Shibukawa's wisdom and culture, in the same light, affected manner, while Banzan added:

'Yes, Kainan's son also lived close by. A very elegant district, I always thought. With well-bred people living there.'

He was now deep in nostalgic reflection, recalling those distant days with some passion, although his main theme seemed to be that, no matter where he went, he always found somebody famous living nearby, or somebody related to somebody famous, such as the cousin of the wife of the Russo-Japanese War hero General Nogi—the implication being that new heroes, men like the former prime minister, for example, were bound to rise from the ranks of those connected with Banzan Onuma. When asked for his comments on the calligraphy of this former prime minister, he nodded and said:

'A man of consequence will produce work of consequence.'

This aphorism called for another drink, and his grey face now began to take on a pinkish hue. Again he meditated awhile before facing the stiff white paper, steadying his breath, then swinging into action and producing some more lines from the "Songs". This time, however, the best of all medicines had its miraculous effect, and he wrote in a carefree style suited to the tone of those ancient love poems. The card was placed up in the rack alongside the other, and after comparing the two he gave his judgement.

'Well, that may be a bit better. In writing, lightness is all-important.'

Perhaps he meant light-headedness, his visitors both thought, but they politely refrained from any comment, merely sighing deeply to indicate their appreciation. But the granddaughters were clearly lost in admiration, which they were only too happy to express.

'Tremendous, Grandad.'

'Before drinking, and after.'

'You ought to do a TV commercial.'

'You really should.'

Banzan beamed at this praise, but eventually dipped his brush in the ink again and produced a few more efforts: all brief, four-character quotations from the same source, extolling the virtues of beautiful women.

'I'm afraid they may be rather a nuisance to carry, but do please take them with you,' he said to Chie, then cast aside his brush, telling his granddaughters to have the cards stamped with his seal. They protested that poor Shibukawa hadn't had one written for him, but Banzan pretended not to hear, although he had no trouble understanding Chie when, after expressing her thanks, she said she had one more favour to ask of him, in addition to letting her companion see the Soejima scrolls.

'Yes, yes, I have heard something about the matter. That should be discussed in private. I believe it has to do with the present government. The scrolls are in the Memorial Hall, and my granddaughters will show Mr Shibukawa the way.'

'What, are you trying to get rid of us, Grandad?'

'You're a sly one, aren't you?'

Banzan seemed indifferent to these remarks, however, and although Shibukawa couldn't quite work out what was happening, he gathered, from the subsequent discussion about whether the person in charge was there or still out somewhere, that the Banzan Memorial Hall (built by subscriptions from government circles) must be nearby and that, besides the more significant works of Banzan himself, there were famous pieces by other people on display. He glanced at Chie, indicating that this virtually enforced separation was not what he'd expected, but she only nodded to indicate she didn't mind.

Escorted by the two girls, Shibukawa had a walk of about five minutes to get there, and on the way they kept up their constant chatter, telling jokes about their grandfather that impressed him as being likely to be true. They laughed, for example, at the way his writing the first time had been so bad that he'd needed an excuse for a drink. They also said he used completely different paper when writing for important people in the political and financial world than he did for people of lesser standing, and Shibukawa assumed this was no exaggeration either but a clear indication of the man's character. Similarly, a story about him watching television (to which he was addicted) and suddenly becoming very upset, muttering that none of the broadcasting companies had ever approached him about making an appearance, sounded true as well, despite the way these girls spoke about him, giggling and agreeing with each other, producing one anecdote after another as if describing the antics of a household cat.

The Banzan Memorial Hall (or, to give it its full name, the Banzan Onuma Memorial Hall of Calligraphic Art) had been designed by an architect from the former prime minister's constituency. He seemed to have been inspired by the concept of a large parcel, for at the very top of the square building was a bird-shaped object resembling a neatly tied ribbon. The bird's beak drooped mournfully open, and in the Tokyo dusk this peculiar building showed to particularly bad effect, partly perhaps because it seemed ridiculous to set up this sort of architecture on such a tiny strip of land.

The interior was clean and uncluttered, however, and the art works intelligently displayed. Unlike other artists of his generation, at least Banzan had the saving grace that he appeared to have made no spurious attempts to be avant-garde, but his works inevitably looked far inferior to those of an earlier period hanging there, Soejima's in particular. At first Shibukawa rather admired the man for having the courage to put things so obviously better than his own in such close proximity, but then it struck him that perhaps this was inspired less by modesty than by the fact that Banzan didn't see his own work as inferior in any way.

After looking round the whole display, Shibukawa returned to the Soejima scrolls. The ones written towards the end of his life were a mixture of pieces done in square Chinese characters and those in the more flowing Japanese style, and in both he'd used abbreviated forms freely, giving a powerful impression of confident, almost reckless freedom, and a total lack of pretension. The overall sense of spareness, even austerity, was certainly attractive, but a decline in actual energy was very apparent, too, and it struck Shibukawa that when a man writes like this he has obviously left the world of active politics. Since the two girls went off together for a while, he was able to give the scrolls his full attention, but eventually they came back again, talking non-stop as usual. He told them a few stories about Soejima, but their favourite was the one about instructing his son to use every possible seal, even though he'd only used four, presumably because their own job was to stamp Banzan's scrolls with his seal.

It was deep twilight as they walked back, and they arrived to find the sushi man just delivering the evening meal, presumably ordered while they were at the Memorial Hall. The girls took the tray of food and paid for it, mentioning the fact that Banzan hated any kind of shellfish but was crazy about tuna and herring. The sushi man said he'd brought exactly what was ordered, laughing as he went away.

All three went cheerfully into the house, finding Banzan and Chie in the living room, seated on sofas placed at right angles to each other, talking peacefully together. It appeared they too were discussing sushi. Apparently Banzan had for a long time had a strong dislike for herring, although he'd never actually eaten any, but then happened to try some and enjoyed it; he now deeply regretted all the years he'd spent avoiding it. For that reason, he made a habit of eating out on the occasion of the first catch of the year, and he invited Chie to come next time to the place in Ginza he went to.

'It's as if you're trying to regain your lost youth,' said Chie lightly, but seeing Shibukawa approach, obviously trying to catch what they were saying, she looked a bit flustered and added hastily: 'Yes, I'd love to go, in the summer sometime.'

Chie and Banzan both smiled. There certainly seemed to have been some reduction in the psychological distance between them, and Shibukawa assumed the discussion about Yumiko's problem had gone well, yet he was also aware of something odd about the atmosphere. So, presumably, were the sisters.

'Did your talk go okay?' the younger one asked.

Neither Banzan nor Chie answered, but they looked at each other and smiled again.

'Oh, that wicked look in your eyes!' the girl went on teasingly, which made Shibukawa reflect that at least he wasn't the only one who thought so.

Preparations for the meal were soon made, and the five sat round the table, with Chie on Banzan's left, her classmate on her left, then Shibukawa and the younger girl. The elder sister was in charge of the tea and the younger of the saké, although this time the saké was drunk out of small porcelain cups. There was certainly more tuna and herring than was normal with the average sushi meal.

Shibukawa praised the Memorial Hall, then the Soejima collection. Banzan acknowledged the compliment with a deprecatory gesture, and said:

'You know, I once had the opportunity to lay my hands on a priceless item when I was young, but as a poor student I was sadly obliged to let it go.'

He turned to Chie and addressed the story to her.

'Soejima was, as I've already mentioned, a descendant of the imperial line of the Han dynasty. In a decisive battle, around 200 B.C., his ancestor Liu Peng finally achieved complete control of the empire, and had the rival he'd defeated kill himself. Soejima was made foreign minister at the beginning of the Meiji era, but when his policy of Korean subjugation was rejected he joined the opposition and spent three years travelling around China. During that time he visited the place where the suicide had occurred, and wrote a four-line stanza, said to be one of his finest.'

He indicated to his granddaughters that he wanted his ink and brush again, then wrote down the quatrain in small, square characters:

> The wild geese cry from withered reeds; the frost
> Will soon descend. Evening turns all things grey.
> Descendant of Liu Peng, I row my boat
> Into midstream, mourning his dead rival.

Having given the translation, he added:

'For its nobility and generosity, this represents all that's best in Oriental poetry. He grasped a moment in time, two thousand years ago, and used it to reflect on the true meaning of history. It could well be the finest example of Japanese writing since the Meiji Restoration, and novelists nowadays, who all seem to make a living from describing the sexual passions of young women, ought to kneel in shame before it.'

At this, the younger granddaughter, then her sister, began to giggle, presumably finding it hard not to connect this stern remark with his obvious infatuation with Chie—unless, as seemed unlikely, they were laughing at the plight of contemporary novelists who were so lacking in distinguished forebears that they couldn't be expected to produce such poems.

Shibukawa, who felt the old man was praising this particular poem too highly, only said:

'You mean, sir, that you were unable to obtain the scroll with this poem on it?'

'Exactly.'

Banzan gave a detailed explanation of the reasons for this, but the story was so muddled that in the end all Shibukawa could do was offer his sympathy, leaving the two girls to start talking about Chie's kimono, as Banzan helped himself to more food and drink.

'We could do with a proper kimono like that.'

'Couldn't we just. I haven't had one made since the year before last.'

This was patently a hint directed at their grandfather, who said:

'Well, we will deal with that question on some other occasion.' Then, turning to Chie, he went on: 'What is of particular note in this poem is the fact that he isn't paying his respects to the memory of his ancestors but appeasing the soul of the man they destroyed. It's in this splendid attitude towards a dead enemy that one can see an essentially Oriental morality; for here it truly exists. This is *bushido*, the spiritual way of the warrior. And it's this quality that the politicians of the Meiji period still possessed.'

Chie managed to indicate her rather cautious agreement while swallowing a mouthful of seasoned sea urchin roe, but the two granddaughters were not to be put off so easily.

' "Some other occasion", indeed, when in fact you're going to forget all about it.'

'Let's settle it here and now.'

'For here we truly exist.'

These complaints were made merrily enough as they ate their

sweetened egg and shrimps, and all the while Shibukawa was mulling over something he urgently wanted to say, something that had occurred to him the previous year, when he had first read this poem, and thought about from time to time since.

The poem by Soejima was certainly moving—grand in scale and generous in attitude—but its power to move depended on the situation itself, in which a man visits the place where his ancestor had won a battle two thousand years before. It wasn't the poetic expression that produced the effect, but the historical fact; the four lines themselves were just a series of clichés. So something else must have caused the Meiji writers of Chinese poetry to praise it so highly, something other than a legendary episode involving ancestors and descendants, and a visit to an old battlefield. That something else, he thought, could only be the traditional Japanese belief in spirit worship.

Ever since the eleventh century, when the vengeful spirit of Sugawara Michizane, who had died in exile, was said to have been transformed into a thunderbolt that fell upon the palace of Emperor Daigo, killing him and several others, it had been believed that the spirits of political failures, if left unappeased, could cause disasters to occur. Furthermore, if they were treated with great courtesy it was thought that, not only would they cease to be vengeful, they would be transformed into guardian deities. This belief, rather than fading, had grown stronger with time, as is shown in the case of Takamori Saigo, one of the founders of the Meiji Restoration who died rebelling against the government. The Meiji government set up a bronze statue to him—a remarkable thing to do, for which the only explanation must be that very need to appease a vengeful spirit. And this itself may have influenced Soejima, since Saigo had been a close acquaintance of his (they both supported the proposed invasion of Korea).

Shibukawa said none of this, however, not wanting to risk offending the old man while the problem of Chie's mother remained, but compensating for his self-restraint by satisfying other appetites instead. The two granddaughters, who helped him in this by ensuring that his cup and plate stayed full, had moved on to a discussion of the merits of French cooking, though admitting that sushi was also okay. Chie, while plying Banzan with saké, joined in the conversation, but Banzan, delighted as he was by her attentions, was quite uninterested in this talk about chicken terrine and lobster fricassée, and decided to change the subject.

'Excuse this abrupt question, but what obituaries has your mother written?'

'I don't think she's written any,' said Chie. 'As I was telling you earlier, she writes editorials.'

'I don't mean ordinary obituaries.' Banzan smiled. 'I am referring to the occasion when a very distinguished person dies and is often written about respectfully in the editorial columns.'

'Yes, the top reporters used to write them,' Shibukawa put in. 'But the practice seems to have died out.'

'Mummy isn't a top reporter,' said Chie. 'She's only just been promoted to the editorial team.'

Banzan waved his hand.

'Ah, I see, I see. I don't seem to read the editorials much these days.'

'He only likes the cartoons.'

'The comic pages on Sundays.'

But Banzan just frowned and ignored the girls.

'On Soejima's death, all the major newspapers devoted their leading articles to the fact, in what I am told was the finest journalistic effort of the whole Meiji period—Setsurei Miyake, distinguished critic and patriot, later awarded the medal of culture, in the *Nihon Shimbun*; Konan Naito, Chinese historian, later professor of Oriental history at Kyoto University, in the *Osaka Asahi*... Now, who wrote in the *Tokyo Mainichi*?... In the *Tokyo Mainichi* ... ah, yes, Ikebe. All powerful wielders of the brush, and all pouring their hearts out in tribute to him.'

'What about the *New Daily*?' his granddaughters asked.

Banzan was stumped for an answer, not wishing to reply in a way that might seem disrespectful towards Chie's mother.

'It hadn't been founded at the time,' said Shibukawa, much to Banzan's relief.

'Ah-ha. Quite. Of course. That is something only a true historian would know, a historian who knows the period backwards.'

This high praise was drowned out by a chorus from the granddaughters.

'Lucky for you he was here, Grandad.'

'You wouldn't have known what to say otherwise.'

This made everybody laugh, and Banzan smiled with such sweetness that at last Shibukawa could see there must be something genuinely attractive in his character. It was presumably this smile that had persuaded politicians to become his pupils. Unfortunately, this small surge of goodwill towards the elderly calligrapher was probably what induced Shibukawa to behave less cautiously than he had up until now, for he began to talk about the obituaries Naito and the others had written about Soejima. No sooner had he embarked on the subject, however, than he noticed that Banzan was looking far from happy, despite making an obvious effort to hide his feelings. Shibukawa realised he must be saying the wrong thing, but it was too late to get off the subject now.

'I've only read the official biography of Soejima, but I was struck by the originality of those obituaries. They are certainly very well done—no doubt about it—but they are also surprisingly anti-establishment. That's what they all seem to have in common—they are all critical of the major establishment figures. Obviously I'm not saying there's anything critical in what they write about Soejima himself; they all admire, even worship him. But towards the leading members of the establishment the writers seem to have felt what one can only call disgust—disgust at their corruption, at their vulgarity ... at the depths to which public life had sunk under them. With the Russo-Japanese War going on, it was almost impossible to attack the government openly, and no opportunity seemed to lend itself to even minor criticism—until, by chance, they were faced with the death of a man who'd failed to toe the party line, who'd been critical of the government, who had also been totally incorruptible—a man of model behaviour and high culture, the perfect vehicle for their needs: Taneomi

Soejima. So the journalists of the time, or at least those who weren't prepared to suck up to the government, took the opportunity to express their discontent ... however cautious they may have been in the way they put it. That's what makes those obituaries really come alive, or at least that's one reason why they were able to excel themselves.'

Shibukawa paused at this point, clearly expecting some kind of response, but Banzan said nothing, merely raising his cup to his lips. The sisters also remained silent, obviously realising their grandfather must be upset, or at least that something was up, even if they didn't know what. Only Chie seemed to find the situation amusing, smiling mischievously, while Shibukawa, unable to understand why the silence should continue for so long, began to wonder if Banzan could have heard properly. Since it would be rude just to repeat what he'd said, he decided the only sensible course was to develop his argument.

'I think this explains why all the obituaries are printed in full in the first chapter of the biography—because they were basically anti-establishment, and critical of the government. Of course, you could also say they provide a convenient introduction for the reader, giving a précis of the broad facts of Soejima's life. Then again, the author of the biography, Kanji Maruyama, had been a journalist himself and was interested in that kind of material. All of this is true—yet surely the most important thing is their common attitude towards the authorities. Maruyama had been working for the *Osaka Asahi* when an editorial (not written by him) was picked on for being irreverent, and there was a ridiculous attempt by the government to accuse the paper of lèse-majesté and close it down for good. The incident had some funny name I can't quite remember ... ah, yes, the "White Rainbow Affair". Anyway, some members of a right-wing group actually tied the chairman of the paper to a stone lantern in his garden, with the result that the *Asahi* published an apology, saying they would take a firmly patriotic line from now on—I'm sure you've all heard about it. A number of journalists resigned from the paper in protest, and one of them was Maruyama. Well, it's just one story from an age when freedom of speech didn't exist, but you can see how a safe subject like the biography of Taneomi Soejima must have seemed the perfect outlet for all that frustration pent up inside him, and I'm sure that's why he undertook it.'

To make it clear that he'd finished, Shibukawa raised his cup to his lips and took two sips, and when it was refilled for him by the younger granddaughter he drank it straight down and set the cup in front of him. But still Banzan said nothing, remaining as expressionless and silent as ever. Chie gave another little smile, apparently unconcerned, and Shibukawa found himself at a loss, assuming it was now a matter of seeing who could hold out the longest. He also felt he'd been stupid to hold forth on a subject like that in front of someone who made his living by fawning on the powerful. Perhaps he had even harmed Yumiko's cause, for the great man was unlikely, in such a bad mood, to look on her case with favour, let alone do anything about it. But he couldn't help that now—the best he could do would be to get the present situation under control. Try as he might, however, he couldn't think of a way out. Eventually it was the elder sister who came to his rescue, turning to her grandfather and, for the first time, speaking in a normal, grown-up way, without the usual 'Grandad'.

'It's getting rather late, and I'm sure you must be tired. If you don't feel like talking any more, then I think the best thing would be for you to say goodnight to everybody and go to bed.'

But Banzan made no response to this either, stubbornly refusing to open his mouth. Since her sister's attempt to take charge of her grandfather hadn't worked, the younger girl now directed her efforts at Shibukawa, using a prim tone of voice that contrasted strongly with her earlier conversation.

'Professor Shibukawa, I do hope you'll excuse us, but Grandfather has reached a very advanced age and tires easily nowadays.'

Obviously the old man, now in his mid-eighties, was in the habit of sinking into silence whenever he felt offended, and the granddaughters were practised at handling such situations. But their transformation was nonetheless remarkable, and Shibukawa saw an astonished look on Chie's face which he was aware only mirrored his own.

It seemed reasonable, given the combined efforts of the two sisters, to expect Banzan to respond at last, but he remained as po-faced as ever, as if he hadn't heard a word they'd said, only eventually muttering:

'Prepare my writing things. Something from the age of chivalry has come to mind.'

The girls bowed at this instruction, going off together to do as they were bidden. Chie tried to pour Banzan another drink, but he firmly declined, although Shibukawa accepted her offer and was quietly sipping from her cup when the two girls at last came back, ushering Chie and Shibukawa into another room, their voices now having recovered their earlier teasing lightness. This room was in pure Japanese style, not very big, with a large framed piece of writing proclaiming Banzan's residence here on the facing wall, the left wall being taken up with bookshelves full of boxes of brushes, paper, folding copybooks and so on, while on the right wall were three hanging scrolls with temporary mountings. Some thick writing paper had been laid out on a faded red writing cloth spread on the tatami, and at its side the granddaughters had set a large inkstone and were busy adding water and rubbing away to produce the right consistency of ink. The old artist faced the red cloth. The granddaughters sat at the top end of the paper, slightly to one side. Chie and Shibukawa sat behind Banzan, one on either side of him. There were no cushions in the room.

Finally, Banzan dipped his brush into the ink and, having prepared himself for the moment of truth, raised the upper half of his body and, with his left hand pressing lightly down and slightly forward on the cloth, wrote one line of five characters in a flowing hand, producing tasteful variations in the thickness of the ink over the whole line. Next to the five large characters he recorded in much smaller writing that this had been done by old Banzan at the age of eighty-five. Then he quietly laid down his brush and read aloud what he'd written:

' "Stealing the fragrance skilfully with one hand." '

'Is that all?' the elder sister asked.

'Yes. And it is well done,' he replied; and the strength suddenly seemed to drain out of him.

The girls took the paper carefully in their hands, stood up, and stuck it to the wall. The elder one turned to the old man, who now, in his rumpled kimono, seemed to have lost all dignity and looked much smaller than he had before, and asked:

'Well, what's that supposed to mean?'

The other girl remained by the wall, complaining that she couldn't understand either, then crooked the index finger of her right hand in a suggestive gesture and wondered aloud if that was what it was all about. This made Shibukawa laugh out loud, even though he was no wiser than they were.

The old man himself said, 'Smile, but make no reply', glancing at Chie as he did so. The elder granddaughter noted this.

'Look, Chie knows what it means.'

'Very suspicious,' said the other, but Chie smiled and shook her head. So the younger girl stood there and wondered again, while her sister brought the poem cards from the living room, stamped them with Banzan's seal, then asked what she should do with the one on the wall.

'That one's not to be given with the others. That's for the Memorial Hall,' he said. 'Well, now I trust you will allow this old man to take his leave of you. Miss Chie, if I am still alive, I hope we will eat sushi together in Ginza next year. Stealing the fragrance skilfully with one hand has given me great pleasure.'

Saying this, he drifted out of the room, while Shibukawa gazed after him as if the clue to this mystery were disappearing before his very eyes, thinking also, as he watched him go, that the act of writing had been some form of retaliation, presumably for what Banzan had assumed to be Shibukawa's criticism of his way of life (though none had been intended) in the account of the obituaries written for Soejima. Another, less immediate reason may have been that Banzan had expected Chie to come alone, and had been very disappointed when she brought a young man along with her. He'd been told about this in advance, so it was unreasonable to get annoyed about it, but then old men were forgetful and liked having their own way. However, even if these two reasons made sense, he still couldn't work out what the actual retaliation consisted of. Certainly the quotation from a poem (if that was what it was) was meant to convey something unpleasant to him but, not having that sort of erudition, he didn't understand what. The old man had expected him to know, perhaps, the implication of the two words 'stealing' and 'fragrance'—some ancient custom no doubt, some pleasure that the old man craved—and this was linked to something he'd said to Chie when they were alone together, or even perhaps to something he'd done: the words could otherwise have no effect on Shibukawa, and thus be no form of revenge. But what could Banzan have done? Chie didn't seem upset at all—indeed, quite the reverse—so it could hardly have been anything too terrible. He was still puzzling over this when their taxi arrived and the two of them got into it.

Shibukawa gave the driver Chie's address, but she found she didn't feel like going straight home. She was exhausted after the hours spent in that strange house, and now felt a sense of relief, as well as an odd kind of loneliness, the reason for which she couldn't understand. In addition to this somewhat confused state of mind, there was also the knowledge that if she went home no one would be there, as her mother and great-aunt were going to pay their visit to the prime minister this evening and would stay overnight in a hotel in Akasaka, while her grandmother was attending a reunion in Hakone.

'Anyway,' she said, 'he's promised to do what he can. He said he'd phone tomorrow. It's very nice of him.'

'Great,' said Shibukawa. 'It should go all right, then—we hope. And your mother and great-aunt are going tonight?'

'Yes.'

'How about the indifferent professor?'

'That's tonight, too. In Sendai.'

'Let's just hope one of these three cards turns up trumps.'

'You're doubtful about it?'

209

'Historians have to be sceptical—it goes with the job.'

'So it could all turn out to have been a waste of time.'

'It could. Banzan certainly seemed to have it in for me. There's no knowing what he'll do.'

'Suddenly going all quiet like that.'

'Mm. And those two girls were odd—all that "Grandad" stuff, then a complete change of tone when they wanted to tick him off.'

They talked about their three hosts for a while, then Shibukawa said:

'I couldn't work out what he meant by "stolen fragrance".'

'Nor could I.'

'Did anything happen?'

'What do you mean?'

'Did he do anything to you ... with one hand?'

Watching her in the semi-darkness of the taxi's interior, he noticed her simply smile in response to his question.

'He must have done something skilful with his hand, I can work out that much. Still, it doesn't matter. If you won't tell me I can find out for myself.'

'How?'

'I'll look through some dictionaries when I get home. If it's not too difficult I should be able to crack the problem.'

'How many dictionaries will you look in?'

'A number.'

'What kind?'

'First the character dictionary, then those in Chinese—the *Dictionary of Ancient Chinese Usage*, things like that.'

'Can you read Chinese?'

'No. But I can sort of guess, just by looking at the characters. Apparently the Manchurian emperor—the "Last Emperor"— used to read Japanese newspapers that way.'

'It sounds fun. Could I watch?'

'You mean come to my place?'

'Yes.'

The idea made his heart leap, and he gave fresh instructions to the driver. One need hardly point out that Chie had never been to his flat before.

The block of flats in which Shubukawa lived was at the end of a cul-de-sac, a smallish building with an old-style gate before it. Beyond the gate was a small garden with a number of willow trees ranged to look like an avenue. Chie thought what a job it must be keeping the place tidy, seeing it was just about time for the leaves to fall. In the lobby she noticed a tray with empty bowls on it under the mail boxes, the remains of someone's dinner ordered from outside.

Shibukawa's place was on the fifth floor. It consisted of two rooms, the large one a combined study and bedroom, the smaller one used for storing books and other things. The large desk was occupied by a word processor, books, notebooks, magazines, empty beer and soft-drink cans, ties, pencils and crayons, a return postcard on which he'd not yet written a reply, a letter written by a man with extraordinarily bad handwriting (presumably it was a man), and a battered box of tissues. On a chair beside the desk were piles of Xeroxed papers, dictionaries, magazines, socks, shirts, and some empty bookcases. All in all, it looked as though he could hardly have had any visitors for ages. In remarkable contrast to this was the bed, which was neat and tidy, with obviously fresh sheets and pillowcases. Chie noticed how out of place this looked and wondered if he hadn't changed the sheets specially, on the off-chance that she might drop in on her way home. Of course, this intuition was correct. Shibukawa had changed the sheets and pillowcases precisely with that in mind, as he'd done on numerous occasions before, when she'd declined his invitations. That this evening had turned out differently perhaps indicated that a direct invitation had been the wrong way to go about it.

He transferred the contents of the chair to the floor, to allow her to sit down. He noticed she gave the room a cursory glance, and thought he should have some pictures on the walls, which made him think about the hanging scroll in Banzan's place and

211

how their first priority was to clear up the problem of the mysterious quotation. So he moved a number of things off the desk onto the floor as well, pushed the word processor up against the wall, and took down the index of the multi-volume *Chinese-Japanese Dictionary*. This he quickly consulted, before putting Volume I on the desk and flicking through its pages. He found what he was looking for, and pointed the place out to Chie:

Toko: To steal fragrance. To have an illicit affair.

She got that far, but the rest of the explanation, apparently involving some legend about a girl secretly giving some perfume to her lover, she only half grasped, while the quotation in Chinese that illustrated the story meant nothing to her.

'I just can't read it, I'm afraid. Like they say, it's Greek to me.'

'I'm not much good at it either. I took a basic course at university but that's about it. This dictionary doesn't make any concessions to non-specialists, either.'

He took down another three books, but these were all genuine Chinese dictionaries, published in China, which only made things worse, until he came across a reference to the work from which the quotation was taken, and found he had that particular book in a Japanese edition, with explanatory notes. The story was about a remarkably handsome young man who was invited to court, where he was spied by a young girl who immediately fell in love with him. She expressed her feelings in a poem, which her maid gave him, and to which he sent back an answer. The young girl was so pleased and happy that her father became suspicious, until one day he caught a whiff of a particularly fragrant perfume on the young man. The perfume apparently was one that only the emperor used, since it had been sent from the West (meaning India) to the Han emperor, but the girl had stolen some to give to her lover as a present. The girl's maid eventually told him the whole story, but it all ended quite happily, with the girl being allowed to wed her young man. Consequently, 'stealing fragrance' meant an (as yet) illicit relationship between a man and a woman.

'Very handy for a romance, the perfumes of Ind.'

'Yes,' said Shibukawa, smiling at her. 'Now we've got part of the puzzle. The only bit missing is what that old man did to you this evening ... with his hand.'

She hesitated at little, then said playfully:

'So that's what he was getting at.'

'Unless it was *you* who did something with your hand?'

'Don't be silly. No, it was him.'

'What, exactly?'

'Do I have to tell?'

'Of course you do.'

'Why?'

'Why? Well, let's put it like this. Firstly, as your guard and escort today I have a responsibility for anything that happens to you. Then there's the fact that I'm in love with you, and I want to know—okay, maybe that's not an acceptable reason. Thirdly, since we're trying to solve the mystery of the quotation together, it's only right that we should pool any information we may have. Your information is essential to the solution.'

'The third reason is fairly convincing. I'm not sure about the other two,' she said, her eyes shining.

As though compelled by the force of logic, Chie then told him what had happened.

'When we were left alone together we went and sat on the sofas. He suggested we sit together on the large one, but I said it would be easier if we faced each other on different sofas, and that's what we did. Then I asked him for his help on Mummy's problem.'

For some reason, she'd found it surprisingly difficult to summarise the controversial article for Banzan, though when she'd first read it—despite her mother's reluctance to show it to her—it had seemed pretty straightforward. Instead of trying, therefore, she decided to skip all the tricky parts and to concentrate instead on the implications of the affair—namely, that it was mixed up with the transfer of government land, that to use this as a lever was a clear infringement of the newspaper's right to freedom of expression, and that since the writer in question was a woman, it was an example of discrimination against members of her sex, which could mean the governing party losing a good part of the women's vote if it got out. Chie's explanation hadn't actually been quite as coherent as this, but anyway she'd ended up by saying that it should be stopped, and that Banzan should talk to two people in particular about it: to the former prime minister, who had been a pupil of his at university and even now was studying calligraphy under him; and to the man who, under the former prime minister's influence, had also become one of Banzan's students, the incumbent prime minister, Tamaru.

Banzan had thought about this for a while, then said:

'So you want me to tell them to stop meddling in the internal affairs of the paper—to stop blackmailing the proprietors and hand the land over...' He stopped and smiled before continuing. 'And if they don't let the paper have the land, women will start a riot and the government will fall...'

'Well, that's putting it rather bluntly, but yes, the end result would be something of that kind.' Banzan chuckled, and Chie added: 'But it's true, you know. They haven't been doing all that well recently, have they?'

Banzan closed his eyes, saying after further thought:

'All the same, it does seem rather a low-grade affair for me to intervene in, don't you think?'

'Does it?'

'Consider, my dear. In the past the ideal of every scholar in the East was to act as mentor to the head of state. It was with this aim in mind that Confucius and Mencius travelled to so many states offering their services to the princes who ruled them, although, as it happened, their services were always declined. In the case of our own country, certain scholars did indeed become mentors to those men who were, in effect, our kings, namely the shoguns, thus realising their deepest ambition. I myself have been tutor to two prime ministers. Consequently, one could say that I have performed an equivalent task. Most people no doubt think of me as a master of the art of calligraphy, but they are wrong. My aim is to teach the Wisdom of the East, by way of that art. My aim is to instruct the leader of this country in the spirit, the soul, of Oriental thought.'

'I see.'

'This being the case, my dear, where does that leave us? For a man dedicated to instructing his ruler, stooping to a matter of this kind would surely be a little—frivolous, shall we say?'

'Yes. I see your point,' Chie said, deciding to play along with him. 'But then it's surely to the advantage of this country that you should remain his teacher for as long as possible.'

'Well, you exaggerate perhaps a little there.'

'We don't know if the next prime minister will be one of your pupils or not. It could be somebody with no taste for that sort of thing at all.'

'Um...'

'It might be someone who would treat you in the way Confucius and Mencius were treated.'

'Uh.'

'For that reason, we need to keep the present cabinet for as long as possible, so that your ideas can have a lasting effect... So wouldn't it be worth having a word with the prime minister about all this?'

'So as not to suffer the fate of Confucius and Mencius? I see.'

Presumably the old man was pleased by the flattery (assuming he saw it as such), or perhaps he had intended to accept Chie's proposal all along and had been putting up a token resistance simply for the sake of appearances, because he smiled and said:

'Yes. You make a convincing case for it. What a clever child you are, my dear. That *is* certainly one way of looking at it, and it deserves serious consideration. Very well, I shall telephone both of them tomorrow.'

Chie felt a sense almost of anti-climax at the ease with which she'd succeeded, but she thanked him with all due deference and appreciation.

'No, no. Regard it as a small offering to that most rare of things in this day and age, a pearl of a woman.'

He waved his hand generously, but then the conversation took an awkward turn, with him noting that, despite his great admiration for her, Chie seemed to resemble none of the famous paintings of beautiful women, in either Western or Oriental art. Apparently searching his memory to find some masterpiece with which to compare her, he gave the names of a dozen works by different artists, including Botticelli's *Primavera* and Fujishima's *Butterfly*, most of which she couldn't place. Chie managed to swallow the notion of herself in the company of these world-famous beauties without too much embarrassment, and the conversation then shifted to famous film stars she didn't look like (Chie took the opportunity of mentioning Aeka Yanagi, but it seemed Banzan had never been particularly impressed by her). This led him to the conclusion that it was somewhere other than in the world of art or film that he would find the reason for the profound attraction he felt towards her. In fact, only last night, having woken around midnight, he thought he'd found an answer: it had dawned on him, apparently, that she must look like his mother, who had died when he was a baby, leaving behind only a tiny, blurred photograph.

'Your *mother*? Oh, you're making that up.'

'You think it's sophistry, do you? Well I studied the Chinese sophists when I was young, and I suppose this might show their influence.' For a moment the old man's fabrication perched on this elevated level, but soon descended as he followed it up with a request: 'Regardless of that, however, I wonder if I might mention a deep desire I have in my declining years, the longing of a man who never saw his mother's face?... I wonder if you would let me touch your tits?'

Chie was so startled by this that she too produced a less than perfectly genteel reply.

'What? What on earth do you think you're on about?'

But Banzan didn't seem to notice, and since he looked so serious Chie began to reconsider. This, after all, she quickly decided, was the man who was going to phone the prime minister and perhaps fix the question of the land transfer. Some token of appreciation was called for.

'All right, then,' she said, and stood up, thrusting her left breast forward slightly. 'But only from the outside.'

Banzan also stood up. He did so with such vigour that one might almost have supposed he was on the point of regaining—if not his youth—at least his middle age. He stood facing her, stooping slightly because of his considerable height. She watched the blotched skin of his grey face, the white hair, eyebrows, moustache, and stubbled chin approach, and then, slowly, he stretched out his hand, which closed on the nipple hidden beneath her thick kimono and thin underwear and, feeling the breast swelling in his palm, began to fondle it. His face turned crimson and his breathing became heavy, causing Chie some anxiety, although the pressure of his hand remained the same and there seemed no threat of violence. But just as she was thinking he'd probably had enough, he said, with a sad little smile and his hand still firmly in place:

'You know, my dear, this isn't really quite enough for me to remember my dead mother by. Couldn't I just slip it inside…?'

'No you could not.'

'I see.'

He accepted the refusal. Chie hadn't hesitated, knowing that if she conceded this line of defence, represented by the two layers of cloth between her breast and his hand, there was no end to what he might ask for. It might even result in his slipping his hand up her skirt (or, since she was wearing a kimono, her skirts).

The old calligrapher grunted in acquiescence, but then said he wanted to try the other side as well. She refused that, too, giving his hand a light tap which made him drop it with a little gasp.

'That's all now,' she said.

'All? All? After such fleeting contact with my mother's breast?'

As he muttered this, however, he lowered both hands obediently and sat down on the sofa again.

'Still, you have been most generous to me. As it says in the *Analects*, "From the hosts of heaven to savage tribes, compassion for the old prevails." A memorable line.'

This attempt to include satisfaction of his feeble sexual desires among the filial duties seemed a bit much to Chie, now seated on the other sofa.

'You see that as an expression of respect towards the old?'

'Certainly. The strange meeting, in this case, of two dutiful children.'

He may have been trying to make a joke, but even if he was it was so inane she wanted to protest. However, she realised if she did there was no knowing how he might respond, and decided to change the subject instead, saying she was beginning to feel hungry. This ploy worked well, enabling him to launch into an account of the tremendous reception he'd been given in China, due presumably to his role as mentor to Japan's prime minister, with a description of all the delicious food he'd been served there, and this led to his telling her which of the noodle shops in the area were best, and how the president (another friend of the prime minister's) of a large group of flour mills had sent him some very special instant noodles which it was just about impossible to get hold of in the shops; and finally he got on to the subject of sushi, at which point the other three had returned.

Having heard her out, Shibukawa breathed a sigh of relief, then grinned and said:

'So there was no illicit affair, after all.'

'Hardly likely, was it? said Chie, pouting. 'I think there must be something funny about that dictionary.'

'Well, that's as may be, but Banzan at least wasn't being funny. Anyway, Chinese poetry traditionally prefers obscurity and vagueness to clarity and realism, blurring everything as much as possible; that's why it makes so much use of the distant past. A poetic rhetoric that deals only with distant events permits considerable breadth of interpretation. So "stealing fragrance" can mean the act itself, and it can also mean putting one's hand on a girl's kimono.'

'Very good. A neat explanation.'

Shibukawa was pleased with the compliment.

'In the original story the girl steals some perfume. In Banzan's version, as written on the scroll, his hand steals your breast. If you think about it too much, the parallel falls apart, so the trick is not to bother—just take it as it comes.'

'Do you think it's a real quotation?'

'Hard to say. It fits the situation so well, maybe he made it up.'

'Why did he write it, then?'

'It was aimed at me. He was scoring a point—probably out of spite, trying to make me feel jealous.'

'I suppose so.'

'Of course he was.'

'He was annoyed about what you said about the Soejima obituaries?'

'Yes. Perhaps he thought I was trying to take his hero down a peg or two, although that wasn't my intention.'

'I suppose he'd never have thought in those terms himself.'

'He'd also have felt it was all a bit too relevant to his own case.'

'Funny way to show anger, though—just clamming up like that.'

'I found it interesting: an alternative way of demonstrating displeasure.'

'You were very patient with him.'

'I was?'

'Yes.'

'I didn't think I was. I thought you were. You were the one who got pawed, not me.'

They both laughed, then went on to discuss all three inhabitants of that eccentric household. They commented on how the two girls treated him like a circus animal, and decided it was possible, judging by their ages, that Banzan was actually their great-grandfather. By this stage they were imitating the way the old man and the two girls talked, which showed how glad they were to have got an awkward subject over with.

'Were you worried when you left me alone with him?'

'I'm not sure. In fact I felt more worried when I came back, wondering if something had happened. Then there was that quotation. It seemed to mean something I didn't much care for. By the way, just how much did he manhandle you?'

The girl stood up and turned so that her left breast was towards him; he stood up as well and placed his right hand on it. They both looked amused.

'A bit harder than that.'

'This much?'

'Yes—ah, now you're going too far.'

But she made no attempt to slap him down and, encouraged, he put his left hand on her other breast. Still she didn't resist, returning his gaze without flinching. Since she seemed to be accepting him, perhaps even tempting him, he took her in his arms and kissed her. Still she didn't object, and they both fell onto the bed. He started to slide his hand inside her kimono, but then remembered something and gave a shout, suddenly getting up.

'What's wrong?' she said.

'My hands are dirty. The dictionaries were covered in dust. I'll just go and wash them.'

Chie's response was to give a yelp of her own.

'What's the matter?' he asked.

'It's my kimono. I can't tie the sash myself.'

'You can't?... That *is* a blow... I know, let's go to a hotel, the kind where they have people to do that kind of thing for you.'

The girl thought a moment without saying anything.

'I know, we'll go home.'

'To your place?' he cried, wondering if she hadn't gone out of her mind. But she explained calmly:

'It's all right. There's nobody there. My mother and great-aunt are spending the night in a hotel after seeing the prime minister, and Grannie's at a reunion in Hakone.'

Realising the only place she could take her kimono off without having to put it back on was at home, he accepted this change of plan.

'I see. All right—let's do that.'

At that same moment Masako Yanagi and Yumiko Minami

were in their hotel room in Akasaka. That morning a message had come asking them to call at the prime minister's official residence at 2.00 A.M. Apparently the prime minister was in the habit of sleeping from ten at night until two in the morning, then getting up and working at his desk for a couple of hours, reading and signing documents, before returning to bed at four to sleep until seven. Yumiko was anxious to find out if Chie was home yet, and was going to phone her when Masako, who was watching television, told her it was about time she realised her daughter was grown up and let her look after herself. Yumiko dropped the idea of telephoning and joined her aunt in front of the television. It was 9.20 P.M., and a documentary about wild animals was showing. Rain was falling on the African veldt. The graceful shapes of a herd of gazelles appeared on the grassy plain. The rain suddenly stopped and a rainbow appeared in the grey sky. There were only three colours, red, yellow and light green, but the thick band filled the screen with an almost vertical arc. The two women, one seventy-five and the other forty-five, gasped at its beauty.

In Hakone, in *her* hotel room, Etsuko Minami and two other women lay on their stomachs on the bedding which had already been set out for the night, occasionally watching television but mainly absorbed in their conversation. They all wore the warm kimonos provided by the hotel. Etsuko's companions were the widow of a scholar and the wife of the president of a smallish company. The scholar's widow saw the rainbow on the screen out of the corner of her eye and told the other two to look. For a minute or so they were all silent. Then, when the scene changed to hippos bathing, the widow said:

'Wasn't that lovely!'

Etsuko agreed, and the president's wife said hesitantly:

'It's as if someone somewhere were saying they were sorry.'

'A gesture of apology, she thinks,' said the widow, and laughed.

'God shows he's sorry for what he's done by sending a rainbow, doesn't he?' asked Etsuko.

'Yes, he's supposed to. But it sounds rather silly when you put it like that,' mumbled the president's wife. She'd had the same feeble habit of immediately retracting what she'd said when they were at college together.

'Still, I know what you mean,' said Etsuko. And she did. Unlike the scholar's widow, she knew the woman had lost her two grandchildren in a traffic accident the year before.

Yokichi Toyosaki was drinking alone in a large room used for private functions in a restaurant called Kohagi in Sendai. The other rooms all seemed to be closed, and the chief secretary of the ruling party, Zenroku Sakakibara, had still not turned up. Toyosaki had expected something like this to happen, so had come prepared with three philosophical tomes (one German, one French, one English), but had chosen instead to read right through three weekly magazines left behind by previous guests.

Meanwhile, Banzan Onuma, waking in the middle of the night, drank some mineral water straight from the bottle and smacked his lips. Then he stared at the palm of his right hand for a while, obviously remembering the feel of Chie's breast. A frown passed across his face. There was something else, something he'd forgotten. He could remember making a promise to the girl, but not what the promise was. He tried all sorts of ways of remembering, but none of them worked, and after half an hour he started to feel sleepy again. Well, it hardly mattered. It had been some trivial affair, beneath the dignity of a man of his standing—mentor to princes. Confucius and Mencius would no doubt have disregarded it.

SEVEN

.
.
.

It was nearly 10·00 P.M. and Sakakibara still hadn't appeared. Yokichi Toyosaki had already had dinner and now sat waiting all alone in a room large enough for thirty people. On the long, low table that stretched almost the entire length of the room a half-moon lacquered tray had been placed before him, containing some dried cuttlefish, sliced fish sausage, chopsticks and a saké cup. A flask of saké was beside the tray, and he noted that it was his third. Occasionally the proprietress or a waitress came to fill his cup. The third bottle had been brought by the proprietress herself, who was wearing a well-coordinated outfit consisting of a blue striped kimono with a sash in various shades of persimmon, her hair held up by a long, jewelled pin. Her age (probably somewhere in the late thirties) and manner were also exactly what one would expect of this high-class, slightly shady establishment. After pouring his saké, she remained kneeling beside him (he was seated on a cushion) to keep him company, commenting:

'So you're pleading the cause of a fair lady. The chief secretary told me. How nice. How romantic.'

The way she spoke, with some amusement, indicated a fair degree of intimacy with the chief secretary, and Toyosaki felt obliged to respond.

'I hope you'll do some of the pleading, too,' he said with a laugh, holding out his small porcelain cup for more.

The lady produced a tiny name card, so he had to pass over his. She gave it a close inspection.

'A professor of philosophy. You have to be very clever to study philosophy, don't you?'

'Actually, the opposite is probably true.'

'You're just being modest.'

'Well, let me give you an example,' he said, holding up his saké cup. 'There must be at least thirty cups in this restaurant of exactly the same pattern and shape, but this one is still different from the others. It's both different and the same, being a cup. That's what's odd, you see: the way things are connected. Then there are all the saké cups in other parts of the country, with various shapes and patterns and colours—but all completely different, yet having in common the fact that they're all cups.'

'But that's rather obvious, Professor, surely?'

'Yes. Very obvious. And philosophy is just rethinking things that are perfectly obvious and taken for granted. It's not something that clever people do.'

She clapped her hands in delight and cried:

'What a clever explanation. That just shows how smart you are.'

Eventually, following her advice, he removed his tie and watch and got down to some serious drinking. The tie was a regimental one he'd bought in New York some years before; he had been standing in front of the window of a menswear shop, having arranged to meet Yumiko there, when the shop assistant happened to open the door, so he went in and bought the tie he'd been admiring. The wristwatch was a cheap thing he'd bought at an airport when he found he seemed to have mislaid his own. When he got home his old watch had turned up among the cleaning things under the sink, but he preferred his new, cheap one.

It is a characteristic of man's basic nature that time passes quickly when an attractive woman is serving him drinks, so it seemed only a short while until the chief secretary entered the room. He had on a dark suit of obviously expensive material, and his taste in shirts and ties seemed quite good, but his face showed little sign of any intelligence, and his features looked more rustic than cultured, perhaps even coarse. Toyosaki started to move to a more subservient posture, but the great man told him to stay as he was, sitting down in the place usually reserved for the most important guest.

'I apologise for being so late,' he said, bowing his head. He added: 'I've had dinner, but I could do with some dessert,' at the same time raising his haunches slightly so that the woman could slip his cushion into place. 'First let me give my regards to your wife for her kind support—and then let's get down to your problem,' he said, rather brusquely, so that Toyosaki, his tie still held in his hand, answered immediately:

'A member of the editorial writing staff of the *New Daily* is to be transferred to the promotions department, after pressure has been applied from a number of sources. Somehow we feel—'

Sakakibara grabbed the cup from his tray and had it filled for him.

'Yes, yes. You want this move stopped and the government land exchange deal renewed,' he said, filling in the points not yet mentioned by the professor, and indicating that no more need be said. Then he thrust out his right hand with the palm upward.

'Still—can't be done for free, you know. Let's have it. Give.'

He moved his hand up and down in front of Toyosaki, while the professor, completely in the dark as to what was being asked of him, and with an anxious expression on his face, tentatively proffered the tie he was holding in his hand.

'No, no, not that,' snarled Sakakibara, with a dismissive wave of his hand.

Toyosaki then slid his watch forward, equally tentatively, wondering why on earth the man could possibly want it when he already had a watch of some obviously expensive foreign make glittering on his left wrist.

'No, not that, either,' he said. The proprietress was finding it hard to keep from laughing, and Toyosaki had to resort to a direct question:

'What, then?—if you wouldn't mind telling me.'

Sakakibara gave a wry smile, had another drink, then explained. He said he really did want to help out, because of the close ties between them, but to get the situation back to how it had been before would require an enormous amount of effort and sacrifice. His wife had been annoyed by the vague answers he'd given her when they'd talked about the situation, so he would tell the professor straight: some sort of recompense was in order, whatever form it took. There had been certain changes in the situation, as he'd heard only yesterday that the old man with the wisdom teeth, who was always poking his nose into party business and hated the *New Daily* and had been heavily involved in the editorial affair, was seriously ill in hospital. Still, to get everyone else involved to drop the issue would take a lot of hard work, and when he thought about it, well, he just wasn't prepared to do it for nothing. He was only being realistic; as far as he was concerned, people shouldn't be expected to do something for nothing.

The professor swallowed, then asked:

'Some suitable recompense?'

'Yes.'

'You mean money, or some kind of … gift?'

'Yes. Money or a gift.'

'But I don't have any money, and I wouldn't be able to lay my hands on any.'

Sakakibara drained his cup again.

'That's all right, Professor. A gift would do.'

'But I don't have anything I could give you, either. I have a few books, but nothing of any value, just plain editions of philosophical works, and with my notes inside, anyway. Naturally if they were Bergson's or Wittgenstein's notes, they would be worth something, but they're only mine … and you couldn't even fool anyone, either, since I was unwise enough to write in Japanese.'

The fact that the books might be of higher value if the annotations were in a foreign language was, however, of no interest to the chief secretary.

'The word "gift" has a wide meaning, doesn't it? I don't mind what you come up with. It could be information. I could do with

226

some good information, if you could supply it—that would be all right.'

'Information?' the professor bleated. 'Really? I could certainly give you information of a kind, but I don't see how it would be worth anything to you. I could tell you who's probably going to get the Nishida Philosophy Prize this year, for example, but I don't suppose that would mean much. I don't imagine you really want to know about the power struggle in the Japan Philosophical Society, either, and why the philosophy chair in the Japan Academy is still vacant. Or the story about the Japanese philosopher, whose name I think you probably know, whose letters were going to be collected after he died. The project was suddenly abandoned when it was discovered he had been in the habit of writing love letters to a number of women, all on the same date, and absolutely identical in content. "Today the smoke rises once again over Mt. Asama, like my love for…"—that sort of thing, sent from Karuizawa to three or four women.'

'That's not a bad idea. I've sent postcards with identical wording to constituents, but I've never thought of doing the same with love letters. Mm … his love was like a smouldering volcano, was it?'

Sakakibara seemed impressed, but not in the way the professor had intended, and he frowned.

'You find that amusing, do you?' He was, in fact, starting to lose his temper, and he emptied his cup in one gulp. 'Look, Mr Sakakibara, if you're going to refuse, just come out and say so, will you? You don't have to be coy about it. It's absurd to expect an ill-paid scholar to be able to produce money or other objects of value, nor is there any likelihood of my being in possession of the kind of information that might be of use to you. It's pretty obvious you're making these demands in order to give yourself an excuse for refusing.'

'No, I'm afraid you've got me wrong there. I'm not just trying to get out of it. What's at stake here is what you might call my philosophy of life.'

'Your philosophy of life?'

227

'Yes. If I'm obliged to any person I like to fulfil that obligation. I don't like to say no. But I'm not prepared to do something for nothing. I think it's wrong to do something for nothing—I think it's bad for both parties involved.'

'Oh…'

'This belief was hammered into me during my political apprenticeship. You could call it the cornerstone of Japanese conservative politics.'

'You could?' said the professor, oddly impressed in spite of himself. 'All right, if you say so. But it doesn't alter the fact that I have nothing to offer. I have no weekend cottage. My car is very old and run-down.'

'You must have something I could use. Some really out-of-the-way information. Some forecast about the future,' he said, raising his cup to his lips again.

'Nothing. No money, no gifts, no information.'

'Some method of improving my golf handicap?'

'I don't play golf.'

After making this blunt reply, Toyosaki happened to notice that the woman who ran the place, still kneeling at the chief secretary's side, had her index finger pointed at her head and was winking energetically at him. This was apparently a broad hint that he should use his brains. He nodded to acknowledge her assistance, and said:

'Well, since thinking is my profession, perhaps I could offer you a few ideas in exchange—ideas that you could actually put to use.'

'Yes, that would do fine. In fact, that was just the kind of thing I had in mind.'

'Would you give me a little time, then? Time to think?'

Sakakibara nodded, then said to the proprietress that they could get in some practice in the meantime, and the two of them stood up and moved to the far side of the room where there was a large gold screen. Toyosaki didn't mean to watch, but he couldn't help noticing that the woman then produced a white plastic stick, of the kind used for beating the dust out of quilts, and handed it to Sakakibara. He grasped this somewhere around the middle, holding it horizontally, and assumed a semi-crouching posture in front of the screen. He seemed to have closed his eyes. Then there came the melancholy strains of some film music, the name of which Toyosaki couldn't quite recall at first but finally realised was the opening theme for the Zatoichi series, a popular TV programme of the sixties and seventies which recorded the amazing sword-fighting exploits of a priest-like blind masseur and gambler. To one side was a karaoke machine providing the accompanying words, which the chief secretary began to read aloud (presumably he'd now reopened his eyes), although his recitation was so wooden that it quite destroyed any emotional impact they might have had.

> Outcasts are we,
> Walking the back roads beyond the Law;
> Gamblers, hired swords, that's what we are,
> Despised and feared the whole world over...

At this point the proprietress of Kohagi burst into song, in a voice that was better suited to 'Funiculi, funicula' or 'Santa Lucia' than to some tired, sentimental Japanese ditty of this sort, while Sakakibara performed a kind of mime. It occurred to Toyosaki that the explanation for all this must be that the politician was an appalling singer, and that since karaoke was such an important feature of supporters' meetings (a haiku poet from his university had assured him that even at haiku gatherings nowadays karaoke skills were what really mattered), he would normally be obliged to sing, and either he or the restaurant woman had come up with this clever way round the problem.

> Refrain, you must, from such futile acts—
> Tell me about it, some other time—
> Relying on smells, relying on sounds,
> Cutting them down, one after another—
> Grief in the shoulders, grief in the shoulders.

At 'Refrain, you must', the chief secretary made the shape of a

229

cross with his forearms, while at 'such futile acts' he gave a casual, dismissive wave of the right hand. 'Tell me about it' was accompanied by a gesture less easy to interpret, involving putting his hands to his mouth and then stretching his arms out in a circular, all-embracing movement; Toyosaki assumed this wasn't in fact meant to be understood as blowing kisses, but was supposed to suggest the sort of word balloon that comes out of people's mouths in comic strips. At 'some other time' he put both hands on his swordstick (or quilt beater), ready to draw the blade from its wooden sheath, and the next two lines allowed a great deal of swishing about, until finally he let his shoulders droop heavily at the repetition of 'Grief in the shoulders' and plodded about a bit, becoming a blind masseur again rather than a brisk dispatcher of his enemies. Then he suddenly snatched at the mike and said:

Ah, how vile a trade is ours.

The woman switched off the karaoke machine and proceeded to comment on his performance.

'Sir, as soon as you've finished cutting them down, you're supposed to put the sword back in its sheath, the way Zatoichi does.'

'Okay, okay,' he said, going through the motions again, this time to copious praise.

Toyosaki, watching this spectacle unfold against the gold screen, gradually lost himself in meditation. Some time later, when he became aware of his surroundings again, he saw the woman coming in his direction, but only to remove two roses from the bowl placed in the alcove and return with them to the karaoke machine, where she picked up the mike, said 'Now let's try section three', and switched it on again.

Refrain, you must, from such sinful acts,
Those heartless deeds, beyond contempt—
But the blossoms scatter, the flowers fall,
By the flash of the sword that cuts as it will,
In the setting sun, in the setting sun.

At 'the blossoms scatter' the lady threw the two roses, which she'd so far kept concealed, high into the air, and the chief secretary hacked away at them, his eyes still closed, scoring a direct hit on one and sending it flying towards the screen, which the red flower struck with a small thud before falling limply to the floor. The politician then raised his hand to shield his eyes from 'the setting sun', no doubt dazzled by its low rays, although since Zatoichi was supposed to be blind this didn't make much sense. However, with this gesture the performance came to an end, and the woman clapped her hands. Toyosaki also applauded, then said:

'Sorry to have kept you waiting, Mr Sakakibara. I think I've got my ideas sorted out now.'

The chief secretary had worked up a sweat with his swordplay, so he now removed both jacket and waistcoat and returned to his seat, where he took a long swig of beer before telling the philosopher to go ahead.

'What I am going to put forward,' said Toyosaki, 'is an idea that goes to the very heart of Japanese politics, namely the question of the constitution. I'm not sure if anyone has already made the suggestion I intend to make, and even if it has been made, no doubt it was done anonymously. In a nutshell, I propose that the constitution be abolished.'

The chief secretary was unimpressed.

'Constitutional reform—everybody's always on about that,' he said, thinking this academic must be very out of touch if he was unaware of the row that had been going on for over forty years now about whether to change the constitution or keep it as it was.

'No,' Toyosaki replied. 'I'm not talking about reforming the constitution. I'm talking about abolishing it—getting rid of it.'

The chief secretary still looked dubious.

'But every country has a constitution. It would have to be a very backward … I mean a very developing country that didn't have one.'

'There is one country among the advanced nations that doesn't.'

'Which?'

'The United Kingdom.'

'Ah, yes. I forgot about that. Britain doesn't have a constitution. Mmm ... not a bad idea. Do the same as the British. Not bad at all,' he said, brightening up. 'Yes, that could go down quite well. When people start complaining about the imperial family they soon shut up if you tell them the royals are the same. Not just that, either. One of my relations, an old fellow, really hated the mini-skirt, but he stopped complaining once he learned the fashion started in England.'

'I thought it was France,' the proprietress said.

'No, England. Didn't you know?' the chief secretary admonished her before turning to the philosopher again. 'Yes, your idea might just work. If we lost all that pacifist rubbish in article nine, we could go to war again if we felt like it. Right—so we drop all talk about revision and go for abolition instead, in line with British ideas on the subject. It's certainly worth thinking about.'

But Toyosaki's reply put a damper on the chief secretary's enthusiasm.

'No, as far as the right to make war is concerned, there are too many risks involved. The real point is the abolition of the written constitution and replacing it with an unwritten one based on the experience of the Japanese people during the forty years and more since the war ended, in which such things as respect for human rights and the preservation of peace would presumably play a part.'

'I see.'

'Britain has no written constitution, but it has executed one king and expelled others, and these acts reflect the wisdom and experience of the nation as a whole. This, in effect—a combination of wisdom and experience—is the constitution of the country. If we were to do the same, then the wisdom and experience acquired by the Japanese since the war would be our constitution, taking the place of the present document. By these standards, the armed forces would become an acknowledged fact, although whether they should be sent to serve abroad is another matter. That's something the general public would need to think about.'

Sakakibara greeted this with some scepticism.

'In that case, what's the point of abolishing the written constitution? What reason is there?'

'There are two. Firstly, there's a section in it that no longer corresponds with matters as they now stand.'

'You mean about not making war?'

'No, I'm thinking of the preface.'

'What part of the preface?'

'The preface states the principles that are to govern our way of life: harmony with all nations, peace, democracy, that sort of thing. And we've stuck to those principles, of course. In particular we've not sold arms abroad, and that's a real achievement. To have reached this degree of prosperity without selling weapons of war is remarkable. But there's something missing, something that goes with those principles—in fact something that precedes them: a more basic, a more fundamental idea.'

'Namely?'

'The idea of exchange.'

'Exchange? Exchange of goods?'

'That's right. What goes on at the end of the year and in the summer.'

'You really feel something like that should be put into the preface to the constitution?'

'It's tremendously important. It's the way we've been living for centuries.'

Professor Toyosaki explained his views to the now bewildered chief secretary by means of the following lecture.

First of all, one had to think about the normal, everyday life of the average Japanese person. It was dominated by the concept of exchange. When you first met someone, you formally exchanged name cards; if you forgot to do so, disastrous consequences could follow. In July and December you sent gifts and got gifts in return; you sent them to the people you knew, your relations, your friends, your superiors. It was a nationwide practice, encouraged by the government and private enterprise, with bonuses being paid to cover the cost. If the practice didn't exist, department stores and delivery services would all go bankrupt.

233

There were other occasions for gift-giving, inevitably involving exchange. Farewell gifts of money for people going on journeys, who would bring presents back with them. The offering of similar gifts at funerals and the receiving of some token in return; gifts given at weddings, again with something given back. Then there was money for children at the New Year, which they returned on Mother's and Father's Day; women giving chocolate to men on St Valentine's Day, returned by the men in the form of underwear on 'White Day' (a Japanese invention which admittedly wasn't all that widespread). One could think of other examples—at concerts, for example, the performers received bouquets from both the management and the audience, something you didn't see in Europe. Kabuki actors threw small towels to their audience, and the women in the sword-fighting scenes in vaudeville shows received money wrapped in twists of paper that were thrown onto the stage. In Sumo the wrestler who has just won offers some water to the next wrestler; then, as he retreats up the gangway, people touch him for luck. The yakuza who has done something wrong cuts off his finger and presents it to his boss. And we give money to our gods and buddhas. Contemporary Japan is the empire, not of signs, but of gifts.

In comparison with this, people in the West wouldn't seem to be particularly keen on presents. Of course, they give them—at Christmas, on birthdays and so on—but the sense of reciprocity is nothing like as strong as it is in Japan, and the presents are much smaller. They are certainly not given on every conceivable occasion, as happens here. The gifts exchanged on the occasion of a death, for example, have no equivalent. Also, the cost of the gifts is inevitably much less.

An acquaintance of his, Toyosaki said, a young student of English literature, spent a year at Oxford or Cambridge—he couldn't remember which—and was invited to an Englishman's house for dinner. He asked a friend what he should take, and was told a bottle of wine. The lady of the house, however, nearly had a fit when she saw the expense he'd gone to, even though he had actually chosen something cheaper than he'd have offered at a similar occasion in Japan.

'Let me give you another example,' Toyosaki went on. 'A Frenchman I know—an engraver—has been living in Kyoto, married to a Japanese woman, for thirty years, and Japanese behaviour, such as expressing your opinion in a roundabout way and always smiling cheerfully, has become second nature to him. As a result, he naturally sends presents to people in July and December, but because these are relatively inexpensive he has acquired a reputation for meanness. The fact is, though, that he isn't mean, but French: he hasn't yet become totally Japanese.

'When I mentioned name cards, you looked doubtful, but this habit of giving cards to all and sundry is something only we do. Not all that long ago, for example, a girl in Thailand went around claiming to be Japanese, and managed to take any number of people in, just by using a name card. Interestingly enough, the practice of exchanging cards on first acquaintance originated in China, but has died out there; it's only with us that it survives.

'Given this national characteristic, the Japanese economy can be said to be kept going by gift-giving. I've already mentioned department stores and delivery services, but there are various other businesses, making things from laver to dairy products and tea bags, that are wholly dependent on the income from gifts, as also are the manufacturers of string, paper and other things used in wrapping them up. And what knocked the bottom out of the securities companies was compensatory payments made to favoured customers—yet another instance of gift-giving. Another is the way firms give top posts to former civil servants from the relevant ministries.

'Politics is the same. It may seem odd to be saying this to someone in active service such as yourself, but I hope you won't mind. Democratic politics are based upon free elections, but the electoral system in this country is dominated by the flow of money. The candidate gives money to the electors, and in return the electors give him their votes. Admittedly, this sort of bribery is forbidden by law, but you have to be really unlucky to be arrested for it, and even if arrests do take place the system is such that the candidate himself avoids any kind of punishment. It's also common for candidates to take coachloads of people from their district to hot-spring resorts or on guided tours of the Diet building, and the number of people who repay such generosity with their vote is probably larger than those who receive money directly. Neither is the custom particularly frowned upon before nomination. No doubt my own wife has enjoyed such visits after joining your supporters' group.

'Since our elections seldom let the voter hear any actual discussion of policies, and since the policies themselves are drawn up by the traditional Japanese process of compromise and negotiation as a solution to all problems, it isn't surprising that votes are decided in a similar way. This applies even when a candidate dies, for example. Whether a progressive or a conservative, his place is taken by his son or wife, and if people cast their vote for his successor it has less to do with sympathy than custom—the custom in this case of offering consolatory gifts at funerals.

'More obvious forms of gift-giving, however, can be seen in the way large corporations provide Diet members with cars, even secretaries. Then, within the system itself, faction leaders provide their supporters with money and jobs. The reason why our ministers stay in office for such short terms is because the supporters of the other factions want to get in on the act as well. Only when the faction leaders all work in concert can a prime minister be found, and presumably this involves a phenomenal amount of gift-giving.

'The government's agricultural policy is essentially one of buying cheap rice at high prices to keep the farmers happy, while regional policy takes the simple form of providing cities, towns and villages with large sums of money. This gift-giving even goes on between the government and the opposition, and there is only one large newspaper that hasn't received land from the government. Japanese foreign policy is little more than a matter of handing out cash to various countries. In other words, one can confidently say that Japanese politics in all its functions is simply a matter of donations.

'Now, how has this strange phenomenon come about? The question is obviously a difficult one, but I can only assume the answer to be that modern Japan is a country in which there remain numerous vestiges of the past, not only on the surface but deep down. We tend to concentrate on those aspects of our society which are the result of modernisation, but the reality is a hopeless confusion of the old and the new.

'Ancient Japan saw gift-giving as a form of contractual obligation between two parties. The traveller filled a special bag with neatly cut strips of silk, hemp, or paper, and left handfuls of them as an offering to the guardian deity of travellers. The well-known lines by Sugawara in the *One Hundred Poems* anthology, about gathering fallen leaves and offering them in place of these strips, are an apology for having had to leave home in a hurry, without being able to make the proper preparations. These scattered tokens represented a kind of spell cast by the traveller, since his soul was in some way attached to them, and the tutelary deity responded by guaranteeing the traveller's safety. The exchange was a ratification of the relationship between gods and men and was thus, in effect, a contract.

'The simplest example of the contractual nature of gift-giving can be seen in the medieval hiring system, which took place once a year on the first of August (by the old calendar, of course). The newly employed or re-employed apprentice would give a small token of thanks to his employer, in the hope that the goodwill shown him so far would continue. During the thirteenth and fourteenth centuries, this custom spread to the warrior class in the Kanto area, and in the following period it reached a point where things of great value—swords, gold and silver, horses—were given by the clan lords to the shogun in return for various favours. Thus a contractual relationship, whereby protection was offered in exchange for loyalty and vice versa, was expressed in the exchange of gifts.

'This method of establishing ties between people remained

intact during the Edo period, up to the middle of the nineteenth century, and indeed persists to the present day. Since ancient times the Japanese have lived in small, enclosed communities, in a state of constant anxiety about their relationships with their neighbours, obsessed with giving gifts in order to receive them, thus constantly renewing the links between each other. If this renewal did not take place every six months, there would be concern about their standing, which is how the habit of giving things in the middle and at the end of the year became fixed; and underlying this habit, one can see quite clearly the earlier contractual custom of making offerings to the gods. The habit of giving presents, year in and year out, to these most important of neighbours made it a natural progression to create similar contracts with their purely human neighbours, and for the idea of breaking such an agreement to be unlikely, even unthinkable. The very wrappings of our presents have a religious feeling to them, as ritualistic as the seal we stamp on all our documents, and the inevitable reciprocation has a similar incantatory quality, as if all these acts were the casting of lucky spells. Our society functions in accordance with all these contracts, creating a structure not unlike the elaborate networks of the express delivery services.

'Now, why should Western societies be less concerned with giving presents? After all, if we go back to the Graeco-Roman period we find enough offerings being made to the gods—meat, cakes, incense, clothing, jewels and so on—for it to seem likely that the same kind of exchange was going on between mortals as well. But just as the advent of Christianity led to offerings to other gods being forbidden, so one can assume that the exchange of gifts between people also declined. At least, that seems a reasonable supposition. The fact is, Christianity could hardly acknowledge the existence of the giver's soul in the gift he gave, since for Christians the soul resides in one place, fixed and immovable.

'So it seems strange that there should be no reference to the essence of our national character in the preface to our constitution, when that part of it is supposed to declare the basic policies and aims of our people. The reason for this omission is simple enough: our constitution was created with the United States in mind, where the giving of presents is seen as a purely private affair carried out on only a minor scale. But it is nonetheless an oversight. We are a nation in thrall to gift-giving. That is our national character. No doubt there are instances where it is done to excess, and excess should, of course, always be corrected, but that is still how we are. It may not be something to be proud of, but neither need we be ashamed. It is also a fact—one might even say a well-established fact—that this propensity has been responsible for many years now of peace and prosperity.

'I admit it would be very difficult to write this into the constitution. No constitution in the world mentions the exchange of gifts in its basic outline, and it seems fair to conclude that the subject is not readily amenable to formal expression. Somehow, it just wouldn't work. Our first "constitution", drawn up by Prince Shotoku in the eighth century, with its seventeen articles, managed only to hint at the truth about gift-giving in a vague admonition to value harmony. That being the case, the wisest plan seems to be to follow the British example, by doing without one, thus saving ourselves the trouble of spelling it out. The British national character, like our own, preserves many ancient aspects, starting with the monarchy. One assumes it was for this reason—that such aspects could never be expressed in writing—that they didn't create a fixed, written constitution. We should learn from this wise and realistic attitude.

'My second reason for wishing to abolish the constitution springs from a desire for the Japanese people to learn to think for themselves. Up until now, all our debates on the subject have been conducted solely in terms of what is or isn't contained in this document. But this respect for what is simply a set of black ink marks on sheets of white paper amounts almost to a kind of fetishism. From now on we need to form our attitudes on the basis of actual experience, not in accordance with the constitution but with our own history since the war, and with our hopes for the future. As I see it, that experience and the lessons learned from it must lead to the following conclusions. First of all, a belief in the paramount importance of human rights; this, I think, nobody would deny. Secondly, a belief that under no circumstances should we make war on another country, nor sell the weapons that allow war to be waged. If people don't agree with that, then the question must be discussed; if, after exhaustive debate, a viewpoint of which one cannot approve prevails, well, one ought nevertheless to go along with it. Instead of conforming to a written constitution, or to arbitrary interpretations of that constitution, in matters both physical and spiritual, it would be infinitely better for our political life to conform to ideas we have worked out for ourselves: not by discussing the wording of a text, but by thinking about reality.

'And that,' the professor concluded, 'is why I believe we'd be better off getting rid of the thing.' And he asked the proprietress of Kohagi for a glass of beer, which he consumed in a series of gulps. Sakakibara, perhaps excited by this drinking feat, also asked for more beer, but downed only one mouthful.

'Very interesting, Professor. One surprise after another. So gift-giving is the thing... Mm. I suppose you could see the eight-headed serpent in those terms, too.'

'You mean that ancient myth of ours, Yamata no Orochi?'

'Yes. When Susanowo made his sister Amaterasu angry, he was exiled to Izumo, was he not? There he met an old man and woman who were weeping because that night their daughter was going to be eaten by a huge snake with eight heads and eight tails. So Lord Susanowo prepared some saké in eight large tubs and waited, and the eight-headed serpent turned up, drank itself silly, and fell asleep. Whereupon the lord cut off all its heads, and from one of the tails there appeared a magic sword.'

'So you see the saké as an offering, and the sword as a return gift?' the professor asked.

'That's right.'

Toyosaki didn't in fact see how this simple example of murder by stealth could have anything to do with the exchange of gifts, but it would have been tedious to explain, and as he still needed to keep on good terms with the chief secretary, he agreed that it was indeed an example of the same principle, an excellent example.

'That's what I thought. I remembered that story while I was listening to you.'

The chief secretary seemed very pleased with this, while the professor could only reflect that you could make anything fit a theory, and vice versa. He cheered himself with the thought that even the eminent philosopher who had written the same love letter on the same day to various women had once admitted, while in his cups, that you only had to step outside for a short walk to come up with a new theory of some kind.

'Another thing that just struck me, Professor, is that our relationship is a pretty good example of what you've been saying.'

'Oh yes, I agree,' Toyosaki replied, feeling secretly that it was a remarkably coercive form of it. 'It's a relationship based on an exchange—or, at least, it is so long as you give me something in return for what I've just given you.'

Sakakibara smiled.

'Well, I've learned a lot tonight. But I've not forgotten that what we're basically dealing with here, Professor, is the offer of public land to a newspaper company in exchange for something of equivalent value, or, to put it more plainly, the donation of government land to that company. That's the issue, isn't it? What you're saying is that, Japan being a society based on the habit of giving each other things, the government should go ahead with the gift of land to the *New Daily*. Make a contract with the *New Daily*, give the land to the *New Daily*—that's what you're saying, isn't it?'

'Spot on,' said the professor in a jocular manner which the chief secretary ignored.

'That's what your theories about the constitution contain, like the jam inside a doughnut. Your ideas are the dough, the government land is the stuff inside. I asked you for an idea, and that's what you came up with. I'm not putting your performance down —it was brilliant—but, let's face it, Professor, the whole thing was just an elaborate joke.'

'Of course it was. And as long as I remain a philosopher anything I say is bound to be one.'

'Is it?'

'I don't know how it was with other philosophers, but Socrates used to spend his days walking around the streets of Athens cracking jokes. I don't expect to achieve anything of the kind he did, but my philosophical aim is the same.'

'Oh,' said the chief secretary suspiciously. 'Socrates was like that, wasn't he?'

'Socrates was gay, wasn't he?' the woman joined in, making Toyosaki look in her direction.

'Yes. But he wasn't the only one. All Greek men of the time liked boys.' Then he turned back to Sakakibara. 'There are those famous ideas about love related by one of his students. Originally human beings had four arms, four legs, two heads, four ears and two sets of private parts, and fell into three types: men plus men, women plus women, men plus women. Now, these human beings rebelled against the gods, and as a punishment each was cut in half. So it's our lost half we seek in love relationships. In those cases where a man has been separated from another man, he seeks another man; in other words, he's gay. In the case of a woman separated from a woman, she seeks a woman, and so she's lesbian. With a man separated from a woman, we get heterosexuality. You've heard of this, haven't you?'

'Yes, I have.'

'Well, it's a typically Socratic joke. It may not sound like one, but there's no way he could have given a theory of that kind any real weight. Still, one can also say that it's this very playfulness that gives his ideas their incisiveness; or, to put it more precisely, that philosophical questions challenge the distinction between seriousness and jest. In contrast to questions of everyday life, the difference between serious and joking remarks ceases to be real.'

'Now you're just trying to bamboozle me,' the chief secretary said, smiling, while the restaurant lady said that was just the way he'd gone on about the saké cups, and urged them both to eat the fruit that had been sitting, untouched, on the table for some time. As he ate some melon, Sakakibara said casually:

'You know, Professor Toyosaki, what you've said has been

remarkably interesting, but your idea of abolishing the constitution is completely unrealistic. Of course, if one took what you might call a macroscopic view of the situation, there's probably a lot to be said for it, but as an immediate, practical policy, well, I've no idea how we could even start to implement it. I think people here want a constitution because it seems to give the country a certain dignity. That's how they are. We Japanese see the Eiffel Tower and we build Tokyo Tower; we go to Disneyland and we want to have one of our own. The reason the British get by without a constitution is surely because they feel it'd be beneath their dignity to copy a former colony. Admittedly, these are difficult questions, but I feel your proposal isn't really quite…'

He broke off. Toyosaki, scooping up a last spoonful of melon, said:

'Oh, that's all right. I never really thought you'd buy the idea. I'm just loosing off, as it were. The real shooting match is going on elsewhere. Not to worry.'

But the chief secretary put an end to these self-deprecating comments with a light wave of his hand.

'No. Despite what I've said, I don't want to drop the idea altogether. How about waiting a little longer so we can chew things over? I never like dismissing new ideas, particularly when they're as original as yours. I'm always open to suggestions from scholars and critics.'

'Fair enough,' Toyosaki replied after a slight pause. It seemed Sakakibara wanted to avoid ending their meeting on a sour note, and the philosopher saw no reason not to comply. He also genuinely believed his own negotiations weren't of major importance, compared with the meeting that was soon to take place between Yumiko, her aunt and the prime minister.

'Yet we ought to have some kind of deadline. Let's say I'll give you an answer in a fortnight's time.'

'I look forward to it,' said Toyosaki, and smiled.

'Shall we have another whisky, then call it a day?'

'An excellent idea.'

As the drinks were being poured Toyosaki said:

'This is merely a piece of idle chatter on my part, and I wouldn't dream of putting anything like it into practice, but I was just wondering…'

'Go ahead.'

'Well, I was just wondering—suppose nothing comes of this in, say, two weeks' time, what would happen if I gave all this stuff to one of the weeklies? I mean, about your being prepared to do me a favour if I offered you something in exchange, like money or a gift or information, or a method of improving your golf handicap? I was wondering if the prospect might bother you in any way…'

The chief secretary drank up his whisky, put the glass down gently in front of the woman to have it refilled, then said cheerfully:

'No, Professor, that wouldn't work, you know. You'd only burn your own fingers. Just have a look at this.'

He handed over a sheet of paper. Typed on it was a clear record of the dates on which Toyosaki had stayed overnight in Tokyo, the names of the hotels, and the precise times at which Yumiko had come to visit him and when she'd left. It even noted that she'd spent some time in conversation with a gang boss in the ground-floor lounge of one of these hotels.

'My goodness…'

'That could be put to use, you see.'

'Ah,' said Toyosaki thoughtfully.

'Private universities are kept going nowadays by Treasury support, are they not? Even though some people maintain it's unconstitutional?'

The chief secretary meant he had only to show the sheet of paper to the university authorities for Professor Toyosaki's classes in Tokyo to be cancelled the following year.

'I see. Somebody's done a very thorough job,' he said, returning the piece of paper with a bemused expression on his face, while Sakakibara said playfully:

'Ah, how vile a trade is ours!'

EIGHT

.
.

The former actress and her niece, the journalist, came out of the hairdresser's in a cheerful mood. It was nice to have one's hair properly done, to be wearing smart clothes and walking in Ginza on a lovely day, and inevitably the two women started chattering away. The aunt was wearing a mauve dress with polka dots on it, although she meant to change before visiting the prime minister. The dress for that occasion was hanging in their hotel room. Her niece had on the Armani suit she'd worn to the office, having come straight from there to the hairdresser's.

They turned a corner and had walked a little way when Masako Yanagi said:

'Let's drop in here and say a prayer.'

You had to look hard to notice the shrine, which occupied the bottom part of a very narrow building. In fact, the building looked as if it had been put up first and the ground-floor frontage removed to accommodate the shrine. A little way back from the street was a white stone arch with a black and gold frame suspended from it, in front of which hung a bell with a red and white rope. Yumiko had occasionally passed this way before but had never noticed it, or perhaps had been vaguely aware of it but decided to ignore it. It certainly seemed a peculiar place in which to find something of this sort.

'Oh, it's a shrine,' she said.

'Even Ginza is part of Japan, you know,' her aunt reminded her tartly, and Yumiko suddenly remembered the shrine on the roof of the *New Daily*. She'd once gone up there to have a photo taken and had been surprised by the odd little structure, with its red arch, stuck away in a corner. According to the noticeboard in front of it, this tiny shrine had been left intact when the *New Daily* offices were first built on this site, on land that had previously belonged to one of the western clans, but had had to be removed when rebuilding took place. The workers in the printing shop (as opposed to the journalists and the office staff, who presumably weren't interested) had clubbed together to pay for its removal up here. Perhaps this meant that the Ginza shrine had refused to be moved up onto the roof, or that the owner of the building was more god-fearing than the president of the *New Daily*…

Beneath the black and gold frame bearing the shrine's name was an offertory box, in front of which, at that very moment, a large man in a black suit, having put his black briefcase to one side, was in the act of praying, his head lowered. Beyond the arch was an oval mirror, set carefully within the semi-darkness of the inner shrine, well polished so that it reflected, in flickers of red, blue and beige, the colours of the clothes of passers-by and of passing cars. Yumiko looked at the row of dusty paper lanterns hung on the left-hand wall, carefully reading the names of the bars, small restaurants and sushi shops written on them, but when she'd finished and looked back she saw the man was still praying.

'He's taking his time, isn't he?'

'He must really have something on his mind.'

They gazed for a while at the man's suit and briefcase, seeing them both as dark containers packed tight with misery, until Masako couldn't wait any longer.

'Let's go,' she said.

'So we're not going to pray?'

'Yes we are. We'll go to the Suitengu. The god there has a higher rank than this one,' she said, and moved briskly away.

As they walked towards the subway station she talked about the time, in her late teens, when she'd been given her first job at the film studios: one of the big stars of the time, Chidori Saho-gawa, had insisted they pay regular visits to that shrine.

'But the Suitengu is for the water god, to do with people in trouble at sea or in childbirth. Why should anyone in the entertainment business go there?'

'Well, I can't really think, except that we're part of the so-called "water trade" and I suppose a water god seemed somehow appropriate.'

They got off at Ningyo-cho, only a few minutes away but very different in atmosphere from Ginza—lower-class, old-fashioned, what people liked to call 'downtown'. Here the old Edo had become entangled with modern Tokyo and no longer knew what to do with itself, although on the surface it seemed to be managing to stay alive. Yumiko had some recollection of having been here once before, although she couldn't remember why. It crossed her mind that journalists could in some ways be considered members of the "water trade" as well, being part of the whole entertainment business (not just the sleazier aspects of it), and she found the idea amusing.

There were few really modern-looking shops, and Masako's attention was drawn to a strikingly old-fashioned confectioner's, but she eventually decided against going inside, saying they'd drop in on the way back. Towering above the confusion of the crossroads before them was the main building of the shrine, with its green-tiled roof, vermilion pillars and white walls, all rather chic-looking. By the stone steps leading up to the grounds a signboard gave the history of the place. Yumiko glanced through it and gave a summary to her aunt.

'The gods worshipped here are Ameno Minaka Nushino Kami, Emperor Antoku, Kenreimon'in, and Niino Ama. The ladies of the Taira clan originally set up this shrine in Kyushu for the souls of the boy emperor Antoku and those of the clan who were drowned in the sea battle of Dannoura in 1185, when the Taira were finally defeated by the Minamoto clan. Then, in

1818, the Lord of Arima had it reconsecrated in Akasaka, and at the beginning of the Meiji period it was moved here.'

'Ah. And who's this Ameno Minaka Nushino Kami?'

'I think I've come across the name somewhere—in the *Ancient Records* probably. Anyway, just some very ancient god.'

'So it's just for the sake of appearances?'

'Yes. An old god comes in handy for that. It's the other three that matter, of course—the emperor, his mother, and his grandmother who drowned with him.'

The two of them then pooled what they knew about these gods. Niino Ama was Tokiko, wife of Taira Kiyomori, head of the clan but dead by the time of the sea battle, so she had become a nun, as her official name of Niino Ama indicated, and Emperor Antoku was her grandson. When the battle was clearly lost she took her grandson in her arms and, saying there was another capital city at the bottom of the sea, leapt into the water with him. Kenreimon'in, wife of Emperor Takakura and mother of Antoku, threw herself in as well, but the warriors from the eastern provinces, the Minamoto, fished her out...

By the time they had reached this point, the two women had arrived at the font, where wooden ladles were provided for visitors to the shrine so that they could perform the correct ablutions (rinsing out one's mouth and washing one's hands) before worshipping. As they stood before the main building, they saw a young woman holding a baby in front of the outer chamber. She was accompanied by her husband and mother-in-law, and was receiving the blessing of the priest, which consisted in shaking a branch of the sacred tree over them. Watching, Yumiko and her aunt also said a prayer, for success in their mission later that day. Yumiko then dropped a hundred yen coin into the offertory box, which seemed to her rather extravagant, although her aunt donated a thousand yen note. Yumiko had felt it had to be a coin, so that there would be a sound as it dropped, but Masako obviously thought the sum too small for their purpose.

There was a rest area in front of the shrine office, and they sat together on a bench there and looked around at the grounds. The husband was taking a photo of his young wife and the baby.

'It's the baby's first visit, I suppose,' said Yumiko.

'Must be.'

'Did I take Chie to our local shrine? I can't remember,' she said, half to herself. Then she suddenly thought of something. 'I don't think it was anything to do with being in the "water trade", you know. That film star, Chidori Sahogawa—didn't she have a child that nobody knew about, hidden away somewhere, and was praying for it to grow up strong and healthy?'

The aunt listened to this, obviously suspicious of this attempt to view the distant past in a new light, finally giving Yumiko an old-fashioned look and commenting that journalists always liked to dig up something nasty—which meant she thought her assumption was almost certainly correct.

'I don't think like that because I'm a journalist but because I'm crazy about films,' Yumiko protested, and her aunt immediately cheered up. Yumiko had worked out long ago that the easiest way to make her happy was to provide an opportunity for reminiscing about the good old days when they knew how to make real films.

They chattered on a while longer, wondering whether to buy some of those little cakes in the shape of a sweet-fish, but deciding they probably wouldn't be available in October, and commenting on a man throwing popcorn to the pigeons despite a large sign saying they shouldn't be fed. While Masako was looking at a distant flock of birds, Yumiko found herself thinking about the shrine's connection with water, and particularly its provision of a tutelary deity for babies, perhaps also linked with aborted foetuses. But she said nothing, concerned that it might make her aunt remember something she'd prefer not to. Then, at her aunt's suggestion, she paid for a horoscope. The slip of paper read as follows:

> *Fortune*: Generally speaking good, but you have a tendency to get muddled, favouring one side over another. If you control your temper, stop having selfish thoughts, and

blame yourself rather than others, your reputation will improve and you will benefit personally.

Wishes: If you persist in wanting two things at the same time, ill fortune will certainly ensue.

She skipped the next three headings to:

Business: On the whole good, but without the prospect of large profits.

'I wonder if wanting two things at the same time means expecting to remain an editorial writer and hoping the company gets its land as well.'

'It could mean that, seeing it also says there's no prospect of large profits.'

After this exchange, Yumiko read the final sections:

Birth: A safe birth is predicted.
Illness: Nothing serious.
Marriage: If you hesitate, you may be too late.

Perhaps as a result of this, she returned to the subject of the drowned boy emperor.

'Still, I can't think why Kenreimon'in should be worshipped alongside the emperor and his grandmother.'

'But she was his mother,' said Masako, looking as if she thought her niece was being obtuse.

'But she didn't die at Dannoura.'

'If she weren't included,' said Masako quickly, with the air of someone pushed into a corner, 'it might seem as if she shouldn't have survived, which would be very unfair.'

'Um, I suppose so,' said Yumiko, pretending she agreed, although in fact she didn't; and then: 'But it does seem strange that we should worship the spirits of people who died tragically, or were frustrated somehow. People have always thought the spirits of those who die full of bitterness turn into ghosts and, if you aren't careful, they'll haunt not just the people who did them wrong but all the living as well. That's why you have to make such a fuss of them, so they won't do anything awful to you. I suppose that's why we put them in shrines, too, so we can give them presents. We raise them in rank, we offer them food, we play them music, we give them Sumo performances, we perform plays about their lives...'

'Putting them in plays is an excellent idea. You know, only the year before last I was asked to appear in a play at the Arts Theatre, but I turned it down. It wasn't much of a part.'

'Oh, you should have taken it. Your fans would have been delighted.'

'Would they?'

'Of course they would. You've still got plenty of them, even now... But you know, Auntie, the interesting thing is, if you take some trouble over these spirits, then they stop doing you harm, turning their spite into sympathy and acting as guardian angels.'

Her aunt expressed some interest in this, and Yumiko explained that all the really popular gods in Japan were former tragic heroes and reformed evil spirits:

'That seems to be the kind of god we like. Still, I can understand why the boy emperor and his grandmother should have been bitter, since they actually died at sea, but what did the mother have to be so upset about? She was pulled out and saved. And then there were the goings-on between her and the enemy commander, Yoshitsune... In fact, before that, while they were swanning about the Inland Sea in one of the Taira warships, trying to escape, there was something going on between her and her brother Munemori. And way before that, even, when her husband Emperor Takakura died, they say she was definitely up to something with her father-in-law, the cloistered emperor Goshirakawa. It beats me how a woman like that, with all those experiences to live down, could be allowed to enter a nunnery, put on the appearance of chastity and, as a result, be rewarded with a purple cloud from heaven when she died, which bore her off to paradise. I can't see what she had to complain about—she couldn't possibly have been full of hatred and bitterness when she died. It doesn't make sense.'

'No, it doesn't,' said Masako emphatically, going on to say, however: 'I don't know about the business with her brother and father-in-law, but I'd have thought any woman would feel life had dealt her a good hand if she had a man like Yoshitsune hanging round her. She couldn't have had any regrets. It's all most peculiar.'

This unexpected response put an end to the conversation as far as Yumiko was concerned. They entered a tiny shop to rest and have a snack, then dropped in at the old-fashioned confectioner's. Back at their Akasaka hotel, her aunt sat and relaxed while Yumiko skimmed through the evening papers. She thought of ringing the press room in the prime minister's official residence to see what she could find out, but nothing of any importance seemed to have happened that day, certainly nothing newsworthy. Both aunt and niece agreed this should mean he would be in a good mood. They didn't dine in the hotel restaurant but had something brought up to their room, then spent the time until midnight dozing in front of the television.

Before going out, they had some of the rather special tea they'd brought with them and a few of the cakes they'd picked up in Ningyo-cho. They both took their best handbags with them, Masako having changed into her other dress. When they finally left in one of the company's cars (they decided to remove the newspaper's pennant, however) it was 1·40 A.M.

Since it was so late, they soon arrived at Nagata-cho. As instructed, they turned at a corner with a small sentry box, just below the prime minister's office, and stopped in front of a tall iron gate. They still had time to spare before the appointed hour of two o'clock and, naturally enough, the person they expected to see wasn't there yet. They had the driver take a long turn round the block, and when they got back a man was standing by the gate, now slightly ajar, a flashlight in his hand.

They tipped the driver, asked him to wait, and got out. The man approached.

'Ms Masako Yanagi, I presume?'

'Yes,' said Yumiko. 'And I'm with her. I'm her niece.'

'Fujimura, the PM's secretary,' the man said, reaching into his inside pocket, but then withdrawing his hand. 'No. I'll save my card until we get into the light.' He smiled and shone the beam into their faces.

Yumiko smiled back in the circle of light and made the sort of polite remarks called for by the situation. Despite the late hour it was quite obvious, even in the darkness, that this man's tie was very carefully knotted. She couldn't see the expression on his face, but she felt fairly certain that he had his suspicions about the prime minister's former relationship with this actress.

'As I said on the phone, I hope neither of you is wearing high-heels,' he said, and shone his light at their feet.

They assured him they were not.

'When someone is visiting the residence in private, we use this back gate.'

After this explanation he produced two more flashlights and gave them one each. He then called out to the man in the sentry box, let them in through the gate, and turned the key in an absurdly big lock. The secretary led the way, and all three kept their flashlights pointed at the ground as they climbed a narrow, sloping path. On either side was what appeared to be a garden, with a scattering of low trees and bushes, not particularly well looked after. In fact, surrounded by the smell of all this foliage, it felt as if they were walking through a forest. For some reason, there was the occasional large hemp palm among the low trees. The path was dimly lit, but only to the extent of providing a grey semi-darkness, and walking was difficult. The secretary had no trouble, however, and obviously knew the way well, for he kept talking as he led them along.

'The PM goes to bed at ten and gets up again at two to look through his papers. Some need to be signed, others have to be reconsidered. Then he sleeps again from four to seven... The radar can catch anything that moves over the whole area; mainly cats and crows, of course. The three of us will be on the screen at this moment.'

But Masako and Yumiko were preoccupied with where they

should put their feet and found it hard to keep up a conversation.

The path turned left, became a little steeper, and they were suddenly out of the thickets and on flat ground, on a lawn like that of a real garden, even if it was only a rather ordinary version of a Western lawn. The lights ahead were clearly those of the prime minister's residence. Immediately, the two of them began talking.

'Are all women guests brought this way?'

'I heard there was a secret tunnel—I was hoping we'd be taken through that.'

'People say there are some big snakes around—I imagine they must be on the hill we've just come up.'

The last two remarks were made by Yumiko, and although they got no response from the secretary, Masako gave a theatrical scream.

The secretary opened a door and led the way inside, into an area filled with light. The two women stood before a staircase that looked familiar from somewhere.

'You probably recognise this staircase. It's where the members of a new cabinet stand to have their group photo taken,' the secretary said, and had them stand on the bottom step, the aunt in her silk dress with its large floral pattern of mauve and pink on a grey background, a thick blue shawl over her shoulders, and carrying a small bead handbag she'd bought in Florence; while her niece wore her collarless Armani suit of dark brown over a purple T-shirt, the gold buttons matching her earrings, holding a cheerful gold-brown bag. The secretary backed away a few paces, formed his hands into a square through which he peered, and asked them to assume appropriately grave expressions. Masako and Yumiko burst out laughing, but soon stopped when they heard their voices echoing through the silent halls of the building.

The secretary now produced his card, giving one to each of them. Masako gave hers some attention, holding it at a distance before handing it over to Yumiko and telling her to look after it. Yumiko, though secretly surprised that her aunt should be treating her as some kind of lady-in-waiting, put it together with the other one in her bag. Naturally she had given the secretary her own card, so he knew her profession. Fujimura handled the situation adroitly, pleasing Masako by saying he'd seen a number of her films, and how lovely she'd looked in them, then turning to Yumiko and wondering if she'd ever worked in the political section of her newspaper. As she hadn't, this was the first time she'd been in the prime minister's official residence.

'If you wouldn't mind just waiting here a moment,' he said, going off but coming back almost immediately and saying briskly: 'There's nobody about, so let's go.'

They left the hallway and went down a wide, deserted corridor, the two women hurrying after the secretary as he led them up a red, fully carpeted staircase. The carpet was worn and stained in places, but clearly this was the main entrance to the building, and Masako and Yumiko felt tense at the thought that there was no turning back now.

They walked a little way down the high-ceilinged, brown-walled upstairs corridor before the secretary suddenly stopped, gestured to them to wait, then disappeared behind a door, also brown, to his right. The two women stood in silence. Fujimura soon returned, saying everything appeared to be all right, and as Masako turned to look at him another door, which she'd thought part of the wall, abruptly opened and a face appeared, obviously that of an elderly man.

'Ah, come in,' he said, and Masako did so, leaving Yumiko facing the partly concealed door.

There was a screen immediately opposite the door, but beyond it Masako saw a large room, some fifty feet square or more, with, on the right, three low tables and six chairs arranged neatly about them, all upholstered in the same colour. In front of her, Shingo Tamaru was now seated on a sofa, and indicated that she should come and join him. He smiled in a natural and welcoming way, but she noticed he also looked a little sheepish.

Masako was overwhelmed to think she hadn't met this man for well over thirty years. But this wasn't just someone who had exchanged his good looks for old age. Certainly he looked older, much older, but he had a new dignity and strength, and he was also attractive in a way that didn't come across in his photographs or on television. He had the serenity of someone watching over things, and it seemed absolutely right that he should be up in the middle of the night going through his papers. He wore corduroy trousers with a rather faded shirt, a cardigan draped over his shoulders, and his casual appearance seemed to emphasise the feeling of energy he generated, the vitality of a man at the peak of his career. His hair, she saw, was not so much white as only half grey, and she felt she ought to revise her first impression that this was an elderly man.

She found herself secretly comparing him with the man, two or three years his senior, with whom she sometimes spent a weekend at Izu. This was someone who owned between a hundred and a hundred and fifty car parks from Kanto to Shizuoka, and managed to live very comfortably on the proceeds of the monthly contracts for them. He was an amiable, considerate person whom she genuinely liked, but now she realised there was something lacking in him. She'd first met him a few years after Tamaru had left her, when he was managing a supermarket. He'd made a number of approaches, but they broke it off just as she was beginning to think she might give in, and then, five years ago, she'd gone to Cyprus at the invitation of a woman friend, found he was staying in the same hotel, and they'd at last started an affair.

Tamaru gestured before him with his hand (something he always did when he wasn't quite sure what to do with a visitor) and said, pointing out the obvious:

'That's the desk I work at.'

On the wall behind the desk were portraits of the emperor and empress, and to one side a tripod holding the national flag, making it all look rather like a headmaster's study, although a headmaster's room would not have been as large as this, of course. He then pointed to another, smaller desk in the right-hand corner.

'And that telephone there,' he said, 'is the hot line.'

Masako gave a little gasp, although she wasn't in the least impressed, or even interested, having no idea what a hot line was. As she wanted to get to the main subject of her visit without too much delay, she said, in a quiet voice that was nonetheless full of emotion:

'The television doesn't do you justice—the lighting is obviously as inept as I've always imagined. Not like the cinema at all. You look far more distinguished, just as one would expect a genuinely important person to look. It feels strange that somebody like me, because of some past relationship, should be allowed to talk to you like this. I feel happy and yet nervous at the same time.'

'Stop it!' the prime minister commanded. 'Masako, I've heard those lines before. In some monster film.'

'Monster film? I never go to see them.'

'But you've appeared in one.'

'I have?'

'Yes. You had the part of a woman who runs a bar in Ginza, and you had a request to make of a Nobel Prize-winning scientist played by some famous actor whose name I've forgotten.'

'I did?'

'Yes.'

'Oh.'

'When the woman was a teenager the great scientist had been a student living in the house next door.'

'Oh.'

'You see?'

'But why should a woman running a bar go and see a scientist to ask for help with a monster? I could understand if it was the chief of police.'

'Or the chairman of the National Security Committee.'

'So why does she?'

'I seem to have forgotten.'

'I can't remember either.'

The two laughed, both remembering how, when they were living together, he would always make fun of the plots of the films she appeared in, and how they would amuse themselves using lines from them as part of their everyday conversation. The seventy-five-year-old woman and the sixty-nine-year-old man felt they had slipped back into the distant past.

Masako gave a sudden cry.

'That monster film was made at least ten years after you were first elected to the Diet. Did you go to see it?'

'Yes.'

'Have you seen all my films?'

'I've seen a good many of them, but probably not all. Some of them I wasn't able to see from the beginning, and some I had to leave halfway through, even though I wanted to see them.'

She was so moved she took his hand, and he seized the opportunity to explain about the past, more than thirty years ago, when he'd sent his uncle to see her, afraid that if he'd gone himself he'd have found it impossible to leave her, and he was really very sorry, truly sorry—while she, with tears in her eyes, forgave him everything. Still holding hands, they indulged in reminiscences about those far-off days: how, during the last days of the war, she'd been so angry every time she listened to the radio news, because of the lies they told, and how he'd pleaded with her to be careful not to talk that way when she was out anywhere or the military police would arrest her; and she teased him about the fact that a man so chronically careful should have grown so careless, constantly making slips of the tongue in public. He smiled wryly at that, explaining there was more than one way to make slips of the tongue, the majority of his own being quite intentional, a means of finding how the land lay, rather like sending up an observation balloon. Then he thanked her for taking an interest, to the extent of noticing the mistakes in his speeches.

Now that the first stage in the negotiating process had been completed, Masako released her hand gently from his and drew a white envelope containing a letter from her handbag.

'Please, would you read this for me? Here and now? It's written by my niece.'

'Ah, the editorial writer for the *New Daily*. I gather she's strikingly good-looking,' he said, taking the letter. 'It must run in the family.'

He went to the desk to get his glasses, and while he was reading the letter Masako looked round the room. In front of the screen to the left was a large globe, which made the room look even more like a headmaster's, and beyond the flag was another entrance, with the door open. The lights were on in what she assumed was his secretariat, although she couldn't see if anyone was in there or not. She stood up and walked about, stopping in front of the small desk to look at a painting on the wall, a mountain landscape with autumn foliage which she didn't think much of, before returning to the sofa and sitting down again. Tamaru looked up when he'd finished the letter, removed his glasses, and smiled benevolently.

'That sets out everything very clearly. It has gone rather far, so it won't be easy, but I'll see what I can do. Please tell her that.'

'But look, Shin—oh, sorry—what *is* the situation, and what are you going to do about it?'

'You must understand, Masako, that in affairs of this kind timing is crucial. It may well be that I won't be able to do anything immediately, in which case I must ask you to be patient and wait.'

'Wait for what?'

'My position inside the cabinet is a bit shaky at the moment. Once that's taken care of—that is, when I'm in a position of strength—then I can clear this matter up straight away.'

Masako pouted, dissatisfied with this half-promise, and asked how long it would take to sort out his shaky position—was he talking about a general election, or what? But he didn't reply, so she went on:

'Oh, come on, you can tell me, surely? Don't be stiff and formal. How long do we have to wait?'

'Six months. Maybe a year.'

'You can't mean that,' she said, clasping her hands together. 'My niece has already put up with this for six months, and now you talk about another six months, even a year.'

'I realise it's hard on her,' he said quietly, trying to mollify her, 'but she has her whole life ahead of her, and we all have difficulties to endure. Diet members can always lose an election. It's how they weather that ordeal that determines what's going to happen in the next one. You have to possess your soul in patience.'

'Oh, don't say that.'

'When you lose an election, there's more than a year to wait.'

'So she's got to carry on going through hell at work?'

'What's wrong with this post in the chairman's office? What was wrong with the job in promotions, for that matter? I don't understand her objection. Papers aren't that rigid—just because she's moved to promotions, it doesn't mean she can't go on writing articles.'

'So you won't do anything for us?'

'I didn't...'

'The newspaper won't get its land, and Yumiko will be blamed for it...'

'I didn't say I wouldn't do anything. Of course I will, out of friendship for you. All I'm saying is, it's going to be difficult right now. I need time, that's all.'

This exchange went on for a while. He explained that he had to save the chief secretary's face, that there were people in the party who hated the *New Daily*, that the religious sect was applying pressure, and there were other aspects that also had to be taken into consideration. You had to be as slippery as an eel if you wanted to get away with anything in politics. Masako felt constrained from putting the kind of pressure on him she would have done on the garage-chain owner. For one thing, he was a more impressive character, and there was also the fact that he'd gone to see those films of hers, even after they'd split up, which she felt very pleased about; then again, he was more experienced in negotiations of this kind, while for her it was the first time, and that was probably the real reason.

'But you must understand, Masako, that affairs of this kind sometimes seem to resolve themselves unexpectedly. So you mustn't give up hope. Just wait and see.'

Vague encouragement of this kind simply made it more difficult to find anything to counter it with, and she didn't know what to say. Finally she remembered her niece waiting outside and asked him to listen to her side of the story, but this the prime minister skilfully refused. There was no time for that, he said, and eventually brought the discussion to a close, saying he had papers to look over before he went back to bed. He stood up and prepared to show her out, but Masako said, also standing up:

'At least let me introduce her to you.'

'Of course. I'd like to see how much she looks like you,' he replied tactfully.

But when he opened the door there was nobody in the silent corridor, and the prime minister and his former mistress were left standing, uncertain for a moment what to do.

Immediately after Masako had disappeared inside the prime minister's room, Fujimura had asked Yumiko if she'd like to see the cabinet room.

'May I?'

'Of course.'

'Then I'd love to.'

He showed her into the room he'd just come out of, and the first thing she noticed was a number of splendid chairs lining the walls.

'This is known as the ministerial reception room. The PM has his photo taken here with his visitors.'

She would have liked to look at the room a while longer, but he opened the door on the right.

'This is the actual cabinet room. Please, come in.'

The room had a number of rectangular tables with chairs beside them. Each table had an inkstone and brush on it so that documents could be signed in the traditional way. This arrangement of tables made the other end of the room seem oddly distant, like a painting in which the laws of perspective have been too diligently observed. Yumiko pointed at the far wall.

'Is that where the prime minister sits?'

'Yes. Of course.'

'Can I go and look?'

'By all means.'

She walked round behind the tables, the secretary following after her and pointing out the PM's seat.

'Wouldn't you like to sit down?'

'I would, since you're kind enough to ask.'

She sat down, but the leather chair seemed slightly damp and a little too soft for comfort. Both her chair at work and the one in her room at home were much more comfortable.

Fujimura stood a little way off, then said, with a polite smile:

'Could you give us a few words, Prime Minister?'

The woman in the dark brown suit and mauve T-shirt adjusted her position, and the earrings chosen to match her buttons glinted as they swayed about.

'Ahem,' she said, and the secretary clapped his hands and smiled.

As they walked back down the room she said:

'I'm surprised to see the chairs all lined up like this.'

'Why's that?'

'Well, I shouldn't really be saying this, but some time ago I met a Mr Hotta, who was then acting as chief adviser in the secretariat, and when I asked him what kind of work he did he said he had to make sure all the chairs were lined up properly for cabinet meetings, and what an awful chore it was.'

'An interesting definition of his work.'

'Naturally I didn't think he moved them all himself, but I still assumed he must have had a hand in it, or at least that somebody must have kept lining them up or rearranging them.'

They laughed quietly, and discussed this Hotta who, according to his obviously more up-to-date information, was now head of some bureau in the Welfare Ministry, until they reached the door to the prime minister's room. He then withdrew, leaving Yumiko alone. There was no sofa, not even a chair, in the long corridor, and she recalled how a woman journalist in the political section had told her there was never anywhere to sit in the corridors of the official residence, presumably to save ministers from being cornered for questioning. She put her ear to the door but couldn't catch what was being said, so went back to the middle of the corridor feeling as if she were back at school and being made to stand there as a punishment. She then started to wish she'd brought a paperback, particularly as her bag was large enough for one to have fitted in quite easily. She looked at her watch, saw it was 2·40, and noticed at the same time that there appeared to be somebody down the corridor, far off to her right. This somebody turned out to be wearing a white kimono with something over it, and was coming slowly in Yumiko's direction, walking with what seemed like a slight limp. It was a woman, apparently an old one.

The kimono was in fact a yukata, the light version used for sleeping in, with a chrysanthemum pattern; over it was a mauve crêpe jacket, and the sash was a narrow yellow one. The strings of the over-jacket were a lighter purple and dangled untied. The woman wore slippers on her bare feet and now looked around seventy, but Yumiko saw she had a strangely innocent, almost childish expression on her face. Yumiko assumed she must be a member of the household, and that she should therefore greet her, since she didn't want to be seen as some kind of intruder. She had forgotten for a moment that this was no ordinary household, feeling like a guest in someone's home. So she smiled and addressed her pleasantly, saying good evening and hoping she hadn't disturbed her in any way. The old woman looked at Yumiko intently, leaned her head slightly to one side, then said in a voice full of emotion:

'How very pretty you are.'

'Oh.'

'Just like a young bride.'

Her words were a little slurred and, like her expression, rather childish.

'Like a young bride?'

'Yes. You're so pretty.'

'But I've got a grown-up daughter.'

'A grown-up daughter…'

263

Yumiko felt rather pleased to think she didn't look her age, and added:

'It's because I went to the hairdresser.'

This attempt to explain why she looked so attractive was deliberately offered rather perfunctorily, to match the tone of the other woman. When there was no reply, she went on:

'In Ginza.'

At this the old woman looked as if she were about to burst into tears.

'I want to go to a hairdresser ... in Ginza,' she murmured.

At last, a little late in the day, Yumiko began to wonder who this was. It was certainly very strange that she hadn't asked herself the question before, but it must have been because the woman's appearance had been disturbing, even a little frightening. At this point Yumiko still wasn't fully aware of the fact that this was the prime minister's official residence, and was still trying to work out who she might be. The woman assumed a coy look and asked in a wheedling voice:

'You wouldn't have a puff, would you?'

'A puff? What sort of puff?'

The old woman opened her left hand and held it in front of her face, as if she were looking into it, pursed her lips slightly, then tapped the fingers of her right hand lightly against both cheeks. As Yumiko watched this mime of applying make-up she suddenly realised this must be the prime minister's wife. Urano had been wrong about her living in the other house, or at least he had been wrong to imply she never came here; most likely she stayed in the official quarters next door and had woken up, got lost in her wanderings, and drifted into this part of the building. Also, her interest in life seemed not to be restricted to food, for clearly she was also interested in looking nice; or, again, perhaps Urano's information had been incomplete, and her current craze was asking people, not for biscuits, but make-up. These thoughts, in various forms, darted through Yumiko's mind like fireworks bursting in swift succession, quite silently, in a distant sky.

'Yes, I have,' she said, producing from her bag the foundation she'd bought the other morning to cheer herself up and had used for the first time today, and handing it to the woman.

'Thanks.'

She took the square gold case, opened the lid, looked awkwardly into the mirror as she tried to enlist the aid of the overhead light, then took the puff in her hand.

'May I use it?'

'Of course you may. I'll give it you.'

The old woman looked so taken aback that Yumiko felt she might not have understood, and repeated her offer.

'I'm giving it to you. Giving it, you see,' she said, placing her hand on her breast and then moving it in the other's direction in a simple mime of the act of giving.

'It's yours. Do you understand?'

The woman stared at her, then nodded, put the puff back, and closed the lid.

'It's very kind of you,' she said, bowing deeply.

Yumiko was moved by this alternation of childish and adult behaviour, and felt hurriedly inside her handbag, producing a lipstick case which was also almost new.

'This too,' she said, giving it to her.

'What? This too? Oh, thank you,' she said, looking very happy and twisting the tube so that the tip of the red stick protruded.

'No, not here. There. Over there,' said Yumiko quickly, pointing in the direction from which the woman had come, meaning that she should go back to her own room and do her make-up there. The woman nodded again and, twisting the lipstick back into the tube and holding it and the foundation firmly in her left hand, indicated with a polite gesture that Yumiko should come with her, looking into her face with a pleading expression, like a small child who isn't sure she will be allowed to do what she wants. Then she took hold of Yumiko's hand and led the way.

Yumiko had no idea where they were going, but went with the old lady to the end of the corridor, where there was a banister and a staircase leading to another corridor; they went down the stairs and turned left along a glassed-in passageway of about fifteen or twenty yards. As she was led slowly along she remembered something she'd been told by the man who had once been in charge of the lifestyle section of the *New Daily* before moving to a sports paper. He was always saying: 'It's a reporter's job to go anywhere, any time, at a moment's notice.' These were the words he had used when he'd sent her off to interview the boss of the Ginza mob, Heigoro Asaoka, for the 'pre-forties' series, and they certainly seemed applicable here. So on she walked, telling herself she was a journalist and there was no need to feel any qualms about wandering around someone else's house, particularly as she was in the company of someone who lived there; and the refrain of 'anywhere, any time' kept pace with the slow march of their footsteps.

There was no door at the end of the connecting passageway, just as there hadn't been one at its beginning, and Yumiko was led by the hand into the first room they came to, feeling that this house was full of surprises. The room itself, however, was very ordinary, with a screen and a cheap round table with one or two magazines on it, and an unopened bottle of beer which looked somehow solitary and dull. To the left was a sofa. Someone had embroidered the face of a well-known cartoon character into one of its cushions.

It seemed to be some kind of ante-room, and Yumiko assumed they would sit down on the sofa, but the woman moved on round the screen. This gave Yumiko a start, although she didn't have time to consider why she should be startled. Beyond the screen was an entrance hall, now in semi-darkness, and to one side of it a small room, door open and fully lit, although nobody seemed to be in there. The radio was on low, playing a song in English, with a man singing and a woman saying something in reply. The room next to it was a rather splendid-looking washroom. On the left-hand side were another two or three rooms matching these, presumably reception rooms.

They passed these rooms, however, and went up a step. Here the carpeting changed from grey to light brown, and the woman changed her slippers, Yumiko also taking off her shoes and putting on some slippers that were obviously provided for visitors, excited at the thought that this was real scoop material. No doubt any number of journalists had entered this area before, but nobody seemed to have written about it, probably because they were interested in the politics of the place—with how somebody or other was rated by the PM, or what his wife had to say about his political opponents—and didn't notice how interesting it was as a house in which people actually lived. Yumiko told herself that she was probably the first journalist to come here who saw it in that way, and she wanted to write about it. She wondered if what she did write would get printed, and then thought that, so long as she didn't mention who had shown her round and what kind of illness she suffered from, there was no reason why it shouldn't come out, and that what she produced would be of genuine interest. It would do very well for the lifestyle pages—after all, this certainly involved a lifestyle of some sort. Lost in her thoughts, she completely forgot she was supposed to be there as a companion to her aunt, who was petitioning the prime minister on her behalf.

They were now in a rock garden with a stone basin and lantern, and some bamboo discreetly illuminated from behind. The wind must get in here from somewhere, for it had brought in a small plastic bag which had got caught between the roots of the bamboo. Yumiko looked carefully around, memorising everything. This was an inner garden which provided ventilation for the house, surrounded by two ordinary and two glass walls. Facing the garden on both sides were two sliding doors, one opening on to a room with a tatami floor. They turned right at this point, into a Western-style room with two sliding wooden doors, and the woman opened the farther one and beckoned to Yumiko to follow. They entered a narrow corridor between two rooms, neither of which had a door, so that there was free access to them. At the end of the corridor was what must be a bathroom, she thought, but she was only guessing. The room on the left was dark, the one on the right brightly lit, and it was into this last that the woman went, with Yumiko following. The place was about twelve feet square, with a Persian carpet, a large bed, two chairs, a chest of drawers, an oil painting of Mt. Fuji, and a dressing table near the entrance. The woman went to the bed, folded the eiderdown, removed the pillow, and rolled up the thin mattress, together with the sheets. Underneath the bed, occupying the area below where the pillow would have been, were a number of boxes made of light wood, of various shapes and sizes, some long, some square, some very small, arranged in a semicircle. Despite her professional interest as a journalist, Yumiko was shaken by all this. Why on earth was she being shown it?

The old lady picked up a long, thin box, opened the lid, and took out a bracelet and necklace, both silver with a heart-shaped design, from the thin paper they were wrapped in.

'Look, how pretty,' she said excitedly, and gave them to Yumiko. The silver was tarnished a little but still had a sumptuous glow to it, or perhaps the slight cloudiness heightened the pathos they radiated at that moment. The objects themselves, which would have looked neat and fragile if they had been of Japanese workmanship, gave an impression of strength, even splendour, despite being so finely wrought.

'Yes, they really are pretty,' said Yumiko who, after looking at them for a minute, returned them to their box.

The next box contained a necklace of plaited gold links, possibly Celtic in design. She couldn't make out the brand name, but it was a wonderfully solid and elaborate piece of craftsmanship.

'Pretty, isn't it?' the woman said, putting it gently into her hands.

'Yes, very,' said Yumiko, and sighed.

It seemed she was expected to admire the woman's various trinkets, perhaps to compensate for the feeling of rivalry stirred up by Yumiko's smart appearance, to show her she had lots of nice things of her own; but it may have occurred her that it was strange to be looking at these things standing up, for she drew up a chair and sat down, while Yumiko sat on another chair, facing her. The woman nodded, to show she was satisfied with this arrangement, and stretched out her hand to the next box.

From this third box came a three-string necklace of black pearls, meticulously sized and arranged like a chorus line, with the large ones in the middle and the others gradually getting smaller towards the ends. The woman held it against her throat, then smiled at Yumiko and gaily offered it to her. Yumiko hesitated a moment, as if asking permission, before going to the dressing table and trying it on in front of the mirror. The rows of black pearls, pleasantly cool against her skin, went perfectly with the sombre brown of her suit; and she reflected that she would probably go through life without ever being able to experience such luxury herself. She noticed the wry smile on her face in the mirror, then went back to her chair.

The next box was small and covered in cloth. It contained a platinum ring set with a large ruby surrounded by diamonds. The old lady put it on her finger and watched it glitter in the light with pleasure. For some reason she didn't pass this to Yumiko, but put it straight back in the box.

From the box of paulownia wood that she kept between the pillow and the headboard she took out an ivory comb wrapped in thick Japanese paper. A white peacock with outspread feathers was embossed on the cream-coloured ivory, providing the kind of embellishment found in the Korin school. Going by its style, it seemed to be late Edo, but since the white peacock was a foreign importation it probably had to be Meiji. The woman proudly passed the comb over to Yumiko, urging her by gesture to put it in her hair. Yumiko tried it on, but the sheer elegance of the workmanship somehow didn't suit her modern hairstyle.

'Pretty, so pretty,' the woman murmured, laying it on the paper in the little box, then repeating the words and taking it out again, sliding it neatly into her own hair. Her hair was untidy, but the comb seemed to fit perfectly, giving her an air of poise and grooming. Yumiko was very struck by this transformation, but she remembered hearing that the prime minister's wife had reached a professional standard in traditional dance, and was no doubt used to wearing ornaments of that kind. The comb was replaced in its box.

The next box was old-fashioned in design and contained a large tortoiseshell comb. When the heavy paper wrapping was removed Yumiko gave a cry of admiration. It was in the form of a bunch of grapes, made of mother-of-pearl, which a bee made of gold lacquer, with other colours cunningly worked into it, had visited, now clinging to that cool, succulent object, half drunk with honey, or rather with the nectar it sipped. This fanciful coupling had been picked out with appropriate elaboration, a display of technical expertise that took one's breath away. It was almost impossible to imagine the kind of hairstyle and dress that would go with something of this sort. The two women could only handle it and sigh, neither attempting to try it in their hair.

Finally out came the last box, even larger and thinner, and worn with age, in what seemed to be mulberry. The lid was opened to reveal a long object wrapped in thick Japanese paper, and this paper contained a traditional hairpin, very long, with ornaments dangling from it. The woman took hold of the brass pin, which was of normal length, all the ornamentation being at one end. This remarkable piece of handiwork consisted of an oval base about the size of two postage stamps and made of gold, to which were attached plum blossoms, one made of coral and five of silver, with a single gold leaf. Below that hung ten clusters of silver beads, each attached to the base of a string of four coral beads.

'Dangle, dangle, dangle,' said the woman, entranced, shaking it lightly, and the bunches of coral and slightly discoloured silver flowers trembled under their golden shade as if swaying in a spring breeze.

'It's lovely,' said Yumiko, praising the performance as well as the ornament itself, and the woman smiled and gave it to her. Yumiko shook the pin, repeating the words 'dangle, dangle, dangle', but since she held it in the middle rather than at the end a spring breeze of some other day touched the flowers, and they swayed in a slightly different way.

Yumiko would have liked to have looked at it a little longer, but the woman held out her hand so she gave it back. It was wrapped again in its paper, placed in the box, and the lid was closed. Then the whole thing was passed over to Yumiko, the woman looking at her uncertainly, even plaintively. Clearly she was giving the box and its contents to her, and it seemed likely this had been her original intention, but when she'd uncovered it among her other treasures she hadn't been able to resist showing them as well. Yumiko was now aware she had been guilty of a serious misjudgement regarding the woman's motives, but that this was hardly the time to indulge in feelings of regret.

'Oh, I couldn't possibly take it, it's much too valuable. And I can see it must mean a great deal to you. That foundation case I gave you was a cheap thing I picked up in a department store.'

But the woman simply thrust it on her, no matter how hard she protested.

'I'm just not the right person to be given something like this. It's too young for me. I'm forty-five and...'

'You're grown up ... grown up...,' the woman said, shaking her head vigorously. Yumiko wondered what she could possibly mean, and then worked out she wasn't saying 'you're' but 'your'.

'For my grown-up daughter?' she asked, and the other nodded in agreement.

'For my grown-up daughter to wear when she gets married?'

The woman nodded again.

'That is incredibly kind of you,' she said, genuinely moved. 'But I still couldn't possibly accept it.'

While this exchange was still going on, the woman suddenly dropped the box on the floor between them with a cry and started searching on the bed for something. Realising she had just remembered the foundation and lipstick but couldn't recall where she'd put them, Yumiko assisted in the hunt, even looking under the bed, and finally the two things turned up, nestling inside the rolled-up eiderdown.

The woman gave a shout of delight, and Yumiko smiled with her. She did, in fact, feel surprisingly happy that her gifts weren't lost. The woman hurriedly took them with her to the dressing table, sitting in front of the mirror and starting to make herself up. This seemed to be a pleasure she hadn't enjoyed for years, for she kept screwing up her face and observing it in the mirror before using the powder puff and then applying the lipstick. When she had finished she came back, apparently satisfied with her performance, but this time she sat on the bed facing Yumiko, no doubt in order to display her improved appearance. As Yumiko looked at the mask-like face she reflected that make-up was difficult if one didn't wash one's face first, and that it was also unwise to put it on as thickly as the woman had done. The lipstick reminded her of the crude look of certain pages in the *New Daily* when they'd first started experimenting with colour advertisements, some years ago.

'You look lovely, really pretty,' she told her, nonetheless.

Delighted by the compliment, the woman nodded again and put the mulberry box on Yumiko's lap. This time Yumiko did not refuse, thinking she'd be able to leave it behind somewhere when she left.

'You're very kind. I don't know how to thank you.'

The woman ignored this gesture of appreciation, merely preening herself like a pleased child, all dressed up to have its picture taken. Yumiko took the hint.

'You really do look pretty—it's you who look like a bride.'

But even as she spoke, she saw the woman begin to tremble and turned, astonished by the sudden change, to see an old man standing there, dressed in a shirt, corduroy trousers and a brown cardigan, looking even more astonished than she. She immediately recognised the prime minister, not because he looked like the figure she had seen in photos or on television, but because he was exactly like the cartoons of him in the *New Daily*, which always showed him with round, startled eyes and a rather goofy expression.

His presence transformed the situation. The moment the man in corduroys and cardigan materialised as Prime Minister Tamaru, Yumiko became a woman journalist in a bedroom deep inside the official residence, and regained an objective awareness of just how extraordinary a scene she had witnessed, being shown all the objects in the boxes underneath that bed. She stood up, producing her card on an automatic impulse, and saying at great speed:

'I'm Yumiko Minami of the editorial writing staff of the *New Daily*, accompanying my aunt who, I believe, may have shown you my letter, in which I have taken the liberty to inform you of matters at the *New Daily* concerning the transfer of government land and also changes affecting personnel. While I was waiting outside your office for my aunt, your wife, as I believe...'

The prime minister silently nodded.

'Your wife appeared and engaged me in conversation, with the result that I gave her some make-up things she was interested in and then came here at her invitation.'

The prime minister nodded again, then slowly examined her card. He looked at his wife, who remained sitting on the bed, her eyes downcast, and said:

'The *New Daily*. I see. Who's the chairman now?'

'Norio Kiriyama, sir.'

'Ah. Kiriyama. I know him. Rather a large man, keen on football. What were you doing before you started writing editorials?'

'I worked on the lifestyle pages, sir. I was also in the financial section for a while, and on the city desk.'

'Political section?'

'No, sir,' Yumiko replied, suddenly aware she was still holding the box. 'Your wife very kindly said she would give me this, and I was just trying to refuse it when you came in.'

The prime minister didn't seem to understand what she was saying, so she opened the box and took out the ornamental hairpin.

'Oh,' Tamaru said, still looking mystified.

'Your wife was so pleased when I lent her my foundation—foundation is a kind of face powder, sir, kept in a compact, as it used to be called—and also lipstick, that I said I would let her keep it. It was all done on the spur of the moment, sir. And then she brought me to this room...'

'Ah, I suppose she got carried away.'

'And just as I was doing my best to turn it down…,' Yumiko went on, placing the box on the bed.

'I see,' he said, and his words hung uneasily in the air after he had spoken. He thought for a moment, then addressed his wife: 'Look, Mother, I've got to talk to our guest. It's about something very important.'

He pointed in the direction of his own bedroom.

'Go to the other room. All right?'

When she hesitated, the expression in his eyes changed.

'Look. Go over there, will you?'

The tone of his voice was gentle enough, but the contrast between his words and the hard look in his long, narrow eyes made Yumiko tremble. His wife got up reluctantly and shambled off to the room next door.

Tamaru, at that particular moment, was in a state of total dismay at finding his wife with this woman journalist. It was Yumiko Minami who was at the centre of the *New Daily* affair, so she would obviously be feeling pretty hostile about the prospect of being kicked upstairs; it was also clear from her editorial that she was a rabid feminist, and no doubt she knew all there was to know about the way he'd broken off with her aunt. There could be no question of her feeling well disposed in any way towards him. She was therefore just about the last person he'd have chosen to have the extraordinary misfortune of meeting his wife and being given this demonstration of her mental problems. He was doubly upset because the reunion with his former mistress, which he'd been looking forward to with some trepidation, had gone extremely well, and he'd wanted to send her away with something more than just a vague promise. But although he was annoyed that this mishap had put an end to his good intentions, his main concern now was to prevent anyone writing about his wife; he would do anything to stop that happening.

He therefore made a swift decision. To stop this person writing about her, he would have to enter into full and direct negotiations in the *New Daily* affair. That would lead to all sorts of unpleasant repercussions, but he would just have to deal with them. In exchange for his intervention, even this woman would surely forgo the satisfaction of exposing his private life in some wretched article.

That in itself, however, would not be enough. He was determined that tonight's events should not be written about, not just now, but ever. Although it seemed virtually impossible that she could sell any of the information she'd picked up to any of the weeklies, since the news source would be so easily identifiable, she might well, for example, produce her autobiography in later years—*My Life as a Woman Journalist*, or some such title. If so, tonight's events must form no part of it. The affair must remain absolutely secret. For the whole nation to hear that the prime minister's wife had left their private quarters in the middle of the night with only her night clothes on, wandering into the public part of the building, right up to the door of his own office, there to encounter a visitor and beg make-up materials off her before inviting her back to her own bedroom, there to apply this same make-up—the story was not so much bizarre as comic, and the idea of its becoming public property made his blood boil. Even more embarrassing than having the whole country know about it was that it might come to the attention of his son, a professor of chemistry in America, and daughter, who was married to his secretary and lived in Tokyo. Both had begged him, any number of times, not to have their mother live with him in the official residence, warning him of the possible consequences, but he had ignored them, making light of their concern and giving them lofty assurances that it would be all right, there was nothing to get worked up about. If, in the evening of his life, in the last year of it perhaps—even after his death—this woman journalist published an account of the episode, it would put paid to any last vestiges of dignity he might still possess. In particular he feared his son, a cynical man, always sneering (about the only thing that was spared his general contempt was opera)—it made his blood run cold to think what he might have to say about it. He saw Yumiko Minami's future book, even if it existed only in the distant future, as something that would destroy the harmony of his family and strip him of parental authority; it was this prospect that made his flesh creep, for that loss was what he most feared.

His mind raced as he tried to come up with a plan that would ensure she never wrote about what had taken place tonight. He was confident he could win her over somehow. As a result, perhaps, of his experiences when young, especially that of living with the actress he had just left in the other building, he was clever at getting his way with women, and he believed this skill had increased as he'd gained more influence and power. And having just successfully negotiated his way around Masako's petition, surely he could handle the problem niece as well. He would have liked more time to think the matter through, but time was what he didn't have. Yumiko Minami was there in front of him, and if she wasn't dealt with forthwith he could lose the opportunity for good. A number of ideas flashed through his mind, but as he tried to weigh their respective merits and flaws he felt on the verge of despair—until suddenly he had a genuine inspiration, a visitation from some familiar spirit, it seemed, and arrived, as he thought, at the perfect plan. In point of fact, however, it was only a variation on something he'd put into effect twenty-five years before.

When Tamaru was still a relatively inexperienced Diet member, a leader of one of the other party factions had asked him if he wouldn't mind looking after an American journalist who intended to write a book about Japanese politics; he had an excellent command of the language, apparently, and wanted to attach himself to a Japanese Diet member for a year and see for himself what went on. This very senior politician had been approached by an American friend whom he found it virtually impossible to refuse, but none of the members of his own faction liked the thought of their affairs being pried into (especially their financial affairs), and so he was hoping Tamaru would accept the job. Naturally Tamaru didn't like the idea of a witness to everything he did either, but this senior politician had done him a number of favours and he felt obliged to agree to the idea. After he'd accepted, he spent a number of days worrying about it, before finally deciding, half out of desperation, that the only way to handle this was to show the man everything, concealing nothing.

The American was a cheerful character in his thirties, with a great liking for fish broiled in salt, noodles, and swimming, as Tamaru soon discovered, since the man lived in his house in his constituency for twelve months, and when they came to Tokyo stayed in a nearby hotel. He got on very well with Tamaru's son, playing catchball with him and taking him swimming.

Tamaru even took the young American to his mistress's house, and let him sit in when money was being paid out to an election broker. There may have been an element in this of showing off just how wicked he was, but the policy paid off. In the same way as the ancient Romans respected courage and self-denial, so this American believed in straightforward honesty. He was impressed that Tamaru made no attempt to lie to him, and showed his appreciation by suppressing anything that could have caused him any real embarrassment, while still producing a very interesting book. There was, it was true, one passage about Tamaru's secretary sending a large quantity of plain brown envelopes from Tokyo to the constituency before the official nomination day, but he assumed this was simply an oversight. The main thing was that his *Japanese Diet Member* was well reviewed in both America and Japan, and Shingo Tamaru established a reputation for himself, particularly in the States, that turned those who had shied away from the job green with envy. The senior politician, for his part, felt so pleased at the way it all showed how well things turned out under his supervision that he gave Tamaru his first ministerial post when he took over the reins of power.

Thinking back over this, Tamaru decided to use the same method now—to tell Yumiko the unadorned truth. So he had her sit down, took a chair himself, and began speaking. His expression was mild enough, but the way he spoke was as effective as if he were staring hard into Yumiko's eyes.

'I have read your letter, and have given the gist of my reply to your aunt, although this is really a matter for the chief secretary, as it concerns questions which I'm not in a position to deal with directly. That is one reason, coupled with the fact that we were in my official work room, where I tend to be cautious in the way I express myself, why I was unable to really get to grips with the matter, with the result that she didn't seem all that pleased. This I found rather upsetting, since I like to be of service to old friends and feel I haven't done so in this case. Still, I can now say this to you…' He looked her straight in the eye and went on: 'Would you tell my friend Mr Kiriyama that I should be very pleased to attend any centennial celebrations of the *New Daily* when they take place … on their new premises…'

Yumiko gave a little cry of glee:

'So we'll be able to have the party in the new building? Thank you so much. I shall tell him straight away—I know he'll be delighted.'

'By that distant date, assuming I'm still alive, I shall no doubt be in retirement, while you, Ms Minami, will still be writing editorials, of course.' He paused. 'I repeat, you will still be a member of the editorial writing staff.' He smiled and added: 'Here's wishing you more power to your pen.'

'I understand. Thank you very, very much.'

Yumiko had been feeling confident that things would work out if the negotiations were left to her aunt, but these words still came as a pleasant surprise. At the same time, however, a slight suspicion entered her mind that perhaps her meeting with the prime minister's wife might have some connection with the way things seemed to have gone.

'I must also thank you with regard to the make-up,' he said, bowing his head, 'and apologise for any trouble it may have caused. I shouldn't really be saying this, but I'm afraid the only things that are of any interest to my wife now are cosmetics and food. It's very sad. If left to herself, she would spend the whole day making her face up, only to take it all off and start again. For that reason we don't buy her any, and consequently, when she sees an attractive woman visitor, she tries to beg some off her. It's all most unfortunate.'

'It really wasn't any trouble.'

'What you gave her must have made her very happy. She wore

278

the hairpin she offered in exchange when she danced the Wisteria Girl, and it means a great deal to her. She was obviously touched by your generosity.'

'There's no need…'

'Normally she would be in my house in Seijo, but she does occasionally visit me here. She's like a child, you see, and one has to let her do what she wants. She wakes up in the night, sees the light on in my room and that I'm not there, and goes all the way to my office if someone doesn't stop her on the way, which she is rather careful they shouldn't do. Once in the past when she felt lonely, she got one of the maids to take her to my office, and that's how she remembers the way. And the maid was someone from back home who had been with us a long time.'

Yumiko said nothing, but nodded, and he went on:

'I'm afraid I'm to blame for the extent of her distress. It will take some time to explain, but if you don't mind…?'

'Of course not.'

'Completely off the record, you realise?'

'I accept that,' Yumiko replied, thinking there was little chance that she'd be allowed to use this kind of material anyway, but also feeling a journalist's satisfaction at hearing information nobody else had been able to get at.

The tone of the prime minister's voice changed slightly, becoming a little gloomier.

'As you will probably have heard from your aunt, my marriage was basically one of political convenience. The dowry I received was my father-in-law's constituency. My father-in-law had his debts paid off for him, and enough besides to make his retirement very comfortable. Well, it's an old story; it happens often enough outside the political world, I believe.'

'Yes.'

'Still, it went quite well, really—at the beginning, at least. In fact it might have gone on well enough for a very long time, only a rather strange incident occurred. To cut a long story short, let me just say that, about fifteen years ago, the deputy mayor in one of the towns in my area said he wanted to be mayor. He was the elder brother of my wife's dance teacher. The younger brother had studios in Nagoya and Tokyo. I told the deputy mayor it was all right by me, but the situation suddenly changed and the party decided to support a different candidate. There's nothing you can do in a situation like that. You don't have that sort of power as an individual.'

Yumiko nodded emphatically to show she understood, and he acknowledged this with a slight nod of his own.

'Of course, I phoned the deputy mayor—the elder brother, that is—and got him more or less to accept this turn of events. I suppose I should have told him he'd be next on the list, made some kind of promise, but it would have been a bit difficult for me, in the position I was then, to keep that promise. But where I really went wrong was in not telephoning the younger brother, the dance teacher. I still regret not doing so. And then the elder brother, who'd told me he didn't intend to run, finally decided he would, and naturally failed to get elected. Up to this point nothing particularly terrible had happened. It was what came next.'

The prime minister stopped to reflect for a moment, but soon went on again, although at a slightly faster pace.

'One month after the election the dance teacher committed suicide in a hotel in Toyama. He took an overdose of sleeping pills. That same day, in our house in Seijo, my wife took a similar overdose, but in her case they were able to save her. Neither left any suicide note. I was on a plane on my way back from America. Without my knowing anything about it, the two of them had been having an affair for two or three years.'

Yumiko's smart handbag of suede and enamel slipped off her lap onto the floor. But she was less concerned about the bag than with what possible reason the prime minister could have for telling all this to a woman journalist, someone he'd only just met and who was, moreover, a virtual intruder in his home. The first thought that occurred to her was that this was an attempt to talk her into something—in fact, to make some kind of pass at her. Her first instinct was always to suspect something of this sort, partly because of past experience, but mostly because she flattered herself that men would naturally take that kind of interest in her. However, she soon decided this wasn't really very likely, considering where they were.

The prime minister leaned forward and picked up her bag. His hair was not as thin on top as she'd expected.

'That's a nice handbag,' he murmured as he gave it back to her. Yumiko thanked him, and said the safest sort of thing in this situation:

'Please go on.'

And he did.

'After that my wife was never very well, always prone to some illness or other. Then, five years later, she fell over and hurt herself, as a result of which she caught a spinal infection—herpes, in fact—and became mentally the same as a child... It was pitiful.'

'I can well imagine,' said Yumiko, still wondering why he should feel obliged to confess so much.

'Everyone—my wife most of all—had a bad time of it. But feeling sorry for her doesn't mean letting her eat as much as she likes, or letting her sit there painting her face for hours—which is why she made such a nuisance of herself with you.'

Yumiko responded quite calmly.

'I wonder, Prime Minister, if I could ask you a question?'

'Of course.'

'I'm curious to know why you have decided to tell me all this, seeing it's only the first time we've met. I imagine it's something you've been keeping secret for a considerable length of time.'

'Yes,' Tamaru replied just as calmly. 'I assume it's partly because I feel I can trust you to go on keeping a secret, since you were kind to my wife. It's as if you're not really a stranger. That's the first reason. Secondly, I can't help being affected by the fact that you look so like Masako when she was younger. But I must confess my principal aim is that you should sympathise with my wife's tragedy, and should refrain from writing, at any time, now or in the future, about what you've seen and heard here tonight.'

'Well, Prime Minister,' she said in a much louder voice than she'd intended, 'you certainly make your intentions very plain. Of course I shan't write about your wife, now or at any time in the future. But I had no intention of doing so anyway, whether you'd told me all that or not.'

Tamaru was obviously relieved to hear this, but his pleasure was spoiled to some extent by the realisation that he'd blundered, that there'd been no need to give her that information after all.

'Could I ask you a few more questions?' Yumiko enquired. 'When I was a cub reporter I was told to pay particular attention to any information given off the record, even though it couldn't be written up. You had to ask questions about it and get all the facts clear in your mind.'

'All right, then,' Tamaru replied easily.

'Thank you. Well, the first thing is, since neither of them left any suicide notes, how did you find out about their affair? Did your wife tell you about it afterwards?'

'I got the story from her old maid.'

'She offered the information freely?'

'No.'

'Then how did you get the story out of her?'

This seemed to take Tamaru aback, and he looked uncomfortable as he said:

'Do I have to answer that question?'

'If you wouldn't mind.'

'Why do you need to know?'

'As I just said, I was taught not to be lazy about stories just because they weren't going to be written up, as laziness could become a habit. Naturally I'm not going to write this story either, but my training as a journalist makes me feel obliged to follow it up properly.'

'And suppose I say I won't answer?'

Yumiko tried to conceal the fact she was trembling as she replied:

'If the prime minister doesn't give me a satisfactory reply, then I might have to look for one elsewhere. Obviously I would tell any other informants that their information was off the record, too.'

'It wouldn't bother you to have to take this up with strangers?'

'No. Morally speaking, of course, it would be wrong to divulge my source, saying I'd heard such and such from the prime minister. There are some people who claim that "off the record" is only a prohibition against writing and doesn't extend to speaking about the matter, but I feel that's questionable, morally. What I would do is tell people there was a certain rumour and ask them what they knew about it. I was told there was no problem if one did that.'

'All right. Then what sort of people do you plan to question?'

'The maid from her home town who was with you for years. Your secretary at the time. Your son in America.'

'He's a fool. He only knows about research.'

'I was told he was rather brilliant in his field.'

'And he doesn't know a thing outside it.'

Yumiko mentioned the name of a Nobel Prize candidate, a chemist who was one of her 'pre-forties', saying he had praised Tamaru's son's research in the highest terms, although he had actually done nothing of the sort.

'Anyway, he hates being disturbed.'

'But I'd only need a few minutes of his time. International phone calls are so easy nowadays.'

'Oh, all right, then—I suppose I might as well tell you. The maid's younger brother was a policeman whose promotion to superintendent never seemed to come through and who was always asking me to do something about it. I remembered that, so I told her I'd do something about her brother if she'd tell me everything.'

'I see,' said Yumiko, turning to the next question, although this was more like a confirmation of what she already knew.

'Fifteen years ago, I believe you said? So your wife would have been in her forties?'

'Yes. I think she was forty-eight.'

'Forgive me if I seem to be prying, but how old was the man?'

'Ten years younger. Yes, thirty-eight.'

'Was he married?'

'Yes, but with no children.'

'Had your wife had relationships of this kind before?'

Again an odd look came over Tamaru's face.

'Why should you want to know that?'

'I do apologise, Prime Minister, but a conscientious journalist is bound to ask questions about any point that isn't absolutely clear.'

'I see.'

Tamaru was reminded of that American writer from a quarter of a century ago and his endless questions on almost any subject you mentioned to him. Probably the worst experience he'd had with him was when they went together to the funeral of some important person in his constituency, where he'd been pestered with questions about Japanese funeral customs. The man was never satisfied with the usual answers, but kept asking 'why' all the time on the way back, like some horrible little child. What Tamaru had found most difficult to explain was the consolatory gift (money, of course). He'd managed to bluff his way out of this with some kind of answer, until he got carried away and stupidly revealed that you were always given half the amount back in some other form, which prompted another chorus of 'whys' until he'd felt like bursting into tears. Remembering those far-off days, he was able to reassure himself that this was nothing by comparison, but his reply was still made in a very cheerless voice:

'I think he was probably the first. I can't be absolutely sure.'

'Did you ask her maid the same question?'

'I don't think I did,' he said, then smiled wryly and added: 'In a case like that you don't have the time or the inclination to go into too much detail. There are questions of face involved.'

'There must be.'

Tamaru decided to divulge a few more details, however, as if he'd rather do this than be subjected to any more questions.

'The dance teacher had always been a bit neurotic, always finding life too much for him. Since he tended to make the worst of everything, he managed to convince himself it was his fault his

284

brother hadn't been chosen as the official party candidate. He was one of those people who just seem to get everything wrong. So there he was, thinking he'd ruined his brother's career through his extramarital activities, and presumably also worried that I might decide to take some kind of revenge on him, which I could easily have done, as I'd helped him out with bank loans and favours of various kinds; added to which there would have been the knowledge that they'd never be able to meet again if the affair was made public. All these feelings must have come to a head, and he killed himself.'

Yumiko nodded but didn't interrupt.

'I don't think there can be much doubt about it. There was what the maid had to say. Then they both took their sleeping pills at exactly the same time. That could hardly have been accidental. It must have been worked out beforehand … as a double suicide.'

Yumiko looked him straight in the eye, and this seemed to encourage him.

'I didn't ask my wife about it. She took a long time to recover, and then she looked so apologetic and nervous about everything I just didn't have the heart to interrogate her. I didn't feel she was really to blame, either. I could see much of the responsibility was mine—I was always caught up in the demands of my career, always too busy to have time for her, and so she felt lonely and that's why it happened. I didn't want to question her about it.'

'Prime Minister,' Yumiko said with a bright smile, 'you said you were always too busy to have time for her, but was this only the demands of your career?'

'Ah-ha.' Tamura smiled back. 'Well, there were other things.'

'How many others?'

'That's a very nasty question,' he said, but looking rather pleased to have been asked it. 'I seem to have been summoned before the house, and the right honourable member for the opposition is determined to give me a hard time. Very well, let's say two, in the main.'

'So there were, from time to time, others besides those two?'

'Yes.'

'Who were the two?'

'One was a geisha, the other an actress.'

'You seem to go for actresses.'

'Yes, I suppose I do.'

'At this point I would like to make a request.'

'Yes?'

'I would like to write an article for the lifestyle pages on the prime minister's official residence from the domestic point of view. I mean just as a house, with no mention of your wife, of course. How would you feel about that? Would I be allowed to come here again for material?'

'I see no reason why not.'

'Thank you very much,' she said, and bowed.

'Oh, look at the time,' said Tamaru, glancing at his watch. It was half past four. 'It's been a funny sort of night, and it all started from the coincidence of my wife's being here and meeting you.'

He appeared to be lost in thought, and this seemed a good opportunity for Yumiko to show what she was made of.

'But you know, Prime Minister, one shouldn't take coincidences too lightly. According to a certain philosopher, ever since Nietzsche announced the death of God, people have treated romantic love as a substitute for Him, and our contemporaries in particular tend to see chance encounters as a revelation of the existence of this new divinity.'

'Yes. He may well have a point there. Human beings manage their lives by attributing meaning to all kinds of accidents. You seem to be quite a reader as well. I'm impressed.'

'I buy books, but I find it hard to settle down to read them,' Yumiko replied modestly, as politeness required, although she was secretly laughing at the idea that the prime minister probably assumed this 'philosopher' was someone like Heidegger or Bergson. She stood up.

'If you'll excuse me, I think I should be on my way. I must thank you again, sir, for all the trouble you've taken.'

'Good night,' he said.

'Good night,' Yumiko replied, but just as she was about to go she heard a remarkable sound coming from the next room, like thick paper being ripped apart.

'What's that noise?' she asked.

'My wife snoring,' the prime minister replied with a grimace.

When Yumiko arrived at the small inner garden, she experienced a strange sensation as she stood gazing at it through the plate-glass window: something of fabulous size (that something probably being space itself, although she wasn't sure) had shrunk and was now compressed into this tiny, commonplace garden. She'd noticed nothing special about it when she'd passed this way before, but now this sad area, with its plastic bag, pressed heavily on her, as if the rock garden were the universe and the stone lantern, basin, and other objects in it the moon and Mars and all the planets, while the bamboo was this earth of ours, and all this was now laid out, in condensed form, before her. She put the palms of her hands flat against the glass and felt radiating from it an energy so strong her head went cold and numb, while the strain in her shoulders was almost unbearable. To stop this numbness and pain she decided she must walk, she must try to walk; and she just managed to do so. Then she remembered her handbag, and picked it up.

As she was changing into her shoes at the step, she felt a surge of joy at the thought that she'd finally won, combined with a heavy weariness which spread throughout her body. Fujimura, the private secretary, was in the ante-room and said their car was waiting in front of the main entrance. When Yumiko peered in through the window, the driver woke up, but her aunt remained fast asleep, snoring only slightly more quietly than the prime minister's wife.

NINE

:

Saturday towards the end of March; six o'clock in the evening. What was to be the last drinking party in the editorial staff room was about to begin. Attendance had been dropping off for some time, and since two of the regulars (the man from the sports pages who was crazy about golf, and the former political reporter who had fallen down the stairs in a bar) had reached retirement age the previous year, the executive committee had finally decided to drop the event. The chief hadn't been too happy about this, hoping it would continue 'for as long as we remain in this building', but nobody took any notice of him. That remark of his did, however, convey something of the company situation at the time: land had finally been acquired; on 1 December the executive section chief had been made head of a standing committee appointed to prepare for the move to the new building; and even without much more than that to go on, the general feeling was that they would all be moving quite soon.

What had happened was this. A few days after Yumiko reported the prime minister's message to the paper's chairman, Chie learned from her friend at the Ministry of Finance, Miyake, that a meeting of the National Property Commission was to be convened in the near future. The same news reached the paper via its journalist attached to that ministry, as well as from a member of the commission itself, among other sources. Ten days later

Miyake rang to say the exchange of land had been ratified by a unanimous vote, which was confirmed the same day via other, more circuitous routes, and not long afterwards the chairman went to pay his respects to the prime minister and the minister of finance. Chie was delighted by Miyake's news, though in view of the way things had developed with Shibukawa, she also felt slightly awkward. Then for some reason, all communication with Miyake ceased. She mentioned this to Shibukawa when she met him early in January, and he grinned and said he wasn't surprised, having seen his friend over the New Year. Miyake had got to know a girl who worked as secretary to the chairman of a large corporation, had fallen in love with her, and the girl was apparently equally keen on him. Shibukawa had taken the opportunity to explain how things were between Chie and himself, and received the other's blessing. Chie, naturally, was relieved to hear this.

'The funny thing is,' he told her, 'he said she had one failing: she likes contemporary music, while he can't stand it. He's also worried that listening to twelve-tone music might have a bad effect on a baby in the womb. Seems a bit early in the day to be bothering about things like that, doesn't it?' Shibukawa smiled and then, on second thoughts, added: 'Or perhaps it isn't.'

That was on the seventh of January; on the fifteenth, around lunchtime, Chie had a phone call from her classmate, Banzan Onuma's granddaughter, which made her burst out laughing. That morning the two sisters had asked Banzan if he'd done what had been asked of him, and he admitted he'd completely forgotten what it was. The girl said she was awfully sorry but would Chie mind telling her, so that she could remind him; and Chie explained that the whole business had been settled and they could relax. This caused a good deal of amusement in Chie's family, though Etsuko, who would soon be seventy-one, muttered something about still being a decade younger than the grand old man.

In the meantime, as hardly needs pointing out, word about the land transfer and Yumiko's position on the paper had soon

289

reached a wider circle of people. At the end of October, for example, the conductor rang from Singapore to offer his congratulations—as did the government politician, the chairman of the company renowned for new technology, and the bureau chief in MITI, all round about the same time. She particularly enjoyed getting a Christmas card from the gang boss Heigoro Asaoka, posted in Rome and arriving on New Year's Eve, apologising for not having been of more service to her and explaining that he had been too busy with some business in the Philippines; he was, however, delighted at the outcome. She tried to think what possible connection there could be between Rome and the Philippines, the only thing coming to mind being the Vatican, and then dismissed the idea as too unlikely.

But the biggest change in her life was that she was no longer called in once a week to be interviewed by the head of personnel. Now that she was free of these meetings, she realised just how miserable they had made her. Sometime in the middle of November she was sitting in the ground-floor coffee shop talking to a visitor when in came Hasegawa. He approached her, smiling, and asked how she was getting on. He looked exactly as he had a month before, very large, with a bad complexion and tiny slit eyes like bits of string, but he also gave the impression he was genuinely pleased to see her. It was probably this that made her praise his smart ensemble of sky-blue suit and navy-blue tie.

One thing that didn't change was her relationship with her immediate boss. He was as affable as ever, giving no indication he'd ever heard anything about the affair, and making no mention of the fact that her transfer had been cancelled. This was in sharp contrast to most other people on the paper, who soon came to understand that Yumiko's position was now secure and changed their former attitude—whether it had been sympathetic, cautious, or embarrassed—to one of casual familiarity in her presence, some even going so far as to congratulate her quite openly.

So it is difficult to pinpoint the exact moment she began to think of leaving the paper. Perhaps it would be safer just to say the idea had always been somewhere at the back of her mind.

One proof of this was that, when the maestro had rung from Paris and suggested she should give up the business altogether, she had certainly found the idea eccentric but at the same time was able to see it as at least one possible solution. Then, ever since that night in the prime minister's house, the thought of resigning had felt more and more a possibility, her whole view of her role as a woman journalist having changed its perspective. When she submitted her notion of an article on the prime minister's residence to the lifestyle pages and it was turned down, as she'd half expected, due to opposition from the political section, she found it didn't bother her; and when, as the first act of the newly formed standing committee preparing for the move to their new premises, a circular came round asking for suggestions, she gave it her serious attention but as a matter involving other people rather than herself, and wrote only very general answers, such as that every journalist should have his own separate desk, as they did on the editorial writing staff. It was during the six months that she was observing herself in this way that her resolve to leave the company became firm.

Naturally enough, she talked over the question with Toyosaki a number of times, but no amount of discussion seemed to establish why she wanted to leave. In fact, the reason became progressively more obscure, much as it does when a reporter is taking down an expert's opinion on the cause of some air disaster. But during one of these sessions together the following happened. Toyosaki was describing how, when he was talking to Sakakibara, the chief secretary, he'd said that, since the idea of exchange was so strong in Japan as to dominate all aspects of social life, it would be very hard to maintain parliamentary democracy. And Yumiko was struck by a related thought: the rise of the newspaper in Europe was obviously linked to the rise of parliamentary democracy, and if Japanese democracy was simply the outer shell of something essentially different, then it followed that there was something fundamentally wrong with Japanese newspapers. As proof of the basic weakness of the Japanese press, one only had to look at this business of the transfer of government land.

'I think that's it, you see. I've come to think of the press here as operating according to a law of its own. Up until now I'd always thought our papers were like those in the West.'

She explained it was these doubts about basic issues that made her want to resign. After six months or a year off, she felt she'd like to write criticism or essays. There were plenty of magazines around nowadays, and they were looking for women writers, so she imagined things would somehow work out.

'But,' said Toyosaki, 'if our parliamentary democracy isn't functioning properly, then that makes the role of the press even more important. Our papers probably are different from European ones, but they're still newspapers. There are all kinds of saké cups, of various shapes and sizes, colours and patterns, all made in different parts of the country. They look different, they feel different, but they're all essentially the same thing…'

Even this argument, already used in the restaurant in Sendai, together with various others pointing to the conclusion that there was no good reason for her to resign, had no real effect on her. Her motives for leaving weren't clearly thought out, so they were hard to contradict.

Yumiko first discussed the matter with Toyosaki in mid-December, and when they met at the New Year she'd already made up her mind. All her family agreed with her. Toyosaki tried once again to get her to reconsider, but now more with the idea of finding out if her decision was serious or not. He understood well enough that her experiences over the short period from June to October must have given her an unusual insight, from a number of different angles, into the newspaper business, and that she could hardly have gone on working there with the same attitude as before; and by February he'd agreed with her decision. She then made a formal application to the company, and although the head of her section and even her old enemy Hasegawa tried to talk her out of it, and there were other complications, the final result was that her resignation was accepted with effect from 31 March.

Thus, on the night before that Saturday towards the end of

March, there had been a small farewell party for her and a few other people, and the man in charge of 'the booze-up' itself had asked her to put in a brief appearance there as well, to say goodbye to them all.

Urano would also be saying goodbye. While investigating the religious sect at Yumiko's request, he'd managed to sniff out some suspicious goings-on at a certain bank, and he appeared to have done enough to ensure that its president would have to resign. This scoop had brought him back into the limelight, and since the projected move to the new building seemed to call for a lot of shifting around of personnel, the upshot was that he was made head of the city desk from 1 April. One need hardly say that he was finding it difficult to conceal his glee.

Being the last drinking party, attendance was high, with even some retired staff showing up, and everything went with a swing. One journalist complained that he didn't see why they should give up these parties when this one was going so well, but the man from the arts pages who always had to have the last word said it was just like the final number of a magazine, which always sold out. Most of them had begun drinking, of course, well before the party officially started.

Editorial adviser Ichiro Anzai was explaining to a large group of listeners how he'd been made visiting professor at a certain university where he only had to teach a graduate seminar.

'At least it means I won't be blocking anyone else's promotion,' he said, in justification for the move.

'I don't think you should hold yourself back that way,' said a former financial reporter. 'Teach all you can. When Keynes was old he was asked if he regretted anything in life, and he said he wished he'd drunk more champagne. It looks as if you'll have to say you wished you'd done more teaching.'

'Which means you think I like the sound of my own voice,' said the scholar of economics, accurately enough.

In due course, the party was officially opened. The chief said a few formal words, one of the deputies called for a toast, and then Urano was invited to say something.

'Ms Minami ought to be first by rights, but I suppose we're doing it in reverse alphabetical order. Anyway, thank you one and all for a very instructive year. I'm really grateful for all you've done for me. The fact is, the year I've spent here has completely changed my life. I know a lot of you will be nudging each other and grinning and making insinuations, but let me assure you it's got nothing to do with anything like that, only with the fact that at last I've learned how to write.' (Laughter and applause.) 'Of course, I admit I'm still not much good, but at least I can do it all on my own now... I can, can't I?' ('He can,' someone said.) 'At this point, I want to say that Ms Minami taught me a lot, somehow persuading me I could do it myself. That bucked me up, you know, it made me want to work away as hard as I could, just so that teacher would have something nice to say to me. The fact that she's leaving the team at the same time as me seems a pretty remarkable coincidence—we joined the team together, too. Still, she's a wonderful teacher. Couldn't ask for better... I found out she only likes intellectuals, and I tried to become one myself, to get on more intimate terms, but unfortunately that didn't work out.' (General laughter.) 'Better luck next time.' (Laughter.) 'But now that I'm going back to the city desk, where there's not much culture to spare, I don't suppose there's much chance I'll ever become an intellectual. At least I hope I don't forget how to write. I'm afraid this speech seems to have gone off at a tangent, but anyway, thanks to each and all, wishing you good health and more power to your pens. Let's keep in touch.'

The assembled throng, all thirty of them, burst into loud applause and hearty laughter, and one former foreign correspondent who had lived in Italy for donkey's years and made great claims to being a member of the intelligentsia, even had to take his hankie out to wipe the tears away. The three secretaries giggled, and Yumiko also smiled, since everybody was looking at her.

When the applause died down, one man (Anzai, the editorial adviser) went on clapping, and when he'd finished he turned to the chief and said:

'There's nothing quite like the confessional element in speeches of this kind. Most amusing, I thought. I expect it'll be all round the building tomorrow. What a good fellow that Urano is! The point is,' he added, turning to the deputy on his left, 'that he said only Ms Minami taught him and not the rest of you, hah, hah. There's the rub, you know. Most amusing…'

While Anzai was enjoying himself in this bantering way, the man in charge of the proceedings went up to Yumiko.

'They're all making such a racket I think we'll have to wait for them to calm down. Let's give it another ten minutes.'

Then Nobuko Konaka came up to her.

'Well, at least you've got a title for your first book: *Composition for the Completely Incompetent*,' she laughed.

Urano now approached, a glass of shochu diluted with Oolong tea in his hand.

'Sorry about that. Still, you know, that's what my year in this place really amounted to. See you later,' he said, and walked off.

The party was now going with more of a swing than ever, even the non-drinkers having something to keep them happy, as food had been laid on at the company's expense. After ten minutes the organiser called for silence and asked Yumiko to say a few words. She was wearing the same dark blue suit she'd worn on 1 April the previous year for her first day in this office, although her blouse was different, a frilly thing in dark grey. The gathering stood there looking at her, glasses and chopsticks in their hands, as she began to speak.

'When I was at school I always wanted to be a journalist, and I feel very fortunate to have been able to do what I wanted for twenty years and more. We have a habit in this country of comparing everything in life to baseball, and I've felt just like a boy who wanted to be a professional baseball player and actually made it into a team, becoming a regular player, even if he was only sixth or seventh in the batting order.' ('A bit higher than that,' somebody said.) 'I've been perfectly satisfied with my place in the batting order, and I want to thank all of you who've helped me to stay there, and to say how grateful I am. Some of you may ask why I want to give up a job I like so much, and all I can say in reply is that I don't really know myself. What I do know is that my year in this office has been a richer experience than the whole of the previous twenty years. It would take too long to describe what that experience has meant to me, so instead I want to talk about something else, something quite personal, which may or may not be connected with what has happened to me here.

'For a long time now my mother has been saying she wants to get a dog. I've always been against the idea, because it goes against the regulations of the block of flats we live in. But recently I changed my mind. "Let's get one," I told her, and we've chosen— well, my daughter has, anyway—a miniature schnauzer, which is due to arrive next week. We're all looking forward to it.

'Now, I changed my mind for two reasons. Firstly, when I took a proper look at the regulations, I found nothing in them about being forbidden to keep pets; all there was was a stipulation about not keeping pets that might be a nuisance to your neighbours. This shows a real laziness on my part about finding out the facts, something I should be ashamed of as a newspaper reporter. The senior people in the residents' association had just over-interpreted what was in the regulations, and misled everybody accordingly.

'Secondly—and this is the funny part—my mother was sent a crate of fruit by somebody, and as usual she decided to share some of it with our neighbours. She called on the head of the association, who, incidentally, is a retired lawyer, and when they opened the door, what should come flying out but a cat!' (General laughter.) 'They'd been keeping one on the quiet.'

The author of 'In a Pensive Mood' applauded vigorously, sounding like a twenty-one-gun salute, and one of the retired journalists, an ancient character, cried out, 'Well done!' Yumiko waited for the commotion to die down, then continued:

'So we decided to keep a dog ourselves, and I started to wonder why I'd always been against the idea, and came to the conclusion it was probably because I worked for a newspaper. Since I was always writing about people behaving very badly, on the one hand, or extremely well, on the other, I couldn't face the idea of being criticised behind my back. I now regret I didn't write about this while I had the chance—I mean, about the desire to keep a dog and the feeling that it was wrong. Obviously it wouldn't do for an editorial, but it would have suited "Starting from Scratch". Desmond Morris, the zoologist, says somewhere that old people who keep dogs and cats have lower blood pressure. I still think it would suit that column.'

At this point the voice (together with a raised hand) of the author of 'News from Another Planet' was heard:

'Let me have the story—I'll use it right away!'

Everyone looked over to where he was standing by the blackboard, and he smiled engagingly at them all.

'Poor fellow. It must be hard finding something new every day,' Anzai said sympathetically, and everybody laughed again.

'All right, I'll send you a copy,' said Yumiko, then resumed her speech.

'I think I had started trying to be better than other people, or at least better than I really was, before I joined this section, but it certainly got worse after I began writing editorials. That may explain why I only started thinking seriously about the real purpose of journalism after I took up this post. Still, it's rather like thinking about baseball while actually playing it—it makes the activity less interesting.' ('I'm with you there,' somebody said.) 'Anyway, there were a number of occasions when I found I wasn't sure whose opinions I was writing. When my own point of view and that of the paper were much the same, the writing came easily but was little more than a string of platitudes in the established house style. Mr Urano was kind enough to praise me just now, so let me return the compliment and say the pieces he wrote were never in the house style, never followed any established pattern, but were always new in their approach, and they taught *me* a lot.

'But I won't go on about that or we could be here all night—mainly because I don't really know how to explain myself properly. Let me just say that things seemed to pile up, and I felt I simply couldn't go on. And so I decided—to extend my baseball metaphor—to drop out of the team. What I want to do now is take some time off—six months or so, maybe a year—to think, then maybe move on to something new. There are a number of subjects I want to write about, and I'm still in perfect health, so there are no worries on that score. In fact, I can promise you I'm not finished yet. So here's wishing us all a bright future. Thank you very much.'

She received even more applause than Urano had, partly because she was leaving, partly because the story about the dog had gone down well, but mostly out of gratitude and admiration at her discretion in not mentioning the squalid business concerning the personnel department, the government land and all the rest of it, which they all vaguely knew about. For that reason, presumably, they were able to overlook her remarks about editorial writing, which applied to them all.

Urano came up to her and, in a booming voice, thanked her for her kind remarks, then lowered his voice and said:

'There's something I want to give you. Let me know when you're leaving.'

One of her colleagues, a man who had spent years reporting law cases and was known for his sullen disposition, smiled and said:

'You find that kind of man, the ex-lawyer in your block of flats, all too often these days, you know, I can't think why.'

But before Yumiko could answer, the man from the arts pages—the fount of useless information who always liked to have the last word—said:

'Ms Minami, Ms Minami, are you going to have that dog's tail and ears trimmed or not?'

And a number of other people seemed to want to say something about how editorials should be written. However, despite being the centre of all this attention, she remembered what Urano had said, and after about thirty minutes made a sign to him and went to her desk, now empty, since she had already cleared her things away earlier in the day. Urano gave her a small package tied with a ribbon.

'But Shirobei isn't here. It's for him.'

'I wonder what it can be,' she said, opening the parcel and finding a small dog collar made of red leather inside. 'Oh, what a clever present—it's charming. How very sweet of you.'

'As I said in my speech,' he said proudly, 'I still haven't given up. If you lose your old tenant, you know where you can find a new one.'

'What an extraordinary way you have of putting things,' she said, glaring, but he smiled back at her, quite unperturbed.

She took the subway to Toyosaki's hotel. He'd been lecturing that afternoon, but was paying for his room himself. He hadn't eaten yet, and she unpacked the various provisions she'd bought before the editorial party. There was an odd mixture—terrine of duck, beef stew, salad, rice, hijiki and fried tofu, spring greens dressed in mustard Japanese-style, and a bottle of red wine. Toyosaki had paid for it, but the choice of what to buy had been hers, although she'd taken into account his penchant for mixed Western and Oriental food. They asked room service to heat up the stew, the hijiki, and the fried tofu in a microwave.

During the short time it took to do this Yumiko showed Toyosaki the present she'd just been given.

'What is it? A bracelet?'

This amused her so much she tried it round her wrist. Toyosaki watched her, at the same time reflecting that he hadn't eaten pre-cooked food of the kind Yumiko had bought for over a month now. His wife had risen from her sickbed, the reason behind her remarkable recovery being that she'd felt sorry for the editorial writer who was going to be transferred, and had rung up the chief secretary's wife about it. Up until then, she'd been avoiding the telephone, but her concern over someone else's troubles had given her own spirits a lift, and from that point on she had decided to face the outside world again. Just two weeks earlier, in fact, when he was writing a short article, she'd knocked briskly on his study door and come in, then said, looking slightly embarrassed:

'I wonder…'

'What?'

'Could I have that back?'

'Could you have what back?'

'You know—what I gave you. The money and things.'

'Ah, that. Now where did I put it?'

As he tried to think, she raised her right hand and pointed at one of the drawers in a bookcase in the far corner of the room. He opened the drawer, finding inside a large envelope with her bank savings book and other things in it. She took the envelope.

'I seem to be all right again.'

'Good.'

'Yes.'

'Everything seems easier when you're well.'

'I know.'

She'd asked him what he wanted for dinner the next day, then left the room.

Toyosaki took the dog collar off Yumiko's wrist and, fiddling with it, praised the thought behind the gift.

'Not something for you to wear, but your toy dog. I rather admire it, the indirect approach. There's something old-fashioned about it.'

'He probably thought it was a good joke.'

'Yes, it has a playful aspect to it, too. When tension is suddenly released, the comic, or rather the absurd, tends to appear. In this case the intensely romantic nature of his infatuation with you has been transferred onto the relationship you have with your toy dog. That's the comic element coming into play, and that's how he hoped to please you. Consequently, the gift is perfectly sincere. I imagine he thought of it on a sudden impulse, but it still shows a nice touch. He had every right to fall for you.'

'This is high praise.'

'Indeed it is.'

He enjoyed being generous with his praise, convinced as he was that this woman had no interest in any other man.

The waiter arrived, Toyosaki uncorked the wine, and their little dinner party began. The wine was surprisingly good, considering its price. The terrine was tolerable.

First, Yumiko told him about the final drinking party, how she had avoided making a direct attack on the editorial policy of the paper only by getting people to laugh at her dog problem and the ex-lawyer. Then she said Urano had been applauded enthusiastically for his little confession, and had told her he hadn't given up hope.

'I see. The man impresses even more, with his depth of feeling. A model for us all.'

He poured out a second glass, and mentioned that Sakakibara's karaoke performance had been written up in a local Sendai paper just the other day. His wife had noticed it and posted it to him. It was only a short article, but the last sentence came as a surprise.

> The philosophy professor Yokichi Toyosaki was privileged to see this performance somewhere in town, and was so struck by it that he sent the performer a research paper entitled 'Dance and the Body'.

What had happened was that Toyosaki had received a letter from the chief secretary's aide saying that his ideas for abolishing the constitution had been considered impracticable, etc., etc., and he had replied enclosing a copy of the research paper in question. He had been amused to see how a prominent politician was prepared to enlist anything in the cause of self-promotion.

'But it's absurd to call what he did dancing, surely,' said Yumiko, glass in hand.

'In evaluatory terms, yes. In categorical terms, no.'

'Explain that, will you?—the evaluatory and categorical stuff. It could come in handy sometime.'

'People say of some cold-blooded murderer,' said the lecturer, getting into his stride, 'that "he isn't human". This is an evaluatory remark, based on the ethical notion that only decent human beings can be considered truly human. The statement is thus a value judgement. But even the most evil of criminals still belongs

301

to that class of primates known as homo sapiens. That's the "category" he belongs to, being neither a lion nor a cockroach, and thus to call him human is a categorical statement.'

'Another of your wonderfully clear explanations.'

'Don't make fun of me.'

'I'd like to see a copy of your paper.'

'I've brought one with me.'

He produced a Xerox of his monograph, and wrote his name and hers on the cover. His handwriting was peculiar, looking both relaxed and neurotic at the same time. In evaluatory terms, one couldn't really call it writing.

While eating the beef stew, Yumiko talked about her aunt who, the week before, had been offered a part in a new film. She'd been reminded of this by the talk about dance. The director, a well-known figure, had flattered her by claiming it had been a long-term ambition of his, ever since his early days as an assistant director, to make a film with Aeka Yanagi; and she herself, delighted it would be a real film, not one of those television dramas, was very excited about it. She would be playing the part of a former prime minister's widow.

Apparently Masako was going round telling everyone what a coincidence this was, and how the great director must have kept himself informed of her affairs. Yumiko couldn't help thinking how useful her own experience with Tamaru's wife might be to her aunt as a way of getting into the role; but eventually she decided not to tell her about it, knowing that if she did the rumour would spread like wildfire.

Toyosaki toyed with his beef stew, paying more attention to the wine and rice.

'I suppose this means both mother and aunt must be pleased with the way things have turned out. That's something to be grateful for. And how has the daughter responded?'

'She seems pretty happy, too.'

'I see.'

Yumiko was about to tell him about Chie and her two young men, but she didn't get the chance because Toyosaki went on:

'You remember telling me what your aunt said about local festivals and the offerings people made to the festival god, and what his reaction must be? That they were all in rather bad taste, but acceptable, even so? I was very impressed by that, although I don't recall what I said at the time.'

'You said you were impressed by the way she spoke from her own experience, and that she'd thought things out for herself.'

'What struck me, thinking about it afterwards, was what your aunt said about the way the god responded: it seemed to embody two major characteristics of our culture, namely tolerance and a strong emphasis on the principle of taste. Shinto has its basis in these two qualities. Tolerance is a belief in not pushing anything or anyone too far. Taking a critical view of it, it could be seen as a form of indifference, of course. It involves trying to understand the position of the other person, trying to avoid conflict, at least so far as people within one's own group are concerned. The emphasis on taste, however, represents a different set of values. The importance of cleanliness in Shinto has nothing to do with morality or hygiene but is purely aesthetic. Things are kept neat and tidy simply because it feels better that way. But when this feeling is intellectualised, it takes on an erotic emphasis.'

'Erotic? How?'

'In the Heian period, aesthetic taste dominated court life and was clearly an erotically based concern. Wasn't that what Genji, the Shining Prince's life was all about? And the same can be seen as a thread running through our way of life at all periods. The essentially erotic nature of *mono no aware*—the sadness of things, *lacrimae rerum*—which Motoori Norinaga summed up in the eighteenth century as the basis of all Japanese thought, has been enlarged upon in this century by people like Shinobu Orikuchi.

'But taste is an elusive subject, just as our ancestral religion has always been particularly difficult to define. Since our ancestors themselves seemed able to communicate with each other without the need to say very much—well, they didn't. In order to make Shinto look respectable in ideological terms it was necessary to go to Confucianism or Buddhism, and that's why we find these religions combined in this country, Shinto fusing with Confucianism, Shinto linked up with Buddhism. Being a naturally tolerant religion, it was easy for it to compromise. Conceptually, it's a mess ... although you could also say its lack of doctrine helps make it all-embracing.'

Yumiko decided to tackle the question from a slightly different angle.

'The gods in the West represent clear ideas of justice and love, which can't be said of our gods.'

'Ours represent ideas of a sort, but in a highly diluted form.'

'Being diluted makes them easier to swallow.'

'Easier to swallow...,' the philosopher repeated, thinking about it. 'Yes. Diluted, almost tasteless. The gods are a bit disappointed by what the public gives them in the way of offerings, but it's easy enough to accept, so they don't get cross about it.'

'Because they're so tolerant?'

'That's part of it, but mainly it's because they realise these ordinary, rather awful things have been offered in earnest. The whole business is a nuisance, but people are seriously trying to please them.'

'They're moved by their sincerity?'

'They're moved, all right, and in more senses than one. After all, the sincerity of prayer has magic in it; it creates a sort of spell.'

'Ah,' said Yumiko. 'But presumably that doesn't mean the gods are obliged to respond to our prayers?'

'No, it doesn't ... there being too many other factors involved. So life remains full of misery.'

'Yes,' said Yumiko, surprised herself at the deep sigh she gave, wondering if she should tell him what was on her mind but deciding not to, since tales of woe don't really suit the dinner table—and particularly not when the food is Japanese, which was the part of the meal they were about to embark upon. But she was afraid he might ask her to explain her sigh, and decided to do so in another way. As she poured out the tea, she said:

'Sometime last week I woke up in the middle of the night and a very strange idea crossed my mind.' She gave him a mischievous look, and went on: 'I thought I shouldn't have been so reluctant to accept that hairpin she offered me. In fact, I should have taken it. It just shows how greedy I must be at heart.'

'It's not a question of greed—merely a quite natural psychological reaction, a harmless piece of wishful thinking. You probably also wanted to see it in Chie's hair.'

'I wouldn't mind wearing it myself.'

'Put your hair up, Japanese style?'

'You think it wouldn't suit me?'

This led to a discussion of wigs and hairpins, of how much wigs cost to hire and other questions, until finally she came out with a genuine revelation.

'There's something I kept secret about that visit.'

'That visit?'

'To the prime minister's house.'

'But that was six months ago.'

'It was a big experience for me. It still seems like only yesterday.'

Toyosaki didn't seem all that interested, commenting on the food they were eating, but Yumiko went on:

'I'd left the room and was passing the inner garden when I had this really strange feeling. I'm not sure how to describe it. It was as if all space, the whole world, had been squeezed into that garden.'

'What?'

'And it made my head ache and my body go numb. I just put my hands against the window pane and waited.'

The expression on Toyosaki's face changed, and he put down his chopsticks.

'Try to tell me in more detail.'

She did, but the words wouldn't come easily, although she managed to give a slow, fragmentary account of what she'd experienced six months earlier. Toyosaki remained silent for a while.

'Was it just my imagination?' she asked.

'No, it wasn't.'

'An illness—feeling faint for a while?'

'I don't think that was any illness.'

'What was it, then?'

'A form of religious experience. A mystical experience.'

'You mean I'm religious?!'

'I don't mean you experienced God. It's more like an intense awareness of the existence of the world and the universe—a pseudo-religious experience, if you like. I don't think there's any other way to account for it. A non-believer's religious ecstasy.'

'It didn't feel much like ecstasy. It was more oppressive, sharper-edged than that; it felt weird. I wouldn't say it was actually unpleasant, though.'

'Exactly. That's what religious ecstasy is. Or that's what it's generally said to be. I haven't ever experienced it myself, so I wouldn't know.'

'Ah.'

'I certainly don't think it was anything pathological. Gardens have always served as a miniature of the world, being created to satisfy our desire to see the world in a condensed form. This could well have sparked it off.'

'When I thought about it later I decided, as it wasn't much of a garden, I was probably just overreacting to the fact that it was in the PM's house—to the aura of political power.'

'No, that's simply a rationalisation, working it all out after the event.'

'Which is probably the reason I kept quiet about it; although not the only reason, perhaps.'

'Politics doesn't come into it. The same response could have been aroused by any garden. It was most likely something else.'

'Like what?'

'Late at night you perform this odd exchange of powder and lipstick for a valuable, traditional hair ornament, with an old woman who has become just like a child; this in itself was hardly an ordinary, everyday event. It would have prepared you for something otherworldly, as if the world you were in had been transformed into one of myth.'

'Would it?'

'It could have done. I don't know,' said the professor, looking as if he found the whole thing slightly distasteful.

When they'd finished dinner Yumiko said she'd stay the night and asked him to leave the room for a moment while she phoned her mother. She obviously still found this kind of thing a little embarrassing. Chie answered the phone, announcing that they'd just been given some cakes by the people next door and were eating them. She handed the phone over to Etsuko, who talked about the dog. Then Yumiko took a bath.

Later that night, Toyosaki had some whisky while she kept him company with a glass of beer. After a while she began to speak in a different tone of voice, indicating she had something serious to say.

'Last week a parcel and letter arrived from Hokkaido. From Chie's father.'

This was how Yumiko always referred to her ex-husband—section chief in the Bank of Japan when she'd first met him and now president of a bank in Hokkaido—on the few occasions she did so at all, this being only the third or fourth that Toyosaki could remember.

'He's got cancer. He's handed in his resignation. The letter's not very clear about it, and I can't remember the exact wording, but apparently the doctors don't think he has long to go.'

'How old is he?'

'Fifty-seven.'

'Only two years more than me. That's young to die.'

'He's having an operation early in April. He'll be in hospital for some time.'

'What sort of cancer?'

'The lungs.'

They talked about cancer for a while, then Yumiko said:

'In his letter he said he was sending something under separate cover that had been on his mind for some time. It was a bundle of my letters. I wrote them during our engagement.'

He told her that these letters of hers had been in a small, very ancient trunk in the store room in his family home. She could remember the dark store room, and thought she could also remember its being crammed with boxes containing scrolls and picture frames. When he remarried he must have been uncertain whether to return her letters, and yet reluctant to burn them, so had sent them to his family home instead.

Her writing in these old letters was so different from now that she'd wondered if they could really be hers, but quite clearly they were—love letters of a sort, written in her own hand. They showed how she had looked up to this man whose chief attribute seemed to be the fact that he was twelve years older than her, how pleased she was to have acquired a fiancé after never even having had a boyfriend, and how disappointed she was not to be in love with him (this last a constant undercurrent, although not expressed directly, of course). As she re-read them she was struck by the silliness and immaturity of what they had to say. They were positively embarrassing, at times conceited to the point of rudeness, since she'd been of that age when one is most wrapped up in oneself. Or maybe she'd just written all those things in order to provoke, to get some kind of emotional reaction. She had, for example, told him not to choose his own ties any more, and she occasionally corrected his spelling mistakes. Besides embarrassment, she also felt sorry for the man who'd had to receive and read the things, and a deep sense of gratitude at the consideration he'd shown in returning them. It was while she was in this state of mind that an idea had slowly occurred to her, a pretty amazing idea by any standards. It was this she now revealed, in a serious, heartfelt way.

'I was thinking of going and nursing him for a while.'

'Oh.'

'Going up to Hokkaido.'

'Ah.'

'It's come at a good time, just after my resignation.'

'I see.'

'I wouldn't go for long, just a couple of months. But it might be of some help to his family. You don't mind, do you?'

'Um.'

Toyosaki's first thought was to wonder how the man would feel about having to put up with something like that in front of his present wife. Surely it could only make matters worse for him if he had to try to convalesce with not only his illness to contend with but this complication as well? Yet she looked so eager he wasn't able even to hint at these objections, deciding to look at the question from the wife's point of view.

'Yes, but what will his wife have to say?'

Yumiko's reply was totally unexpected.

'Oh, she's delighted with the idea.'

'You mean you've already been in touch about it?'

'Strike while the iron is hot.'

'You can say that again,' he said, smiling with a composure he didn't feel.

'I phoned yesterday and she said it would be a great help, and I really must come up—I'd be very welcome.'

He was impressed by her apparently unswerving optimism, but on further questioning it turned out that relations of a kind had been established three years before, when Chie had gone to spend a week in Hokkaido (the wife's idea) and had got on very well with her half-sisters. Naturally Yumiko hadn't been invited, but she'd rung the wife to pay her respects, and that had made it much easier to phone this time. Toyosaki could only feel they were both looking a bit too much on the bright side, but he didn't say so, deciding to try a different gambit.

'What about him, what's his name?...'

'Nakahara.'

'Yes, what does Mr Nakahara think about all this?'

'There was another phone call, and he said he was really pleased.'

'He said so himself? Over the phone?'

'Yes. He sounded quite well, but then he started coughing, poor thing. He said he'd never dreamed I might offer to look after him.'

Toyosaki sighed. He couldn't help feeling that, although everyone was behaving in a very generous fashion, there was still something unnatural about it all, particularly when you considered the fact that the man seemed to be on perfectly good terms with his wife. Could it be the journalist in her coming to the surface —the pursuit of some special objective blinding her to other considerations? But although he couldn't approve of the idea, he had nothing in particular against it. His own view was that Mrs Nakahara would find all sorts of difficulties when it came to it, that two women nursing one man wouldn't work, and that she would come to regret not turning the idea down immediately. Her husband, for his part, would be exhausted at being caught between the two women, and would long to be left to die in peace, alone, as we all have to do in the end anyway. Toyosaki could see all these consequences, but it was nothing to do with him personally so he decided to let it go. He realised Yumiko was set on going, and that there was no direct connection with their own relationship, so what did it matter?

He opened a second miniature bottle of whisky and mixed himself another drink, and, seeing Yumiko's bottle of beer, remembered a debate he'd had last summer with a professor of philosophy from Kyoto, about whether beer in a bottle tasted better than beer in a can, although he couldn't remember which view he'd held.

'Well,' he said, 'the situation would have been just about impossible in the past. It's very hard not to feel sorry for someone who has to spend his last days like that.'

Yumiko interpreted these veiled remarks as indicating approval of her plan.

'As divorce becomes more common, so will cases of this kind,' she maintained, also mentioning that the family in Hokkaido had asked for Chie to visit more often. Since Toyosaki had said quite clearly that he was strongly in favour of the daughter seeing her father, she began to think he must surely feel the same way about this other scheme of hers and started to outline how she saw the coming two months. She'd be spending long hours in a sickroom, and would be there some time, so she'd need a place of her own as a base and had decided to take a room in a commercial hotel.

She'd probably return to Tokyo a couple of times over the period as a whole, and would stop off in Sendai on the way. Toyosaki could even come up to Hokkaido if he could find some excuse.

'Yes, I suppose so. I'll just have to get used to the fact that we won't be able to meet every week,' he said, and started describing the various rooms he'd stayed in in commercial hotels while attending academic conferences in different parts of the country. When this harmless digression had ended, Yumiko said, looking at the beer glass in her hand:

'I'll do the same for you sometime,' smiling kindly at him and speaking so calmly that the remark seemed all the more astonishing, a genuine bolt from the blue. For a moment he was unable to take it in, sitting there with a dumbfounded look on his face.

'I'll nurse you.'

'When I've got cancer?'

She nodded silently in response. At this point, he could have saved the situation by saying, casually, that he'd be very glad when the time came, or by indicating gently that he'd prefer not to talk about it, taking her hand or even kissing her to suggest how painful he found the idea of never seeing her again. He could even have turned the whole thing into a joke by asking her if she had no intention herself of dying one day. But instead he found himself thinking that if he did get cancer his wife's depression would return, she'd take to her bed again, and life for him would become another round of cooking, dish-washing, cleaning the house, planning meals, and traipsing off to the supermarket where, in between long periods spent speculating on our perception of three-dimensionality (the current topic of debate between philosophers), and wondering why they always chose a simple six-sided object to discuss, and coming to the conclusion (clearly erroneous, because lacking any philosophical basis) that it was dice they had in mind, he would be obliged to tackle the more pressing question of whether the cheap salmon here, which looked more appetising than the expensive kind over there, really was so, without being able to come to any firm decision. The thought of those dismal days returning sent a cold shudder through him and for some peculiar reason made him ignore the fact that he was the one who was supposed to be suffering in future from cancer. So disturbed was he by this image that he produced exactly the wrong kind of answer.

'I shouldn't bother to do that, really.'

Her expression changed immediately, as did her tone of voice.

'Why not?' she said caustically. 'Why wouldn't you want me to?'

'But they're quite different—his situation and mine.'

'They're almost exactly the same.'

'No they aren't.'

'What's different about them?'

'Lots of things.'

He went on to explain, in a manner that was deliberately cool and quiet, what these differences were. First of all, the bank president had been her husband, which Toyosaki never had. Of course, he was stressing this only as a legal, not an emotional, fact; the emotions involved were irrelevant here. Secondly, the wife in Hokkaido knew about her husband's relationship with Yumiko, whereas Toyosaki's wife did not. These factors alone were enough to set their situations apart.

'So what you're saying,' she said, rather loudly, 'is that you don't want your wife to know about us, even if you're dying of cancer.'

'Yes, that's right,' he replied, having thought about this.

'That's ridiculous. It's completely irrational—and you call yourself a philosopher!'

'Why?'

'Don't you understand? All right, I'll explain. We've been going on like this for years now, always being careful no one should see us together. It's all right to go to the cinema because it's dark in there, but not to the theatre. All that stupid caution got on my nerves, but when I said so what did you say? You said if we got found out we'd have to give each other up. You said if we were to go on with it, then it would be best to keep it all secret. That's what you said, didn't you?'

'Would you mind lowering your voice a little?'

'Well then,' she said, continuing to shout, 'if you were dying of cancer, there'd only be one place we could meet, wouldn't there? There'd be no choice—it would be your sickroom or nowhere.'

'Yes, that makes good logical sense.' He tried to ease the tension by smiling as he spoke, but she went on glaring at him, with the same hard expression on her face. 'Still, you were in perfect agreement with the idea that our relationship should stay secret. You yourself said, if I remember rightly, that the fact that there were no rumours about us, and that nobody knew who your lover was, stood you in good stead on a number of occasions. Take this present, for example.' He pointed at Shirobei's dog collar. 'The man who gave it to you didn't know about me, and felt encouraged in his affection for you…'

'You mean, he'd have got scared and backed off if he'd known he had a character like you to deal with?' she said, but he ignored this facetious comment.

'That's why he put so much effort into investigating your problem…'

'There's no logical necessity about that. Now look who's arguing after the damn event,' she said, giving a howl of triumph, which was followed by a loud knocking on the wall from the next room, obviously objecting to all the noise.

Toyosaki shrugged his shoulders and forced himself to smile, making a gesture with his hand that was meant to pacify her, but judging by the look on her face, she was clearly unappeased. For a moment he found himself thinking how much he'd have preferred to have the person next door complaining about a cry of ecstasy.

'You talk about love,' she went on, her voice slightly more subdued, 'but you only see me when it suits you—when you can fit me in alongside something else.'

'That's one way of looking at it, I admit; but the world isn't made up of one colour. It's a variety of them, a spectrum.'

'Well?'

'Well, it is. And life can't be all one shade either: it isn't either

313

black or white—or grey, for that matter, which they often say the various gradations of light and shade boil down to in the end. That's just a figure of speech, an oversimplification. Life is variable, changing in different lights, now pink, now blue…'

'You're just playing with words.'

'So from one point of view you could say I met you only when it was convenient. But, from another, I'm someone who has constantly arranged his life so that he could see you. Almost everything in my life, just to see you.'

'Look at all the times we couldn't even have dinner together.'

'Sometimes that was because it didn't suit you.'

'We've hardly ever been anywhere together. All we do is go to bed. How can you call that love? Have we ever been to the opera together? Have we ever been to see Kabuki?'

'I'm afraid not.'

'Not once in ten years.'

'We went to the Noh once.'

'That was before all this started!' she yelled, jumping up from her chair. Immediately the banging from next door started again, as if replying before he could get a word in.

'Please,' he said. 'Do try not to make so much noise.'

She gave a surly nod and sank into silence, while all he could do was drink in silence, too. Then she started again, keeping her voice down this time.

'Haven't you ever thought you'd like to go on a trip somewhere with me?'

'We went to New York.'

'Was that your idea?'

'I don't quite get you.'

'You said you were attending a conference in New York, and I said we could meet there because I was going to the States on company business. I made that all up.'

'You made it up?'

'Yes.'

'You mean, you paid your own way—the plane ticket and everything?'

'Of course I did.'

'Good heavens!'

'I always wanted to go somewhere with you.'

'I see.'

'I hardly wrote anything about America. You don't think they'd have sent me all that way for that amount of work, do you?'

'Mm.'

'And all for just a fortnight.'

'Well, that couldn't be helped.'

'I suppose not. Anyway, you can always work out from one experience what all the others would've been like.'

'I ... I'm sorry ... I don't know what to say.'

'During the past year,' she said, getting back to her original complaint, 'have we ever been to an exhibition together? How many concerts have we been to? Not one. When people go to things together they talk to each other about them, they have fun together. Just getting into bed's no fun.'

'Well, you know...'

'I want our relationship to be ... cultured. All right, people laugh if you say something like that, but it's true. It's nice to go to things together; it's good to have experiences to talk about together. And yet...'

'Yes, I agree. You're right. I've been wrong about that, I admit. Still, I did talk about lots of interesting things to you.'

This annoyed her again, and she shouted at the top of her voice:

'Philosophy? Edmund Husserl? The crisis in European studies and the role of transcendental phenomenology? Are you crazy? How was I supposed to remember any of that when the only times you ever talked about it was after we'd had sex!'

Toyosaki's response to this outburst was complicated. First, he was shaken by it, by the force of her objection, and inclined to admit that his own remark had been a clumsy form of self-defence, and that maybe it *was* inappropriate to talk to a woman for such a long time about Husserl. All the same, he wanted to say that he hadn't done so straight after they'd had sex; usually forty or fifty minutes passed before anything was said, and if she asked him any questions he naturally replied, sometimes getting carried away and going on for too long, but only because she seemed to be enjoying it. Yet even as he tried to justify his behaviour in this way, he also began to feel ashamed of himself. He was unhappy about the image that now appeared before his eyes—the image of a man with a narrow range of conversation, not just a bore but a boor, a clumsy intellectual. Simultaneously, however, he felt he had something more immediate to worry about: the remarkable volume of noise she was capable of generating. That last shout had been incredibly loud, the worst so far, and it made him nervous. He was afraid that, this time, whoever was next door wouldn't just rely on a fist but start hammering away with a slipper, a shoe, even a chair. Fortunately, though, nobody banged on the wall, and peace descended. Even Yumiko, astonished herself at the sound she'd managed to produce, sat stupefied by the eerie silence.

Just as Toyosaki, pulling himself together, was about to say something, however, the bell on their door gave a long ring. Someone was standing outside with a finger on that bell. The philosopher stood up, straightened the lapels of his dressing gown, then went to the door, prepared for the worst. But when he opened it nobody was there, so he stuck his head outside and saw someone's back (a man, of course) retreating slowly down the corridor, about ten yards or so away, a tall man in a dark suit moving in a deliberate and leisurely fashion without pausing to look round. Toyosaki was wondering what this was all about when he saw a white envelope just in front of the door. He opened it and withdrew a sheet of paper. On it, in a fairly educated hand, was written:

> You are having problems, I gather
> I shall go for a walk for an hour
> Hoping something can be worked out
> Before I get back.

He went back to his chair and read it again.

'What is it? Show me,' Yumiko said, taking it from him. 'Neatly written,' she added with a sigh.

'Yes, very. Obviously no fool.'

'It's like a poem.'

'A poem? Ah, because the lines are broken up.'

He described how the man had walked away down the long corridor.

'It all seems somehow significant. Symbolic of something.'

Yumiko sat with her eyes closed. She stayed like that, quite motionless, for a long time. Then she opened them and said:

'I can see him very clearly, slowly moving away.' And then: 'I think I'll go and wash my hair.'

'Yes, that's a good idea,' he said as she stood up.

'That letter's taken the wind out of my sails.'

'I'm not surprised.'

'But I'm still angry.'

After he'd watched her disappear into the bathroom, he opened another little bottle of whisky and, imagining the sounds she would be making washing her hair (he couldn't actually hear a thing through the closed door), he began to think things over, reconsidering the last ten years and what had happened tonight, and thinking of women, of men, of love and death.

Looking back, he recalled that, during the ten months since June of last year, Yumiko had never once lost her temper, which could only mean that what he'd said tonight must have hurt her deeply, that the strain of those months and her concern about the future had created a tension that had finally snapped. In which case, the way she'd behaved over that period was pretty remarkable, and he admired her for it, even if he could hardly approve of the way she had taken it out on him just now.

This reflection was a prelude to a consideration of her many virtues. She was good-looking, elegant, intelligent; her shouting at him during an argument could hardly be condemned as just bad-mannered, given the special circumstances involved, and if she was a little plump, well, that was inevitable considering her age. As he lined up the points in her favour, he began to realise how painful it would be to lose her. Then he remembered that experience of hers, when she'd felt the whole of space squeezed into that ordinary little garden. The strange poignancy of it had touched him to the quick: it revealed an aspect of her he'd never known about (neither had she, presumably) and suggested a woman with some dark shadow deep in her soul, which only added to her attraction.

While he was reflecting in this way, the idea crossed his mind, quite suddenly, that the reason she'd come up with this extraordinary plan to go and look after her former husband might be the result of a growing dissatisfaction with how little time they spent together. The thought was so startling it was hard to analyse or gauge its accuracy: at times it seemed quite plausible, at others absurd, based on a self-conceit which he ought to feel thoroughly ashamed of. Although he couldn't resolve the question, however, the process of trying to do so was by no means unpleasant, and he allowed himself to enjoy it, thinking at the same time what a mistake it would be to let a woman like this, who seemed so fond of him, slip through his fingers, and that he'd have to make quite certain of her affection or some other man (the new head of the city desk at the *New Daily*, for example) might step into his place. This idea he found unnerving, and he began to see this journalist, whom he'd never met or even thought about before, as a distant threat, a suave and sharp-witted figure, like that man in the dark suit disappearing down the long hotel corridor.

In this state of mounting fear, uncertainty and, most of all, affection, he made up his mind. He would tell her that, if he got cancer, he would ask her to look after him. That would serve as an apology for his earlier lapse, and with her happy again things would return to normal between them. Still, there was a knack to saying something like that; you had to get the tone just right. It had to be done cheerfully, in a casual, carefree kind of way, as if you were almost joking. If he got it right, though, she would realise that her offer was unrealistic and would regret ever having made it, recalling that, after all, theirs was a love affair between

318

mature, responsible adults; she would reply in similar joking terms, and the ritual of reconciliation would be safely accomplished. Yes, that seemed the way to do it.

But suppose she interpreted it as a serious promise—what then? If she took it seriously and he did develop cancer (which could happen next week, for all he knew), he would find himself in the position of having to explain things on his sickbed, with Yumiko and his wife going at it hammer and tongs in the intervals between operations and chemotherapy sessions and drip-feeding—and he trying to sweet-talk them, apologise to them, even as he faced the most harrowing of all life's experiences.

Just as his imagination reached this point Yumiko came out of the bathroom and sat down on the chair next to his. He immediately made a compliment about her hair.

'Oh, we are being polite, aren't we?' she said, but he ignored the sarcasm.

'Yes, I am. And since I'm being polite, I'll be even politer. Which means I apologise for what I said. I'm sorry. I eat my words. If I get cancer, you're welcome to come any time.'

He smiled as he said this, keeping his eyes fixed on her face. She smiled, too, but that was all. She said nothing. Her expression was like his idea of space (or that garden in the prime minister's house): nebulous, inscrutable, mysterious, suggesting some meaning that lay beyond one's grasp. He tried to grasp at that meaning but couldn't, and at that moment found himself praying that he would die of some illness other than cancer, this hope being based on the hasty and literal-minded assumption that another illness would not be covered by the promise he'd made, and that he would be spared the desperate situation he'd so clearly imagined. Myocardial infarction, subarachnoid haemorrhage, cerebral apoplexy, amyotrophic lateral sclerosis and scleroderma—all those illnesses that end in a sudden or placid death filled the horizon of his future, giving it a rosy hue.

He poured her a glass of beer, and she downed half of it in one gulp with obvious enjoyment. He also had some of his whisky, still looking at her face, his mind now toying with the thought that pouring her a drink was part of the ritual of giving each other things. So, of course, was her offer to nurse him, a gift made in all sincerity, while he on his side was like a god embarrassed by an offering he'd have preferred to refuse but couldn't. He started to wonder what it would be like to be a god, and this led to further reflections on the linked existences of gods and men, his thoughts alternating between logical reasoning and the occasional imaginative leap.

His starting point was the idea that at one time men, when trying to emulate the gods in their manner of speech, had used a type of sacred language transcending the vernacular, and that was poetry. Just as the gods made their proclamations in poetry, so men petitioned the gods in poetic forms, too, and it was a vestige of such ritual that one saw in the poetic act today. When a poet wrote a poem he became a kind of god; even that man in the dark suit just now had fulfilled the same role, unknowingly of course, when he left behind that letter in the form of a poem. It may have been prose in origin, but an unconscious desire to be poetic had surely shaped its appearance. Poems are for people who seek to be gods; prose is for ordinary people. The one is ancient; the other modern.

In the same way, the buying and selling of goods is a modern activity, practical and human, but the giving of gifts is ancient and incantatory—men playing the parts of gods. It would be stating the obvious, he thought, to say that gift-giving was an objective correlative of mutual esteem, but the essential homeomorphism of such acts was worth underlining. When offerings are made to the gods, the person who makes the offering assumes the dignity of a pseudo-deity. In the middle ages, when a samurai made a vow of allegiance to his commander, both men in their own way behaved as gods; and the same still applies today when people exchange gifts, for a contract is made, the basis of which is a hallowing of the relations between people, a renewal and a reapprehension of its sacred nature.

This was particularly true of the relationship between lovers.

Since they existed on the heightened plane of passion, they dressed accordingly, behaving like gods and goddesses. The bouquet of flowers a man bought at the florist's was an article of commerce, but when he gave it to a woman it became a sacred offering. In the early and medieval periods of Japanese history, a man wooed a woman poetically, and the woman responded in kind, their poems having the dual function of being in the language of the gods and using the language of the gift, both when given and when returned.

But unfortunately men were not gods; they were only amateur gods, acting the part. Among these amateur actors there were skilled and clumsy performers, and even the skilful actors sometimes blundered. His failure to accept his goddess's offer of nursing him on his deathbed was one such blunder, and the goddess herself could have been more sensitive to the specific circumstances surrounding them…

Toyosaki had reached this point when he found himself imagining a *New Daily* cartoon of Yumiko and himself as two god-like figures in one of the ancient Japanese myths: Yumiko dressed in a white over-robe with a white train, a thin veil trailing from her long hair, and her crescent eyebrows raised in anger as she glared at him; while he quailed before her, dressed in white jacket and pantaloons with the ends of his belt dangling loose, and his hair done in two ponytails, one above each ear. The picture made him smile.

'What's so funny?' she asked.

'I was just thinking about presents … philosophically speaking.'

He was thinking how she'd probably get angry again if he told her what his thoughts had been, but her response wasn't what he expected. She gave a loud cry, quickly lowering her voice as she said, eyes shining:

'That would make a good book. A book about presents. You ought to write it.'

'You think so?'

'In paperback. Something easy to understand.'

'Ah,' he said happily, though his happiness was due entirely to her change of mood.

'It's bound to sell.'

'If it sells I'll take you out to dinner.'

'A nice French restaurant.'

'Mm.'

As they talked about it, the book gradually started to take shape in his mind.

'I shall call it *The Indifferent Guide to Gift-Giving*.'

'*The Philosophy of Presents* would be better. Women perk up when they hear the word "present".'

'They do, do they?'

'Men do as well, of course.'

'It wouldn't surprise me.'

'It's only natural, after all.'

'In that case,' the philosopher said, 'I'll do it, I suppose.'